Arlene James has been publishing steadily for nearly four decades and is a charter member of RWA. She is married to an acclaimed artist, and together they have traveled extensively. After growing up in Oklahoma, Arlene lived thirty-four years in Texas and now abides in beautiful northwest Arkansas, near two of the world's three loveliest, smartest, most talented granddaughters. She is heavily involved in her family, church and community.

Gail Gaymer Martin is a multi-award-winning novelist and writer of contemporary Christian fiction with fifty-five published novels and four million books sold. *CBS News* listed her among the four best writers in the Detroit area. Gail is a cofounder of American Christian Fiction Writers, a keynote speaker at women's events, and she presents workshops at writers' conferences. She lives in Michigan. Visit her at gailgaymermartin.com. Write to her online or at PO Box 760063, Lathrup Village, MI, 48076.

Deck the Halls

Arlene James

&

Upon a Midnight Clear

Gail Gaymer Martin

HARLEQUIN® LOVE INSPIRED®

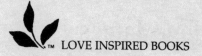 ™ LOVE INSPIRED BOOKS

Recycling programs for this product may not exist in your area.

ISBN-13: 978-1-335-19996-6

Deck the Halls and Upon a Midnight Clear

Copyright © 2017 by Harlequin Books S.A.

The publisher acknowledges the copyright holders of the individual works as follows:

Deck the Halls
Copyright © 2005 by Deborah Rather

Upon a Midnight Clear
Copyright © 2000 by Gail Gaymer Martin

www.Harlequin.com

Printed in U.S.A.

CONTENTS

DECK THE HALLS

Arlene James

For my husband, who has taught me how real
and rewarding love can be.

Shew me thy ways, O LORD;
teach me thy paths.
—*Psalms* 25:4

Chapter One

The voice on the answering machine, while obviously feminine, sounded curt and cheeky.

"Come to your old apartment and get your mail before I trash it. Never heard of mail forwarding?"

Vince smacked the heel of one hand against his forehead. Where was his brain? He hadn't given a single thought to having his personal mail forwarded. In the past few weeks he'd been too busy settling into the new house, replacing his business accountant and hiring enough mechanics to fulfill a city maintenance contract to think about his personal mail.

Just about everything important came to the offices of Cutler Automotive, but that was no excuse. He should've realized that the new tenant of his old apartment would have to deal with his share of circulars and the other junk that routinely clogged every mailbox in the Dallas/Fort Worth Metroplex. Besides, something important did occasionally find its way into his residential mailbox. In fact, the materials he'd been expecting about the spring singles' retreat at his church would undoubtedly be among the papers waiting for him at the old apartment.

He hit a button and listened to the message again. Her irritation couldn't have been more obvious, but he found himself smiling at the huskiness of her voice melded with the tartness of her tone. He heard both strength and vulnerability there, an odd combination of toughness and femininity. Since he was still wearing his jacket over his work clothes, he decided that he might as well go at once, make his apologies and relieve her of the unwanted burden of his mail.

Picking up his keys from the counter, he jauntily tossed them into the air, snatched them back again and retraced his steps through the new, sparsely furnished house to the garage and the shiny, white, three-quarter-ton pickup truck waiting there. Glancing at the sign proudly painted on the door, he climbed inside and started it up. The powerful engine rumbled throatily for a moment before he backed the truck out onto the drive and in to the street.

As he shifted the transmission into a forward gear he tossed a wave at his next-door neighbor Steve, who was taking advantage of the clear, early-November weather in the last hour of daylight to walk his dog. The Boltons were nice people. Wendy, the missus, had been one of the first people to welcome Vince to the neighborhood. They were about his age and the proud parents of a sixteen-month-old curly-top named Mandy, who took most of their time and attention, but Wendy seemed determined to "fix him up" with one of her single friends. Steve had confided that his wife found Vince too "tall, dark and delish" to be still single at twenty-nine, but that she'd have felt the same way if he'd been a "bald warthog."

Vince didn't know about being "tall, dark and delish," but he didn't think he was a "bald warthog," either. He'd happily give up the single state the moment that God brought the right woman into his life. So far he hadn't stumbled across her—not that he'd exactly been out beating the bushes for the future Mrs. Cutler.

He was a busy man with a booming business, three garages and a large extended family, including his parents, four sisters and half a dozen nieces and nephews, with one more on the way, not to mention the brothers-in-law and innumerable aunts, uncles and cousins. That, church and a few close friends was about all he could manage, frankly.

As he drove toward his old apartment building, a feeling of déjà vu overcame him. He remembered well the day, almost a decade ago, when he'd first moved into the small, bland efficiency apartment. A heady feeling of liberation had suffused him then. He'd felt so proud to have left the home of his parents and struck out on his own, leaving behind two pesky younger sisters and two nosy older ones.

Of course, with more freedom had come greater responsibility. Then had come the hard-won understanding that responsibility itself could be counted even more of a joy than any foolish, youthful notions of "freedom" that he'd once entertained. A fellow could take pride in meeting his responsibilities and meeting them well, whereas freedom—as he had learned—could become an empty exercise in keeping loneliness at bay.

Other lessons had followed. He'd found his best friends in moments of difficulty rather than fun, though that was important, too. Most significant, Vince had learned that those who truly loved him—his family, particularly his parents—were bulwarks of support rather than burdens of bondage. The mature Vince possessed a keen awareness that not everyone was as richly blessed in that area.

For the life he had built and the man he had become, he had his parents, with their thoughtful guidance, patience, loving support and Christian examples, to thank. For his parents, he could only thank God, which was not to say that from time to time they did not make him wish that he lived on a different continent, particularly when it came to his single status.

By the time he pulled into the rutted parking lot of the small, dated, two-story apartment building, Vince was feeling pretty mellow with memories. He was by nature a fairly easygoing type, but he possessed a certain intensity, too, an innate drive that had served him well in building his business. Looking around the old place as he left the vehicle and moved onto the walkway, he saw that nothing whatsoever had changed, only his circumstances.

Onward and upward, he mused, setting foot on the bottom step of an all-too-familiar flight of stairs. His heavy, steel-toed boots rang hollowly against the open metal treads as he climbed. After passing three doors on the open landing, he stopped at the fourth and automatically reached for the doorknob. Only at the last moment did he derail his hand, lifting it and coiling it into a fist. Before his knuckles could make contact with the beige-painted wood, however, the door abruptly opened and a feminine face appeared. Obviously she had heard him coming.

"Who are you?"

Vince looked down into clear green eyes like pale jade marbles fringed with sandy-brown lashes. Large and almond-shaped, they literally challenged him. He backed up a step, lowering his hand and took in the whole of her oval face.

It was a bit too long to be labeled classically pretty, just as her nose seemed a bit too prominent to be called pert. But those eyes and the lush contours of a generous mouth, along with high, prominent cheekbones and the sultry sweep of eyebrows a shade darker than her golden-brown hair made a very striking, very feminine picture, indeed. The hair was the finishing touch, her "crowning glory," as the Scriptures said. Thick and straight with a healthy, satiny shine, it hung well past her shoulders, almost to her elbows.

Vince suddenly had the awful feeling that his mouth might be agape. He cleared his throat, making sure that it wasn't, and finally registered her question.

"I'm, uh, Vincent Cutler. You left a message on my—"

"Well, it's about time!" she exclaimed, sweeping her wispy bangs off her forehead with one hand and then instantly brushing them down again. "I've got a whole bag full of your mail here. You must be on every mailing list in the country."

He nodded in thoughtless agreement, but she whirled away too abruptly to notice. He watched the agitated sway of her hips as her long legs carried her across the floor. She moved toward the narrow counter that separated the tiny corner kitchen from the rest of the single room and he instinctively followed.

"I tried dropping it off at the post office," she complained, "but they just kept sending it right back to me. Doesn't matter that it hasn't got my name on it. It's got my address. That's all they care about apparently."

"Guess so," Vince mumbled, shrugging.

A raised ten-by-ten-foot platform set off by banisters

denoted the sleeping area, and the remaining floor space served as dining and living rooms. A small bathroom containing a decent-sized closet opened off the latter. He knew all this without bothering to look, the apartment being as familiar to him as his own face in a mirror. Besides, his attention was fully taken by the tall, slender, feminine form in worn jeans and a simple, faded T-shirt, mostly obscured by the fall of her hair.

When she bent to open a cabinet door and reach inside, gentlemanly impulse sent his gaze skittering reluctantly around the room. Color jolted him as his eyes took in a bright-yellow wall and a neat, simple plaid of yellow, red and green against a stark white background. Potted plants were scattered about, and he registered a smattering of tiny checks and a few ruffles, but the room was not overly feminine, as his mother's and sisters' houses were inclined to be. The furnishings were sparse and dated, obviously used, but the overall effect was surprisingly pleasing, much better than the drab, often cluttered place that he had inhabited.

"Wow," he said, and the next thing he knew, she was flying at him, both hands raised.

"What are you doing? Get out! Get out!"

She hit him full force, palms flat against his chest, propelling him backward. Vince threw his arms out in an attempt to regain his balance and then felt them knocked down again as he stumbled backward through the door, which summarily slammed in his face, just inches from his nose. Automatically reaching up, he checked to be certain that it hadn't taken a blow and felt the small familiar hump of a previous break. That was when he heard the bolt click and the safety chain slide into place.

For another moment, he was too stunned even to

think, but then he began to replay the last few minutes in his mind, and gradually realization came to him. He slapped both hands to his cheeks. Good grief! She hadn't invited him in; he'd just followed her like some lost puppy, right into her home! *Her* home, *not* his, not any longer. No wonder she'd freaked! He dropped his hands.

"Oh, hey," he said to the door, feeling more and more like an idiot. "I—I didn't mean to alarm you. I would never…that is, I—I used to live here," he finished lamely.

She, of course, said nothing.

He closed his eyes, muttering, "Way to go, Cutler. Way to go. Probably scared the daylights out of her."

Shifting closer, he tried to pitch his voice through the door without really raising it; he knew too well how thin the walls were around here. "I'm sorry if I frightened you."

He waited several seconds, but there might have been a brick wall behind that door rather than a living, breathing woman. Actually, he had no idea if she was even still in the vicinity. She might have been cowering in the farthest corner of the room, though he couldn't quite picture her doing so.

No, a woman like that wouldn't be cowering. More likely she was standing there with a baseball bat ready to bash in his head if he so much as turned the doorknob. Clearly, a prudent man would retreat.

Despite recent evidence, Vince Cutler was a prudent man.

He turned and walked swiftly along the landing, then quickly took the stairs and swung around the end of the railing toward his truck. A certain amount of embarrassment mixed with chagrin dogged him as he once more climbed behind the wheel, his errand an obvious bust.

Yet, a smile kept tweaking the corners of his mouth as he thought about the woman upstairs.

She was all dark gold, that woman, dark gold and vinegar. Spunky, that's what she was. He recalled that the top of her head had come right to the tip of his nose. Considering that he stood an even six feet in his socks, she had to be five-seven or eight, which would explain those long legs. It occurred to him suddenly that he didn't even know her name; that, more than anything else, just seemed all wrong.

As he turned the big truck back onto the street, he also turned his mind to mending fences. She still had his mail, after all, and he couldn't let things lie as they were. Good manners, if nothing else, decreed it. The question was how to approach her again. Frowning, he immediately sought solutions in the only manner he knew.

"Lord, I don't know what happened to my good sense. I scared that girl. Please don't let her sit there afraid that I'd hurt her. The whole thing was my fault, and if You'll just show me how, I'll try to make up for it."

Just then he drove by a minivan with the tailgate raised. It was parked in an empty lot and surrounded by hand-lettered signs touting Tyler roses, buckets of which were sitting on its back deck. A strange, unexpected thought popped into his head, one so foreign and seemingly out of nowhere that it startled him, and then he began to laugh.

That's what happened when you relied on God to lead you. As his daddy would say, when you ask God for guidance, you'd better get out of the way quick. Now all he had to do was pick his time and his words very carefully. That was to say, very prayerfully.

* * *

Vince polished the toe of one boot on the back of the opposite pants leg, not a work boot this time but full-quill ostrich, one half of his best pair of cowboy boots. Armed to the teeth with two dozen bright red rosebuds, he took a deep breath, squared his shoulders and rapped sharply on the door. He counted to six before the door opened this time.

Green eyes flew wide, but he thrust flowers and words at her before he could find himself facing that door again.

"I'm so sorry. I didn't meant to frighten you or seem disrespectful." When she didn't immediately slam the door in his face, he hurried on. "I guess I just lived here so long that it seemed perfectly natural to walk inside. I didn't think how inappropriate it was or how it would seem to you." She frowned and folded her arms, giving her head a leonine toss. He found himself smiling. "Honest. I feel like a dunce."

"You're grinning like one," she retorted, and then she sniffed.

His smile died, not because she'd insulted him—he didn't take that seriously—but because she'd obviously been crying.

"Oh, hey," he said, feeling like a real heel. "You okay?"

She swiped jerkily at her eyes and lifted her chin. "Yeah, sure I'm okay. You going to beat me with those flowers or what?"

"Huh?" He dropped his arm then quickly lifted it again, saying, "These are for you."

One corner of her mouth quirked, and humor suddenly glinted in those clear green eyes. "Yeah, I figured."

"For, uh, your trouble." He shifted uncertainly. "The mail and all."

"And all?" she echoed, arching one brow.

He gave her his most charming smile and waggled the roses in their clear plastic cone. "I said I was sorry."

She reached out and languidly swept the flowers from his grasp, drawling, "Right. Thanks. I suppose you want your mail now."

He nodded and fished a folded card out of his pocket, offering it to her. "I've already turned in one, but I thought you might want to drop that in the box yourself, so you'll know for sure that it's done."

She glanced at the change-of-address card, and that brow went up again. "That's you? Cutler Automotive?"

Nodding, he dipped into the hip pocket of his dark jeans and came up with a couple of coupons. "That reminds me. Maybe you can use these sometime."

She tucked the change-of-address card into the roses and took these new papers into one hand, cocking her head to get a good look at them.

"Hmm," she said, reading the top one aloud, "Fifty percent off service and repairs." She looked him right in the eye. "This on the up-and-up?"

"Absolutely."

"No catch? I don't have to spend a certain amount or agree to some extra service?"

"Nope. You just present the signed coupon, we knock fifty percent off your bill."

"No strings attached?"

"We don't accept photocopies," he pointed out, calling her attention to the smaller print at the bottom of the paper. "But that's it."

She nodded, apparently satisfied. "Okay. Great. If you wait right here, I'll get your mail."

"These feet are not moving," he promised, but the instant she turned her back, he craned his neck to get another look around.

She'd done wonders with the old place. Despite the dated furniture and faded fabrics, the apartment had a homey, put-together feel about it that he quite liked, and he told her so.

"Never looked this good when I lived here."

She laid the flowers on the counter and turned to face him. "No?"

He shook his head and shrugged. "Guess I just don't have the knack."

"What guy does?"

"None I know of, not many women, either, from what I can tell."

"You pay attention to that sort of thing, do you?" she asked, seeming surprised. It had sounded a little odd, now that he thought about it.

"Lately, I do. Since the move."

"Ah."

She bent and extracted a small shopping bag from the cabinet.

"This is it," she said, carrying the bag toward him. "Two more pieces came just today."

He reached through the open doorway to accept the bag. It was stuffed with papers.

"I'm sorry about this. I usually take better care of business."

"I just hope there aren't any overdue bills in there," she said dryly.

"Naw, I try not to have any of those."

"We all try," she quipped wryly, but he detected a troubled note.

"Not all," he said, wanting to reassure her somehow. "You'd be surprised how many people make no attempt to pay their bills."

"Maybe they can't."

"Maybe," he admitted, "but if they try, we work with them."

She tilted her head and her brows bounced up and down at that. "Cutler Automotive, you mean."

"Yes, ma'am."

"Huh."

After a second or two it became apparent that she wasn't going to say anything else, and he couldn't for the life of him think of any way to rectify that. He shuffled his feet in place.

"Well, you have a nice evening."

She reached for the door. "Yeah, you, too, if you can with all that to go through." She nodded at the sack in his arms. "If any more comes, I'll send it on your way now that I have a good address."

"I don't mind coming after it again," he assured her quickly, "if you'll just call."

"I'll send it," she stated decisively.

Defeated, he nodded. "Okay. However you want to handle it."

"That's how I want to handle it," she said flatly, backing up to push the door closed. "So long, Vincent Cutler."

He put up a hand. "Wait a sec. I'd like to know your name, at least. I mean, if you don't mind." He shrugged. "Seems strange bringing flowers to a woman whose name I don't even know."

She considered a moment longer then said, "Jolie."

"Jo Lee," he repeated carefully.

"No." She rolled her eyes. "Jolie. J-o-l-i-e."

"Ah. That's pretty. Jolie what?"

She flattened her mouth, but then she answered. "Jolie Wheeler. Jolie Kay Wheeler."

He smiled again for some reason. It just sounded… right. "Jolie Kay. I'll remember that."

"If you say so."

His smile stretched into a grin. "Good night, Jolie Kay Wheeler. Maybe I'll see you around."

"I doubt it."

He didn't. He didn't know why, but even as that door closed to him once again, he knew somehow that he hadn't seen the last of spunky, pretty Jolie Wheeler. Strangely enough, that thought was quite all right by him.

Jolie reached into the cabinet overhead and brought down a big pickle jar to serve as a vase. After filling it with tap water, she turned to the counter where the tightly budded roses waited. No one had ever brought her flowers before. Figured it would be some goofball like Cutler. First he doesn't bother to have his mail forwarded, and then he strolls right in as if he owns the place, as if an open door is an automatic invitation to invade the premises.

The good-looking ones were always like that, thought they had a right to the whole world just because they were easy on the eyes. He was easier than most, with that pitch-black hair, lazy, blue-gray eyes, square jaw and dimples. More polite than most, too.

He had immediately apologized yesterday for invading her space, but her heart had been slamming against her rib cage so violently that she hadn't found enough air to reply. Then embarrassment had taken over, and she'd mulishly let him stand there and wheedle until he'd given up and gone away.

Actually, he seemed harmless enough. Now.

The day before when she'd looked up and found him standing there in the middle of her apartment as if sizing up the joint, he'd appeared eight feet tall and hulking. Today, of course, he'd been his usual six-foot—or thereabout—self. She hadn't imagined those broad shoulders and bulging biceps, though, or the slim hips and long legs. The truth was, she had panicked, which wasn't like her, but then she didn't know what she was like anymore. Nothing was as it had been. Without Russell.

She pushed away thoughts of her nephew, rapidly blinking against a fresh onslaught of tears.

This was getting to be a habit. She'd be okay for a while, and then something would remind her of that sweet baby face, that milky, gap-toothed smile and little hands that grasped so trustingly, coiling themselves in her hair and shirt. The loss still devastated her. More, it made her angry, at herself as much as at her sister and brother.

She should never have let herself love little Russ so completely. She should have treated him as nothing more than a foster child, his presence in her life temporary at best. After all, she knew only too well how the game was played. Ten years of experience on one side of that equation should have prepared her better for the other.

Oh, she had been placed with foster families who had truly tried to make her feel a part of the group, but she had always known that it would end. Something would happen, and she would be on her way again, shuffling from one home to another with heart-numbing regularity.

Somehow, though, she hadn't let herself think that it could happen with Russell. When Connie had first gone to prison, pregnant and unwed, she had talked about giving up her child for adoption. Then, after his birth, when she'd asked Jolie to take him and give him a good home, saying that he ought to be with family, Jolie had seen her opportunity to really have someone of her own.

She and Connie had never discussed what would happen after Connie got out. For one thing, Jolie had never dreamed that a judge would actually hand over the child whom she had raised as her own to her misguided younger sister, no matter that said sister had given birth to him. It wasn't fair, and to have their adored big brother Marcus side with Connie had been the unkindest cut of all.

Jolie was still grieving, but she supposed that was to be expected. It had only been days since she'd last seen him, eleven days, two hours, in fact. She could know how many minutes if she was foolish enough to check her watch, which she wasn't. Of course she was still grieving. She'd grieved her mother's absence for years, until she'd found out that Velma Wheeler was dead. Strangely enough, knowing that her mother had died was easier than believing that her mother had simply abandoned her children to the uncertain kindness of strangers.

Jolie shook her head and willed away the tears that had spilled from her eyes, telling herself that she would get on top of this latest loss. She'd had lots of practice.

Reaching for the roses, she slid them from their plastic cone and began arranging them in their makeshift vase. She did not realize, as the pleasing design began to take shape, that she made it happen with an innate, God-given ability which those lacking it would surely treasure.

Never once in her entire life had she ever imagined that anyone could admire or envy anything about her.

Chapter Two

Jolie picked up the two small rectangles of heavy paper from the counter top and studied them again, each in turn. One was the fifty-percent-off coupon that Vince Cutler had explained to her. The other promised a free tow. She wondered again what the catch might be, but she wasn't likely to find out until she had need of the services offered. And the need was very likely to arise.

Her old jalopy was a garage bill waiting to happen. The thing had been coughing and gasping like an emphysema patient lately. She'd literally held her breath all the way to work this morning.

If the dry cleaners where she was employed had been situated just a little closer to the new apartment, she'd have walked it every day just to save wear and tear on the old donkey cart, but five miles coming and going on a daily basis was a bit more than she could manage, especially with the evening temperatures hovering in the thirties. Just to be on the safe side, Jolie tucked the coupons into her wallet—never know when they might come in handy—before going back to the ironing with which she augmented her meager income.

Since the death of his wife, Mr. Geopp, owner and operator of the small, independent dry cleaners where she'd worked for the past six years, had chosen to out-source the delicate work rather than invest in the new machines that could handle it properly, and he'd stopped taking in alterations and regular laundry altogether.

One day, Jolie mused, Geopp would retire, and then what would she do? Her heart wasn't exactly in dry cleaning, but she didn't seem to possess a single exploitable talent. It was a familiar worry that she routinely shoved aside.

With the tip of one finger, she checked the temperature of the pressing plate, judged it sufficiently cooled not to damage the delicate silk blouse positioned on the padded board and carefully began removing the wrinkles from the fabric. Her mind wandered back to the coupons.

If she took in her car for an estimate, would she see Vince Cutler again?

She glanced ruefully at the flowers he had given her. They were a pretty pathetic sight now. The buds had opened and half the petals had fallen, but she couldn't bring herself to toss them just yet. Not that she was harboring any secret romantic fantasies about Vincent Cutler. She wasn't in the market, no matter how goodlooking he was, and he was plenty good-looking. Why, the only thing that saved the man from being downright beautiful was the little hump on the bridge of his nose.

She couldn't help wondering how his nose had been broken, then she scolded herself for even thinking about him. Vince Cutler was nothing to her, and she intended to keep it that way. Secondhand experience had taught Jolie that romantic entanglements were more trouble than they were worth.

Her mom had been big on romance, and all that had gotten her was three kids by three different men, none of whom they could even remember. Still, every time some yahoo had crooked his finger at Velma Wheeler she'd followed him off on whatever wild escapade he'd proposed, often leaving her children to fend for themselves until she returned.

Sometimes they were out of food and living in the dark with the utilities shut off when she'd finally remember that she had a family. One day she simply hadn't returned at all, and eventually Child Welfare had stepped in to cart Jolie and her siblings off to foster care.

For years Jolie had harbored the secret fantasy that her mother would come back a changed woman, determined to reunite their scattered family, all the while knowing that Velma would have had to learn to care for them a great deal more in her absence than she ever had while present. Then one day Jolie had been told that her mother had died in a drunk-driving accident and been buried in a pauper's grave somewhere in Nevada. A simple typographical error had resulted in the misspelling of her name and an incorrect filing of records. Her mother had been gone four years by that time.

With Velma as their lesson, Jolie and her sister Connie had sworn that they would not go from man to man. Then Connie had somehow settled on that jerk Kennard and doggedly refused to give up on him. Jolie understood that Connie had feared being a serial loser just like their mom, but only after Kennard had gone to prison for the rest of his life, taking a pregnant Connie along with him, did she turn away from him. Of course, Connie had claimed that she hadn't even known that an armed robbery was being committed that day, let alone a mur-

der, despite the fact that she had been sitting in front of
the bank in a running car.

Jolie had been inclined to believe Connie at the time.
Now she just didn't know.

Maybe if Connie had made a better choice than Kennard…but then, Jolie reminded herself, she wouldn't have
had Russell. It was worth any hardship to have a little
boy like that. Wasn't it?

Jolie shook her head. Thinking that way could get a
girl in trouble. Better just to go it alone.

Jolie had learned that lesson the hard way after the
authorities had split up her and her siblings when sending them into foster care. At first she and Connie had
been placed together, but that hadn't lasted for very long.

Oh, they'd maintained contact. The department was
good about that sort of thing. But the years had taken
their toll. Jolie had been nine, Marcus only a year older
and Connie just seven when their mom had disappeared.

Two decades later, Jolie was again alone.

With Russell to fill her days and nights and heart,
it had seemed that she had family again, but only for a
little while. Now all she had was a pile of other people's
clothing to iron and a single room with a private bath to
call her own—so long as she could pay the rent.

That thought sent her back to the job at hand, and
for a time she lost herself in the careful placement and
smoothing of one garment after another. Funny how you
could take pride in something so small and insignificant
as smoothing wrinkled cloth, but a girl had to get her
satisfaction where she could.

"Come on, baby, just a little farther."

Jolie patted the cracked black dash encouragingly,

but the little car sputtered and wheezed with alarming defiance. Then it gave a final paroxysm of shudders and simply stopped, right in the middle of rush-hour traffic.

"Blast!"

Someone behind her did just that with a car horn.

"All right, already!" she yelled, strong-arming the steering wheel as far to the right as she could. The car came to a rolling halt against the curb.

Tires screeched behind her. Another horn honked, and then an engine gunned. A pickup truck flew by with just inches to spare. Jolie flinched, put the transmission in Neutral and cranked the starter, begging for a break. The engine turned over, coughed and died again. The second time, the engine barely rumbled, and on the third it didn't do that much. By the fifth or sixth try, the starter clicked to let her know that it was getting the message but that the engine was ignoring its entreaties entirely. Jolie gave up, knowing that the next step was to get out and raise the hood.

She didn't dare try to exit the car on the driver's side. Instead, she turned on her hazard lights, put the standard transmission in first gear, set the parking brake and released her safety belt to climb across the narrow center console and the passenger seat to the other door. Stepping out on the grassy verge between the curb and the sidewalk, she tossed her ponytail off one shoulder and kicked the front wheel of the car in a fit of pique. Pain exploded in her big toe.

Biting her tongue, she limped around to the front end of the car to lift the hood and make her situation even more visible to the traffic passing on the busy street. After that, all she could do was plop down on the stiff brown grass to wait for someone to come along and offer to help as there was no place around from which to make a telephone call. Looked like she might be trying out those coupons from Cutler Automotive sooner rather than later. Provided someone with a telephone stopped.

More than half an hour had passed and her toe had stopped aching before a Fort Worth traffic cop pulled up behind her aged coupe, lights flashing. Traffic moved into the inside lane to accommodate him as he opened his door and got out. He strolled over to Jolie, a beefy African-American with one hand on his holster and the other on his night stick.

"Ma'am," he said pleasantly, "you can't leave your car here like this."

"Sir," Jolie replied with saccharine sweetness, "I can't get the thing to move."

He rubbed his chin and asked, "Anyone you can call?"

"Could if I had a phone."

He removed a cell phone from his belt and showed it to her. Heaving herself to her feet, she walked over to the car to take her wallet from the center console. Pulling out the coupon from Cutler Automotive, she handed it to him. Nodding, he punched in the number and passed her the phone.

The number rang just twice before a voice answered.

"Cutler Automotive. This is Vince. How can I help you?"

Vince. She swallowed and shifted her weight. "This is Jolie Wheeler."

"Well, hello, Jolie Wheeler. Have you got mail for me?"

"Nope. I've got a coupon for a free tow."

"A free tow?"

"That's what it says. Any problem with that?"

"No, ma'am. Where are you?"

She told him, and he said he'd be right there before hanging up. She handed the phone back to the officer and thanked him. He nodded and turned to watch the passing traffic, trying to make small talk. They'd covered how the car had been acting and where she was going and where she'd been and the state of disrepair of the Fort Worth streets by the time the white wrecker, lights flashing, swung to the curb in front of her crippled car.

Vince bailed out with hardly a pause, and Jolie's heart did a strange little kick inside her chest. Then he walked straight to the grinning cop, ignoring her completely.

"Jacob," he said, shaking the other man's hand.

The policeman smiled broadly and clapped Vince on the shoulder. "How you doing, my man?"

"Staying busy. How're you?"

"Likewise, only with very little sleep."

"New baby keeping you up nights?" Vince asked, flashing his dimples.

It was at this point that Jolie folded her arms, feeling very much on the outside looking in.

"Oh, man, is he ever!" came the ardent reply. "Rascal's got a set of lungs on him, too, let me tell you."

"Well, he sure didn't get those from his soft-spoken mama," Vince said with a grin.

"Soft-spoken?" Jacob the cop echoed disbelievingly. "Soft-spoken? My Callie? Man, you know better than that. You've sat in front of her at a football game."

Vince just grinned wider. "I'm going to tell her you said that."

"Not unless you want to attend my funeral." Both men laughed and back-slapped each other before Jacob moved off toward his patrol car. "You're in good hands now, ma'am," he called jovially to Jolie as he sauntered back to his vehicle.

Vince shook his head, still chuckling, and parked his hands at his waist, striking a nonchalant pose before finally turning to Jolie.

"Well, I'm glad you got a nice visit out of this," she said sarcastically.

Vince Cutler arched his brows, but his smile stayed firmly in place. "Jacob and I attend the same church, but because of his schedule we don't often get to the same service, so I'm glad to have seen him. Now, what's the problem with your car?"

She threw up her hands, disliking the fact that he'd made her feel glad, jealous and petty all in the space of a few minutes.

"How would I know? The hateful thing quit, that's all."

"Uh-huh." He stepped up to the bumper and looked over the engine. Gingerly, he wiped a forefinger across one surface and rubbed it against his thumb. "No oily emission."

"Is that good?" she asked anxiously, her concern about her transportation momentarily overcoming all else.

"It's not bad."

Whatever that meant.

She flattened her lips and tried to see what he saw as he leaned forward and fingered first one part and then another, poking and prodding at hoses and wires and other unnameable organs. Finally he turned to lean a hip against the fender.

"So what happened, exactly, before it quit running?"

She pushed a hand through her bangs, tugged at her ponytail and sucked in a deep breath, trying to remember *exactly*. Finally she began to talk about how the car had been coughing and sputtering by fits and starts lately and how the dash lights had blinked off from time to time.

He listened with obvious attention, then asked, "Any backfiring?"

She considered. "No, I don't think so."

"Okay." Pushing away from the car, he moved toward the driver's door. "Keys in the ignition?"

"Yes."

He opened the door and folded himself into the seat behind the wheel. The starter clicked for several seconds then stopped.

Vince spent a few moments looking at the gauges on the dashboard, then he got out and walked back to the wrecker, returning quickly with a small tool box and a thick, quilted cloth, which he spread on the fender before placing the tool box atop it. He opened the box and extracted a strange gizmo that resembled a calculator with wires attached, which he carried back into the car with him.

Jolie walked around to the passenger window and looked in while he wedged himself under the dash and began pulling down wires. He separated several little plastic clips and attached leads from the gizmo to them, then he studied the tiny screen before turning the ignition key on and off several times in rapid succession.

"What is that thing?" Jolie asked, curiosity getting the better of her.

"I call it my truth-teller."

"Oh, they sell truth at mechanic's school, do they?"

"They sure do," he drawled, ignoring her sarcastic tone.

"That's not what I heard."

"You heard wrong, then."

He removed the leads, reconnected the clips and tucked everything back up under the dash. Then he rose and carried his equipment around to the front of the car again. Jolie joined him there, more curious than ever. He didn't keep her waiting.

"You've got a sensor going out, and I'd guess that the alternator needs to be rebuilt, too."

Dismay slammed through her. She covered it by rolling her eyes. "And what's that going to cost?"

He shrugged. "Can't say without checking a parts list."

"More than a hundred?"

"Oh, yeah. Plus, you've got half a dozen hoses ready to spring leaks and at least one cracked battery mount that I can see. That'll have to be replaced before your next inspection. And if I were you, I'd have the timing chain checked."

She caught her breath, stomach roiling. How would she ever pay for all that? she wondered sickly.

"I've reset the sensor," he went on, "so it should behave for a little while, and I'll give you a jump to get you started, but you really ought to bring the car in soon as you can because this *will* happen again. Just a matter of time."

Jolie bit her lip. Maybe he was just shilling for the garage. Maybe this would be all it took. Whatever, she had zero intention of taking the car in for repairs until she had no other option. She folded her arms again as he went back to the wrecker and returned with what looked like a battery on wheels.

"How much is today going to cost?" she wanted to know, not that she had much choice at the moment.

"This? *Nada.*"

Jolie blinked. "Nothing?"

"I can charge you if you want," he said, mouth quirking at the corners.

She wrinkled her nose. "Thanks, but no thanks."

He smiled knowingly, dimples wrinkling his lean cheeks. "Okay, then."

With that he got busy hooking up everything. Finally he got in and started her car. The engine fired right off and settled into its usual, uneven rumble. Jolie almost dropped with relief.

"Thank goodness."

He started disconnecting and packing away gear.

As he dropped the hood, she lost a short battle with herself and asked, "You won't get in trouble with your boss, will you? For not charging me, I mean."

Vince wiped his hands purposefully on a red cloth that he'd pulled from his hip pocket, holding her gaze.

"No problems there."

"You're sure?"

"Jolie, I *am* the boss."

She felt a tiny shock, but she'd practiced nonchalance so long that it came easily to her.

"Well, if you say so."

He folded the cloth and stuffed it back into his pocket with short, swift movements, saying, "Fact is, I own and operate three garages."

She blinked, impressed, but of course that would never do.

"All by yourself?" she quipped blandly.

He chuckled. "Not exactly. I have twenty-two employees, not counting the outsourcing, of course."

"Outsourcing," she echoed dully.

"Um-hm, bookkeeping, billing, that sort of thing."

"Ah."

And here she'd figured him for a regular joe. Just goes to show you, she thought, eying his dusky-blue uniform with reluctant new interest.

"If you call the shop tomorrow," he told her casually, "I can work you in." She lifted her eyebrows skeptically, and he went on, prodding ever so gently. "You really ought to have that work done."

Now she *knew* it was a scam. Soften up the mark with a little freebie, make her think you're as honest as the day is long, then get her in the shop and soak her good. Resetting that sensor was probably all the car had ever needed.

"We'll see."

"Okay," he said lightly. "Well, I'll be seeing you."

"Oh, really?" She tilted her head, studying him for signs of dishonesty. Had he somehow sabotaged her car so that she'd have to bring it to his shop?

He glanced away pointedly, his sculpted mouth thinning. "You know, not everyone in the automotive-repair business is a crook. In fact, despite our reputation for rip-offs, most mechanics are honest and highly trained."

To her absolute disgust, color stained her cheeks. "I didn't say you were a crook."

He just looked at her, his smoky-blue eyes flat as stone. "No, but you were thinking it."

Her chin rose defensively. "You have no idea what I was thinking."

"Don't I?"

He just stood there, staring at her, until she suddenly realized what he was waiting for. Her hauteur wilted in a pool of mortification. Still, she wasn't about to apologize.

"Okay, maybe I was thinking it, but you don't know how often someone like me gets ripped off."

"Someone like you?" he echoed uncertainly. "And what makes you so different from the rest of us?"

"I'm a single woman, for one thing."

His expression grew suspiciously bland. "I had noticed that."

"And I don't have a lot of money for another," she snapped, trying to offset the little thrill that his droll comment had produced.

"I would think that would make you less of a target for the unscrupulous, frankly," he said calmly.

Bitterly, she shook her head. "You would think wrong."

"I'm sorry to hear that."

She gulped at the sincere tone of his voice. "The thing is, I don't know enough about cars to guard against getting ripped off."

"You could learn," he suggested lightly. It sounded almost like an invitation.

She looked down at her toes. "I doubt that. I'm not the mechanical type."

"Just the suspicious type," he countered dryly.

Rolling her eyes up, she met his gaze. "I have reason to be."

"I wouldn't know about that," he said, his voice softening, "but I know this. You have nothing to fear from me, Jolie Kay Wheeler. On any score. Ever."

Now what could she say to that? Apparently he didn't expect a reply, for he started toward the wrecker.

"Well, you try to have a good evening."

"Yeah, you, too," she grumbled, disliking the mishmash of feelings that swamped her.

He flipped her a wave, climbed into the truck and drove off, leaving her standing there in the gathering twilight like some oversized, ponytailed traffic cone. Glancing around self-consciously, she made her way to the driver's seat of her little car and dropped down into it.

A sedan flew by with the blare of a horn. Traffic had moved back into the outside lane the instant Vince and his flashing lights had pulled away, but she had barely noted that fact. Shaking slightly, she switched on her headlamps, jammed the transmission into gear, put on her blinker, turned off her hazard lights and prepared to merge.

It hit her then. Like a ballpeen hammer to the back of the head.

She had never thanked him. A handsome, apparently successful man had gotten her car running for free, and she hadn't even had the grace to thank him properly. She tried to remember all the reasons why she had been right to suspect his motives, but somehow they didn't quite ring true.

Jolie brushed her bangs up, then down, blowing out a stiff breath and closing her eyes until the world righted itself and equilibrium returned and she could look at the situation dispassionately.

On second thought, it just didn't figure. He had to have some ulterior motive, something so slick and cagey that she couldn't even think of it. And maybe—good gracious— maybe he was just a nice man who liked to help people. Stranger things had happened.

Somewhere.

Sometime.

Telling herself that it didn't matter, she took a last measuring look at traffic, then pulled away from the curb.

The problem was, somehow it did matter. A lot.

Enough to make her feel small and petty and unreasonable.

She was halfway home before it occurred to her that she still had both of those coupons.

Vince shifted in his seat, the safety belt biting into his shoulder. He craned his neck, trying to work out a kink there. It was ridiculous, getting this worked up over a little thing like having his motives questioned. Everyone was suspicious of everybody, at least until they got to know one another. He'd been accused of having ulterior motives before, though not in quite some time. It wasn't pleasant, but it wasn't fatal.

So she didn't trust him. So what? The world was full of people who expected automotive repairmen to rip them off. It was foolish to think she would be any different. And what difference did it make, anyway? God had obviously brought her into his life so that he could get her old car running for her again, and that was just what he'd done. End of story.

The thing wasn't going to run for long, though. With just a cursory inspection he'd found enough wrong under that hood to keep him busy for days, but he'd only mentioned the worst of it because it was obvious that she didn't have much money. It was just as glaringly obvious that she wouldn't be easy to help, either.

Maybe that was the point.

If so, he'd definitely be seeing her again. He believed that God had a purpose in all that He allowed into the lives of His children. So if he never saw her again, so be it. It wasn't his business, after all, to second-guess God, and he was just fine with that.

So why was he fighting the urge to turn around and

give her a lecture on the stupidity of looking a gift horse in the mouth?

Ridiculous. Just ridiculous.

He didn't know her well enough to be this disappointed in her attitude. And he probably never would. A hole seemed to open in his chest, burning hot around the edges.

Vince sighed and tried to concentrate on his driving. He passed an intersection on a green light and immediately heard the screech of tires followed at once by the crunching of metal. Automatically, Vince flipped on his warning lights and pulled out of traffic.

Looking around, he saw that two cars had collided in a grocery-store parking lot across the street. It didn't seem serious, and it wasn't impeding traffic, plus, he was off-duty. The fact was, he didn't make wrecker runs anymore. At least he hadn't until Jolie Wheeler had called. Well, that would teach him.

Shaking his head, he began making his way across the busy street to the parking lot. What was he going to do? Leave without making certain that no one needed his assistance? Not his style. Then again, neither was embarrassing himself, but he'd managed to do that twice now with Jolie Kay Wheeler. Twice was quite enough. Why couldn't he just leave well enough alone?

He reached the scene of the mishap, killed his engine and slid out onto the tarmac. Two women were glaring at each other over the hoods of their tangled cars. Vince put on a smile and waded into the fray.

"Can I help, ladies?"

Almost an hour later he'd managed to uncouple their bumpers and pull out a fender so both could be on their way, still angry but maintaining their civility even as they each contemplated a hike in insurance rates. Twenty bucks richer—the one with the crumpled fender had insisted on compensating him—Vince swung the wrecker through a fast-food lane to pick up a burger to eat at home. Alone.

He could've dropped in on his mom or one of the girls. They were always willing to set an extra plate at the table for him, but they were always wanting to know where he'd been and who he'd seen lately, too, and he just wasn't in the mood to answer questions about his nonexistent love life or hear how he worked too much. He wasn't in the mood to eat alone, either, but those were the options. With a sigh, he resigned himself to the latter.

It was only later as he bit into his burger at the kitchen counter that he wondered if Jolie would call on Cutler Automotive when her old jalopy finally conked on her again, because conk it would—and she still hadn't redeemed those coupons.

Feeling a little better, he enjoyed the rest of his burger.

Chapter Three

❧❧❧

"Aaargh!"

Jolie smacked the steering wheel with a closed fist. Not again! This time the engine wouldn't even turn over. No cough, no sputter, nothing.

She'd have cried if it would've done any good, but tears wouldn't pay for automotive repairs. Air wouldn't either, and that's what was in her checking account at the moment, with payday still two days away and rent due next week.

To make matters worse, she was going to miss at least a few hours of work this morning. The week was not starting out well. Sick at heart, she wrenched her keys from the ignition and crawled out of her old four-banger—*no*-banger at the moment—to head back upstairs.

Her first telephone call was to Mr. Geopp, who told her only to get into work when she could. He was a pleasant enough employer but somewhat distant personally. His late wife had been easier to talk and relate to. She'd cut Jolie every possible break, especially after Russell had arrived.

Jolie would stay with Geopp for no other reason than

loyalty to the memory of his wife. She just wished that he would display a little more emotion, if only to let her know for sure where she stood with him in moments like this. It was one more worry on a long list of worries.

Jolie sat down to think through her options with the car. It had started before with a simple jump from a battery charger. Maybe that would work once more. She judged her chances of getting it done for free a second time at slim to none, however, especially if she called Cutler's again. After questioning Vince's integrity, she doubted that he'd cut her a break. Then again, neither would any other emergency service in town.

She thought of the coupons and shook her head in resignation. Cutler Automotive probably jacked up the price twice as high as normal before giving their fifty percent discount, but at least the towing would be free. They couldn't jack up free.

Sighing, she reached for the telephone once more. This time a perky-sounding female answered the call.

The wrecker arrived twenty-four minutes later.

Jolie was sitting on the bumper tapping one toe against the pavement when the familiar white truck swung into the lot. Her stomach lurched in anticipation, but then a stranger opened the driver's door and got out.

"You Ms. Wheeler?"

Nodding, Jolie tamped down her disappointment and straightened away from the car to look over this newcomer.

He seemed roughly the same age as Vince and had a shock of very dark hair falling forward over his brow, but that was where the similarities ended. This fellow was shorter and wider than Vince with a noticeable bulge around the middle and a slight under-bite that made his lower jaw seem overlong. His brown eyes twinkled merrily as he thrust out his right hand.

"I'm Boyd. What can I do for you?"

"You can make my car go."

"Well, let's have a look," he said noncommitally, taking a toolbox from the truck, "and while I'm looking, why don't you tell me what's been going on with it?"

Jolie started with that morning's fiasco and worked her way backward over the past couple weeks, leaving out only Vince's diagnosis. By the time she was through with her tale, he was nodding his head knowingly.

"Sounds like the alternator and probably a bad sensor. I'll try resetting the sensor and jump-starting it."

Jolie breathed a sigh of relief, but it was for naught. The sensor would not register, according to Boyd, and the jump did no good.

"Well, I'll tow her in and see what a full diagnostic turns up," he said blandly.

"What's that going to cost?" Jolie asked, fishing the coupons from the hip pocket of her jeans. "I have these."

Boyd took the coupons, kept the one for the free tow and handed back the other, saying, "These'll help."

"So how much?"

He shrugged. "Provided it's what I think it is and we don't find any other problems, I'd say about three hundred, but a lot depends on the parts. This is a domestic car, but a lot of the parts are foreign-made, so…" He shrugged again.

Jolie felt physically ill.

"Is that three hundred before or after the discount?"

He looked at her sympathetically. "After."

She momentarily closed her eyes.

"I can't afford that!"

"Aw, don't worry," he told her. "The boss will cut you a deal."

That would be the boss whom she'd practically called a crook.

"I wouldn't count on it," she muttered.

Boyd chuckled. "No, really. Vince is a good guy. He helps people out all the time. Between you and me, he'd probably give the business away bit by bit if I didn't keep reminding him that he was supposed to be making a profit. But then, the way I figure it, God takes care of His own."

Jolie didn't know about that. She just knew that life had suddenly gotten immeasurably more difficult for her personally, and it hadn't exactly been a walk in the park to begin with.

"I don't know how I'm going to manage this."

"Listen, just call the shop later and speak to Vince," Boyd urged. "Use the second number on the coupon. Okay?"

"Sure."

The two of them were probably working the scam together, she thought sullenly, and the nice-guy acts were just a carefully coordinated part of it.

Then again, the car wasn't faking it. The thing had been bugging out on her since well before Vincent Cutler had showed up on the scene.

Boyd had her put the car in Neutral so he could push it out of its parking space and "get a good hook on it." A few minutes were all that were required to secure the towing device. Then he just started up the automatic winch, and they stood there watching the front end of her car slowly rise off the ground.

"I have to find a ride to work," Jolie muttered to herself.

"Yeah? Where do you work?"

She told him, and he jerked his head toward the cab of the truck. "Get in. I'll drop you."

She brightened. That was the first bit of good news she'd had today.

"Really?"

"It's on the way."

"Great."

She climbed into the cab of the truck while he finished securing the tow. It was spotlessly clean, despite a gash in the vinyl of the bench seat, and sported a two-way radio, GPS system and some sort of miniature keyboard attached to the dash with an electronics cord.

As soon as Boyd slid beneath the steering wheel, he picked up the keyboard and typed in some letters and numbers, then he triggered the radio and informed whoever was on the other end that he was headed back to the garage with a car in tow, rattling off both make and model.

Soon Jolie was standing in front of the dry cleaners watching her car move away behind the wrecker, its front end pointing skyward. Mindlessly, she swept her bangs back and then smoothed them down again before turning to enter the shop. Bumping into one of their regular customers, she pasted on a smile. A glance showed her that the shop was full and the counter vacant while Geopp evidently searched for garments to be picked up. She went to work.

"How are you, Mrs. Wakeman?"

"Arthritis just gets worse and worse" came the usual doleful reply.

"That's too bad. How many pieces today?"

"Three, and be careful of the gold buttons on the blazer. They tarnished last time."

"Yes, ma'am."

The rest of the morning proved as busy as those first few minutes, but Jolie's mind was never far from her troubles.

Immediately after lunch, she called the garage, using the number on the card that Boyd had given her. Vince answered this time.

"Cutler Automotive. This is Vince speaking. How can I help you?"

She gulped inaudibly. "This is Jolie Wheeler again."

"Oh, hi. We've got the car on diagnostics now."

He sounded perfectly normal, as if she hadn't insulted him, as if they were friends or something equally ridiculous. For some reason that rankled, adding a dry edge to her voice.

"So you still don't know what's really wrong with it?"

"We don't have confirmation, no."

"And when will you have confirmation?"

"Shortly."

"Call me as soon as you know what it's going to cost," she demanded.

"All right."

"*Before* you do any work."

Several seconds of silence followed that, and when next he spoke, his voice was tinged with annoyance.

"No one's going to take advantage of you, Jolie."

She went on as if she hadn't heard him.

"Because I really can't afford a big repair bill." Or any repair bill for that matter.

He sighed gustily.

"I realize that. Look, why don't you just come by the

shop after work? I'll show you exactly what's wrong with your car and what it's going to cost to fix it, and we'll figure out how to take care of it. Okay?"

He couldn't have sounded more reasonable, so why did she feel like needling him?

"And just how would you suggest I get over there without transportation? Take the bus?"

It was an entirely plausible possibility, which made what happened next all the more inexplicable.

"I'll pick you up," he said lightly. "What time to do you get off work?"

She didn't even balk, which in itself was appalling.

"Six o'clock."

"Okay. See you then."

They quickly got off the phone after that. Jolie stood staring at the thing for a long moment, wondering what on earth had possessed her to agree that he should pick her up, but then she shook her head.

Why shouldn't he? He had her car, after all. She hoped she could wangle a ride home out of it, too. Beyond that, she just refused to think, period.

Vince pulled up to the curb in front of the dry cleaners at precisely three minutes past six. The shop had obviously seen better days. Its storefront looked outdated and rather dingy, but the area was clean and safe. Because he was in a ten-minute loading zone, he kept the engine running and settled back to wait.

He didn't have to wait long. The door opened just moments later, and Jolie burst out onto the sidewalk. He grinned at her dropped jaw. Her ragged little car was purring like a contented kitten.

"It's fixed!"

He laughed at her delight, but then her face turned thunderous. Her hands went to her hips, and he *knew* what she was going to say. Even as she spoke, he released his safety belt, opened the door and stood, one foot still inside the car, one hand on the steering wheel.

"I did *not* authorize any work."

"No, you didn't," he interrupted, "but it had to be done."

"You said we'd talk about it first!"

"Jolie, how would you get back and forth to work without your car?"

She put a hand to her head, ruffling her bangs and then smoothing them again. Vince tried not to smile at what seemed to be a characteristic gesture, something she did without conscious thought.

"I can't pay for it!" she suddenly wailed, as if he didn't know that.

The sidewalk was not the place to talk about it, however.

"Get in," he told her, indicating the passenger seat. For a moment she just stared at him. "Get in," he repeated. "My truck's back at the shop. We can talk on the way."

She trudged around and got into the car with all the enthusiasm of a prisoner on the way to her execution. He chuckled despite his better judgment.

"It's not funny," she grumbled as he dropped down into the seat and clipped his belt once more.

"It's not tragic, either."

"Shows what you know," she snapped. "When was the last time you had to choose between paying the rent and other obligations?"

"It's been some while," he admitted, "but I have been there."

"Then you understand that there's just no way…" She gulped. "A—a few bucks a month, maybe, if I—"

"Will you just listen for a minute?" he urged, laying his arm along the back of her seat in entreaty.

She frowned at him, worry clouding those jade-green eyes.

"I have an idea about how we can square this."

Her mouth compressed suspiciously. It was a very pretty mouth, wide and mobile and full-lipped, but he couldn't help wondering what or who had fostered that mistrustful expression.

"How?" she asked.

He glanced at the front of the dry cleaners.

"Well, if it's not a conflict of interest for you, I need someone to do my laundry."

She blinked.

"Laundry?"

"Yeah, you know, dirty clothes and shop rags, some linens, that sort of thing."

The clouds were beginning to lift from her eyes, but her tone was tart as she retorted, "I know what laundry is, but why should I do yours?"

She buckled her safety belt, and Vince put the transmission in gear, turning away so that she wouldn't notice that he struggled with a sudden grin.

"Garages are dirty places," he began, nosing the car into traffic, "and I own all the uniforms that the guys wear. I thought I could do the washing myself, even bought a top-of-the-line, extra-capacity washer-and-dryer set, but it just doesn't get done in a timely manner."

"And you want to pay me to do it."

"Something like that."

She flipped the end of her ponytail off her shoulder, obviously thinking.

"I get it. You're talking about a barter arrangement, basically."

He nodded and signaled with the blinker that he was moving the car over into the next lane.

"Unless, like I said before, it's a conflict of interest for you, given that your regular job is with a dry cleaner."

"Not a problem. Mr. Geopp stopped taking in laundry a few months ago after his wife died."

"That's too bad, about his wife, I mean."

"Yeah, she was a good lady," Jolie said lightly, but something about her tone let him know that she honestly grieved the woman's passing.

"Were you friends?"

"Not really," Jolie replied, looking away. "About the laundry…"

He took the hint and dropped the subject.

"I have to warn you, there's lots of it."

"Good. That means I'll get the debt worked off sooner rather than later."

He nodded, signifying that they had come to an agreement in principle at least.

"Okay, so all we have to do is negotiate the particulars. I understand that laundry costs are figured by the pound or by the piece."

"That's right."

"I don't have any way to weigh it, so I say we go by the piece, then, if that's agreeable to you."

She named a price that was very much in line with what he'd expected, given that he would be providing the equipment and the necessary supplies. He proposed drawing up a debit sheet so she could mark off her work and subtract the cost of it from the repair bill, which would reflect the fifty-percent reduction that she'd been promised and that would include some extra repairs to her car that he felt were necessary but which he had not yet done.

"I only have two days a week to devote to this," she warned him.

"And what two days would those be?"

"Sunday and Monday. Those are my days off from the dry cleaners."

He shook his head.

"Sundays are for church. I'll be content with Mondays."

"No matter how long it takes for me to work off the debt?" she pressed.

"No matter how long it takes," he assured her.

She stared out the window for a long time, her expression hidden from him. He waited, confident of her decision. Finally she looked straight ahead.

"Okay, it's a deal."

He let her see his smile.

"Let me show you where you'll be working, then."

"Might as well." She sat up a little straighter.

"Obviously this street is Hulen," he pointed out, slowing to make a right turn. "We're going to take the Interstate up here and head west for about a mile."

She nodded, obviously making mental notes as he drove and talked her through the route.

When he turned the car down his street, she drew her brows together and said, "This can't be right."

"What do you mean? It's right up here."

"Here?" she echoed uncertainly, indicating the neighborhood around them with a wave of her hand.

The development was brand-new, not even half occupied yet, but that didn't explain her confusion to him. He let it go long enough to pass by the two empty lots between the corner house and his own at the top of the rise.

"This is it."

He couldn't help the note of pride in his voice.

By some standards, it was a modest home, but it was everything he had ever wanted, bright, roomy, well-appointed and undeniably attractive with its gabled metal roof and exterior of natural stone and rich red brick. He'd labored over every detail, probably to the point of driving the architect and builder nuts, but this was the place where he intended to live out the bulk of his life and, he hoped, one day raise a family.

Most folks didn't look at a first house as a long-term home, but Cutlers weren't the sort who "traded up." They were the kind of people who put down roots, sank them deep and let the years roll by in relative contentment. They believed in God, family, personal integrity, hard work and generosity, all notions that he'd once found boring and mundane. He'd gotten over all that, and he hadn't questioned his values again—until he saw the look on Jolie Wheeler's face as he turned her old car into his curving driveway.

She hated the place; he could see it on her face, and his gut wrenched. Disappointment honed a fine, defensive edge onto his voice.

"What's wrong with it?"

"What's wrong?" she echoed shrilly. "It's your house!"

"You expected me to take you to someone else's house?"

"I expected you to take me to your *business,* one of your garages!"

He stared at her, realization dawning.

"You thought I'd put a washer and dryer in one of my shops?"

"Of course I did!"

He stroked his chin, thinking. Guess he hadn't ever said that the appliances were at his house, and he *had* mentioned uniforms and shop rags and dirty garages.

"Never thought about putting a laundry room into the shop," he mumbled. "Might not be a bad idea. I'll have to look into that."

She threw up her hands, clearly exasperated.

"And in the meantime?"

He shrugged. "In the meantime we've got what we've got, don't we?"

She dropped her jaw, trying to see, apparently, just how far it could go without dislocating. He clamped his back teeth together and mentally counted to ten before drawing a calming breath and reaching way down deep for a reasonable tone.

"Look, I didn't mean to mislead you. The thought of putting a laundry room in the shop itself never even occurred to me."

"And you assumed that I understood you were taking me to your house?"

"Yeah, actually, I did."

She rolled her eyes at that.

"If you prefer," he offered grimly, "you can take the stuff to a commercial laundry somewhere."

"And who's going to pay for that?" she demanded.

"I will," he gritted out, hanging onto the wispy tail end of his patience, "but first you really ought to take a look at what my laundry room has to offer and what you'll have to haul around town if you decide that you just can't stand working here."

She turned her head to stare out the passenger window, drumming her fingers on the armrest attached to the door. He didn't know what else to say, what she expected him to say now, so he just waited her out. After some time she abruptly yanked the handle and popped up out of the car. Vince breathed a sigh of relief. He didn't know if his relief stemmed from her cooperation or the possibility that her disapproval was not directed at his home after all.

He killed the engine as she moved around the car toward the walkway. He got out, tossed her car keys to her and followed her along the curving walk to the front door. He didn't usually go in this way, preferring to park in the garage at the side of the house and enter through the back hall and kitchen, but he'd always admired the professional landscaping. In the summertime the flower beds beneath the front windows would blaze with purple lantana. Now he looked at it all with an especially critical eye, wondering what she thought of it, though why he should care was beyond him.

To put it bluntly, the girl was a charity case, and as prickly as a cactus. What difference did it make whether or not she approved of his house? Or him, for that matter? And yet it did. He couldn't help wondering why, but when it came right down to it, he was almost afraid to know.

Chapter Four

Jolie tried not to be impressed by the sprawling structure sitting proudly atop the gentle hill, but that wasn't easy. It rose up gleaming and perfect, like something out of a storybook, with its rock and brick exterior and shining metal roof. The walkway underfoot was constructed of the same red brick and brown stone as the house and was flanked by billowing hillocks of greenery and clumps of a spiky plant that looked like a big, spiny artichoke to her. She didn't know one plant from another, but she knew money on the ground when she saw it.

She couldn't wait to see the inside of the place, even if the hair had stood up on the back of her neck when she'd first realized where he'd brought her.

His house, for pity's sake!

What'd he think, that she would be so impressed she'd just fall all over him?

Not likely. No way. Uh-uh. She had better sense than that, thank you very much.

But, oh man, what a place.

Vince slipped past her on the brick porch, which was deeply inset beneath a tall arch, and jammed a key into the lock, giving it a quick twist. The tall, honey-colored wood plank door, inlaid with artistically rusted nailheads and iron bands, swung open soundlessly, revealing stone floors and smooth walls plastered in pinkish-tan adobe. The tall narrow windows flanking the door were made of stained glass depicting two spiny cacti in a delicate green with blossoms of rose red.

He stepped back to let her pass, and she'd have wiped her feet before entering if there had been a mat of any sort. As it was, she wiped her hands surreptitiously on the seat of her worn jeans, just in case they were dirty, then tugged on the hem of her T-shirt to cover the self-conscious action. She tilted her head back in the foyer, looking up at least twenty feet to the ceiling, past an elegantly rustic wrought-iron chandelier with cut-glass shades.

To her left was a hallway. To her right stretched a huge room set off by tall arches. It was completely empty except for a pair of light fixtures, larger versions of the one hanging over her head, and a leafy fern that sat on the floor in front of a window covered by a faded bed sheet. Straight ahead Jolie spied the back of a nondescript sofa and the overhang of a bar topped in polished granite.

"This way," he said, leading her through the foyer and into what was obviously a den.

The sofa sat in front of a massive stone fireplace. Flanking the fireplace was an equally massive built-in unit which could easily contain a television set as large as a dining table. Upon it were a small framed photo of several kids with mischievous grins and a pile of paperback books. The only other furnishings in the room were a low, battered table and a utilitarian floor lamp.

At least here the windows were covered with expensive pleated shades in a dark red.

The bar, she saw, opened onto a large kitchen, as did the arched doorways on each end. Louvered, bat-wing doors stood open to reveal an island containing a deep stone sink. Behind it rose enough cabinets to stash away all the cookware usually offered for sale in a small department store.

The brushed-steel fronts of the appliances announced that no expense had been spared in outfitting the space, but the countertops were bare except for a small toaster and a coffeemaker. At the end of the kitchen, surrounded by oriel windows and two doors, one that opened to a hallway and another leading outside, was a dining area large enough to dwarf the small round table and two chairs situated beneath another unique light fixture.

"Who lives here?" she wanted to know.

"I do."

She rolled her eyes at him. "Besides you."

"No one."

Bringing her hands to her hips, she stared at him in disbelief.

"You've got how many bedrooms in this place, two, three?"

"Four, actually."

"And you live here all by yourself?"

"That's right."

She looked around her, dumbfounded.

"It's a little bare," he said sheepishly, and that was putting it mildly. "I really need to get somebody in here to help me do it up right. Just can't figure out who."

Good golly, Miss Molly, what she could do with a place like this!

She couldn't imagine living here, but it was practically empty, almost a blank slate, and she could see just what ought to go where, starting with a pair of big, leather-upholstered, wrought-iron bar stools so company could sit there at the counter enjoying a cold drink while the host prepared dinner. And that island just begged for a big old pot rack, something sturdy and solid, not that the place lacked storage.

"Hire a decorator," she told him. Obviously he could afford professional help.

He wrinkled his nose at that. "I don't know. I'm not much for trends and themes. It's not a showroom, after all, it's a home."

"But the right decorator could do wonders in here," she insisted.

"Yeah, but who is the right decorator?" he asked rhetorically. He then effectively closed the subject by lifting a hand and saying, "Laundry room's this way."

He led her through the kitchen and into the hallway. After pointing out that the garage lay to the left, he turned right. The second door opened into a laundry room large enough to sport not only a top-of-the-line, front-loading washer-and-dryer set but also a pair of roll-away racks for hanging clothes, a work table for folding and an ironing board, plus a sink and various cabinets.

Dead center on the tiled floor lay a heap of clothing big enough to easily hide a full-grown man. Sitting up. Jolie's jaw dropped.

"How long have you been accumulating that?" she asked, pointing at the pile.

"Week, week and a half," he said mournfully. "By Friday there'll be about half that much again."

"Good grief!" she exclaimed, mentally rolling up her sleeves. "Looks like I've got my work cut out for me."

He lifted his hands. "So do I load it up or not?"

"In what?" she asked dryly. "You got a dump truck around here?"

He chuckled. "Not that I've noticed."

"Well, then," she said with a sigh, "I guess we'll do it your way."

He just grinned, blast his good-looking hide, and well he might. In his place she'd be grinning, too. She was smiling on the inside as it was. Working in a place like this was going to be an out-and-out pleasure, even if it was only temporary. If he tried anything funny with her, she'd just walk out and leave him and his laundry high and dry without the least qualm.

Looking at it that way, she couldn't lose, because whatever happened, her car would be fixed. She almost hoped he *did* try to take advantage of the situation, but not until her debt was paid off because she didn't like owing anybody anything.

Yes, sir, smiling on the inside.

For once, things were going to go her way.

"This one?" Jolie slowed the car as they drew near the corner. Vince shook his head.

"No, the next."

She sped up again, laughing when the little car responded with more pep than usual. "I can't get over how much better it runs."

"It'll drive even smoother with the tires rotated and balanced," he told her. "You might notice a little improvement when we get all the hoses replaced, too, but probably not. You won't have to worry about another breakdown anytime soon, though."

"Music to my ears," she said, and he couldn't help smiling.

She drove as she seemed to do everything else, he noted, with an innate wariness. It certainly kept her on her toes and gave him some confidence in her safety on the road, but it also made him a little sad because she seemed to be constantly expecting trouble and catastrophe.

Over all, Jolie Wheeler struck him as a woman who'd had a lot of hard knocks in life, which was, he supposed, nothing new. The odd thing was that he didn't much like thinking of it.

The way she'd taken in his place had told him that she was unfamiliar with some of the more recent building trends. Later, she'd seemed to be mentally furnishing and decorating the space, and yet she'd remained oddly detached, admiring but certainly not gushing with compliments. He had sensed a kind of assumption on her part that she was out of her element in his house, and that had irritated him a little. Okay, a lot.

He was proud of his home. It was no mansion, but it was comfortable and spacious and extremely well-built. For the life of him, he didn't see why she shouldn't feel perfectly at ease in such surroundings, especially as he'd been particularly struck by how *right* the place felt for her. Maybe that accounted for the new idea noodling around in the back of his mind.

What he'd told her about needing help with furnishing and decorating the place was true. In fact it had begun to take on a certain urgency as his mother and sisters had started pressing him to let them have a go at it. He shuddered mentally, imagining what that might mean. If he wasn't very careful he'd walk into his own house one day soon and find it outfitted in chintz and lace and filled up with kitschy knickknacks.

He liked what Jolie had done with the apartment much more than what his mother and sisters had done with their respective homes. Could she be talked into giving him a hand with his place? He was trying to think how to broach the subject when his stomach gurgled and growled—more like roared, actually. It was so loud that Jolie burst out laughing.

Mildly embarrassed, he clapped a hand over his belly.

"Feeding time at the zoo, I take it," she teased.

"Hey, I'm a hardworking man, and it's dinnertime, okay?"

"Okay by me," she grinned.

Suddenly his heart was beating a little too pronouncedly as he made a spur-of-the-moment decision. He shifted in his seat, wondering if it was wise but knowing that he was going to do it. Fearing she could get the wrong idea, though, he made the suggestion as casually as he could manage.

"Listen, there's a pretty good restaurant up here on the right. Why don't we stop off and grab a bite?"

For a second, he got no reaction. Then she made a face, and he was sure that she was going to tell him to go soak his head. To his surprise, though, her answer was fairly ambiguous.

"I'm not really fit for going out after a day at the cleaners. It's dirty, smelly work, and—"

"You look good to me," he blurted and then could've bitten his tongue off—until she slipped him an almost hopeful glance out of the corner of her eye. "It's a casual sort of place," he added quickly. "I'm, uh, not exactly dressed for anything fancy, either." He indicated his uniform with a wave of one hand.

They came to a red light, and she gave him another one of those sideways looks.

"Just dinner," she said.

It could have been a question or a warning, but he decided to take it as the former, quipping, "Sure. You didn't think I was going to insist on going roller-skating afterward, did you?"

Her mouth quirked up in a smile.

"Do people still roller-skate? Isn't it all roller-blading now?"

He relaxed.

"Doggoned if I know. If you don't do it in a garage or on a field, I haven't had much experience with it."

They both chuckled and drove on in silence for a couple more blocks.

"That's it right up there," he said, and she turned off the street into the parking lot. "Best chicken-fried steaks in town," he told her as she parked.

After killing the engine she said dryly, "Let's hope there's something a little healthier on the menu."

"Well, sure," he teased, "they've got fried chicken, too."

She rolled her eyes as she climbed out of the car. Chuckling, he let himself out on the other side.

"The menu lists a bunch of salads," he assured her as they walked toward the restaurant. "I've even been known to eat one a time or two."

"I'll bet it had fried chicken on top of it," she retorted as he pulled open the door and held it for her.

So it had, but he let his grin be his admission, to her obvious amusement.

The hostess hurried toward them. A teenager in baggy cargo pants a size too large and a T-shirt a size too small, she wasn't dressed any better than they were. She greeted them with a smile and led them to a booth with bench seats and a plank table.

Vince ordered iced tea, chips and salsa as an appetizer and the chicken-fried steak for a main course. Jolie went for an Oriental salad with grilled chicken and mandarin oranges. They both asked for extra lemon with their tea.

Business seemed unusually slow, so the service was especially prompt, leaving them little time for talking. Even at that, he did most of it.

"So, Jolie Wheeler, tell me something about yourself."

She shrugged and said, "Not much to tell."

"What about your family?"

She looked down at the thick paper napkin in her lap. "Don't have much. What about you?"

"Too much." He chuckled and took it back. "Naw, not really. Thing is, I've got four sisters, and I'm smack dab in the middle."

"That must be trying at times."

"At times," he admitted. "The older two want to baby me all the time, and the younger two think their big brother is supposed to baby them. At least I got four brothers-in-law out of the deal."

"So they're all married then?"

"That's right, and they hate that I'm not. It's like their mission in life is to see that I am, theirs and Mom's."

"And why aren't you?" Jolie asked lightly.

He shrugged. "Haven't found the right lady yet."

"Oh, like you've been out searching high and low for her," she said, sounding very skeptical about that.

He rubbed his palms against his thighs and admitted, "Not lately. I'm open to it, though."

She seemed surprised by that.

The chips and salsa arrived then, and he was hungry enough to dive in, but from long habit, he bowed his head first and silently said grace over his food. When he looked up again, reaching for a crisp triangle of fried-corn tortilla, she was sitting with both shoulders pressed to the back of her seat, her mouth compressed in a straight line.

"What's wrong?"

"I…were you *praying* just then?"

"Yeah. What of it?"

"Nothing." She shook her head and glanced around. "So you're, like, a God freak or something?"

"You could say that. What about you? Aren't you a believer?"

His stomach muscles clenched as he waited for her answer.

"Yeah, I am." She did that thing with her bangs, and then she positively astounded him, muttering, "Actually, my brother's a minister."

"No kidding!"

She nodded, then looked away and back again.

"I never asked you, how do you like your shirts done?"

The abrupt change in subject startled him.

"Oh. Uh."

"Starch?"

"Well…"

"They stay cleaner longer, but it takes extra time," she told him matter-of-factly. "Spray starch gives it a nice finish, but a lot of men like the extra weight and feel of the real thing."

"Spray starch is fine," he said, realizing that she was trying to avoid talking about her brother. Or God. Vince wasn't sure what to think about that. Either way, it troubled him, but since she was obviously unwilling to get into it, he had no choice but to let it go.

His stomach growled again, and he loaded up one of the chips, inviting her to help herself. They'd emptied the basket by the time the main course arrived, and he'd told her his sisters' names and those of his nieces and nephews, except the one on the way, but she hadn't said another word about her own family or much of anything else.

"So how'd you get into the car-repair business?" she asked as he cut up his plate-sized steak.

"Went to school, went to work, saved up some cash, made an investment. I reinvested that and started looking for a property. It grew from there."

She stabbed a piece of lettuce with her fork.

"You make it sound easy."

He shook his head, chewing the tender steak, and swallowed.

"Lots of hard work and pinching pennies."

She waved a fork around and asked, "You do this sort of thing all the time?"

"What sort of thing?"

"Bartering with people who can't afford to pay cash for their car repairs."

He shrugged. "It seems a good way to take care of the problem."

"Seems chancy to me. How do you know you're coming out even?"

He laid down his knife and fork and rested his fore-arms on the table. "Listen, I'm not ashamed to say that I've worked hard because I have, but the truth is that I've been very richly blessed in life, too. It would be pretty selfish and self-centered of me not to try to work with folks who haven't had my breaks. Don't you think?"

"Yeah," she admitted bluntly, "I do."

He chuckled at her refreshing honesty and got down to some serious eating.

At least they agreed on *something*. So what if she was wary and kept her distance? Maybe she wasn't a "God freak," as she'd put it. She obviously had some standards, and that was okay by him.

If his stomach muscles sometimes clenched around her, well, he'd figure out what that meant later. Mean-while, they were both getting their needs met. She needed her car in good running order; he needed his laundry done. And maybe they could help each other in additional ways, too. Time would tell.

"About Monday," he said, preparing to step out of her car in front of his office, "I'll be there to let you in, and if I'm not there when you need to leave, you can just lock up on your way out."

"All right."

"Meanwhile, I'll expect you to drop the car by on Sat-urday morning to get those hoses changed."

She nodded. "I'll do that." He had his head out the door when she impulsively stopped him. "By the way…" He relaxed back into his seat and turned to face her.

"Yeah?"

She felt awkward saying it, but she knew it was the right thing to do.

"I wanted to thank you. For everything. I—Including dinner. I really didn't expect you to buy."

He smiled. "No biggie. Consider it my way of apologizing for failing to tell you up front that you'd be working at my house."

"All right."

"That mean I'm forgiven?"

"Let's just say I'm willing to overlook your lapse in judgment. Again."

"Ouch."

She laughed, so he wouldn't figure it was too big a lapse in her estimation.

"Take care now," he said, getting out of the car. He flipped her a jaunty wave and walked toward a big white pickup truck with the shop's name and information painted on the sides. Thoroughly bemused, Jolie put the car in gear and headed home.

She had to say this for Vincent Cutler. He was one of a kind. First he'd frightened her, then he'd charmed her, then angered her and then charmed her again. That ought to be a recipe for distrust and disaster, but somehow she felt that he was basically harmless. In fact, he seemed like a real nice guy.

More puzzling still, he seemed actually to like her, and she hadn't really given him anything much to like. That made her wonder if he didn't have a hidden agenda, but if he did, she couldn't figure out what it was. He didn't seem to be the self-righteous, pie-in-the-sky type that she'd too often found religious people—including her brother Marcus—to be. Then again, he didn't appear to be out for whatever he could get, either. He just seemed to be…well, so far as she could tell, he was just a really nice man, which, in more ways than one, was surprising.

For one thing, Vincent Cutler was a handsome man, and he had the easygoing self-confidence that all handsome men seemed to possess. In addition, he was ambitious, but in a hardworking, down-to-earth way, not at all as if he figured the world owed him success for being what he was.

It didn't quite seem fair that on top of all that he should also be nice. Could be for show, of course. He might be the most clever of con men, but somehow she didn't think so.

She owed him money, and he was willing to barter for services rendered, but what assurance did he have that she'd even bother to show up for work? The majority of the repairs that her car needed were already done, and since she hadn't actually authorized any of them, she could pretty much tell him to take a leap if she was of a mind to, which she was not.

So, okay, she had to figure that he was a good judge of people, too, but that didn't explain why he'd done what he had. He'd fixed her car, knowing that she very probably would not be able to pay him and had not authorized the work but would likely try to do the right thing. That made him kind, willing to take a chance and a good judge of character.

His list of attributes was getting longer all the time, not that it mattered one tiny whit. She honestly didn't expect to see him much after tonight. They'd made their bargain, and she would fulfill her end as he'd already done his, and that would be that. Wouldn't it?

Somehow she sensed a flaw in her reasoning.

All right, so she'd be working in his house. That didn't

mean he'd have the time or the inclination to babysit her. The man had a business to run, and obviously he wasn't worried about her stealing from him. Why should he? She was no thief.

Of course, he couldn't know that at this point. But she couldn't very well steal a house, and she hadn't seen much inside worth the taking, which made it all the more remarkable, even suspect, that he was willing to go out on a limb for somebody like her.

What did he hope to get out of it? Except a fair exchange of services, that is.

Truth to tell, she just didn't know what to make of Vince Cutler, and maybe she never would. What did it matter anyway, so long as her car was running well and she wasn't choosing between eating and paying a mechanic's bill?

It should not have mattered at all.

But somehow it did.

She told herself that she didn't like surprises, that the world was easier to navigate if people just stayed in their assigned boxes and did what was expected of them. The truth was, though, that Vincent Cutler was turning out to be something of a godsend, and she really didn't want to think about that.

After all, if God was looking out for her, how did she explain losing Russell?

Chapter Five

When he opened his door to her on Monday morning Vince couldn't help smiling. She just looked so good standing there in her simple jeans and a faded red tank top under a soft yellow, short-sleeved shirt hanging open down the front. Her biscuit-gold hair, loose except for the narrow band that held it neatly behind her ears, flowed down her back. Without so much as a dab of makeup or a single piece of jewelry, and dressed for a day of real work, she still managed to look every inch a woman, a woman who was not best pleased, if her frown was any indication.

He supposed it had to do with the dirty, dark-blue shadow on his chin and jaws. His mother and sisters certainly scowled if he went around unshaven, but sometimes a fellow just couldn't face a razor in the morning, and Monday was the one day of the week when he didn't have to, provided, of course, that he didn't have errands to run or a meeting of some sort.

Today was such a day, which meant that he'd seen no reason to shave. Now, rubbing his prickly jaw with one hand, he wished he'd lathered up anyway.

Putting on the best face that he could under the circumstances, he broadened his smile and bade her a cheery, "Good morning."

"Morning," she muttered, glancing down at his bare feet before sliding past him into the foyer. "Am I too early?"

He closed the door. "Not at all. I like an early start on the day myself."

"Hmm, well, I'll just head to work and let you finish getting ready to leave."

His smile wilted.

"Uh, I'm not going anywhere."

Her chin jerked up, eyes wide as saucers.

"Not going anywhere?"

She couldn't have looked more appalled. Vince shifted his feet.

"Monday's my day off, too. Didn't I make that clear before?"

She folded her arms.

"Obviously not."

He brought his hands to his hips, fighting down a surge of irritation, though whether he was more irritated with himself or her he didn't know. How many times and in how many ways could he mess up with this woman?

"I guess I assumed, since we're both in service industries, that you'd naturally figure…" He broke off, reaching deep for patience. Grasping it, he said, "If it'll make you more comfortable, I'll find somewhere to go."

"Why don't you just do that, then," she retorted, lifting her chin so high that he found himself practically staring down her nostrils.

"Fine," he snapped. "If that's what it takes to make you happy."

Grinding his back teeth together, he stomped off toward the back of the house, across the den and through the shallow alcove that opened onto the master bedroom.

Of all the testy, high-handed, downright unfriendly women in the world, he told himself, Jolie Wheeler purely took the cake.

Ripping a shirt from a hanger in the large walk-in closet, Vince yanked it on over his white T-shirt then went to the dresser to locate a pair of clean white socks. Plopping down on the side of the bed, he jerked on one of the socks. He was about to poke his toes into the other when he heard the front doorbell chime again. Rising, he managed to get the second sock on and take a step toward the door in the same movement.

He hadn't even made the den when one of his sisters—Olivia, he thought, or maybe Sharon, he couldn't always tell the voices of the older two apart—called out, "Hey, Vince! You decent?"

Wincing, he answered. "Yeah."

Great, that was all he needed, his nosy sisters barging in right in the middle of another misunderstanding with Jolie.

He hurried into the den, relieved to see that Jolie was absent. Maybe she hadn't heard the commotion.

Helen, the sister just younger than him, walked into the den. Olivia, the sister just older than him, was on her heels.

"Where are your boots?" Olivia asked, as if he was a two-year-old who'd forgotten where he'd escaped from his shoes.

"Waiting for my feet," he told her dryly. "Actually I was just getting ready to leave."

Maybe that would get them on their way.

Fat chance.

They looked at each other and said in unison, "Hope it's not important."

Obviously no one was going anywhere anytime soon.

Vince stifled a sigh. His sisters were often exasperating, but they were all so crazy about him that he couldn't be unhappy to see any of them. Opening his arms, he wrapped each of them in a one-armed hug and quickly bussed their cheeks, hoping to get them on their way none the wiser.

Heaven knew what they'd think if they were to clap eyes on Jolie.

"Okay, what's up? You two are out and about awful early."

"Earlier than you," Helen teased, rubbing the spot where his unshaven chin had grazed her.

"Like I've never seen either of you running around at mid-morning in fuzzy slippers with curlers in your hair."

Helen chortled and Olivia sniffed, tossing her dark curls.

"That's different," Olivia argued. "I've got three boys to corral."

"And who's corralling those hooligans today?" he asked, grinning at the thought of his nephews.

"Mom."

"But she's got Bets to help her," Helen added with a grin. Vince laughed.

Four-year-old Elizabeth Ann, known affectionately by the family as Bets, effectively commanded the coterie of Cutler grandchildren, numbering six in all. An only child, to the growing dismay of her parents, she'd never had any trouble holding her own against her five older cousins, four of whom were boys.

Now that Donna, Vince's youngest sister, was expecting, however, Bets was showing signs of insecurity at losing her position as the baby of the family. As a result, she'd become a bossy little termagant whose orders the older five obeyed slavishly in an unspoken conspiracy to reassure her.

The whole thing was rather sweet to behold and would resolve itself, everyone was certain, in time.

"So what's got you two over here hassling me at this early hour of the morning?" Vince tried again.

Olivia slipped out of his embrace and moved to the center of the sparsely furnished room, holding out her arms.

"Do you even have to ask? My goodness, Vince, you might as well still be living in that little cracker box of an apartment."

"This house needs proper furnishings," soft-spoken, light-haired Helen added, leaning into him.

"And since you show no signs whatsoever of finding a wife to take care of the matter for you," Olivia began sternly, "we'll just have to do it."

Vince felt a spurt of panic. The very last thing he wanted was his sisters outfitting his house for him. Just the possibility made him shudder.

"Now, look here, sis—"

"Don't you look-here-sis me. I've wiped your snotty nose, not to mention your—"

"Olivia!"

Undaunted, she wagged a finger at him.

"You still haven't bought so much as a throw rug! If we leave it to you, you'll be sitting here alone ten years from now on this same old ratty couch eating your supper out of a can. Now, the alone part you'll have to fix yourself—with God's help, of course—but the other we're willing and able to take care of. So, you can either come shopping with us, or we'll do it without you, whichever you prefer."

He rolled his eyes, preferring a hard jab with a hot poker to either alternative, and caught sight of Jolie's head easing around the casement of the kitchen door. An audacious idea burst into his mind, one he'd been mulling around in some fashion since he'd gotten a look at what she'd done with his old apartment. He knew that the idea was born of desperation and would likely blow up in his face, but he let it out anyway.

"As a matter of fact, that won't be necessary," he said calmly. "It's already in hand."

He beckoned Jolie, weighting the gesture with a hopeful look that he prayed his sisters would miss. She frowned at him but edged into the room, her cheeks a becoming shade of pink.

"I, uh, didn't find any color-safe bleach in the sack of supplies you left in the laundry room."

"No? Could've sworn I picked some up. I'm sure it was on your list."

Actually, he was positive that it was on her list of needed supplies and that he'd bought a big plastic tub of the stuff on his way home Saturday evening. It appeared that her curiosity had gotten the better of her and that she was too embarrassed to admit that fact, which suited him just fine in the present circumstances.

He waved her further into the room, saying to his sisters, "Girls, I'd like you to meet Jolie Kay Wheeler. She's helping me out around here."

Two heads pivoted and tilted. Jolie might have been

a bug under a microscope, the way they were studying her. Vince cleared his throat.

"Jolie, these are two of my sisters. Olivia." He nudged the elder, and she jumped as if he'd stuck her with a hat pin. "And Helen."

His sisters looked at him, then each other and finally at Jolie again. Both melted into smiles.

Helen leaned forward slightly and asked in her sweetest voice, "Would that be *Miss* Wheeler?"

"Uh. Um-hm."

Suddenly those smiles were beaming around the room with the force of a lighthouse on a dark and moonless night at sea, and the next thing Vince knew, they'd swarmed her like a pack of locusts, both chirping at once.

"Oh, it's so nice to meet you!"

"He hasn't said a word, the brat. We spoiled him rotten, you know, only boy and all that."

"But he's really very sweet, not half as stubborn as he seems. A little impulsive, maybe, but manageable."

Vince rolled his eyes at that, but no one paid him the least mind.

"Are you a professional decorator?" Helen asked.

"Have you known each other long?" Olivia wanted to know.

"All right, all right."

Vince waded into the fray and rescued Jolie with a hand firmly cupping her elbow to draw her to his side. She glared daggers up at him, and he could see the demand in her eyes. What was going on?

He tried to think of a way to explain it and came up only with the truth. "I, uh, I've been meaning to ask you if you'd help me outfit this place. I mean, yours looks so great." He shot a desperate volley at his sisters, saying, "I really love what she's done with her apartment. It's just my kind of thing, you know? Very tasteful, very…chic."

He wouldn't know chic if it bit him, but he didn't think it involved being upholstered in chintz or layered with doilies.

Jolie stared at him for a full five seconds before she slowly asked, "You want *me* to help you furnish and decorate this place?"

"Yeah. Sure. Absolutely."

She put a finger to her chest. *"Me?"*

"I know it's a lot to ask," he told her, instinctively pulling her closer, both elbows cupped in his hands now. "But I really like the look of your apartment. I like it better than anything else I've seen. And I *really* need the help." He slid a glance over her head toward his sisters before bringing it back to plumb those soft jade eyes. "Please."

Jolie dropped her gaze, lifted a shoulder in a casual shrug, and lightly conceded, "Okay."

He could have kissed her. He might have kissed her, if his sisters hadn't been standing there grinning like idiots and soaking up the whole thing. As it was, his right hand just sort of slipped around to the center of her back, finding its way beneath the heavy, silken fall of her hair.

He beamed at his sisters.

"See. Good as done."

They ignored him, as usual.

"Now, sugar," Olivia said to Jolie, stepping closer, "if you need anything at all, you just give a yell. All four of us would be delighted to pitch in and help out."

Jolie inched closer to Vince, apparently intimidated by the gleam in his sister's eyes. What could he do but slide his arm around her? He couldn't help noticing that she was a perfect fit.

"In fact," Helen was saying, "why don't you come to dinner on Sunday so we can talk about it all together? Mama would be thrilled, wouldn't she, Vince?"

"Oh, uh, sure."

It was the bald truth, never mind that what his sisters were assuming was not.

"I—I couldn't intrude," Jolie said, obviously unprepared for this full-frontal assault.

"No intrusion!" Olivia exclaimed, seizing and squeezing both of Jolie's hands. "Really, the whole family would be thrilled." She abruptly switched tactics. "Make her come, Vince."

"Oh, please come," Helen added to Jolie.

"All right. Okay. Enough," Vince interrupted firmly, literally putting himself between Jolie and his sisters. "I'll take it from here." He reached out and started sweeping them toward the door with one arm. "Thanks, girls. I appreciate your stopping by, but frankly you're holding up the show now, so if you don't mind…"

"Yeah, yeah, we're going," Olivia conceded drolly.

She pecked him on the cheek and strode for the entry, beckoning Helen to follow. Helen paused long enough to go up on tiptoe and throw her arms around Vince's neck. He bent forward to accept her kiss and hear her whisper in his ear.

"I'm so glad. She's very pretty."

"Um," he answered noncommittally, feeling terrible about misleading them and ironically pleased at how it had gone so far.

"It was very nice to meet you, Jolie," Helen said with a last smile in Jolie's direction.

With her light-brown hair and dark-blue eyes, Helen was the sweetest and most soft-hearted of his sisters and at times his favorite, though he could say the latter of all of them at various moments.

"Nice to meet you, too," Jolie murmured, nodding.

It struck Vince that she actually meant it, and an unexpected feeling of warmth swirled through him. He sent her a grateful look and hurried after his sisters to see them safely out.

He knew that the whole family would soon be thinking, as Olivia and Helen must, that Jolie was his girlfriend, which meant they'd naturally assume that they would see her on Sunday at dinner, and he wouldn't disabuse them of that notion. Yet.

He didn't mean to lie to them. He'd just make the truth clear to them a little later, like after he'd gotten Jolie to agree to help him out. He really did want, need, her help decorating and furnishing his house, and who knew? She might even be willing to come over to his mom's for Sunday dinner. Wouldn't hurt to ask. He hoped.

Jolie stood right where he'd left her until he returned from seeing his sisters out. She'd gotten over her embarrassment at being caught eavesdropping—mostly, anyway. When she'd heard the doorbell and then female voices, curiosity had simply gotten the better of her.

For a moment she'd thought that some girlfriend, or two, had come to call, but she'd quickly realized that they were his sisters. It had become obvious that he didn't want them decorating his house, and she hadn't minded helping him out with that, but of course, he wasn't serious about her doing it. Was he?

She couldn't imagine what had made him desperate enough even to suggest such a thing.

"So what's the deal with your sisters outfitting this place?" she demanded the moment that he reentered the room.

"None at all," he said quite happily, "that's the point."

She glanced at the battered, mismatched furnishings in the room.

"No offense, but you could use some help, not to mention some decent furniture."

"Don't I know it, but not from my family. And with you to help me, they won't have to."

"But you don't really want me to help you furnish and decorate this place," she said confidently, only to watch his face rearrange itself into a blank mask.

"That mean you're backing out on me?"

She gaped in astonishment. He really meant it!

"I'm not a professional decorator," she pointed out.

"So what? Neither are any of them."

"That's not the issue!"

"What is the issue?" he asked sharply. Then, before she could even answer, he turned out both palms beseechingly. "Look, I'll pay you for your help. All right? How would that be?"

"But I'm not a professional decorator!" she repeated, more forcefully this time in case he'd missed it the first.

"I know that!" he retorted. "I don't want a professional decorator. I want a helping hand from someone whose taste I appreciate."

What was he talking about? She didn't have any taste; she couldn't afford *taste*.

Didn't he understand that she'd never had two whole nickels to rub together? Whatever "decorating" she'd done at her place she'd managed with old sheets and stuff. It was all done of necessity. She'd never had the luxury of actually picking out things.

Her world was one of make-do. His was… She looked around her and gulped. This house was a palace, an empty palace.

"You can't mean it."

He thumped the side of his head with the heel of one hand and muttered at the far wall, "I know I'm speaking English, so it couldn't have gotten lost in translation."

She parked her hands at her hips, too astonished to take issue with his jibes.

"You actually *do* mean it."

"Hello! Houston, we have contact."

She flattened her lips and narrowed her eyes at him to let him know that he wasn't funny, at least not to her, but her heart was suddenly racing.

"I don't get it. You've got family ready, willing and able to help you. Why ask *me*?"

"Because I've got family ready, willing and insisting on helping me."

She noted that he had not said able.

He sighed gustily.

"Have you ever seen those old fifties movies where the walls are all papered in big bouquets of flowers and even the lampshades have ruffles on them?"

Jolie made a face, disliking the picture he'd created in her mind.

"I love my mom dearly," he went on, "but she has never met a doily or a chintz pattern that she didn't like. As for my sisters, it's the same song just different verses. They've all got their themes, you know? With Sharon, it's chickens."

"Chickens?" Jolie echoed, eyebrows rising.

"Chickens everywhere," he told her. "The throw pillows in the living room have chickens on them. Chicken-patterned chintz."

He shuddered, and Jolie's mouth twitched.

"With Olivia, it's cows," he went on blandly, "black-and-white cows. Black-and-white cows with red in the kitchen, black-and-white cows with blue in the living room, black-and-white cows with green in the bedroom. Black-and-white cows with yellow in the bath. My brother-in-law swears that late at night he can hear mooing."

Jolie snickered and clapped a hand over her mouth, but despite his woebegone expression, he seemed to be enjoying himself.

"Helen, now, Helen's more sedate," he said. "Helen's whole house is tan. Even the flowers on her chintz sofa are tan. The flowers on the wallpaper are tan. The flowers on the throw rugs are tan."

"Oh, no." Jolie bit down on a sputter of laughter.

"But Donna," he managed to say, despite his own grin, "she's the avant-garde one. Her chintz is polka-dotted. Navy blue on white. Or white on navy blue for contrast."

Jolie guffawed, imagining his house done up in flowered chickens and polka-dotted cows in every color of the rainbow. With doilies.

"S-so you can s-see my problem," he chortled. Swallowing, he managed a serious tone. "Hey, I'm just trying to avoid hurt feelings. And chintz of any sort."

He shuddered spastically, and Jolie nearly fell over, laughing so hard that her sides hurt. He threw an arm around her for support, burbling and bumping hips with her.

"I—I'm a desperate man," he managed, sucking air.

After a moment they both calmed somewhat.

He caught a breath and wiped an eye, saying, "I really don't want to have to hire a professional. I don't want a showplace. I want something homey and comfortable but *me,* and I know I'm more apt to get that with you than with any of them. For one thing, I can be honest with you."

She nodded and dabbed at her eyes with the back of one wrist.

"Okay, I get it now."

He clapped his hands together and turned his face up to the ceiling.

"Thank You, God."

She shoved an elbow into his ribs.

"Get serious."

"Sweetheart, I *am* serious," he told her, sounding it.

She ignored the *sweetheart* part—just a figure of speech, after all—and the little thrill that came with it, concentrating instead on studying her surroundings. She discovered, to her surprise, that she really wanted to do this thing.

Suddenly, her mind was hopping with ideas.

"I just don't know how much good I can do for you," she admitted forthrightly. "I don't have much experience."

"You've got style, though, and it more or less mirrors mine, or what I'd like mine to be, anyway. And I meant what I said about paying you."

She shook her head. "I can't take money for something I'm not trained or qualified to do."

He held out both hands again, this time in a stalling motion. Then he snapped his fingers.

"Tell you what, let's stick with the barter plan. I'll

give you a year, make that two years, of free automobile upkeep for your help."

Her eyes widened, but before she could reply to that generous offer, he held up an index finger.

"This time, though, there are strings attached."

She grinned.

"Let me guess. No chintz."

"That's one, but there is another."

She folded her arms in mock resignation.

"Let's hear it."

He dipped at the knees, scrunching up his face in a wheedling gesture.

"You have to come to dinner on Sunday."

Was that all? She opened her mouth to ask, but he hurried on.

"My family will be disappointed if you don't. The girls are used to getting their way, frankly, but they always mean well, and after refusing their help with the house, I just don't want to have to explain why I couldn't convince you to accept their invitation to Sunday dinner."

She was ready to capitulate after the first sentence, but she didn't let him know that. Vince Cutler groveling was a very pleasant experience.

"Well," she mused, stroking her chin, "I guess I could."

"Great!" He clapped his hands together. "How's this? I'll pick you up for church and afterward we'll go straight to Mom's."

Jolie frowned, suspicion instantly rearing its ugly head again.

"Church? Who said anything about church? I thought we were talking about dinner."

"Dinner's always first thing after church," he told her, matter-of-factly. "Mom usually puts something in the oven or slow-cooker before she leaves the house for services, and it's ready when she gets back."

Jolie bit her lip. What was it with this guy? Every time she thought she had him figured out, he threw her some sort of curve. Was this about his sisters' expectations, his empty house or getting her to church?

What was it with church people, anyway? They came on as caring, then turned on you. Marcus had.

"I don't know," she muttered, more to herself than to him.

"Fine," he said lightly. "I'll pick you up immediately after the service. Just be ready and waiting. Mom hates it when we're late to the table. It's her all-time pet peeve. But it's not too far from your place. If we hurry we'll be there in time."

Jolie figured she'd be nuts to refuse. Two years of no worries about her old car! Plus, she'd have the pleasure of outfitting this grand house.

She nodded decisively.

"Just tell me what time."

"Twelve o'clock noon," he told her, sounding relieved. He smacked his hands together again, rubbing them as he glanced around. "Oh, man, I can't wait to get started. When can we, do you think?"

She shrugged, considering.

"Well, I suppose we could do some preliminary window-shopping as soon as I get the laundry done."

"In that case," he exclaimed, turning toward the kitchen, "I'll help you."

"That's not necessary," she told him, laughing and hurrying to catch up as he strode off on stocking feet.

"I can at least help you sort," he insisted, forging ahead.

Jolie paused to roll her eyes. What kind of guy got this excited about decorating his house? In some ways, she was afraid to find out.

She swept into the laundry room to discover him knee-deep in the pile. He'd started tossing clothes every which way. She stood shaking her head, her hands on her hips, until he plopped a pale-blue dress shirt that would look stunning with his eyes into a pile of jeans. She plucked it out again, then started making a few more corrections, and somehow they fell into a pattern.

Before she knew it, they were standing side by side at the work table treating stains at her direction with one of a trio of products.

When the first load was ready, Vince picked it up and stuffed it into the washer while she measured the correct amount of liquid detergent. She poured it into the dispenser and turned some knobs to adjust the water temperature; then he pushed a button, and water started to fill the tub.

An odd sense of satisfaction settled over her, but she didn't have long to enjoy it. He grabbed her hand and tugged her toward the door.

"Come on," he said, "I want to show you the rest of the house."

She put on a smile, nodded and prepared to be delighted, but that had nothing whatsoever to do with Vince. It was strictly about his house and the unexpected pleasure of getting her hands on it. At least that's what she told herself.

Chapter Six

"Might as well start at the beginning," Vince said, dropping her hand.

He felt all too aware of her for some reason, but he simply wouldn't think about it: better to concentrate on the house.

"You've probably guessed that this big empty space at the front is supposed to be formal living and dining," he quipped, then went on to explain, "I wanted everything open for entertaining, you know? This way, even the entry, which is often just wasted space, becomes a part of the whole, flowing right into the den with the beverage bar and, of course, the kitchen. At Mom and Dad's we're always hanging out in the kitchen."

He glanced over his shoulder as they passed beneath one of a pair of tall, wide arches that opened off the foyer. Leading her to the center of the long space, he let her take the room's measure.

"You could hold a ball in here!" she finally exclaimed.

"I don't think it's that big," he muttered sheepishly. Smiling, he pointed out what seemed to him to be the salient architectural touches.

"The set-backs are perfect for displaying things, figurines maybe or... I don't know."

"Plants," she mused, looking over the nooks and crannies that stair-stepped up the front wall, creating a deep inset for the tall, multipaned window, "and maybe some pottery."

"I like the look of leaded glass," he went on, drawing her attention to the window itself, "but I didn't want anything too formal, so we went with this oxidized surface on the metal parts." He chuckled. "Mom says rust is not a decorative finish, but I think it looks cool."

"Like it's been around a long time and will be forever," Jolie commented, lightly brushing her fingertips over the window casing.

He couldn't have been more pleased.

"That's it. That's it exactly. Besides it just seems more..." He curved his hands, trying to grasp the right word.

"Masculine," Jolie supplied.

He felt a tiny shock at that. He hadn't realized that was the effect that he'd been going for until now.

"Yeah. Yeah, it is at that."

"Which means we can throw in a little elegance without making the room too feminine."

He liked that thought. Elegant but not frilly.

"That sounds right. Now, back here..."

He hurried her across the foyer and into the hall branching off it.

"This first door, that's the powder room."

She craned her neck around a bit before he herded her away.

"These three rooms on the front are bedrooms. The first two share a bath."

Walking her through quickly, he threw open empty closets and pointed out the window seats before moving back into the hall.

"The last one here at the end I think of as the guest room because it has its own bath."

He let her look around for a moment, though the room was basically an empty box with a nice window. The small bath contained a tub with a shower in it, unlike the other two full baths in the house, which boasted both tubs and shower stalls.

They started back down the hall on the other side, toward the powder room.

"This," he said, pushing wide double doors, "is what I call the study."

It was a long room with a single window in the end, lots of bare bookcases and two built-in desks. A computer sat rather forlornly atop one, but he hadn't gotten around to hooking it up yet. Didn't see the point until he at least got a desk chair. Jolie wandered into the room, her jaw dropping.

"You have your own library!"

"I would if I had any books," he said. "I thought this would be a good place for the kids to do their homework and maybe play some video games, that sort of thing."

"Kids!" she exclaimed, whirling on him. "You have *kids*?"

For a moment he wasn't sure what she was asking. Maybe she wondered if he *wanted* kids. Or was she saying that she didn't want them? Then again, it was a pretty straightforward question, even if it didn't make any sense.

"Of course not. How can I have kids when I'm not even married?"

She literally snorted.

"In case you haven't noticed, you don't have to be married to have children."

"*I* do," he stated flatly, frowning.

She stared at him for several seconds, as if verifying the truth of what he'd just said.

Apparently satisfied, she nodded briskly and swept past him, muttering, "Good for you."

His jaw descended. Had he seen the sheen of tears in her eyes? Before he could think better of it, he went after her, catching her by the elbow just as she reached the foyer.

"Jolie, are you okay?"

She nodded, but she didn't look at him.

"I guess it's your religion that makes you think like that. Lots of men don't."

"It's my faith, yes," he said, "but it's common sense, too. Plenty of men feel the same way. They know that children should have two parents."

"But lots of them don't."

"And most of them turn out fine," he conceded, "but it means twice the effort for a single parent."

"True." It came out barely more than a whisper.

He caught her chin with the crook of his fingers and angled her face so he could gauge her expression. For a moment she stood with her eyes downcast before suddenly lifting her eyelids. The jade of her irises sparkled with tears.

"Jolie?"

He was almost afraid to ask why she cried, but she pulled away from him and gave him an answer anyway.

"My sister has a little boy." Her voice cracked at the

end. "His father's in prison for killing an off-duty policeman during a robbery."

Vince pushed a hand over his face, horribly relieved
even as he drawled, "Aw, Jolie, I'm sorry to hear that."

"Russell's better off never knowing him," she asserted
defiantly.

"I'm even more sorry about that," Vince said quietly.

She turned away then, and he watched that steel rod
slide into her spine.

"We don't all get the ideal parents," she told him almost grudgingly.

He wondered about her parents, but he didn't think
asking would get him anywhere just then, not with her
defenses back in place.

"I'm sure there are times," he said carefully, "when
one parent is better than two. I was speaking in gener-
alizations before."

"I know." She glanced at him and moved away, mum-
bling, "I should check the laundry."

"Sure. We can finish the tour later. There's just the
master suite."

He stood there until she disappeared into the kitchen,
then he sighed and jammed his hands into his pockets.

What would he have done, what would he have said,
if it had been her and not her sister? It wasn't his place
to judge, of course, but he did believe that his values
were right, and it made his belly burn to think that she
might have been used by some man and then abandoned
by him.

He went into the living room and sat down to think,
but Jolie Wheeler couldn't be puzzled out with what little information he had. He bowed his head and let the
Spirit guide his prayer.

He asked God why Jolie Wheeler was suddenly a part of his life. She'd said that her brother was a preacher, but she spoke about faith and God as if she didn't quite understand them, almost as if she carried certain resentments. Was he supposed to help her deal with that somehow? Or did God have something else entirely in mind?

There had been moments when he was showing her through the house just now, when being with her had felt exactly right. Then there were those moments of confusion, like now.

He shook his head, asking God not to let him do anything foolish until he had this thing figured out. Oh, and he could use some help keeping his temper, too, because she had a way of setting him on edge, which just went to show how confused he really was.

Vince rarely lost his temper, rarely even felt the emotion of anger, but he seemed prone to step wrong where she was concerned, and then the yelling started. He hadn't raised his voice to a woman other than his sisters in his whole life, and he hadn't done it with one of them since he was maybe fourteen.

What was it about Jolie Wheeler that got under his skin?

Jolie slipped into the kitchen some time later, not quite sure what she expected. It wasn't to find him making lunch.

"What are you doing?"

He turned a glance over one shoulder, smiled and waved a knife smeared with mustard.

"What does it look like I'm doing?"

She folded her arms, relieved at his bantering tone.

"It looks like you're building a wall with bread and meat."

"There's lettuce and tomato in there, too," he told her with mock defensiveness, nodding at the gargantuan sandwich, "and pickles and cheese and bell peppers, even some sliced mushrooms." He slid one half of the monstrosity to the side. "Hope you like mustard."

She blinked, oddly touched, and barely bit back the words, *For me?* They sounded mewling and pathetic even inside her head.

"You want to get that cantaloupe out of the fridge and carve it up?" he directed, pointing with his chin. "I'm in a cantaloupe mood. How about you?"

She walked over to the refrigerator and opened the door.

"I like cantaloupe."

"You can use that paring knife there on the counter," he said. "I rinsed it after I sliced the peppers. Oh, and grab that pitcher of iced tea. There's a bowl of sliced lemon in there, too. Got a white lid on it."

"I see it."

She placed everything on the counter, then carried the melon to the sink, where she split, cleaned, peeled and sliced it, dropping the crescent-moon-shaped slivers into a plastic bowl which Vince had set out for her. While she worked, he got down mismatched plastic tumblers and filled them with ice, tea and lemon, then put the sandwiches on plates and carried everything to the island in the center of the room.

Producing a bag of chips, he leaned a hip against the counter, munching, until she rinsed and dried her hands. With a swipe of one foot, he pulled out a short, rather wobbly stool for her. Then he hopped up onto the counter and lifted his plate onto his lap.

"I could eat a horse," he said, spearing a piece of melon with a fork.

"Is that in here, too?" she teased, eyeing the sandwich mountain on her plate.

He didn't answer, and when she looked up, it was to find his head bowed. She quickly looked down again.

"We thank You, Lord," he said easily, "for Your many blessings. I especially thank You for saving me from the chintz squad and, most importantly, giving me a way to keep from hurting their feelings. You know I love them, Lord, and I know they mean well, so thank You for bringing Jolie along to help me out. Amen."

She didn't know what to think about him mentioning her in his prayer, but what she said was, "Do you always do that?"

"Pray before I eat?" he asked, and quickly devoured the melon slice in two bites. "Yep. Don't you?"

She answered him honestly, but for some reason it made her uncomfortable.

"No."

"How come?" He wrapped his hands around the enormous sandwich. "Wasn't it the done thing at your house?"

"I never had a house," she blurted.

He lowered the sandwich.

"Around your home then."

"Can't say as I really ever had one of those, either."

"You had to grow up somewhere."

She picked up her own sandwich and took a bite just so she couldn't answer him. He did not, however, let the subject drop, just changed his tack.

"Guess your folks weren't the praying kind."

"Wouldn't know. Probably not."

"How is it you don't know something like that?" he asked softly, shifting his plate to the countertop.

She felt her shoulders lift in a shrug, and that was when she knew she was going to answer.

"Never even met my father," she said with a swallow, "and Mom was gone at least half the time."

"Where was she gone to?"

She studied her sandwich, but in truth, her appetite had disappeared.

"The better question is *who* was she gone *with*."

"Who?"

His voice could be so gentle, so warm, sometimes. It made her own sound harsh and sharp.

"Some man or other."

He said nothing for a moment. Then he moved his plate to his lap again and picked up his sandwich.

"Who raised you then?"

She picked a pickle slice out of the sandwich and popped it into her mouth.

"The system."

"The system?" he echoed.

"The state. Child Welfare."

"Ah. I have a real good buddy who was raised in foster homes. You met him, I think. Boyd."

She looked up in surprise, and he bit off a huge chunk of sandwich.

"Wasn't he the guy who towed my car?"

Vince nodded.

"Doesn't he work for you?"

"Um-hm."

"And you still call him a real good buddy?"

He worked the food in his mouth and swallowed.

"What's so odd about that? We were friends before he came to work for me."

They were both aware that she was steering the conversation away from her and back to him, but Vince didn't seem to mind. She let herself relax somewhat.

"Isn't it hard to keep the business part separated from the friendship part?"

"Don't know," he said succinctly, readying his sandwich for another assault. "Never tried."

She rolled her eyes, suddenly enjoying herself again. "Now that's some attitude for a business owner."

"What's wrong with it?"

"What's wrong with it? Somebody has to be the boss, that's what's wrong with it."

"You sound just like Boyd. Sissy and I are always telling him that he's more concerned about my business than I am." He chuckled.

"Who's Sissy?"

"Boyd's wife. We grew up together, Sissy and me. She ran tame with my sisters, Helen and Donna. You probably wouldn't like her. She's sweet as sugar and soft-spoken as a running brook."

Jolie huffed, knowing full well that she was being baited but enjoying herself too much to care.

"I have been insulted. You have just insulted me, Vince Cutler."

He laughed and leaned forward, confessing, "Actually, she spits and hisses just about as much as you. The two of you would either get on like a house afire or you'd rip each other to shreds, and I'm not taking bets on which." He winked then and added, "But she's not as cute as you are."

With that he hopped down from the counter and carried his plate across the room, where he ripped a paper towel from the roll and proceeded to wrap his sandwich for easier handling.

Jolie inwardly sputtered for a moment, but then she blinked and let an unfamiliar feeling wash over her.

Cute. He'd as much as said she was cute.

She began pulling the filling from between the slices of bread, poking it into her mouth bit by bit, and found that it was difficult to chew and smile at the same time.

"I've been thinking about it," Vince said, checking his rearview mirror, "and we don't really have to do those two bedrooms up front. Let's concentrate on the living and dining room for now, and then the den and kitchen."

"That's fine," Jolie said, feeling as though she was sitting on top of the world there in the cab of that big, brutish pickup truck.

She didn't like leaving the laundry unfinished to go shopping, but Vince Cutler could be *very* persuasive. She didn't even like to think how persuasive he could be, so she put her mind on the business at hand.

"However," she said, "the first thing you should do is get some drapes up, especially in those two front bedrooms. Until you get those windows covered, the house is going to look empty from the street."

"I hadn't considered that." He rubbed his cleanly shaven chin, glancing at her. "Where do we find them?"

Jolie considered a moment.

"I've heard there's a store down on Camp Bowie that specializes in window treatments."

"Camp Bowie it is."

"I don't suppose you know the measurements of the windows?" she asked hopefully.

He shook his head. "Not off hand, no, but I think I'm still carrying around a set of house plans tucked behind the back seat."

"Then I'd say we're in business," she told him confidently.

Famous last words.

It turned out that the windows in Vincent's custombuilt house were not standard sizes. A persistent questioning of store personnel elicited the name of a custom draper, who was only too happy to show them styles and fabrics and quote prices, astonishingly high prices to Jolie's mind. In just over two hours at the draper's shop, however, they gained a good idea of what it was going to take to get the windows covered, but they were no closer to actually having done so.

"I think I'm going to have to put together a budget," Vince said thoughtfully, letting the shop door close behind him.

"A budget's good," Jolie agreed, moving across the sidewalk to the truck, which was parked directly in front of the building. The prices of custom-made draperies had shocked her, and her mind was reeling in search of alternatives. "You know, I've got an old sewing machine that I picked up at a garage sale. It's not fancy, but it does a good job, and I've been sewing up curtains and such for years now. Maybe I should—"

Vince cut her off in midthought. "Nope."

He stepped up to her side, and she frowned at him.

"No? Why not? You saw the price of those things."

"Yes, I did, and they're high, but there are other drapery shops." He lifted one booted foot to the front bumper of the truck and balanced his forearms atop his knee. "Besides—and I don't mean any offense—I want this done right *and* quick. Now, I know you'd do good work, but you don't have time for sewing. You're already working three jobs, remember?"

Four counting the extra ironing, she thought, and one of them she'd left unfinished. Piles of laundry waited for the washer back at his house. Still…

"It's going to cost an awful lot of money."

"I'm aware of that. I figure at this point maybe five thousand for window treatments and three, maybe four, times that much for furnishings."

Several seconds passed before Jolie realized her mouth was hanging open. Even then some effort was required to snap it shut again, and she had to swallow before she could speak.

"That's your idea of a budget?"

He dropped his foot to the ground.

"I told you, I want it done right. I'm looking for quality, classic furnishings that won't need upgrading every couple years."

"And you're just going to toss me that much money and expect me to produce what you're looking for?"

"No," he said reasonably, "I intend to oversee every purchase. I want you to tell me what works best where."

She let out a long, slow breath.

"Man, oh, man. Did you ever pick the wrong girl for this job. That's more money than I've made in the past year."

"Jolie," he told her, "I've been planning and saving a long time for this, and I want to get it right. Your job is to tell me what you think will look good. I know what

I like, but I'm not sure which of the things I like will go together."

She shook her head, insisting, "You ought to hire a professional."

"We've been through this. I don't want a professional." He strode for the driver's door, fishing in his jeans pocket for his keys. "Now are you getting in or are we camping on the sidewalk?"

She got in.

"Want to take a look at some furniture?"

"Guess it won't hurt to look," she muttered.

Wrong again.

They hit four different stores before a helpful salesman finally directed them to a place that actually carried the rustic Western style that they both seemed to be envisioning. Vince declared the store perfect for their purposes the instant that they walked into the showroom, but Jolie took one look at the price of a leather sectional and insisted that they could do better elsewhere.

"I've seen handmade, one-of-a-kind pieces in this very style at the outdoor market for half the price," she hissed.

"What outdoor market?" he asked in hushed tones.

"Over in Dallas, downtown in the warehouse district. They open these big sheds on the weekends, and the artisans and craftsmen haul in their goods." Vince looked down at his toes. "I can get a Friday off if I ask in advance," she whispered, all but pleading. "We can at least look."

He tucked his fingertips into his waistband, rocking back on his heels.

"This Friday?"

"I'll see," she promised. "Maybe. I haven't had to ask

off lately." She held back a wince at that. She hadn't had to take time off from work since she'd lost Russ. Pushing aside thoughts of her nephew, she fixed her mind on the issue at hand. "I'm sure I can get at least half a day."

Vince caught her arm and steered her toward the door, calling out to the anxious salesman, "Gotta run. We'll catch you later. Thanks for your help."

"I don't know why I didn't think of it sooner," she said once they reached the sidewalk. "I guess I didn't know exactly what you were looking for until you honed in on that last piece."

"Now that," he said, hooking a thumb over his shoulder, "is my idea of a comfy couch. It seats six and has recliners in each end."

"Two pieces would be easier to shift around," she pointed out cautiously. "Besides, that's better suited to the den than a so-called formal living room."

"Hmm, maybe you're right about that. See there." He beamed at her. "You do know what you're doing."

She turned away, rolling her eyes.

"Can I get back to some real work now?"

He chuckled, following her across the parking lot.

"You act like that laundry is going somewhere."

"Not unless I get it done, it isn't."

He unlocked the door and handed her up into the tall cab before making his way around to the driver's seat.

"You'd think we were spending *your* hard-earned cash," he teased.

"Yours is not as hard-earned as mine is or you'd feel the same way," she grumbled.

He shook his head and drove her back to his house, where he busied himself elsewhere while she worked at the laundry and envisioned, room by room, what she really wanted to do with the place. It didn't take long for her to realize that what she needed was a comprehensive list of what it would take to achieve the look she was after. Just knowing how much money she had to play with set her imagination whirling.

She hadn't realized what fun simple dreaming could be.

Chapter Seven

Jolie was at the ironing board, down to the last dozen shirts in need of pressing, with a load of laundry in the washer, another in the dryer and two more still heaped on the floor, when Vince strolled into the room.

"Enough," he ordered. "The rest can wait."

She straightened to work a kink out of her back.

"At the very least, the pants have to be hung or they'll wrinkle and need pressing, too. And the towels have to go into the dryer before I can leave."

"Okay, I'll help you finish up. Then I want you to get out of here," he ordered, "or else I'm going to make you dinner."

"Ooh," she quipped, shuddering theatrically, "how diabolical."

"I should inform you that the sandwich constitutes the sum of my kitchen skills."

"Yuh," she said, perfectly serious, "how diabolical."

"It wasn't that bad!"

She giggled. "It wasn't bad at all, especially if you happen to be a giant—or eat like one. But I couldn't let you feed me twice in one day."

"I don't see why not."

"Meals are not part of our deal, that's why not."

"Speaking of that," he began, "I think we ought to approach this new project from a different angle. What do you think about making a list of everything we know we're going to need and—" He broke off when she burst out laughing.

"That's just what I've been doing." She tapped her temple with the tip of one forefinger. "Just haven't got it down on paper yet."

"There you go," he said, grinning. "Great minds thinking alike."

"I don't know about that," she retorted playfully, "but I have a suggestion. Why don't you make your list, and I'll make mine, and on Friday we'll compare them, provided I can get time off from the cleaners."

"Sounds good to me. Then on Sunday we'll have something to show the girls. You do remember that Sunday comes with a meal, don't you?"

"Of course I remember."

"I see, so it's okay for my mom to feed you but not me. I think that's some sort of double standard."

She rolled her eyes. "It's not about the meal. It's about showing your family that you're making headway on furnishing this house."

"Don't be surprised if you have to make a progress report."

"That I'll leave to you."

The buzzer on the dryer went off, indicating that the load was finished, and she hurried to pull out the uniform pants before they could wrinkle.

He went for the rolling rack of hangers, saying, "So

I'll pick you up at the cleaners about noon on Friday unless you call to cancel. Right?"

"Right. I'll have my list on paper by then."

"Me, too."

They worked for several minutes, folding, creasing and hanging the pants. The washer stopped before they were finished, and Jolie shifted that load into the dryer. All in all, it had been some day.

"Take off now," he ordered, "and I'll see you Friday."

"Yes, sir, boss, sir."

He brought his hands to his hips in a sarcastic pose.

"Right. You and Boyd, great respecters of my authority."

She just grinned, unplugged the iron and gathered up her handbag and keys.

"See ya." She turned for the door.

"Hey, Jolie."

She whirled in midstride.

"Yeah?"

He rocked back on his heels, gaze targeted on his toes. Then he looked up at her from beneath the smooth jut of his brow.

"Just wanted to say that I'm glad you moved into my old apartment. And got overloaded with my mail. And needed work on your car and…you know, all the rest."

Warmth spiraled through her, followed quickly by a spike of pure fear. She was getting caught up in something that she didn't quite understand here, and she wasn't sure how to feel about it, so she just nodded and went on her way.

It would have been a lot easier to deal with if she could have convinced herself that she wasn't glad about how things had turned out, too.

* * *

They spent an hour at a table in a favorite chain restaurant of his, comparing their lists and debating the contents until they came up with a master list. The girl was nothing if not stubborn—and close with a buck.

Since it was his buck that she was wringing, Vince couldn't be too put out about her thrifty ways, especially since it was a habit which she obviously had developed from pure necessity. Strangely enough, that only made him want to spend more, either to irritate her or to delight her, he wasn't entirely sure which.

The tentative excitement lighting her eyes when she talked about actually picking out articles for purchase seemed reason enough to splurge all by itself, but he couldn't deny that arguing with her had become something of a favorite pastime, especially once he'd figured out that her tough exterior was just that, a front that she used to protect herself.

The question became by what, or whom, did she feel threatened?

Vince had no answers for that, but he exercised his better judgment and curbed the impulse to dump wads of cash on her, sensing that she wouldn't find the actual spending of it as enjoyable as he would find watching her spend it. That didn't mean that he wasn't tickled by her building enthusiasm for the project, however, and try as she might, she couldn't hide the evidence of it. At times, she practically bubbled, and it was in those moments that Vince found himself almost aching for the woman he glimpsed behind those jade eyes.

They spent the balance of the afternoon in Dallas wandering around old warehouses and new sheet metal barns. The mid-November weather was glorious, with bright sunshine overhead and air crisp enough to feel like autumn while requiring nothing more onerous than a sweater or light jacket. It was Vincent's favorite time of the year in Texas.

The suffocating heat of summer had waned with September and the weather had run mild for weeks, gradually cooling. The trees were ablaze still, though some of the leaves had started to fall, but the weather would hold, maybe even right up into December, when the temperatures would take a plunge. Winter would bring one or two ice storms, but they would be brief and would lack the danger of the spring tornado season.

Yes, autumn was the heavenly season in Texas, at least as far as Vince was concerned. Jolie called it "perfect shopping weather."

He liked what he saw at the market. Much of it was imported from Mexico and, to a lesser extent, other countries, but most of it came straight out of workshops in Texas or one of the surrounding states. He absolutely went nuts over an easy chair covered in deerhide, manufactured by a retired aerospace engineer in Fort Davis, west of the Pecos River. The vendor stuck a hold sign on it for them, and they tore through the rest of the market putting together a complete roomful of furnishings built around that one chair.

Problem was, he wanted that chair in the den where he could relax in the evening and watch a little TV or read. Jolie carped about deviating from their plan, but he could be stubborn, too, and in the end he got his way without too much tussle. Then she found the perfect dining-room suite, which sent them off on another search for coordinating pieces.

Vince wasn't completely sold on the living-room stuff

that she picked out, but the vendor assured them that anything they didn't love once it was installed in the house could be returned. They arranged for delivery on Monday, and before he knew what had hit him, Vince found himself the proud owner of half a houseful of brand-new, handcrafted furniture, for much less than he'd have paid in a regular retail store.

All in all, it had been a very productive day.

"Wait until the girls hear how much we've gotten accomplished," he said as he drove Jolie back toward her car at the cleaners.

Jolie chewed her lip for a moment before saying, "I hope they won't think I've been extravagant."

"If they think anybody's been extravagant, it'll be me," he pointed out. "It's my house and my money, after all."

"Yes, but it's my plan."

"What difference does that make? I have final say. Besides, it isn't any of their business."

"If you really believed that you wouldn't have insisted that I go to dinner on Sunday with your family."

"I didn't insist! I asked politely, and you kindly agreed." He narrowed his eyes at her. "You're not backing out on me, are you? Because I've already told Mom that you'll be there."

"Who said anything about backing out?" she demanded indignantly.

Vince laughed. He couldn't help it. Even their arguments—and they were constant but completely without rancor—engaged him in a way that no interaction with any other woman ever had. He fought the impulse to reach across the cab of the pickup and chuck her under the chin, but he couldn't deny himself the occasional glance.

She was growing on him, this Jolie Kay Wheeler, prickles and all. He found himself wondering if she might be the one, but then he reminded himself that he still knew little about her. God had not yet revealed His plan. Still, Vince couldn't deny a growing undercurrent of awareness between them. At least he suspected that it was mutual.

Then again, it wasn't wise to take anything for granted where Jolie was concerned.

Vince dropped Jolie off at her car behind the cleaners. It was later than they'd anticipated returning, so the rush hour was well past. He offered dinner, but Jolie said she had much to do. He didn't question her, but he did insist on following her home just to make certain that she got there safely.

She told him that he was a sexist, high-handed Neanderthal, and that she'd been taking care of herself for a quarter of a century at least, which prompted him to drawl, "I didn't think you were that old."

"I'm twenty-seven, thank you very much, and don't change the subject."

"And what is the subject? Oh, yeah, my gentlemanly impulse to see you safely to your own front door."

"Whatever," she replied with a huff, slamming the door to the cab.

He grinned, enjoying himself, and followed at a discreet distance until she turned her little jalopy into the apartment parking lot.

Twenty-seven, he mused. That seemed to him just about the right age for a woman. Funny, but in some ways she seemed younger. And in some ways she seemed older. It was as if she maintained some measure of innocence while carrying the weight of the world on her slender shoulders.

"Lord," he prayed, "show me how to lighten her load."

She was trembling. He felt it in the hand that he placed at the small of her back as he began the first of many introductions to be made.

"Mom, Dad, this is Jolie Wheeler. Jolie, these are my parents, Ovida and Larry."

Jolie timidly offered her hand to his mother, who clasped it and held on for dear life as if afraid that her one chance for a daughter-in-law would escape before they could get her well and truly tied down.

"Sugar, you are as welcome as rain in the summer! My, isn't she a pretty thing, but of course Vince could always have his pick."

Vince groaned inwardly when Jolie shot him a startled glance. Why hadn't he set them all straight? He'd meant to, but somehow it hadn't seemed important. He should have realized that his mother would make her assumptions obvious. His dad had always said that Ovida was about as subtle as her flaming-red hair.

The hair that curled softly around her squarish face had faded over the years, but Ovida remained as bluntly spoken as ever. Vince cleared his throat, hoping she'd get the hint, and all but wrenched Jolie from her grasp, moving on to his eldest sister and her husband.

"This is Sharon and Wally and their two kids, Jack and Brenda. You've met Olivia, and this is her husband Drew and their three boys, Mark, Matthew and Michael. Helen you also know. That wild man she's married to is John."

"Don't you believe a word of it," John put in, winking at Jolie and giving one corner of his beloved mustache a tweak.

Vince playfully tugged the other corner of his old running buddy's facial hair and kept going.

"The little redhead is Bets, and finally here's my baby sister Donna and her crackbrained other half Martin, whom we lovingly refer to as Chrome Dome."

Unperturbed at the teasing insult, Marty rubbed his perfectly bald head, wrapped his arms around his wife and patted her distended tummy, saying, "And this is either Anthony or Ann."

"We wanted to know which, but the baby didn't cooperate," Donna divulged, having inherited both her mother's red hair and frank manner. "Must take after Marty."

"Man, let's hope not," Vince retorted, straight-faced.

"Now, y'all get to the table," Ovida ordered. "The gravy's jelling."

The family turned en masse and swiftly moved into the dining room, leaving Vince and Jolie to bring up the rear. He dropped a reassuring smile on her, figured that he knew what her beetled brow was about and felt a hole open in the pit of his belly.

What on earth, he suddenly wondered, had possessed him to throw her into the arena with his family like this? He knew perfectly well that they all thought she was his girlfriend. It wasn't like him to exacerbate unfounded assumptions. Trouble was, he'd started thinking that maybe it shouldn't be unfounded.

The family scrambled for seats, leaving two places at the top of the *T* for him and Jolie. Vince had hoped that his mother would put the kids in the kitchen as usual, but instead she'd opted for the "holiday seating," which meant that the kitchen table had been carried into the dining room and fitted to the longer table there so that the two formed the shape of a *T.* The whole had been laid with her very best china. He wished that for once the good dishes had stayed in the hutch.

The Cutlers were solidly middle-class folk who lacked for nothing and wanted for little, but their lives seemed embarrassingly rich to Vince just then with all seventeen of them—Jolie made it eighteen—crowded around a table practically bowing beneath the weight of food. Obviously his sisters had pitched in even more than usual, and Jolie was looking a bit overwhelmed by it all. As if worried that she wasn't dressed well enough, she kept tugging on the hem of her simple white blouse, which she wore with black slacks and black loafers.

He pulled out a chair for Jolie and patted her arm in a gesture of encouragement. She didn't so much as glance at him but kept her gaze targeted on her lap. Bets howled about something, was gently scolded by both her parents and shushed by all her cousins, but then everyone settled into place.

His mother disappeared into the kitchen and quickly returned carrying two huge steaming bowls of hot biscuits draped with matching white dish towels. She placed one on each table and took her seat at the end of the top of the *T* opposite his father.

"Daddy, give us the blessing please."

Larry cleared his throat and bowed his salt-and-pepper head and delivered the requested prayer of thanksgiving. The rest of the family echoed his "Amen," and Vince squeezed Jolie's hands, realizing only then that he'd reached over to cover them where they were clamped together in her lap. He quickly withdrew his hand, hoping that no one else had noticed, only to catch several knowing smiles.

For some time, conversation was curtailed by getting everyone served. Eventually, however, the "interview" began. It would be, of course, Olivia who fired the opening volley.

"So, Jolie, where do you work?"

Vincent watched as casually as he could the very careful manner in which Jolie swallowed and laid aside her fork.

"Actually, she's doing some work for me," he blurted. "Laundry, decorating the house. I think I mentioned that when you came by the other day."

Jolie pressed her heavy linen napkin to her mouth and spoke.

"Mainly, I work for Geopp's Dry Cleaners."

"Oh, I know that place," Ovida said brightly. "I used to take our things there all the time, but I thought it closed down after sweet little Mrs. Geopp passed."

"Just for a couple of weeks," Jolie said softly.

"I'll have to start using them again, then."

"I'm sure Mr. Geopp would appreciate that."

It was Sharon's turn.

"Do you have family?"

Jolie toyed with her fork.

"An older brother and a younger sister. And a nephew."

"That's nice," Ovida gushed. "Do they live around here?"

"Yes, ma'am, but, um, we're not really very close."

"Oh, that's a shame."

Jolie hunched a shoulder in ambiguous reply.

"What do you do for the holidays?" Donna wanted to know, and again Jolie merely shrugged.

"Well, you'll just have to spend Thanksgiving with us," Ovida announced brightly.

Vince nearly choked on a hunk of steamed carrot.

"Oh, no," Jolie replied quickly. "I couldn't impose."

"As if one more will make a difference around here," Ovida said dismissively. "Now, I won't take no for an answer, seeing as how you have no other plans. Vincent, take a drink."

Vince croaked out a "Yes, ma'am," and gulped down half a glass of tea.

At least no one had asked about her parents. That was information which he preferred to impart privately. In fact, he should have done so before today. He wondered why he hadn't. Then he realized that he had wanted them to get to know her first, to *like* her first, not that they would hold her raising against her. He just wanted them to see her in the very best possible light.

This was getting a little scary. He couldn't remember another time when he'd felt this way about a woman.

The impulse to try to control the situation was very strong, so strong that he heard himself asking, "Have I told you how Jolie and I met?"

Of course, he hadn't, so he did so now.

"She leased my old apartment, and like a clunkhead I forgot to have my mail forwarded."

"I didn't know you got any mail there," Sharon said.

"Not much," he admitted.

"Not much!" Jolie yelped. "I'd accumulated a whole shopping bag full of his stuff before he finally came and got it. The post office and I played ring-around-the-rosy with it until I went to the library and looked up his phone number on the Internet."

Laughing stiltedly, Vince said, "Guess idiocy pays

off sometimes." He caught Jolie's questioning glance and added, "You should see what she's done with the old place. That's what inspired me to have her help me out with my place. Why, if the apartment had looked that good when I lived there I might have stayed."

This brought groans and comments from all around the table.

"Took us ten years to get him out of there."

"And it still looked like a room in a frat house."

"At least he took down the pizza boxes."

"Yeah, how's that for decor? Pin empty, flattened pizza boxes all over the wall."

"I'm not sure he even scraped the cheese off first."

"Okay, all right," Vince objected, holding up both hands as if to fend off further comment. "The pizza boxes went the first year, and you know it."

"Then it was pages out of sports magazines."

"I wasn't even old enough to vote!"

"Hey, he could've gone to hamburger wrappers," Jolie quipped, and everyone laughed.

"So he's 'cooked' for you, has he?" Donna teased, crooking her fingers to indicate quotation marks.

Vince no longer tried to restrain his rolling eyes as everyone laughed at his expense.

"Y'all leave him alone," his mother scolded without the least heat before abruptly changing the subject. "So, Jolie, where do you go to church, hon?"

Jolie coughed behind her hand, smoothed that hand over the napkin in her lap and mumbled, "I, um, haven't been in awhile."

Vince felt a welling of unreasonable panic and didn't even realize that he was going to speak until he opened his mouth. "Her brother's a preacher, though."

Jolie shot him a look that lanced straight into his heart.

"Is that so?" his mother gushed avidly.

With a strained smile, Jolie said softly, "He has a small church in Pantego."

Ovida Cutler literally beamed. "How interesting. What kind of church is it?"

"What difference does it make?" Vince asked quickly, picking up his fork. Almost at the same time, Jolie answered, so that they talked over one another.

"You're right," Ovida said with a smile. "What difference does it make?"

Vince knew from the gleam in her eye that she was pleased. Jolie, on the other hand, was not, and he couldn't blame her. He wondered all over again what he was doing—and how likely he was to get in trouble by doing it.

All in all, dinner was a trial, but somehow they made it through. Jolie insisted on helping clean up afterward, which caused Vince some uncomfortable moments. He resisted the urge to follow her into the kitchen and run interference for her with the Cutler women, but just barely.

It seemed he need not have worried, however, for when they all trooped back into the den, where the guys were watching television, they were chatting like old friends. Then Jolie retrieved the folder of papers that she'd left with her purse and invited his sisters and mother to take a look at what she'd accomplished so far with his house.

They all exclaimed over the prices she'd given for the furniture.

"That's amazing!"

Jolie beamed, assuring them, "It isn't junk, either."

"Well, of course not," Ovida said. "Vincent wouldn't settle for junk."

"Oh, right, like that ratty piece of horsehair he's been sitting on all these years isn't junk," Olivia said.

"That was Grandma Sledge's sofa," Vince pointed out.

"Sentimental junk then," Sharon retorted.

"Oh, dear," Jolie worried aloud, "does that mean we shouldn't get rid of it?"

"No!" his sisters all exclaimed in unison.

"It really should be retired," Ovida agreed, and they all laughed. Vince took himself off to the safe company of the menfolk.

Some time later he realized that Jolie and his sister Donna had put their heads together for a fairly lengthy discussion, and once more his protective instincts stirred, but when he wandered over to ask what was up, Donna smiled secretively and answered only, "Girl talk, big brother, girl talk."

He knew too well what that meant, as did every other male in the room, but just in case he'd missed it, John translated for him.

"In other words, it's none of your business."

Vince did not agree, but he figured it was best not to probe too deeply at that moment. He'd survived this harebrained scheme so far by the skin of his teeth, but he was well aware that it could blow up in his face at any moment, which was nothing less than he deserved, frankly. Once he figured out what the dickens he was doing, he'd have some confessions to make, not to mention some apologies. Until then, he might just do best to keep his mouth shut, and thereby keep his head attached firmly to his shoulders.

He hoped.

Chapter Eight

Later, driving Jolie home at twilight, Vince figured that it was safe to ask what she'd thought of his family.

"Oh, they're great," she replied easily, "and your sisters and mom actually seemed to like what we're doing with the house."

He nodded, surprised but pleased about that himself.

"So what were you and Donna talking about for so long?"

Jolie smiled enigmatically, and he resigned himself to disappointment on that score, but then she said, "Decorating, of course. What else?"

He snorted at that. "I can think of a few dozen subjects I'd just as soon she didn't bring up, frankly."

Jolie laughed. "She just wanted to know what sort of furniture she could find at the market where you and I shopped."

"And?"

"And I expect that she and Martin will be spending some time in downtown Dallas next weekend."

It was his turn to laugh.

"Remind me to rub it in when Marty's griping about her buying new furniture."

She tilted her head to one side.

"Don't you like your brother-in-law?"

"Love him like a brother. I actually introduced him to my sister."

"Really? Just so you can irritate each other?"

He grinned. "It's a guy thing."

She arched an eyebrow but said nothing else, which was just as well, because he felt keenly the need to broach another subject. Shifting in his seat, he decided how to phrase it.

"I know it's none of my business, but I can't help wondering what's going on with you and your family."

Her eyes frosted, and she lifted her chin. "You're right. It is none of your business."

Like that was going to stop him, he thought, amazed at himself.

"I was just wondering if there was anything I could do to help. Family is important, and you seem so sad when you talk about yours."

Her gaze dropped to her lap, and she muttered, "There isn't anything you can do, believe me."

He was prepared to let it drop after that. What he wasn't prepared for, even after she turned her gaze out her side window and fussed with her bangs, was the tears that streamed down her face when she finally looked back to him. Instinctively he whipped the truck off the street and into the empty lot of a defunct car wash.

"Jolie?"

She shook her head, biting her lip. He slammed the transmission into Park, words tumbling out of his own mouth heedlessly.

"Honey, what's wrong?"

She gulped, and he leaned across the center console to wrap his arm around her shoulders.

"It's all right. Please don't cry."

"I c-can't help it," she finally whispered.

He brushed aside a strand of hair caught in the moisture on her cheek.

"I'm sorry. I didn't mean to make you cry."

"It's not you. It's…my life."

"Won't you tell me about it? You can talk to me, you know. I mean, we're friends now, aren't we?"

"I suppose we are."

She blinked and dabbed at her eyes with the edge of her sleeve. He scrambled in the console for a tissue and came up with a creased paper napkin.

"Thank you." She sniffed and pressed the napkin to her cheeks. After a moment she sighed and let her hands fall to her lap. "I told you that my nephew's father is in prison," she began softly. "What I didn't tell you is that my sister went to prison, too."

Vince rocked, knocked back by this revelation.

"Oh, man."

"They got her for abetting a crime," Jolie went on, "but Connie's always sworn that she didn't know what her boyfriend was doing when he went in to rob that bank branch, and she did turn him in when she heard on the news that he'd shot a guard."

"Well, that's good," Vince murmured, wanting desperately to say something positive, though he felt completely out of his depth here. Prison, for pity's sake.

"The guard was an off-duty police officer," Jolie went on, "and he died, so they sentenced her to five to eight years, but she actually served less than two."

"Sounds like she behaved herself."

"Model prisoner, they said." Her voice dwindled away with the next words. "That's why they gave Russell back to her."

Jolie choked and began to sob.

Russell? Vince's mind was whirling. Obviously he didn't have the full story yet, but all he could think to do at the moment was to wrap his arms around her and croon sympathetically.

"I'm so sorry. I really hate to hear this. I—I mean, I'm glad that she did well, but…you've obviously been though a great deal."

About the time he ran out of comforting words, Jolie calmed, turning her face into the hollow of his shoulder.

"I knew you'd understand."

Understanding had not yet been achieved, actually, but he didn't say so. Instead, he opted to ask the question uppermost in his mind, "Who, um, is Russell?"

That set her off again, and he could've kicked himself— except he still didn't know what it was all about. He figured all he could do was wait out the tears, and eventually she gulped, wiped and pulled in a shuddering breath.

"Russell is my n-nephew."

Her nephew. So that's why they'd given Russell to her sister; the sister was his mother. Vince sighed, pretty sure that he knew now where this was going, and already his heart was breaking for her.

"You took him, didn't you? While she was in prison."

Jolie nodded, blinking rapidly.

"C-Connie found out she was pregnant not long after she went in, and e-everyone thought it would be best if the baby was with f-family." She pulled in a deep breath and went on more calmly. "So I got certified as a foster parent and found us a little house. The state gives you a monthly stipend, you know. It was enough for two bedrooms and a little yard." She closed her eyes as if remembering. "He was perfect, just perfect. We were so happy, the two of us." Her hands plucked at the damp napkin. "Then just before Connie got out, my brother came to see me." She shrugged. "I didn't think anything of it. We saw him often."

"What happened?" Vince asked.

She closed her eyes and pinched the bridge of her nose. "He wanted to talk about Connie and Russell, about reuniting them. I couldn't believe it!"

Vince tightened the loop of his arms about her, feeling torn. On one hand, he couldn't argue against reuniting a parent and child, provided there was no history of abuse. On the other hand, Jolie had evidently cared for that boy for over a year, presumably from his birth. Did no one consider her feelings or what was best for her? Had no one prepared her for the day that the child's mother would reclaim him? However it had happened, it was plain that Jolie had been terribly hurt.

"So your brother helped your sister take back the boy," Vince surmised, and she nodded miserably.

"I guess I should have expected it, but the caseworker was always talking about *if* Connie could reclaim the child, and it just didn't make sense to me that she could go to prison and come out somehow a better parent than *me*!"

Vincent laid his head against hers, feeling her pain and the neediness that she tried so hard to keep hidden behind that tough-cookie mask of hers. Maybe she'd set herself up for disappointment, but that didn't make her grief any less real or poignant. Plus, she'd done a very good thing, caring for her nephew for at least the first year of his life. It must seem grossly unfair to be paid back with such a loss.

"I'm so sorry," he said against her temple. "And I'm sure you *are* a wonderful parent."

"You've no idea how much I miss him," she whispered, leaning into Vince. "I just couldn't believe they'd take him away."

"I guess there was a hearing?"

She nodded, becoming animated. "And Marcus testified on Connie's behalf," she said bitterly. "He talked about her 'spiritual maturity' and how she took parenting classes and college courses. He even let her and Russell move in with him! What hurt most of all was when he said that he feared it would be 'unhealthy' for Russell to be left in my care."

That, Vince could not imagine, and he was almost shocked by how easy it was to feel outraged on her behalf.

"Pure nonsense. Surely he didn't mean it the way it sounds."

"Maybe not," Jolie conceded, "but that doesn't change the fact that Russell is with them now, and I'm alone again."

Again. What a wealth of information and meaning that one little word contained.

"You are not alone," he protested automatically, tilting her face toward his with a finger curled beneath her chin.

"I've always been alone," she whispered, and he saw by the tortured look in her eyes that she really believed that.

"God never allows His children to walk through this world alone," Vince assured her, believing it wholeheartedly.

He'd once heard Hell described as complete and utter separation from God, and he shuddered to think of an eternity spent bereft of the slightest nuance of love. Somehow he understood that Jolie had felt too little love in her lifetime and too much separation.

Could he convince her that he wasn't going anywhere? Should he even try? Any words he might have given her to that effect seemed abrupt and premature, so he did the only thing he could think of to show her that he wanted to be a part of her life. He lifted one hand and cradled her cheek.

The impulse to kiss her shook him right to the marrow of his bones, but he subdued it.

Even as she drew away, color staining her cheeks, he understood that he was taking a big risk by opening himself up to the possibility that they could be more than friends. They were from very different backgrounds, and she did not seem able to trust. Yet.

She had issues to be resolved and wounds to heal, and he suspected that it would take a lot of patience and some very deft handling on his part to get them both to the place where they would have to be for anything more than simple friendship. But he couldn't ignore what he was feeling.

"I can't believe I told you all that," Jolie said with a grimace. "I hate it when people feel sorry for me."

"I don't feel sorry for you," he corrected firmly. "I feel sorry for what you've been though."

She smiled softly. "How is it that you always say the right thing?"

"We both know better than that," he said, "but if I got it right this time, I'm glad. In fact, I thank God."

She blinked and looked down shyly. He watched her pull together her usual bravado, enjoying every instant of the transformation. She was plucky, this woman. *His* woman?

Maybe. In time.

She fluffed her bangs and nervously smoothed them again, saying, "I'd better get home."

He took the hint and leisurely settled back behind the wheel.

He'd see her tomorrow, after all, and as often thereafter as he could manage until they both understood, individually and together, everything that God had in store for them.

Jolie had finally gotten a handle on the ever-plentiful laundry, so they were able to spend Monday afternoon shifting around the newly delivered furniture until everything was placed just right.

Vince was delighted to see that Jolie had been absolutely correct about the living-room stuff, and he told her so, which made her loft her eyebrows practically into her hairline.

"Frankly, I'm not sure which one of us is more surprised," she admitted, and suddenly he found himself slinging an arm around her shoulders as they both laughed.

Then she looked up at him, and he caught his breath as awareness sizzled in the air. Before he could figure out what he should do about it, she had whirled away, ducking down slightly to extricate herself from the loop of his arm.

"About Thanksgiving," she said, glancing away.

He reached for a nonchalance that he couldn't quite find and asked, "What about it?"

"I don't think I should come."

He caught his frown before it fully developed. "Why not?"

She shrugged. "Your family could get the wrong idea about us."

"My family's had the wrong idea since my sisters first walked in and found you here."

"Have you tried to tell them different?" she asked pointedly.

He wouldn't lie to her. "No."

"How come?"

"I don't know." He laid a hand against the nape of his neck. "You've met them. Do you figure it would do any good?"

She looked him square in the eye. "Probably not."

"Well, then, what's the point?"

She bit her lip. "I don't want to mislead anyone."

"Neither do I."

"So I'd better not come," she said decisively. Yet, he heard the faintest note of question in her tone.

He looked down at the toes of his boots and said baldly, "I want you to come."

"Oh?" She sounded a teensy bit hopeful.

He stuffed his hands into his back pockets and nodded. "I couldn't enjoy myself knowing you were sitting home alone at holiday time."

"No?"

"Not a bit."

She seemed to consider. Then, she shook her head. "It's not your problem."

"What's that got to do with it?" he wanted to know. "You'll still be alone, and I'll still be thinking about that instead of enjoying myself."

She rolled her eyes, and he scuffed a toe on the carpet.

"Unless there's a chance you might join your own family, after all."

"No chance of that," she stated flatly, folding her arms, "and I told Marcus so."

Vince felt a jolt of shock. "You mean he invited you to join them?"

She lifted her chin. "Surely, you don't think I could!"

He didn't know what he thought at the moment, but if she was determined not to join her own family, she'd just have to make do with his because he really couldn't enjoy Thanksgiving knowing that she was sitting out the holiday alone. He pulled out the big guns.

"Mom will be awfully disappointed if you don't come, you know, and how am I supposed to explain your absence? Saying that you can't abide being mistaken for my girlfriend would go over big."

She threw up her hands, as if it was all a great inconvenience, and exclaimed, "Well, I guess I'd better come then!"

He bit back a smile, sensing that her capitulation was less onerous than she pretended. "I guess so."

"I certainly wouldn't want to offend your mama after she's been so kind to me."

"Thanks," he drawled wryly. She didn't seem to have any qualms about offending him, but he'd take what he could get at this point. "Well, that's settled then. I'll pick you up about ten o'clock Thursday morning, if that's okay. Mom says we'll eat as close to noon as possible, but she likes everyone to be there early."

Jolie muttered something about sleeping in, but she nodded her agreement and left soon after, almost running to her car.

He chuckled about it, but later he sat in his special

deerhide chair and thought about her or, more to the point, his feelings for her and whether or not he was supposed even to have them.

Looking around at the changes she had already wrought in his home, he tried to decide whether or not God meant her for him, or if he was supposed to somehow help her settle her differences with her family. Apparently they were willing, or at least the brother was.

Maybe that was all there was to it.

Or maybe this was about mutual need. Maybe she was just someone who could literally help him get his house in order, and maybe he was just someone who could fix her old car.

And maybe he would never know why God had brought her into his life.

All he could do was pray for guidance and trust that understanding would come when it was meant to—and that he wouldn't do something stupid like getting his heart broken in the meantime.

Jolie set down the iron and sighed, wiping her brow. She was beginning to hate ironing with a passion. Iron, iron, iron, that was all she seemed to do. That and laundry and planning designs in her head and shopping and arranging and...daydreaming about Vince Cutler.

In the beginning she hadn't wanted anything more than simple friendship from him, if that. Truth be told, she'd have settled quite happily for a cordial working relationship, but somehow one thing had led to another and before she'd known it, they were friends. From there, one short step had brought her to the possibility that they might be more to each other, which was ludicrous.

For one thing, she didn't want anyone in her life. Car-

ing for people just got you hurt. She'd learned that all too
well. For another, she was not the sort for Vincent Cutler. Vince came from a nice, normal family. He would
definitely want a nice, normal girl, and that sure wasn't
her, not with her background and her baggage.

Disgusted with herself for even briefly entertaining
the idea that she might be more to Vince than a charity
case, she turned her back on the ironing board and went
to the sink for a cool drink of water. The outside temperatures were in the low forties, but in this tiny apartment
standing over a hot iron, the air felt downright sultry.

So why did she feel cold inside?

She didn't have to look far for a convenient answer.

It was all Marcus's and Connie's fault. They'd used
her and then betrayed her. They'd let her take care of
Russell and then taken him away from her.

How could Vince even think that she'd accept an invitation to spend the holiday with them?

Wandering over to the counter, she picked up an envelope. Twice now she'd started to peel back the flap,
and twice she'd stopped, telling herself that she didn't
care what was inside. She'd recognized the handwriting
on the front immediately. God knew that she and Connie had corresponded often enough in the past two years
for her to know her sister's handwriting at a glance. She
should have dropped the envelope in the trash the moment she'd realized who had sent it. Instead, she ripped
the back flap off completely.

The card inside slipped out easily into her hand. The
front was embellished with a cross and a white dove
bearing an olive branch, symbols of peace and forgiveness. As if she had anything to be forgiven for, she
thought resentfully, flipping the card open.

The verse printed inside was a quotation from Genesis 31:49. "May the Lord watch between you and me when we are absent one from another."

Jolie thought of her little sister's big green eyes and elfin face, and a lump rose in her throat. Willfully, she pictured Russell's bright coppery head and beaming smile, and the lump turned bitter. Quickly, dismissively, she scanned the short message that her sister had written.

It was all about how Connie missed her and wished they could have a "real family Thanksgiving." She asked Jolie to call her and wrote how sorry she was for "the misunderstanding between us." Some misunderstanding, Jolie thought disdainfully. She had been used, plain and simple, by her own sister. And brother. She wouldn't forget his part in it. They had used her and then cast her aside.

Even knowing that, however, she'd gladly do it all over again, just for Russell's sake. Even knowing that she would eventually have to give him up, she could never have walked away from the fat, cherubic little bundle who had been placed in her arms that day. Only hours old, he'd squinted and blinked at the bright world, pushing his tiny pink tongue against his lips hopefully, and she had instantly wanted for him all that she had missed: a stable and loving home, healthy meals, safety, laughter, a true sense of belonging.

She had tried so hard to give him those things, and he had been happy, so happy. Did he miss her? she wondered wistfully. She loved him enough to hope that he didn't, and yet her heart cracked open a little wider at the thought that he might not.

Closing the card, she stuffed it back into the envelope and dropped it into a drawer. Out of sight, out of mind.

Please, God, she prayed silently. *I just can't bear to think about it.*

Then she remembered that God did not answer her prayers. If He did, she'd still be chasing Russell around on the floor, removing dangerous objects from his reach, rocking him to sleep, playing giggling games of peek-a-boo.

Emptiness overwhelmed her.

In the silence she heard the faint click of the thermostat kicking off or on inside the iron as it attempted to regulate the temperature of the pressing plate. Jolie gulped and swiftly moved back to the ironing board and the work at hand, desperate for anything that would take her mind off Russell.

She concentrated on placing and ironing the next garment, on getting the lay of a lace applique just right. Her hands moved by rote, and her mind wandered to something more challenging. The kitchen in Vince's house was bare and bland. He needed some attractive but useful items to scatter about the place. She tried to remember what he had, what he could use. She remembered the sandwich he'd made for her, the easy way in which he'd leapt up onto the counter to eat his share, the way his gaze moved over her face from time to time.

The slight dilation of his irises as he'd leaned close, his hand warm against her cheek, his arm about her shoulders.

With a jerk she realized that she was fantasizing again about that moment in his truck on Sunday evening when it had seemed that he might kiss her. Just as it had then, her heart beat a rapid staccato inside her chest and heat rose up all the way to her cheeks.

What was she doing?

She already knew that she was not the sort for Vincent Cutler. No man was the sort for her. Any man whom she might want would never really want her, and she would not be like her mother, constantly used and tossed aside. She'd had enough of that already. She wouldn't be foolish enough to open herself up to more. Never would she wind up like her mom or even Connie.

Never would she have a child of her own.

Russell had been her one chance at real family, at motherhood. Without him she had nothing, not even the brother and sister to whom she had clung for so many years, despite the separation of different foster homes.

She was alone in the world, but at least she was safe from the pain of loving and losing.

Still, if she didn't have the Cutlers to spend Thanksgiving with this year, she wasn't sure how she would make it through the holiday.

The Lord never allows His children to walk through this world alone.
The Lord watch between you and me while we are absent one from another.

"Please, God," she whispered, "just this once. I can't go on thinking about them anymore. Isn't it enough that I've lost my family? Can't I please just have some peace now?"

God, it seemed, was just not on her side.

Chapter Nine

"Evening."

"I see you're ready to shop," she said wryly, looking pointedly at his uniform as she slipped through the door of his house.

It was easier than looking at his face. Staring at that handsome face was much too dangerous. Besides, for some reason he looked especially inviting with a five o'clock shadow, very virile. Steady, she told herself. Vincent Cutler was just another guy, nicer than most, maybe, but in the end as much trouble as all the rest of them.

He shifted his feet self-consciously. "Look, I got held up at work. The drapery shop closes at seven, and I've got prayer meeting tomorrow evening, and with Thanksgiving being the next day, it's either tonight or wait until next week to check out this place, so I didn't take time to change. Do you mind?"

She rolled her eyes. The uniform was rumpled but clean and neater than her work clothes, which consisted of an old T-shirt and jeans worn to a pale gray-blue.

"I'm just teasing, okay?"

He lifted his brows at her tart tone but made no rejoinder.

"We'd better get a move on," he said, shepherding her through the house toward the garage. "It's not far, which is why I asked you to meet me here."

"And how did you hear about this place, again?"

"The fellow who built this house for me brought his car in for repairs today, and it occurred to me that he might have a lead on a good drapery place, so I asked him for a recommendation."

She nodded as he handed her up into the truck.

Not forty minutes later, she was climbing back into it, thoroughly disgusted. "And we thought the first place was high!"

"They *were* on the expensive side," he agreed, sliding behind the steering wheel. "Oh, well, nothing ventured, nothing gained."

"Nothing gained is right," she grumbled, buckling her safety belt. How dare that builder waste their time like this? she fumed silently. He probably knew what Vince was worth and figured he could afford such ridiculous prices. "Probably getting a kickback or something," she muttered, folding her arms.

Vince slid her a glance but said nothing. They drove back to his place in silence. Thankfully, it was a short trip. Jolie hopped down out of the truck and let herself into the house before he had the brake set. He caught up with her in the foyer, halting her progress toward the front door with a hand clasped around hers.

"Whoa," he said, drawing her around to face him. "Now why don't you tell me what's really bothering you?"

In the space of four weeks—and it was four weeks

to the day, she realized with a jolt—he had somehow learned to read her like a book. Moreover, she seemed powerless to stop him.

"You're in a snit, and it's got nothing to do with over-priced drapery."

"I am not in a snit!" she defended hotly, but then she caught the concern in his gaze and gave up. "Oh, all right. I'm in a lousy mood, and I admit it. Happy?"

"Not until you tell me why."

She sighed gustily, but she told him. "I got a card in the mail from my sister Connie yesterday."

"I see." He led her into the living room, not releasing her hand until they were seated side by side on the couch. "What did she say?"

Jolie dropped her gaze, her fingers smoothing over the supple leather at her side.

"Not much. She's sorry for our 'misunderstanding,' like she didn't know taking Russell away from me would break my heart."

He didn't exactly rush to condemn her sister's actions. "Is that it?"

Jolie swallowed, feeling petty and frankly irritated about it. What had happened to her was *not* petty, but he was right to think there was more. "She wants me to call her."

"Are you going to?"

"No! Of course not!"

"How do you know it's not about Russell?" he asked softly.

Folding her arms, Jolie reluctantly told him, "She says that she wants a 'real family Thanksgiving.' As if we've ever had such a thing."

"Maybe it's time to start."

Her gaze zipped to his face. "How can we possibly? Connie and Marcus took Russell away from me!"

"And this might be a way for you to have him back in your life," Vince argued gently.

She couldn't believe what she was hearing.

"For moments here and there? I don't think so. It would be like losing him all over again every time we parted!"

Vince placed a comforting hand on her shoulder. "Don't you want to know if he's well and happy? Wouldn't it *help* to know that he's well and happy?"

She hungered for even the tiniest detail about Russell, but every thought of him still brought pain. Far worse, however, was the worry.

"And what if he isn't well and happy?" she whispered.

"Then you go to bat for him again," Vince said placidly. "You contact his caseworker, report what you've seen…"

She'd started shaking her head as soon as he mentioned the caseworker.

"They won't do anything! It would mean admitting that they were wrong."

"You don't know that."

"I can't do it!" Jolie leapt to her feet and began to pace. "I can't put myself through that again. You don't know what it's like to love a child and lose him, to finally be part of a family and have it ripped away! I'm better off alone."

He came to his feet beside her and stopped her in her tracks, his hands clamping her upper arms.

"You are not alone. You have never been alone. You never will be alone."

She cut him a scathingly skeptical look. "You're a

great guy, Vince. You're kind and generous and caring, but I haven't lived the kind of life that you have. I didn't have model parents and a stable home. I didn't have a home, period!"

Dropping his hands from her shoulders, he said, "Maybe not, but that doesn't mean you were alone. You had your brother and sister, didn't you?"

"So what? I don't have them now, and don't try to tell me that it could be any other way, not after what they did to me!"

"What about God, Jolie?" he asked. "God is our constant companion. He's always there, always here. You just have to reach out to Him."

She could tell that, like Marcus, Vince was utterly sincere, and she wanted to be contemptuous about his beliefs, but she couldn't. Instead, she found herself being honest.

"Don't you think I've reached out? If God is here for me, Vince, then why did He let me lose Russell?"

"I don't know, honey," Vince admitted, "but I have to believe that He has a reason, a plan, and I know that God cares for you. I can prove it."

She was shocked by how much she wanted him to do just that, so much that when he led her back to the couch and gently seated her, she did not resist. Sitting down next to her, he wrapped an arm around her shoulders and bowed his head. Without even thinking, she bowed her own.

"Gracious Lord God, please help Jolie feel Your presence. I know how much You love her, but she's in so much pain that she can't feel it. She needs the peace and healing that come from truly knowing how much You love her. It's so easy to lose sight of that fact when we're hurting, but no one can understand her pain better than You can, and no one but You can heal her heart. Please help her to see, to feel, that she's not alone. Help her to accept that she is loved, truly, deeply, constantly loved. Amen."

As he prayed, Jolie felt a warmth flow through her, and for a moment, just a moment, she did believe. Then doubt reared its ugly head.

She told herself that the warmth she felt was nothing more than Vincent's arm and her own wishful thinking. Trusting in God's presence and care would just leave her open to more disappointment because she wasn't the sort whom God could love, not *personally.*

She wasn't even the sort a mother could love—or a man like Vince.

She didn't say so. Instead she smiled limply, thanked him and said that she had to be going. Vince didn't argue, but she saw the disappointment in his eyes.

"I'll pick you up tomorrow morning at ten," he reminded her solemnly.

She smiled and flicked her hair off her shoulders with a toss of her head. "Sure."

How long would it be, she wondered as she left him, before Vince cut her loose just like everyone else in her life had done?

"Hold on there, scamp!" Vince snagged his nephew Matthew by the collar of his shirt and hauled him to a stop. "I'm pretty sure I heard your mom tell you to stop running in the house."

Matthew turned up his freckled snub of a nose and regarded his uncle with impish defiance. "Nuh-uh."

"Oh, right," Vince said, bending to bring himself muzzle-to-muzzle with the little miscreant. "That was *me.*"

Matthew giggled uncertainly, his mind processing

the backhanded order. When he had reached the obvious and only safe conclusion, he sobered conspicuously.

"Okay, Uncle Vince."

Vince smiled and straightened, patting the boy on
the head.

"Good choice. Spread the word. The next one I catch
running in here is going to be the *last* one to the table."

Matthew's face registered horror, and he went off at
a fast walk to deliver the edict. Vince glimpsed Jolie
hovering uncertainly just inside the kitchen door, where
his mother and sisters churned around like marbles in
a blender.

Jolie had been all smiles that morning, as if she
couldn't be bothered to spare a thought for her estranged
sister and brother or her absent nephew, but Vince knew
that wasn't the case. He'd prayed long and hard about
the situation the evening before, and he'd come to the
conclusion that until Jolie made peace with her family,
she wouldn't be able to trust anyone else. And he wanted
her trust, wanted it very much.

Matthew's mother exited the maelstrom with a plate
of deviled eggs. On the way to the dining room she patted Vince's cheek and teased, "Practicing to be a parent, are we?"

"Chapter and verse, son," his dad called over his
shoulder from the easy chair in the den, his gaze never
leaving the fuzzy picture on the old television set.
"You've got to read 'em chapter and verse."

"For all the good it'll do," Matthew's father, Drew,
said dryly. The other brothers-in-law had gone out front
to look over a neighbor's new boat.

Vince changed the subject. "Hey, did I tell y'all that
I've decided to get me one of those new big-screen TVs?"

"Excellent," his father said, glancing in his direction. "Super Bowl party's at your house this year. But aren't those sets pretty expensive?"

Vince shrugged. "Jolie's saved me a bunch of money on the house decorating, but I'm still shopping around. I figured I'd better do it while I'm in a spending frame of mind."

Abruptly Drew bolted upright on the couch and hooted, pumping his fist in the air while Larry flopped back in his chair and groaned. Vince switched his attention to the television, becoming aware at the same instant of a presence at his side.

"What happened?" Jolie asked, looking to the set.

Controlling his surprise, Vince answered calmly, "Drew's team scored." Jolie wrinkled her nose, and he laughed. "What? You don't like them?"

"They've got the lamest uniforms in the NFL," she complained. "Just look at that logo. I know what it's supposed to be, and I still can't identify it."

"That's no reason to dislike a team," Drew protested.

"Yeah, well, their quarterback's got a shallow draft," Jolie went on knowledgeably. "He falls back only two steps, and then he does this double-pump thing that totally alerts the defense to his target." She shook her head and added, "He'll run out of stunt plays soon, and then the other team will clean his clock for him, I don't care how good his line is." With that she turned back into the kitchen.

Vince blinked, aware that his brother-in-law and his father were staring at him with mouths slightly ajar. It had taken concerted effort and drastic measures to get his sisters even minimally interested in live football, and they still wouldn't watch more than five minutes of a televised game. His mother had no interest, either, and in her case nothing seemed to make a difference, not tickets to a pro game, not autographed photos, not detailed explanations. Jolie, on the other hand, came already programmed. Vince grinned and shrugged at his father and brother-in-law, letting them know that he was as surprised as they were.

Drew shook his head as if to say that it wasn't fair. Then a roar from the television yanked them all back into the game. It was Larry's turn to hoot.

"Hey, Jolie!" he crowed. "The game's tied! Ran it all the way back from the kick-off!"

She popped her head out of the kitchen in time to catch the replay. Afterward she dismissed the play with a dry comment.

"Lucky break. Special teams have been sputtering all season."

Vince and Drew laughed at the look of consternation on Larry's face.

As soon as she disappeared again, Larry looked at Vince and admitted softly, "Too bad she's right."

"I heard that," Jolie informed them loudly.

Larry ducked his head, grinning as everyone else laughed.

Vince privately marveled. Who'd have guessed that she could fit in like this? He leaned back against the wall and perked up his ears, wondering how it was going in the kitchen with the female half of the clan.

As usual, they all seemed to be talking at once, but he heard Donna say, "Mmm, Jolie, these potatoes are good. What'd you put in them?"

"A little broth. Cuts back on the fat."

"Don't let Dad hear you say that," Olivia counseled wryly.

"It's Thanksgiving," Sharon said, mimicking their father's voice. "It's a feast. We're *supposed* to eat fat."

"And do we ever!" Helen chortled.

"They're yellow enough. He'll never know the difference," their mother said. "Somebody turn up the oven. These rolls are almost ready to go in."

"I'll do it," Donna volunteered. Vince heard the screech of chair legs against the floor and pictured his heavily pregnant sister hauling herself up out of the seat into which she had dropped earlier, complaining of a backache.

Just then a blood-curdling scream erupted from the closed-in back porch where the kids were playing. Olivia somehow recognized the voice of her youngest and yelled, "Michael?"

Drew popped up onto his feet, announcing loudly, "I'll go." He headed toward the back of the house. "Michael? Matthew? Mark? What's going on out there?"

Content that Jolie was holding her own for now, Vince wandered over and dropped down onto the end of the sofa that Drew had just vacated. His dad leaned forward, propped his elbows on his knees and jerked a head toward the kitchen.

"So what's her story then?"

Vince didn't pretend to misunderstand him. He'd been prepared for this question. He gave out the capsulized version.

"So she's not close to her brother and sister," Larry surmised correctly. They were much alike, father and son, not only in build and coloring, but in attitude, too.

"Actually, they're estranged," Vince admitted, still

very troubled by that. "Long story short, for various reasons Jolie wound up taking care of her nephew for the first year or so of his life. Then a few months ago, her sister took the boy back and their brother helped her do it."

"That's tough." Larry shook his head sorrowfully.

"The thing is, she can't seem to come to terms with it."

Larry clucked his tongue. "Well, give her some time, son. I know women as well as any man can, and I figure she's dealing with a real sense of loss and betrayal right now. Those are especially big issues for women, and given what you've told me, it must be even more difficult for her than most."

"Yeah, I suspect you're right there."

He worried that if she didn't soon find peace with her situation and form some reconciliation with her family she would grow even more angry and resentful than she already was. She'd close herself off entirely then, and he didn't want that. He just didn't know what to do about it. God could and would help her accept, forgive and conquer her pain, if only she was willing to let Him. Getting her back in church seemed to be a logical first step in the right direction, but she'd already refused one invitation to attend with him.

Lord, how do I reach her? he prayed silently.

Before he could follow that thought, his mother rushed into the room, a dripping ladle in one hand, a wild look in her eyes.

"Larry, get the car!"

"What?" His father twisted around in his chair.

Ovida didn't answer him. Instead she abruptly addressed Vince. "Get Marty in here. Now!"

Vince stood, still not sure what was going on, and

caught the murmur of concerned voices in the other room. He glanced through the doorway, straight into Jolie's pale face, and suddenly he knew.

Bolting for the front door, he heard his mother's exclamation. "Her water broke!"

Forget the turkey, they were having a baby!

Jolie stood with her mouth open like some spectator at a train wreck.

It was pandemonium, with the women cramming food into the refrigerator and shouting out instructions to one another, the men zipping around in the background, and the kids crowding around the kitchen door to stare at the laboring mother as if expecting the baby to burst from her belly like some alien in a horror movie.

The only calm one of them, Donna herself, was right at the center of the storm. Despite her white lips, guttural moans and roiling belly, she managed to sit patiently, smile and work her way down a mental checklist while her family careened around like Keystone Kops in a panicked attempt to shut down dinner preparations and get her to the hospital.

"My suitcase is all packed and sitting inside the closet door," she said to no one in particular. "The doctor's telephone number is programmed into Marty's cell phone. All I've had to eat is a hard-boiled egg and crackers. There's a list of people to call on my bedside table."

She looked right at Jolie, who couldn't seem to do more than gape, as she said that last. Then she reached out, sucking in a sharp breath at the same time. Instinctively, Jolie wrapped her fingers around Donna's and squeezed.

Sinkingly aware of the others rushing from the room, she asked, "Are you all right?"

Panting, Donna nodded, gulped and gripped Jolie's hand even tighter. "St-strike the family names from the list," she instructed. "That'll leave the church and two others. Vince can make those calls after we get to the hospital. Okay?"

"Uh-huh."

Marty skidded through the doorway into the dated but homey kitchen, Vince on his heels. He went down onto his knees at Donna's side, demanding, "What's wrong?"

"Nothing."

"B-but Vince said—"

"I'm having a baby," Donna snapped. "It's perfectly normal."

"But it's not due yet!"

"Tell that to the baby!" She grimaced at his look of worry and added softly, "A month early is nothing to worry about. Everything will be fine."

He placed his hand on her belly and fervently said, "From your lips to God's ears."

Stepping up behind Jolie, Vince cleared his throat and said, "John's sedan is waiting out front." His hands settled gently upon Jolie's shoulders, and she fought the most astonishing urge to lean back against him.

"Who's behind the wheel?" Marty asked anxiously.

"Dad."

Martin shook his head. "No, no, he's too slow. You're the wheel man. I want you."

Donna rolled her eyes as Vince flexed his hands on Jolie's shoulders. "No problem," he said mildly. "Let's go."

Donna tugged on Jolie's hand as she began pushing

her way up out of the chair. Bracing herself, Jolie helped haul her up, Marty hovering solicitously at his wife's side.

"Mom sent Sharon for a clean robe for me to wear, and Helen's gone for towels," Donna said, plucking at her wet clothes. Jolie blinked. She'd missed those details entirely.

"Let's head for the door," Vince said, stepping back to make way. "Mom and Olivia are herding the kids into Wally's van."

"Oh, I can stay here with the kids," Jolie offered, glad to have something to contribute.

Donna just laughed. Vince squeezed her shoulders again.

"Thanks, hon, but it would take a battalion of armed soldiers to make that work. The Cutler clan descends en masse for every family event."

"Just hang on," Donna instructed. "They'll need every hand at the hospital."

"Oh, no," Martin moaned. "I think I'm going to be sick."

"For Pete's sake, Marty," Donna chided, her free hand on her belly as he hurried away. "Make it quick, will you?" She lifted her arm. "Vince, lend a hand."

He slid to her side, wrapped an arm around her back, murmuring, "I've got you, sis."

"Nothing new there," she muttered and kissed his cheek.

The trio sidled through the door, Jolie taking up a position on Donna's other side. Helen rushed past with the towels, shouting, "John, put Bets in the car with us. Vince and Jolie are going with Donna."

"Tell Dad I'm driving," Vince called out as she disappeared through the front door.

"Good grief, Marty," they heard her say. "Could you do that in the grass?"

Donna moaned, then she laughed. "Poor Martin. You be nice to him, Vincent Cutler, or I'll pull your ears off your head."

"Me?"

"Don't pretend you won't tease him," Donna scolded.

"Never occurred to me." Vince winked at Jolie over the top of his sister's head, and a smile quirked her lips. The next instant she was blinking back tears.

Jolie couldn't help thinking about Connie going into labor all alone and in a hostile place instead of surrounded by loving, teasing family. They were like nothing she'd ever known, these Cutlers. Donna was so fortunate, and Jolie sensed that she knew it and also that even now, in the midst of happy crisis, she was doing her best to make Jolie feel included.

Sharon met them at the front door with a black bathrobe.

"Here you go, sugar. This won't show stains."

"Isn't this Dad's?" Donna asked, pausing to shove her arms into the wide sleeves.

"He never wears it," Sharon told her dismissively, "so don't you worry about it. Where's Marty?"

"Throwing up on the lawn," Vince answered smugly.

Sharon laughed, and to Jolie's surprise, Donna sniffed and a tear rolled down her nose.

"He loves us so much," she said in a happy, shaky voice, rubbing her belly.

"Of course he does," Vince said solicitously, shoving open the screen door. "Here we go."

What would it be like, Jolie wondered enviously, to feel such love?

She stuck to Donna's side as they again negotiated a doorway.

It was chilly in the shade of the porch, but the sun shone brightly overhead despite the clouds scudding along pushed by a brisk wind. An ashen Marty wore a jacket draped about his shoulders, and Sharon's husband Wally was busily dispensing coats to everyone else.

"Over here," Vince called, holding out one hand. "The corduroy and the denim."

"And the fur," Sharon added, striding forward to receive all three coats. She draped the bronze-colored faux fur around Donna, did the same for Jolie with the ivory corduroy walking coat and tossed Vince his denim jacket as they drew up at the car. Larry was waiting with the rear door open and the motor running.

"Marty, you go around," Donna said, presenting her cheek for her father's kiss. "Vince is going to drive, Daddy."

"Whatever you want, doll." He went around her and got in on the passenger side.

Donna ducked down and carefully edged into the car, the seat of which was lined with towels.

"We're right behind you," Sharon promised, moving toward another vehicle.

Jolie hung back hesitantly, until Vince placed a hand at the nape of her neck. She looked up at him, and he dropped a smile on her, saying, "Let's go, sweetheart. Hurry."

Sweetheart. Once or twice he'd called her honey or hon, but sweetheart seemed so…so…*romantic*.

Gulping, Jolie slid in next to Donna, who immediately gripped her hand again, despite the supporting arm that Marty had wrapped around her shoulders. Vince quickly swung down behind the steering wheel, reaching for his safety belt.

"Okay, let's get this show on the road."

"Owww," Donna moaned as the car backed out of the drive.

"Isn't this happening too fast?" Marty asked Jolie worriedly. Before she could formulate an answer for that, Larry reached into the back seat and covered Donna's and Jolie's linked hands and began praying aloud for a safe delivery and a healthy mother and child.

The other family members echoed his "Amen." Then Donna gasped and dropped her head onto her husband's shoulder.

"Let's move it!" Martin ordered, suddenly taking charge. Vince flicked on the hazard lights, pressed down on the horn and gunned the engine through a yellow light at the corner.

Donna was going through her mental checklist again by the time they pulled up under the canopy at the hospital. It seemed to help her keep the pain at bay.

"Suitcase in the closet. List on the bedside table. Oh, and the vent in the baby's room should be opened. We want the nursery nice and warm when we get home."

"I'll take care of it," Marty promised, bailing out, but as he disappeared into the hospital, Donna turned to Jolie.

"Tell Sharon. She'll see it gets done."

"Sharon," Jolie promised. "A-and Vince is to call."

Marty reappeared with a nurse pushing a wheelchair. Larry got out and hurried around to the door that Marty had left open. Donna scooted forward, pausing long enough to pat her brother on the shoulder.

"Getting off easy, buddy, with all the family in one place."

"Yeah, considerate of you," Vince cracked, glancing into the rearview mirror. "Take care of yourself, sugar," he added as Donna slid awkwardly out of the car. "See you soon."

"Fifth floor," Marty informed them, closing the door as his wife settled into the wheelchair. Vince sighed and readjusted his mirror to meet Jolie's gaze.

"Never a dull moment," he quipped, and started the car forward again.

That, thought Jolie, was as gross an understatement as she'd ever heard. How very blessed the Cutlers were!

Chapter Ten

Vince found an empty spot and parked. His family members were already piling out of vehicles in other places as he opened the back door of the sedan for Jolie. She took his hand as she rose to her feet.

"Are you sure I should be here?" she asked uncertainly, eyeing the horde of Cutlers swarming toward the hospital.

He looked down at her, brushed a strand of hair from her cheek and clasped her hand tightly in his.

"Yeah," he said. "Yeah, you should."

Suddenly, Jolie knew that there was no other place in the world where she would rather be. Perhaps it was odd, but she felt welcome. The Cutlers had a way of doing that. They were probably like that with everyone, though, not just her. Still, she felt special, included.

"Why would you think you shouldn't be here with the rest of us?" Vince asked.

Jolie shrugged. "It just seems odd." A heartbeat later she softly and unexpectedly added, "I wasn't there when Russell was born."

Out of the blue, longing stabbed her, so sharp that

it felt like a knife between her ribs. One moment she was fine, and the next she'd have given her last breath to see Russ. And Connie, Marcus, all of them. How she missed them!

Despite all that had happened, she missed her brother and sister. How weird was that?

Vince slipped his arm around her and turned her to follow the others at a rather sedate pace, telling her, "You were there when it counted most."

"I guess so," she murmured uncertainly.

"You did a good thing with your nephew, Jolie," he told her firmly, "and I'm sorry you got hurt because of it, but it grieves me that you aren't at peace with your family. Won't you consider seeing them, trying again?"

Her heart swelled painfully at his gentle words, but then it contracted with fear.

"I'd just be letting myself in for more heartache," she said tremulously.

Vince dropped his arm and strolled at her side, silent for the moment.

"It's a risk, I admit, but isn't the possibility of mending the rift worth it?"

He couldn't understand how it would be, how it had always been for her and her brother and sister.

"Vince, you have a big, wonderful family. You can't know how much I envy you. But the Wheelers aren't like the Cutlers. Our parents were never there for us, and we kids haven't really been close since Child Welfare split us up."

"What about before that?"

"Before that," she echoed, remembering with sudden clarity.

She didn't even realize that she'd come to a halt as the images and sensations flowed over her.

Connie had been little more than a baby with her pale, wispy locks and frequently trembling chin. Jolie remembered the urgent strength in her thin, ropy arms as they'd banded about her, seeking solace and reassurance. Only two years older, in many ways Jolie had felt responsible for her sister. Unfortunately as Connie had grown and matured into a very beautiful girl, she had continually reminded Jolie that she was not *that* much older, the implication being that she was not that much wiser and shouldn't give advice.

Marcus had been an avenging angel during their childhood. How fierce he had been! When the other kids had made fun of their mismatched clothing and perpetually runny noses, he had lifted his chin and pressed back his shoulders and stared them down with fists clenched. Every time their mother disappeared he'd solemnly taken over the task of caring for his sisters, and Jolie had believed that he could do no wrong.

With adulthood, his thick hair had warmed to a light, toasty brown which just missed blond. His solemn green eyes no longer seemed overly large for his face, a face that had been too thin and rawboned for a boy. He had changed in other ways, too. He was calmer, more confident. How calmly he had stated his case against her and devastated her world!

In retrospect, she realized that it wasn't the first time. Their world had come apart the day that Marcus had gone next door to beg food from the neighbors.

With the gas cut off and no groceries, they'd had to force down macaroni without cooking it. The bread had been growing blue stuff, but they'd eaten it anyway. Finally, all they'd had left was a mushy piece of tomato. Marcus had said what they'd all known, that their mother was not coming back, but Jolie couldn't believe it when he'd said that he couldn't take care of them anymore.

Rage swamped her all over again at the memory of it.

Strong, hard hands closed around her upper arms.

"You're trembling."

Jolie shook off the difficult memories, saying automatically, "It seems to have gotten cooler."

"Let's get inside." He linked his fingers with hers and tugged her toward the brown brick building.

"Are you sure I won't be in the way?" she asked again, dragging her feet.

Surely she didn't belong with these nice, normal people.

"Hey, what's one more when it comes to the Cutlers?" Vince replied teasingly.

"Remind me to ask the nurses that," Jolie retorted, giving back as good as she got and falling into step beside him.

Vincent grinned. "They're probably shuddering to see us coming. It's not the first time this has happened, you understand."

"Obviously."

"And it won't be the last," he added, squeezing her hand.

Jolie's heart fluttered, and she dared not even wonder why. All she knew was that she'd somehow gotten swept up in the Cutler universe and, oddly enough, that she liked it. She didn't know how that had happened, but she did know that it couldn't last.

Nothing good ever did, not for her. But at least she

was a small part of something normal and happy now. She supposed that was as good as it was going to get.

"Oh, man, look at that, will you?"

Vince pressed his palms against the glass partition between the waiting area and the nursery. His newest nephew lay screaming, tiny limbs flailing beneath the taut blue blanket, his face a jowly mask of pasty red flesh below a tiny, white knit cap.

Beside him, Jolie stood very still, her hands splayed against the glass partition. Vince could feel the ache in her. He knew that she was remembering her nephew as a newborn, and his heart went out to her.

She cleared her throat and commented in a voice that was almost normal, "Your dad says they're going to name him Anthony."

"Anthony Martin," Marty confirmed proudly, coming through the door that he'd been popping in and out of for almost five hours now. He hadn't stopped beaming since he'd first given them the news.

"How's the new mama doing?" Larry wanted to know.

"Mad as hops," Marty announced happily. "Doc's told her that she has to stay flat on her back for several hours when she wants to be up rocking the little squaller in there. Ovida's making sure she stays put for now."

"She'll be praying for somebody to keep her down this time next week," Olivia observed dryly.

"Hopefully it won't be too bad," Marty said, "My folks are on their way from Tulsa, and Mom's planning to stay a couple of weeks. You know how first-time grandparents are."

"God bless them," Sharon said with a nod, and that started a mild squabble about how she, as the oldest daughter, had gotten the lion's share of attention and assistance after giving birth to the firstborn grandchild on *both* sides of her family. In the midst of it, a nurse pecked on the nursery window.

"They're going to let me take him in to her again now that they've got him all cleaned up and charted," Marty said, disappearing once more through the door.

"That'll make mama happy," someone said.

A general silence descended. Then Drew suddenly asked, "Has anybody thought about the game?"

That brought several exclamations from around the room. Vince's was among them.

"Hey, that's right. It's just ten days away. Will Donna be able to go, do you think?"

"I wouldn't count on it," Helen answered.

"Doubtful, very doubtful," Olivia confirmed.

"Even if baby Tony had come on time, she was cutting it close," Sharon pointed out. "She told me that if she couldn't go they were planning to give her ticket away."

"Maybe Marty will take his dad in her place," someone said.

"He's declined in the past," Drew noted. "I think the only sport he cares for is golf."

"Well, Larry, looks like you'll get to be one of the sibs this year," Wally said, but the family patriarch shook his head.

"Naw, naw, that's a deal for the younger generation. I'll stay home with Mom as usual. Y'all take Jolie there. She's a football afficionado."

All eyes, save those of the children who were standing with their noses pressed to the nursery glass, turned to Vince and Jolie. It hadn't occurred to Vince even to mention this Cutler family tradition to Jolie, but the opportunity to include her suddenly seemed golden, for more reasons than one.

"What do you say, Jolie? Want to see a pro football game?"

"You're kidding."

He shook his head. "Not at all. We've been attending the first local game after Thanksgiving for years. Used to be just us guys, but gradually the girls got in on it, too."

She looked thunderstruck. "You're serious? A live pro game?"

"We buy the tickets at the beginning of every season," he confirmed. He was sure that Marty would be glad to let him take this year's extra off his hands.

"You're going to love it," Drew assured her, leaning back as best he could in his stiff, shallow chair.

Vince could tell from the look in Jolie's eye that she was afraid to get her hopes up.

"Don't worry," he said. "It's a week from this coming Sunday."

Her eyes brightened. A weeknight would have been problematic, but she didn't work on Mondays, at least not at her regular job. He could guarantee that her other "boss" would understand and be extremely flexible about starting times.

"Thing is," he went on mildly, "there are strings attached. The deal includes church."

"Church," she echoed uncertainly.

"Yeah, see, the timing's a little sticky so we'll all be attending early service together and leaving straight from there."

She nodded, biting her lip. "Uh-huh. Are you sure they haven't made other plans for the ticket?"

"No, I don't think so," Sharon said.

"I think Donna was holding out in hopes of making it herself," Helen said with a glance at her sister.

Sharon shrugged. "Maybe so."

"What do you say?" Vince asked Jolie. "Want to go?"

She took a deep breath—and smiled. "Sure! I'd love to go."

"Excellent."

Vince clapped his hands together and breathed a silent sigh of relief. He'd tried to get her to go to church before, but she'd resisted for one reason or another. He had sensed her ambivalence, even anger, though he doubted she would admit to it, and he could understand to a certain extent, since her brother was a minister. She had reason to be hurt, and he knew that the anger she was feeling directly resulted from her pain and loss. Unfortunately, he suspected that until she released the anger, the pain of her loss would not release her, and it seemed to him that the way to do that was to get her back into church. At least he hoped so.

Lord, let this be a first step in that direction, he silently prayed, even as the conversation continued.

"Wear flat shoes," Sharon warned her.

"And bring some warm pants," Helen added. "I always wear two pieces, like a sweater and a skirt. Then I just slip my pants on in the ladies' room after church, tuck the skirt into a bag, and I'm good."

"And don't forget your coat and scarf," Olivia warned. "The seats are about halfway up in the stadium, and it can get real chilly."

"Especially if the weather turns," Wally said, prompting a discussion about the year an errant wind had driven sleet through the hole in the roof of the stadium right into their faces.

The air was thick with jolly reminiscence by the time his mom stuck her head through that door and waved at his dad.

"Grandpa, get in here."

"About time," he exclaimed, getting to his feet.

"Wally and Sharon, you're next."

"I want to go!" Bets pleaded as Larry moved swiftly past her. "I want to hold the baby."

"Not today," Helen said flatly.

"Please, please, *pleeease*."

"She can go in my place," John said, and that set up a wail from the other kids.

"Brenda can go in for me," Wally announced.

"Just let the girls go," Drew proposed.

"No way," Vince said. "I'm going in."

"What about you, Jolie?" Sharon asked. "You ought to get to go in."

Feeling her immediate withdrawal, Vince piped up again. "She'll stick with me."

"Oh, no, that's all right," she began, but he sensed that this was something she needed to do, whether she realized it or not.

Seizing her hand, he bent his head close to hers.

"Donna will expect it. You don't mind, do you?"

She gulped, and he prodded a little harder, keeping his voice low.

"I know it's difficult, but it would be a shame not to see this thing through to the end. Come on. He's just a little baby."

Finally she drew a deep breath and nodded uncertainly.

"That's my girl," he crooned, sliding an arm around her. He realized as he said it that it was true, at least he'd like to make it true. Against all odds, Jolie Wheeler had somehow carved out a niche for herself in his life. She'd lodged herself in his heart, and he instinctively wanted to keep her there. Whether he could or not remained to be seen. Vince knew himself to be an all-or-nothing kind of guy, and he understood that the make-it-or-break-it point of any new relationship could be just around the bend, but there was no turning back now, not for him.

He draped his arm casually around her neck and drew her closer. It was something he might have done with his sisters, and she seemed to take it that way, but he let himself imagine what it could be like if she was his girl. Full of hope, he listened to his family's banter and held Jolie at his side where, God willing, he meant to keep her.

It was, no doubt, a mistake to hold little Anthony Martin, but when Ovida matter-of-factly dumped the impatiently fussing little guy into her arms, the weight of him felt so right cradled against her chest that Jolie hadn't possessed the strength to immediately pass him on. She thought of Russell and his sweet, placid nature.

How frightened she had been when he'd first been placed in her arms. Then she had looked into his blinking, unfocused eyes and fallen head over heels in love. She would never feel that again, never hold a child of her own. How could she when she was obviously meant to live her life alone?

They were a touchy-feely lot, the Cutlers, always hugging and kissing each other's cheeks, patting and holding hands, so she wasn't particularly surprised when Vince stepped up behind her and casually surrounded both her and the baby in a loose embrace. Looking over her shoulder, he cooed to the baby, who blinked his big, navy-blue eyes and stopped mewling long enough to listen to a voice other than his own.

Suddenly what she would be missing hit Jolie with the impact of a bullet fired at close range. She felt as if she was bleeding from the heart. It wasn't just Russell whom she was missing. It was all those children she would never have.

Unless…

She turned away from the temptation of that thought and gave up the baby to one of his aunts. When Vince patted her shoulder, she knew that he understood at least some of what she was feeling.

Somehow that made it even worse.

Friendship was one thing; a future was something else again. She must not let herself believe that she could have the kind of future for which Vincent Cutler was obviously destined. She was not meant for that kind of life; nothing in her experience had prepared her for it.

Sidestepping, she put her back to the wall as if making room in the crowded hospital suite. Vince folded his arms.

When Donna declared that she was too exhausted for company and that they all needed to get out so she and little Tony could rest, Jolie was secretly relieved. If she could have found a polite, subtle way of doing it, she'd have gone home, but when she hinted to Vince that she, too, was tired, he insisted that she couldn't skip the Thanksgiving meal even if it had been delayed.

They convoyed to the Cutler home, and everybody pitched in to reheat the food and get it on the table. The family seemed determined to make a great celebration, even without Donna, but Jolie's heart was no longer in it.

Marty stayed only long enough to gulp down a plate

of food, and Jolie toyed with the idea of asking him to drop her off on his way back to the hospital, but his eagerness to return to his wife's side would not allow her to impose. Besides, she felt duty-bound to help with the clean-up.

Finally, Vince drove her home. When he casually inquired if she had plans for the weekend, she felt a spurt of annoyance. All she wanted at the moment was to be alone with her misery.

"What weekend?" she retorted, implying that she'd be working Friday and Saturday as usual. "If you mean Sunday, I intend to do nothing at all."

The truth was that Geopp had elected to shut down the business for a couple of days so he could visit with relatives in Louisiana. Ever since she'd learned of this unexpected holiday, she'd been wondering what she was going to do with herself. Now she only wanted to lock herself away until her defenses were shored up again.

One corner of Vince's mouth crooked upward in what could have been a grimace or a grin, but he said nothing more on the subject.

Relieved, Jolie told herself that she needed the time to rest. She felt emotionally and mentally drained. Indeed, by the time she climbed the stairs to the landing, she was practically asleep on her feet. She fell into bed and dreamed of infants wailing forlornly as she tore through hospital corridors searching for something she could never find.

She woke in the morning to despair. Her thoughts turned immediately to Russell and to Donna and baby Anthony. And to Connie and Marcus. And to Vince. And to everything else she had spent her life wanting and could never have.

Chapter Eleven

When the telephone rang on Saturday afternoon, Jolie's first thought was that it was Vince, but the caller ID revealed that the call originated from her brother Marcus's number. After a surprising moment of agonizing indecision, she let the machine get it and then erased the message without listening to it and turned off the telephone.

Why not? She had no more business talking to Vince than to her brother or sister. There was not a single person in the world that she must talk to, and it was better that way. A solitary life was safest, simplest, easiest. She didn't have to get her heart broken repeatedly to learn that lesson.

By Monday morning, she'd convinced herself that she wanted no deeper involvement with Vince Cutler than a casual friendship, which was as it should be. They had made a business deal that was mutually beneficial, and as honest people of good will, they had formed a friendly working relationship, nothing more. The dinner invitations with his family and the upcoming football game were incidental offshoots of their business relationship, and it would be beyond foolish to seek anything more. She resolved to keep her distance.

It should have been easy.

When she arrived at his house for work, he was dressed and ready to go out. That was fine by her. In fact, it was preferable to having him underfoot all day.

"I see you're ready to leave," she said airily, moving toward the kitchen and the laundry room beyond.

"Not me," he said, snagging her hand and drawing her to a halt. "We. Or have you forgotten about the drapes?"

She had. She'd forgotten everything after the events of Thanksgiving, everything but the laundry waiting for her. "I have work to do now."

"You sure do," he agreed, towing her toward the garage.

She dug in her heels. "First things first. Let me get the laundry done, then if there's time—"

"We'll make time," he insisted, bringing his hands to his hips. "The laundry can wait a little while. I'll help you with it later."

"It's *my* job," she reminded him sharply. "I'll do it."

He tilted his head, studying her. "Fine. Then you'll do it *later.*"

Jolie set her back teeth, gritting out, "You're the boss," as she swept past him. What he said under his breath she didn't catch, mostly because she didn't want to.

"You going to glower at me all day?" he asked, following her into the house after another unsuccessful shopping trip.

"I'm not glowering at you," she snapped. "I'm frustrated. Doesn't this town have a reasonable drapery supplier hidden away somewhere?"

"I don't think it's the store owners who are being unreasonable," he muttered.

She rounded on him. "That's a hateful thing to say! I'm only looking out for your best interests! You may like being cheated and ripped off. I don't!"

Irritation flared. "Face it, Jolie," he told her flatly. "The drapes are going to cost what they're going to cost. We've been to every shop in town. Pick one, and let's get this thing underway."

"You pick one!" she shot back. "It's your house." With that she whirled and flounced down the hallway to the laundry room.

He let her go, not trusting his own temper at the moment, and trudged into the kitchen. His intuition told him that something more than the obvious was going on here. She'd been stiff-arming him all day. Why didn't she just set up barricades and tattoo Do Not Touch on her forehead? So much for taking the next step toward a real relationship.

Rubbing his own forehead with the heel of his hand, he leaned against the counter and told himself that he shouldn't have backed off after Thanksgiving. At the time he'd thought he was giving her room to decompress after all the excitement of the baby coming early and the family reaction to it. On a normal day the Cutler crew could overwhelm a person, even him! A self-contained soul like Jolie didn't stand a chance. Obviously she'd used the weekend to reinforce that protective shell she'd built around herself. Now he'd have to chip another hole in it.

He bowed his head and asked God to show him what to say and how to say it. The answer was quick in coming. With a sigh, he turned and ambled into the laundry room. She was stuffing a load into the washer as if it was trying to escape.

"I'm sorry," he said to her back.

She froze for a moment, poked a few stray ends and bits into the tub and slowly shifted around to face him.

"I know you're doing your best for me," he went on, "and I know that it goes against your grain to pay more for something than you feel you should. I'm sorry I let my impatience get the better of me."

She gulped and turned her back on him again, busily dumping detergent into the washer and twisting dials.

"It's not your fault," she finally said without turning around. "I'm in a lousy mood. But you're right, I don't like paying more than I think I should. I don't like for *you* to pay more than I think you should, either. And don't bother saying that you can afford it. That's beside the point."

"Is that really what this is about?" he asked cautiously.

She turned, shrugged and leaned back against the washer, arms akimbo as she braced her hands on her hips. "What else?"

He let the possibilities percolate for a minute. "You get another letter from your sister?"

She immediately got busy cleaning out the lint trap in the dryer. "Nope."

He wasn't fooled. "Your brother?"

"No." But she hesitated first.

"One of them call or come by?"

She balled the lint into her fist, closed the dryer door and walked over to the trash can. "He might have called."

"Might have?" Vince echoed.

She dropped the ball of lint into the trash and then watched it lie there. "I saw his number on the caller ID."

"But you didn't talk to him."

He hadn't meant it to sound accusatory, but she evidently took it that way. After slitting a quick glance at him from the corner of her eye, she pinched the bridge of her nose.

"Look," he said, "I'm not spoiling for a fight. I understand the situation with your brother and sister. I'm just wondering what this mood of yours is really about."

"What mood? I don't know what you're talking about."

"I think you do. I think you know I like you. A lot."

She shot him a quick, sharp look, too quick for him to tell if it was astonishment or dismay.

"Well, I—I should hope so."

"And I think you like me, too," he forged on.

"Of course." She said it lightly.

He wasn't fooled. "I think you like me a lot," he went on doggedly, "a lot more than you want to."

She turned to face him again. "That's ridiculous."

He had her now. "Oh, good." He rocked back on his heels. "Then there's no reason you won't go to dinner with me Thursday night."

She blinked. "Uh."

"You're not busy Thursday night, are you?"

"Uh."

"Friends do that, you know, have dinner together."

Her lips flattened. "Friends. Right."

"Excellent! I'll pick you up about six-thirty, give you time to change after work."

"We can talk about the drapes," she said emphatically, obviously trying to set boundaries.

"Right," he said, grinning. With that, he walked away and left her to her work.

They could talk about anything they wanted to talk about, anything at all, the weather, the economy, philosophy. They'd talk about whatever pleased her, but they would be talking as more than mere friends this time. Of that he had no doubt.

Jolie feared that he'd drag her off to a showy, upscale restaurant and spent hours trying to figure out what to wear. In the end she chose a pair of black jeans faded to charcoal gray and a simple burnt-orange turtleneck. It wasn't fancy, but it was the best she could do.

Vince showed up in jeans, complimented her looks with a casual comment and took her to a popular chain restaurant serving Mexican food.

After ordering, they talked about what sort of drapes she had in mind for the house and what they were obviously going to cost. Jolie had accepted the fact that the draperies were going to cost more than she'd like. After that, it had been a relatively simple matter to decide which of the custom drapers should get the work. Vince approved her choice and suggested that they make an appointment to revisit the shop on Monday. Jolie agreed, and he said he'd take care of it.

When the food came, he prayed over it as usual, but this time he took her hand before he did so. Jolie felt compelled to bow her head alongside him. She really had nothing against speaking a blessing over her meal, and she could admit privately now that a part of her previous reaction to his habit had been aimed, not at him or the act of praying, but at her brother.

Sometimes it seemed that she could not escape Marcus or reminders of him no matter what she did. She'd see a pair who looked similar in appearance and wonder if they were brother and sister. Even children, who were easier to identify as siblings, caused her a pang because she couldn't help remembering how close she and Marcus and Connie had once been.

It was no different that night. As soon as she lifted her head after the prayer, Jolie came eyeball-to-eyeball with a little girl sitting next to her older brother in a booth across the way. The child smiled, rattling her appetizer plate against the ta-bletop, and the boy calmly dropped more tortilla chips on it without interrupting the parents' conversation. Jolie had to look away.

Only when she pulled her attention back to her own table did she realize that Vince still held her hand in his. He gave her a sympathetic look and squeezed her fingers. Quickly she smoothed her napkin in her lap, requiring both hands to do so. It disturbed her that he seemed able to read her thoughts so easily, but she couldn't deny, even to herself, that his concern left her with a warm feeling.

Despite her best intentions, she found herself relaxing, and that made conversation flow more easily. Soon they were bantering and teasing like…well, like the friends they were. The food disappeared, and the check was settled, and yet they lingered at the table, talking and laughing—until the little girl and her family across the way rose and began to leave the restaurant.

Jolie couldn't help glancing at them one more time, and that prompted Vince to say, "You must miss them. I know I'd sure miss my sisters if something happened to drive a wedge between us."

She didn't pretend to misunderstand.

"I do miss my brother and sister, but this is not some silly childhood argument. Frankly, I've never been so hurt or disappointed in anyone."

He nodded and changed the subject, sort of.

"One day when you have your own children, you can use this to help them value their relationship and get along."

Jolie opened her mouth to say that she would never have children of her own. She'd have to fall in love and get married before that could happen, and she had no intention of letting herself get that close to anyone. Still, she couldn't seem to force out the words. She told herself that it was because he would almost assuredly try to talk her out of her decision to remain alone, but the truth was that saying it aloud felt too much like making it real.

She settled for an inarticulate, "Mmmm," smiled and said, "We probably ought to go and free up the table."

He nodded, rose and held her chair while she slipped out of it. Then he helped her with her coat and escorted her from the building. She tried to recapture the mood, but she kept thinking of what he'd said about using her experiences as a parenting tool. That made a certain sense—for a person planning to make a family, a person whose experience had taught her that family was not for her.

Before he dropped her off at her apartment building, he reminded her that the football game was coming up on Sunday and that she would need to be ready by eight o'clock in the morning. She assured him that she wouldn't forget, and assured herself that Sunday would be about fun and friendship only.

She awakened early after yet another restless night. Marcus had called the afternoon before and left another message. She'd stood there and listened as he'd spoken to her answering machine, but she hadn't picked up the telephone, telling herself that there was no point in doing so. If she hadn't slept well, she chalked it up to the excitement of attending a pro game.

Never in her wildest dreams had she ever imagined that she would do such a thing, but then much about her life seemed beyond her imagination. That thought preoccupied her throughout the morning, so that when Vince knocked on her door, she was in an agony of indecision, despite having thought she'd resolved the issue of what to wear.

"Does this sweater go with this skirt?" she demanded of him anxiously.

He answered automatically. "Sure."

Irritated and impatient, she stomped a foot, brought her hands to her waist and demanded, "Look at me! I'm trying to figure out what to wear."

He let his gaze wander from her feet upward. By the time it got to her face, he was smiling. "No, I guess the sweater does not go with the skirt, after all."

She threw up her hands and whirled away, snapping, "Why didn't you say so?"

He just chuckled as she hurried into the bathroom to change the sweater for a simple, tailored blouse which would work well with the double-breasted navy wool coat that she'd picked up at the military surplus store.

It was hard to justify spending good money on a fashionable winter coat in Texas, but she did her best to dress up the outfit with a wooly scarf. After stuffing knit gloves into her pockets, she took one last look in the mirror, adjusted the dark-blue knitted headband that she wore to keep her hair out of her face, fluffed her bangs and went out. Vince was standing exactly where she'd left him, his hands in the pockets of his brown corduroy jacket.

"I'm ready."

"You look terrific," he told her. "Stop worrying."

She rolled her eyes. "I'm not worrying, but thank you."

"You're welcome. Shall we?"

He offered her his arm. She linked hers with it and went out to embrace what she hoped would be a red-letter day.

She didn't expect church to be the highlight of the outing. Feeling betrayed, Jolie had stopped going to church when Marcus had first broached the subject of returning Russell to his mother. She'd told herself that if God didn't care enough about her to keep Russell with her where he belonged, then God didn't care whether she was in church or not. Ever since she'd accepted Vince's invitation, however, she'd secretly felt a certain relief.

As it turned out, Vince's church provided an eye-opening experience. For one thing, Vincent Cutler, good as he looked, good as he was, couldn't carry a tune in a bucket. She, however, could.

Jolie had always enjoyed singing along with the radio, and Russell had seemed to like her voice well enough, but she'd learned to love singing hymns at Marcus's small church. Vince's church was quite large, large enough to boast a hundred-voice choir and a state-of-the-art sound system, with a large video screen that showed the words to each song. Given the season, the place was packed, even for the early service, and all those voices lifting heavenward in praise made her feel as if she might float right up to the ceiling.

"We usually sit down there on the right near the front," Helen had whispered before the service had begun. She'd pointed over the balcony rail. "The pastor likes to leave the back seats for visitors. You know, so they don't have to go searching for an empty spot in a strange place. That's him there."

When the hymn-singing portion of the service had concluded, the pastor stepped up to the pulpit, bade the congregation rise for prayer and read off a list of names of those in need. Next he read a list of those with praises. When he mentioned that Donna, Marty and the new baby were home and well, he waved up to the balcony, and quite a number of heads turned to smile and offer silent congratulations to the family. Most of those seemed to take note of Jolie standing beside Vince.

As if in answer to a collective question, Vince took her hand in his, so that they stood side by side, hand in hand, with heads bowed throughout a long but eloquent and obviously heartfelt prayer.

Once they sat down again, a quartet provided special music. Jolie couldn't imagine hearing better vocals. At the end of the selection, the pastor returned to the pulpit and placed his burgundy Bible atop it. After instructing them to turn to the twenty-fifth psalm, he began to read in a strong, dramatic voice.

Jolie hadn't remembered to bring the Bible that Marcus had given her for Christmas some years earlier, but Vince leaned forward slightly and laid his own Bible in her lap, open to the correct passage. He lifted one arm about her shoulders and with the other hand pointed out where they were. She took the Bible into her hands, and her eye picked up on the fourth verse.

"Make me know Thy ways, O Lord. Teach me Thy paths. Lead me in Thy truth and teach me,

for Thou art the God of my salvation. For Thee
I wait all the day. Remember, O Lord, Thy compassion and Thy loving kindnesses, for they have
been from of old. Do not remember the sins of my
youth or my transgressions. According to Thy loving kindness remember Thou me, for Thy goodness' sake, O Lord."

The preacher looked up and asked a simple question.
"Have you asked God to teach you His ways?"

Jolie felt a thunk, as if something had dropped from
her chest into the pit of her belly. She forgot about
Vince's arm draped casually about her shoulders and
let the preacher's words fill her.

"If not, why not?" he went on. "Our God is the God
of salvation, the God of compassion, a loving, kind God
who forgets, just wipes out, our sins and transgression,
all for the asking. 'Well, pastor,' you say, 'if I ask to know
God, He's going to expect something of me.' I don't deny
it. On the other hand, friend, if you ask to know God,
He's going to *make* something of you."

Jolie listened, fascinated, and what the pastor had to
say made a lot of sense. This was very different from
what she had experienced from time to time as a child,
when church had seemed a confusing, often boring, kind
of punishment, and from what she'd known at Marcus's
church. As his sister, she'd often been more concerned
with how others saw and heard him than with the contents of his sermons or how they might apply to her.

She wondered with a pang if she had been unfair to
Marcus. He had often urged her to consider the words
that he delivered from the pulpit, but she'd had a difficult
time doing so. He was her brother, not some oracle from

God. She'd been proud of him, but she hadn't wanted to take his sermons seriously. Why not?

The answer came in a blinding flash of insight, and suddenly she found herself caught up in a maelstrom of emotion. Tears welled into her eyes, and even as she listened to the pastor with suddenly sharp ears, she came to a clear and abrupt understanding of herself. She hadn't listened to Marcus because she'd already been angry with him.

"Some of you don't want to know God," the preacher was saying, "because you don't want to know yourselves. You want to maintain your illusions. You think you've got the world and yourselves figured out. Knowing the Maker of both would just confuse things, throw your little make-believe world into a tailspin. Well, make-believe is a prison, ladies and gentlemen. Always remember that the truth is what sets us free."

The truth was that even before Marcus had sided with their sister and taken Russell from her, Jolie had been angry with him. Deep down, she'd been angry with him for years. Ever since the day Child Welfare had arrived to cart them off to foster care, she and Connie to one home, Marcus to another, Jolie had been bitterly angry with her brother.

He had gone to the neighbors. He had abdicated his place as their protector and caretaker. Her heroic, solemn, big brother had turned out to be only a boy, after all. The protracted absence of their mother had given him no choice, really, but at the time it had seemed to Jolie to be the ultimate betrayal. She'd known it was unreasonable even then, and perhaps that was why she was only just now facing that anger.

"You push God away," the preacher was saying. "He's

reaching out to you, but you keep pushing Him away with your indifference and your defensiveness and your cynicism and your wrath. This world isn't perfect, so you label God a tyrant, unfair, uncaring. 'What's He ever done for me?' you say. It's a very long list, but I'm going to give you a one-word answer that says it all. Jesus."

Jolie shuddered with something she couldn't describe, not an emotion really but a knowing, an opening. It left her feeling shaken and vulnerable, and suddenly she yearned with a startling ferociousness for her brother. She heard his voice inside her head just as she'd heard it on the answering machine the previous day.

"Hello, Jo," he had said, sounding sad and wistful. "Hope you're well. We're all fine. Russ is growing like a weed, really running around the place now. You did good by him, Jo, he's a happy, loving little boy. We were wondering, Connie and I, what your plans are for Christmas. We missed you Thanksgiving, but we prayed that you didn't spend it alone. Every day I pray that you'll pick up the phone and call. Please, Jolie, let's be a family again. Please think about it."

She did think about it. For a moment, she could see and feel it so clearly, how it had been to be a real family. Then she realized that everyone was getting to their feet. They sang another hymn, and she managed to go through the motions, but she was too distracted by thoughts of her brother, sister and nephew to make sense of the words. She felt as if she were reeling, and she reached mechanically for the old pain and resentment, anything to steady herself.

Surely, she told herself petulantly, Russell missed her as much as she missed him. How could Marcus say that he was fine? How could any of them be fine after all that had happened?

And how could they ever be a family again? Too many years and too much hurt had gone by since they had been a real family. Maybe if they hadn't grown up in different foster homes, maybe if Connie hadn't gone to prison, if they hadn't teamed up to take Russell away from her after she'd stepped in to care for him, if her mother had just once thought of her children instead of the latest man to whisper promises in her ear...

"You okay, hon?"

The sound of Vince's voice jolted her. "Huh?" She looked around to find that the building was quickly emptying.

"The girls are going to change for the game. Did you want to go with them?"

"Yes!"

She grabbed her bag and turned to follow Helen along the curving row of seats and out into the crowded aisle, aware of Vince watching her, his hands at his waist. She dared not look back. Everything seemed to have bobbed to the surface, all the hurt and anger and longing that she'd suppressed all these years, and if he saw her face, he would undoubtedly know.

Following along in Helen's wake, Jolie carefully tucked away all her mental and emotional corks, but something told her that it would only be a temporary fix at best.

Chapter Twelve

Inside a stall in a surprisingly opulent ladies' room, Jolie changed into her jeans. The sisters did the same, chattering about Donna's Thanksgiving baby and how little sleep the new mother had gotten since they'd come home from the hospital. Several others had crowded into the small space, and Sharon made a few introductions, but Jolie knew that she'd never remember who was who despite the friendly smiles and speculative looks.

Finally the foursome hurried out to greet the men, throwing on their coats. Sharon and Olivia seemed especially enthusiastic about the game. Helen, who was the quietest of all the sisters, seemed to be missing Donna. She and her husband John automatically fell into step beside Vince and Jolie, who suddenly realized that Marty was missing, too.

"Is Marty meeting us there?" she asked as they pushed out onto the sidewalk.

John shook his head, and Vince said, "Guess he didn't want to leave Donna and the baby. He called this morning and told us to give his ticket away."

"Give it away!"

"Sure, why not?" Vince asked, taking her hand as they crossed the traffic lane and moved toward the parking lot. "If he's not going to use it, somebody else might as well."

"He's not going to try to sell it or anything?"

"Scalping is illegal," John said matter-of-factly.

"Technically," Wally added over his shoulder. "There are ways around that."

"Yeah, and one of them is to give the ticket away," Vince said. "Marty says he has too much to be thankful for to worry about missing a game and losing a few bucks."

"I think it's a nice thing to do," Helen put in. "Why don't we all pitch in and pay him for it, then we'll each have a part of giving it away?"

"That's a good idea," Olivia agreed, turning around to walk backward as they made for her minivan. "If each couple gave just twenty-five dollars, that would leave Marty and Donna with an equal stake. Then we'd all be giving away the ticket."

Everyone agreed to that, everyone but Jolie who stopped dead in her tracks, gaping at the thought of a ticket that cost a hundred and twenty-five bucks! It took everyone a moment to realize that she wasn't with them, then they all stopped and Vince walked back to ask, "What's the matter?"

"Who paid for my ticket?" she wanted to know.

She hadn't really thought about it before. Somehow, though, she'd assumed that the family had bought the tickets together and that they'd cost maybe thirty or forty dollars each, which seemed like a lot to her. Three or four times more seemed outrageous, and she couldn't let Donna and Marty give that kind of money to her!

Vince reached out and fingered the lapels of her coat, stepping close.

"Better face the facts, Wheeler," he told her softly. "I paid for your ticket because you're my date." He stepped closer still, bringing his forehead near hers and staring down into her eyes. "It's better than letting Marty take the hit for two tickets he couldn't use, isn't it?"

His date. A couple. How on earth, she wondered wildly, had this happened? She shook her head, thoroughly confused, but then his face clouded and she found herself nodding. Vigorously. He grinned and grabbed her hand, turning back to the others and dragging her along with him.

"What are you waiting for?" he asked loudly. "We've got a game to go to!"

That seemed to light a fire. Wally pumped his fist, and the whole group piled enthusiastically into the van. Jolie and Vince crammed into the back seat with Helen and John, leaving Sharon and Wally to the shorter middle one and Olivia and Drew to the front buckets. Vince sat on the outside edge, crossing his legs and extending his feet out into the space between the shorter middle seat and the van's sliding side door.

On their way to the stadium and while inching forward into the parking lot, they talked enthusiastically, the men dissecting the opposition, the women anticipating the food and the people. Sharon and Helen entertained Jolie with stories about fan hijinks, and it became clear to her that they watched the crowd more than the players. They all talked over one another, joking and laughing and generally just having a good time.

That laid the pattern for the remainder of the day. After hiking in from the "back forty" as Drew called the parking area to which their seats entitled them, they gave Marty's ticket to a grateful young couple who traded the seat in for a cheaper one and used the difference to pay for a second. After making their way to the seats, the women shed their coats and handbags and announced that they were going for food. Vince crammed bills into Jolie's hand and asked for nachos, sausages (plural), a burrito, a large soda and a dill pickle, adding that she should get herself anything she wanted.

She looked at the money in her hand and wondered if he expected her to order filet mignons, then she got a look at the actual prices and wondered who in his right mind would spend that kind of money for junk food! The Cutlers apparently, because the sisters loaded up, teasing one another about wearing the goodies on their hips as they made their way back to their seats.

"Good thing we only do this once a year," Helen remarked.

"Speak for yourself," Sharon quipped drolly. "You can look at my fat behind and know this isn't a rarity for me."

Sharon was pleasantly rounded, like her mother, but Jolie didn't think of her as "fat." The other girls, who took after their father, as did Vince, immediately protested the self-description, and by the time they rejoined the men, Sharon was prancing around like a beauty-pageant contestant, dipping and swirling comically.

As soon as the bounty was passed out, the group huddled together for a quick prayer, then settled into their seats just as the opposing team emerged from the locker room. Jolie had never felt quite so avid. Vince glanced at Jolie's single sausage on a bun and asked if that was all she was going to eat.

"It's not even lunchtime yet," she said.

"But it's game time!" Drew crowed, stuffing a dripping nacho into his mouth.

"Yeah, if you're going to hang out with this crew," Olivia said, leaning forward to peer around Vince, "you're going to have to learn to pig out."

"How else can you date our pig of a brother?" Sharon piped up. Jolie looked down. Was she dating Vince or was it all for show on his part? Just then Vince reached around Jolie to lightly smack his oldest sister in the back of the head just as she was about to bite into her hot dog. The result was chili on her chin and nose and a lot of laughter.

The home team burst onto the field just then, and the crowd rose to its feet, including the Cutler contingent. Vince took a napkin and cleaned Sharon's face for her. She stuck out her tongue at him, then darted around Jolie to kiss him on the cheek. Jolie couldn't help feeling a little envious of the easy, teasing camaraderie that the siblings and their spouses enjoyed.

She would never again have the same with her own brother and sister. *Unless I can somehow forgive,* she caught herself thinking. Immediately, she tried to push that thought away. How did she put away her hurt and anger?

The question stubbornly clung to the back of her mind throughout that long and amazing afternoon.

Vince slung an arm across Jolie's shoulders companionably as they strode toward his truck in the church parking lot. Behind them, Drew tooted the horn of the minivan as it turned onto the street. Lifting his free arm high in farewell, Vince gave in to the impulse to pull Jolie a little closer.

"So what do you think?"

"About the game?" she asked, smiling.

"The game, the crazy Cutlers…the service this morning."

"It was great, all of it," she replied sincerely.

Vince smiled. "So, what was your favorite part?"

She shook her head. "This whole day has been… words fail me."

She'd laughed with the rest of them all afternoon, and she'd really gotten into the game, making some astute judgment calls about various plays and rulings. She'd even loosened up enough to splurge on fajitas. Still, throughout the day he'd sensed that she was experiencing some sort of emotional turmoil. It could have been his imagination, of course, but he decided to go with his gut feeling.

"Want to talk about it?" he asked gently as they drew near his vehicle.

She stiffened, but her reply was flippant. "Sure. Let's see." She struck a pose, one arm folded across her body, one finger tapping her chin, as he fished out his keys and unlocked the passenger door. "We should not have lost that game," she concluded, climbing up into the seat.

Vince chuckled. He'd given her the perfect out. Next time he'd choose his words a little more carefully. After walking around the truck, he inserted himself behind the steering wheel, unsurprised when she took up right where she'd left off, rattling on and on about the game.

"The team's just too young, you know. Can't take the pressure."

Vince nodded agreement. Really, he couldn't quibble with her assessment, but that wasn't why he let her get away with dissecting the game play by pivotal play as he drove her home.

At one point he interrupted long enough to ask, "How'd you get so into football, anyway?"

"What else is there to do during football season? I mean, that's all that's on television Sunday afternoons and Monday nights."

"Which just happen to be your two days off from your regular job." And of course, she would not have cable, he added mentally, making her pretty much a captive audience of whatever stations she could pick up with a pair of rabbit ears.

"There you go," she confirmed matter-of-factly.

He smiled, thinking that he had unintentionally benefited from her straitened circumstances, while she launched into a story about Sharon's hips or some such thing. He wasn't really paying attention any longer. Instead, he was weighing the advisability of pressing her to reveal what was actually going on inside that pretty head of hers.

By the time they reached the apartment building, he'd concluded that no good cause would be served by letting the matter go. Sooner or later, she would have to deal with some of her issues—or he was going to have to reconcile himself to simple friendship with her, something he didn't want to contemplate. He sent up a silent prayer and shut off the engine.

"Can I come up? We need to talk."

She blinked at him, frowning slightly. "Sure."

Smiling to let her know that this didn't have to be a frightening conversation, he let himself out of the truck. She was already doing the same, so he waited for her to join him. Side by side, they headed for the stairs.

As they entered the apartment, she flipped on the lights and asked if he wanted something to drink, but he groaned at the very thought.

"I am stuffed. I won't have to eat or drink for at least two days."

She arched a censorial eyebrow, announcing airily, "I am not surprised."

Laughing, he said, "Come on, let's sit down."

He lifted a hand, but instead of putting hers in it, she turned toward the sofa and dropped down onto one end of it.

"What's wrong?"

He sat down next to her and calmly replied, "That's what I want to know."

She shook her head, gaze skittering away. "Not following."

Carefully considering his words, he folded his hands.

"There were moments today when you were somewhere else entirely, and I don't think it was a happy place."

She sighed and rubbed her hand through her bangs, muttering, "Nothing gets by you, does it?"

"Couldn't say. All I know is that I like to keep it real, especially between us, and when something's bothering you, well, seems that it bothers me, too." Surprisingly, tears sprang into her eyes, and without even thinking, he slid close and drew her into the circle of his arms. "Hey, now, it wasn't my intention to upset you."

She gave him a watery snort, insisting, "I'm not upset, I'm...confused."

"What about?"

She bowed her head, and for a moment they simply sat together. Finally, she spoke.

"It's almost too much, you and your family, me and my family, what the preacher said today."

He lifted his arms from about her and locked his hands, meshing his fingers.

"Let's start at the end and work backward. What exactly did the pastor say that's got you thinking?"

She spoke hesitantly at first and then with growing agitation. Who could really know God? Why would He forget the bad things we do? Vince answered her patiently and in some detail. Knowing God, he told her, was a lifelong process. One had to believe, of course, and then ask and keep on asking to know God's will. Most importantly, one had to pay careful attention to God's replies.

"As for forgetting our transgressions," he explained, "it pleases God to forget how those whom He loves hurt Him. Again, all that is ever necessary is that we ask for His forgiveness, and afterward He wipes out our sins as if they never existed."

Jolie admitted that she just didn't understand how that could be.

"Don't make the mistake of saddling God with our human weaknesses," he told her. "And understand now that His strength is also ours for the asking."

"But why?" she demanded.

He considered for a moment.

"Let me ask you a question. Don't you want to forget the pain?" Her eyes widened. "Our sin pains God, but He loves us, so why would He want to remember our sin?" Vince went on. "God *chooses* to forget, but before forgetting must come forgiveness. If you want to forget your pain, Jolie," Vince said, "first you have to forgive."

Her brow wrinkled, and she whispered, "I'm not sure I can. If it was rational, maybe, but…"

"If what was rational?" he asked. When she hesitated, he urged, "Tell me."

To his gratification, she trusted him with the story of her childhood, with the anger she had discovered only that day. Coupled with what she felt was her brother's betrayal in the matter of her nephew, the realization obviously rattled her. He listened until she had talked herself out, sometimes weeping, sometimes bitter, more often just plain hurt and confused. Afterward, they sat quietly, taking comfort in each other's company until the emotional storm had truly calmed and Vince felt that he could broach the last difficult issue.

"You know, this whole tangle might unsnarl itself if you'd just see your brother and sister."

"How can I do that?" she demanded, sitting up straighter. "How can I risk that kind of heartbreak again?"

Vince leaned forward, bracing his elbows on his knees.

"Doesn't it make a difference that you wouldn't be coping with it alone this time?" She blinked at him, and he saw immediately that she was as afraid to trust in that as in anything else. "No, of course, it doesn't," he answered himself.

He sat up again and turned slightly to face her, praying that what he was going to say was the right thing.

"Has it occurred to you that this isn't about you? You're hurt. All right, I understand why that is so, but what if this really is best for your nephew? What if knowing his mother loves him is more important than knowing that you love him? And why shouldn't he have both?"

For a long moment, she stared at him as if he'd sprouted horns. Then she shifted around until their knees touched. "Do you really believe that?"

"I don't know," Vince told her softly, "but I believe that God always has a reason for allowing what goes on in our lives, and it makes sense to me that Russell could only be better off for having a loving relationship with both his mother and his aunt."

"I want to forgive," she said after a moment, "but I don't know how."

Vince smiled and took her hands in his. "It starts with a prayer," he began.

They slipped to their knees, and Jolie poured out her heart, all her hurts and fears and failings. She begged God to help her forgive.

After a long while, they rose

"Thank you," she whispered to Vince, dabbing at her eyes with a tissue pulled from her pocket.

"My pleasure. I hope this means that you're willing to talk to your brother and sister now."

"Forgiving and opening yourself up to more hurt are two different things, Vince," she hedged uncertainly.

"Just think about it," he urged, "and while you're considering it, I'll be praying for you."

She nodded, half smiling. He saw a glimmer of trepidation in her eyes and knew that she had not yet conquered her fears. He understood instinctively that she must, but it was only as he drove himself home a little later that he realized why.

Not only did her happiness depend on it, but theirs together did as well.

And they *could* be happy together.

In fact, Vince was beginning to believe that they *should* be happy together. It seemed to him that God was blatantly leading them in that direction.

At least his heart seemed to think so.

Vince ran a fingertip around the rim of his cup and glanced up just as his father came through the door of the coffee shop. Waving, Vince snagged Larry's attention and sat back into the corner of the booth, one elbow propped atop the edge of the seat back. As he slid onto the bench opposite Vince, Larry turned up his coffee cup and signaled the waitress with a look.

"Cold out there," he commented, rubbing his hands together.

Vince noted that his father's fingers had grown knobby and stiff.

"Arthritis acting up?"

Larry nodded. "Yeah, that twenty-two-degree temperature drop last night kicked it up a notch."

"Well, that's Texas for you."

"You're telling me? I've seen it drop forty degrees in two hours and without a cloud in the sky."

"Blue norther," Vince recollected, but then he changed the subject. "I need your advice."

"Figured something like that," Larry said, pressing back in his seat as the waitress arrived with the coffeepot. She poured the steaming black liquid, ascertained that they didn't want anything else and departed again. "What is it then?" Larry asked, leaning forward to hunker around his cup. "Jolie?"

Vince smiled wryly. "How'd you know?"

"Well, it wouldn't be business. Nothing I can tell you

there. And if it was about the family, you'd be talking to your mother. So I figure it's got to be Jolie. You in love with her?"

Vince nodded matter-of-factly. "Yeah. Yeah, I am."

"How come?"

The blunt question momentarily shook Vince, and to his surprise he found himself growing angry.

"How come? What do you mean, how come? What's wrong with her?"

"I didn't say there was anything wrong with her."

"She's a little rough around the edges, okay?" Vince retorted defensively. "Who wouldn't be, given all she's been through. In fact, it's a wonder she's not selling herself on some street corner, but instead she's managed to maintain her dignity. She lives her life with a certain sense of honor, and if that makes her a little standoffish, then who are we to judge?" He pecked himself on the chest. "I've lived a life of pure bliss compared to her, and I know that if our roles were reversed I'd be the worst sort of thug. If you really want to know the truth, she's too good for me!"

Larry sat back with an air of satisfaction.

"Well, that answers that question. Now how about her? Is she in love with you, too?"

Rubbing the back of his neck, Vince ducked his head and admitted, "I don't know. I think she could be if she'd let herself."

"Trust issues," Larry commented mildly, lifting his cup. "Not surprising."

"Big trust issues," Vince confirmed morosely, "and it's all centered on her family. I know in my gut that if she can't patch it up with them, we can't go forward."

"What are you going to do?"

Vince toyed with the spoon on his saucer. "What would you think about me arranging a surprise meeting with Jolie and her brother and sister?"

Larry kept his eyes averted while he considered, but then he shook his head. "An emotional ambush isn't the answer, even if your motives are good. That would just make her mad at you."

Vince scowled and shoved a hand through his hair. "I wouldn't mind her being mad at me for a while if it patched up her family."

"Except it might not work that way," Larry pointed out, "and forever afterward she'd know that she could count on you to try to handle *her* business *your* way."

Vince grimaced. "I see your point, Dad, but—"

Larry lifted a hand, palm out. "No buts, son. This is where you give your own faith a real workout. God's in charge here. Let's keep it that way. I have an inkling that she'll come around when it's the right time for her to do so. If your patience gets a little test in the meanwhile, well, you must need it."

Vince's mouth crooked into a lopsided smile at the twinkle in his father's eye. "You're right. You're absolutely right. It's just that I feel so strongly that if she can't open herself up to her family again, she'll never be able to open herself completely to me."

Larry nodded sagely, saying, "Then we'll pray that way and trust God to work it out."

"And until He does, I guess I'm cooling my jets," Vince muttered with a resigned sigh.

"I don't see that you have much choice in the matter, son. She's got to resolve these issues before she can be the wife you want and need. That is what we're talking about, isn't it?"

"Yes, and I know you're right, but I'll admit that I was hoping for something else."

"I'll make a covenant with you," Larry said, placing both of his gnarled hands flat on the tabletop. "I'll pray for both of you every day until God works this thing out. In fact, let's start right now. Okay?"

Vince copied his father's posture and bowed his head. While Larry softly prayed aloud, Vince thanked God for the man sitting across from him, for the life he had led, for the wisdom to which he was privy and for not having had the sense to forward his mail.

Chapter Thirteen

Christmas rushed toward them. It spilled out of the shops and onto the sidewalks in sometimes garish displays of tattered decorations and sometimes poignant and surprising beauty. Neither moved Jolie, who had never enjoyed Christmas.

The so-called joy of the season had always eluded her. Oh, once or twice her mother had found a way to provide a modest celebration for her three children, but even the best of those memories were pretty dismal.

Jolie recalled cupcakes with sprinkles, a bitter red punch and a doll with matted hair and gaps in her eyelashes.

Once Marcus had gotten roller skates so old that the leather had been cracked, but he'd skated around their barren little apartment, careening into walls and wobbly furniture, until he'd outgrown the things. He hadn't dared skate outside for fear of the junkies and thugs who would as soon have robbed a child of his battered old skates as shoplift a candy bar.

As for Connie, she had wagged around a huge plastic piggy bank for a couple of years, and for a time they'd all scavenged coins conscientiously. Unfortunately, their cache had been raided so often that they'd never been able to fill more than the piggy's plastic feet.

Usually, their holiday gifts had been nothing more than cardboard puzzles, cheap boxes of crayons, new socks or cans of soda, if that. Sometimes the holiday had passed without anything at all to mark it. Then at the end, their mother had not even bothered to be at home.

Christmas with the various foster families had been more rewarding gift-wise, but Jolie had always felt like an outsider and a fraud at those celebrations. The gifts had never felt personal or appropriate, and she had gone out of her way to destroy more than a few of them, which she now realized had only served to make her seem ungrateful and incorrigible, as she had, in fact, been.

Since she'd reached adulthood, Marcus had routinely invited her to spend the holiday with him and his foster family, with whom he maintained a close relationship. Jolie had tagged along with him the year that she was eighteen, but not since. It hurt too much to see the easy, affectionate manner with which he and his foster family dealt with each other.

Marcus had actually found himself in a family who had truly wanted him, but they obviously hadn't wanted two mulish little girls to go along with their five boys, natural, adopted and foster. As Marcus had explained many times, she and their sister wouldn't have "fit in." She understood *now* that the house had been small, and that the boys had slept dormitory-style in one large bedroom, but she still couldn't escape the idea that Marcus's foster parents hadn't wanted her. So far as she could tell, *no one* had wanted her or Connie.

Maybe that was why Connie had latched on to Russell's low-life father, and why she, Jolie, couldn't seem to latch on to anyone at all. Until now.

She still couldn't quite fathom how it had happened, but somehow Vincent Cutler had become such a large part of her life that when Marcus called on the Tuesday following the big game to say that he and Connie and Russell would be celebrating the coming holiday at home and would like her to join them, Jolie had used Vince as an excuse.

If she hadn't been expecting Vince to call and if she hadn't had her hands full of ironing, she wouldn't even have answered the phone without checking the caller ID first. As it was, she found herself actually talking to her brother for the first time in months.

"Um, Vince probably has other plans," she said into the phone in instant reply to Marcus's rushed invitation to join him and Connie for the holiday.

It wasn't a lie; she hadn't said that Vince had plans which included *her*, but she realized now that she was hoping he did.

"Vince?" Marcus echoed. "Is that your boyfriend?"

Boyfriend. The word had a dangerous, incredulous ring to it. She took a deep breath.

"Uh, more just friend, really, and sort of my boss. Sort of. Temporarily."

Marcus seemed to brush that off. Even more surprisingly, he seemed genuinely pleased that she might have someone in her life.

"That's great, Jo! Tell me about him."

For one long, troubling moment, Jolie fought the urge to do just that, but then she reminded herself that she and Marcus weren't really on speaking terms. He had no right to know about her life.

She said flatly, "I don't think so."

"He must be good to you," Marcus surmised correctly, gently probing. "Otherwise, you wouldn't put up with him." His voice softened, lowered, then. "I've always admired that about you, Jo. You know your own worth."

"And what am I worth, Marcus?" she retorted bitterly. "Whatever it is, it doesn't make me good enough to raise a child, does it?"

"Jo, you know that's not true," he said, sounding pained. "Neither Connie or I would ever have placed Russell with you if we weren't absolutely convinced that you would be a great parent."

"Then why take him away?" she wailed.

She could feel her brother's exasperation, but his voice was mild, gentle when he said simply, "She's his mother, Jo."

"I've been more his mother than she's been!"

His voice dropped a chord, as if he didn't want to be overhead on his end.

"He's her only chance, Jo. Can't you see that?"

"He was *my* only chance!" she cried just before she hung up, but even as she said it, some part of her knew that it wasn't necessarily so. At least she was starting to believe that it might not be.

You wouldn't be coping with it alone this time.

The implications of that were breathtaking. She wanted to believe that Vince had been talking about more than friendship, but he hadn't said that. Somehow she'd gotten the feeling that his reticence had to do with her situation with her family, and that felt patently unfair to her.

Couldn't he see how she had been treated? In a very

real sense, she had been used by her own brother and sister, used and then discarded.

Well, all right, not quite *discarded*, but the same as. Almost. Except she had been the one to turn her back on them, a little voice reminded her. And why shouldn't she? she countered angrily. After what they'd done, who could blame her? Why should she feel guilty about it?

She did, though. Worse, she couldn't quite deny the subtle yearning that had begun in her when she'd first heard Marcus's voice on the telephone. Yet how could she ever trust her brother and sister again? How could she bear seeing Russell and then letting him go home with them?

Suddenly she wanted two things very, very badly. She wanted to fold little Russ close, even knowing that they would take him away again afterward, and she wanted Vince to do the same with her.

When Vince showed up at the cleaners on Friday, Jolie abandoned the presser to greet him.

"Hey!" She couldn't help smiling because he was smiling, his mouth bracketed with the grooves cut by his dimples.

"Hey yourself." He leaned on the counter to talk to her. "You busy?"

She leaned backward to catch a glimpse of Mr. Geopp, who at the moment was pretending to be deaf, dumb and blind.

"I can take a minute. What's up?"

"Two things. Everybody's going bowling tonight. Want to come?"

She wondered just who "everybody" was, but the words that fell out of her mouth were, "Of course."

Dimples again.

"Excellent."

"But, um, I'm not very good," she put in quickly. "I've only tried a couple times."

"No problem."

"Oh, well, if you're sure."

He reached out and tapped the end of her nose, saying, "Absolutely positive. Now then, question number two." He briefly held up two fingers before tucking his hands into his coat pockets. "Mom wants to know if we can count on you for Christmas."

A tiny thrill mingled with relief shot through Jolie. To cover it, she glanced at the frosted window and the paper snowflakes that Mr. Geopp had taped to it.

She'd once expected to spend the holiday with Russell. Without him the whole Christmas season had seemed like a huge insult, something to be endured. She'd been dreading it more than she could even let herself admit, but since Thanksgiving she supposed that she'd been waiting for Vince to invite her to spend the holiday with him and his family.

He was like a glimmer of light at the end of what felt like a long, dark tunnel. She blinked and let her smile brighten.

"Thanks. I'm not big on Christmas really, but I'll try not to put a damper on the fun."

He chuckled. "Don't count on as much excitement as Thanksgiving. We're not expecting any new little bundles of joy. That I know of."

She laughed. "Just a humdrum Cutler holiday, hmm?"

He scratched an ear, admitting wryly, "I wouldn't count on humdrum, either."

She laughed again. "No? Really?"

He nodded in acknowledgment of the absurdity of a humdrum Cutler gathering of any type.

"The schedule usually goes something like this. Christmas eve supper around six at Mom and Dad's, followed by the reading and then the gift exchange and church at ten."

"The reading?"

"You know, the Christmas story."

"Oh, of course."

"We do it in parts so everyone gets at least one line."

"Ah."

"Anyway," he went on, "Christmas eve is the big do at our house. Mom puts on a lavish buffet for Christmas Day, and people pop in and out all day long, but Christmas eve is reserved for family. The sisters sometimes drop by on Christmas Day and sometimes don't, depending on the families of the son-in-laws. Or is it sons-in-law? I always forget."

"Sons-in-law," Jolie murmured automatically, still wondering about the reading, but it was the gift exchange thing that truly gave her pause. "Listen, Vince, I—I can't really afford…that is, there are so many of you to buy for."

He lifted a placating hand.

"Don't worry. You'd only have to buy one gift, and nobody goes overboard. We draw names because no one can buy for everybody. Mom and Dad always get together a little something for each of the grandkids, but no one else does. We do a little name-drawing ceremony that we jokingly call the family lotto. That'll be this Sunday after church. Or if you want, this year we could keep the gift thing just between the two of us."

This year. Jolie's heart kicked. This year. As if they'd

be doing this again next year. As if they might actually have some sort of future together.

"I—I don't mind drawing names," she replied a little breathlessly.

"Does that mean I can count on you for church Sunday?"

She felt an unexpected spurt of eagerness. "Sure. Why not?"

He grinned. "Better and better. I'll tell Mom to expect you for dinner. We'll draw names right after."

"If you're sure it's no trouble."

"You know better than that," he told her cheerfully.

The lovely part was that she really did believe she'd be welcome.

"But, ah, there's just one thing. I-if I get you or one of the other guy's names, you'll have to give me some idea what to buy. I've never…"

"Never bought a guy gift before?"

"Only for my b-brother."

She held her breath, wondering if Vince would bring up the situation with Marcus and Connie again, but he just smiled and rocked back on his heels.

"Good. That's good."

"Is it?"

"Oh, yeah."

She couldn't account for the shyness that slipped over her then. Suddenly she couldn't quite look him in the eye any longer—not with Mr. Geopp just there on the other side of the gliding rack hung with recently cleaned garments arranged in alphabetical order according to the last name of the customer.

"Tell you what," he said, "I'll give it some thought and

be prepared to dish out advice after the name-drawing. How's that?"

"That's fine." It came out almost as a croak. She cleared her throat before asking, "What time should I be ready for bowling tonight?"

"Six-thirty too early?"

She shook her head. "Gives me just enough time to get home and change."

"Then I'll pick you up at the apartment at half past six."

"Okay."

"See you then." He gave her a wave and turned to go. She wasn't really ready to let him.

"Vince?"

He swung around, as eager as a puppy.

"Yeah?"

Her heart beat so pronouncedly that it almost strangled her.

"Thank you. For Christmas, I mean."

"You bet."

"And thank your Mom for me, too."

He chuckled. "Okay. See you later."

She nodded, smiling, and he turned with a wink to pull open the door and move swiftly through it.

Jolie watched him stride down the sidewalk and out of sight, his image blurred by the frosting that had been sprayed on the window. Lifting a hand to her chest, she marveled at the way her heart had sped up at the first sight of him.

It was ridiculous, really. Just because he was handsome and kind and caring, that was no reason to overreact. Why, it was almost as if... Surely she wasn't... hadn't...

She sat down hard on the tall, three-legged stool that Mr. Geopp kept behind the counter for when his legs were aching. Her face felt flushed, and her pulse rapped a quick staccato as the truth hit her.

So this was what it felt like to fall in love.

Oh, no. This was awful!

Or so she told herself.

It didn't feel awful, actually.

It felt hopeful, so very hopeful that it was terrifying.

She closed her eyes and thought, *Dear God, oh, please don't let me be like my mother. Please don't let me be like that.*

She could almost understand now why Velma had chased after every man who had come along. She'd been chasing this feeling, this sense of hope in an otherwise hopeless life. But Vince was different from all those losers her mom had hooked up with.

Vince was good, genuinely good.

So what's he doing hanging around with you? asked that pesky little voice she'd been hearing so much from lately.

Panic swept through her. He wouldn't hang around for long. Of course he wouldn't. No one ever did, not her father, not her mother, not Russell, not one of the foster families with whom she'd lived. Why should Vince be any different? Unless…

"Oh, God," she whispered, without even knowing what she was pleading for, "Oh, God, please." And it came to her then that Vince was in her life because he wanted to be.

She hadn't pursued him, just the opposite. In fact, she'd been downright disagreeable in the beginning. Yet gradually, patiently, he'd made himself a place in her life and in so doing had worked his way into her heart.

Now she could only pray that he didn't break it.

Jolie released the ball and watched it fly down the very center of the lane, gradually straightening as it whirled nearer its target. She was a better bowler than she'd known. Then again, she hadn't had an expert like Vince to show her what she was doing wrong until now.

She backed up a step, afraid to breathe lest it affect the trajectory of the spinning ball. It plowed into the head pin, just slightly to the right of center, and sent every pin but two flying in different directions.

"You can do it," Vince called encouragingly. "It's the same spare as before. Half step to the right. You can do it."

Jolie lifted her ball from the return, scooted right and hefted the ball into place just below chest height. Taking a deep breath, she stepped off, swung her arm back, bent and released.

Once more the ball whirled straight down the alley, this time knocking out the remaining two pins. Jolie leapt straight up into the air, coming down again into Vince's arms as he had rushed forward to congratulate her. They almost toppled onto the floor, but he planted his feet and anchored them both, laughing, before releasing her.

"That's my girl!"

Jolie tried not to read too much into that while the others either applauded or groaned dramatically, depending upon which team they were on. The group consisted of Helen and John, Drew and Olivia, Donna and Martin and Vince's friend and employee Boyd and his wife, Sissy.

Neither Donna nor Helen were bowling, Donna because it was still too soon after the baby and Helen because she seemed to want to keep her sister company.

Sissy had immediately latched on to Jolie, and Jolie found that she quite liked the extremely tall, rather plain woman. Sissy was slender to the point of emaciation, though she ate like a stevedore, and had lank, dark-blond hair that hung to the bottoms of her ears on the sides and was spiked rather unflatteringly on top.

"Thyroid condition," she'd announced cheerfully as she'd consumed her second order of onion rings, having already downed a double-meat burger and a large soda.

Sissy sauntered up to bump hips and elbows with Jolie in a goofy kind of congratulatory dance, seeing as they were on the same team with Vince and Boyd. Her hip bones were like blades.

"Trust Vince to come up with the only true sportswoman in the bunch," Marty groused good-naturedly.

Sissy took issue, planting her bony hands on her bony hips. "Hey! I'll have you know that I played varsity volleyball all through high school and college."

"Now if only she could bowl," Boyd cracked with a straight-faced sigh.

"Her score's better than mine," Jolie pointed out as Sissy glowered.

Suddenly Boyd grinned and pulled his wife down onto his lap.

"I know. I just like to see her bristle."

Her long, skinny arm wound around his neck as she giggled and kicked her feet. The two were obviously mad about each other. It gave Jolie a warm, cozy feeling, especially when she felt Vince's hand slide possessively into the dip of her waist.

"Want a cola?" he asked softly.

She shook her head and leaned into him a little. Just having him close was reward enough for that spare or any other achievement she could dream up, for that matter.

He gave her a smile and asked loudly, "Whose turn is it?"

"Does it matter?" John replied drolly, getting to his feet.

"Only to the winners," Vince retorted goodnaturedly.

Actually they were behind by three pins, but nobody seemed to be paying much attention to the score. It wasn't about competition. It was about fun and fellowship.

The "midnight" leagues actually started at ten o'clock, so they were out of there by nine-forty-five. Their team had lost by six pins, but the others magnanimously refrained from rubbing it in.

Marty and Donna hurried away, saying that it was time to feed the baby. Donna gave Jolie an absent-minded peck on the cheek before making for the parking lot. Helen did the same, then hurried back to ask Jolie if she wanted to join the sisters for a Christmas shopping junket the next day.

"Oh, I have to work on Saturday."

"Rats," Helen said. "Well, maybe another day."

"Monday afternoons are about the only time I have," Jolie began.

"Excellent!" Helen said, "the stores won't be so crowded and we'll know whose names we've drawn by then."

"Oh, I didn't mean...that is, I'll be working at Vince's on Monday afternoon," Jolie went on apologetically. "We haven't quite finished the house."

Helen frowned. "Ah, that's okay. I just remembered

that Mom can't babysit on Monday, and Donna won't leave little Tony with just anyone."

"I'll keep the baby," Vince offered.

"Really?" Helen brightened.

"But what about the house?" Jolie asked uncertainly. "We still have the library and your room to do."

"We'll do them later."

"Are you sure?"

"Absolutely. I'll even go over to Donna's place to keep the little guy there."

"It pains me to say it," Helen told him, kissing his cheek, "but you are the best big brother."

"You used to say that when I'd loan you my sweaters to wear, too," he reminded her, "then you'd return them with stains and smelling like cheap perfume."

Helen ignored that, saying to Jolie as she hurried away, "I'll talk to the others and call you."

"Does she even have my number?" Jolie wondered, waving.

"I'll give it to her," Vince said as they walked toward his truck. Obviously, he approved of her spending time with his sisters. Jolie tried not to think what that might mean. Given the gregariousness and generosity of the Cutlers, probably nothing out of the ordinary.

Olivia and Drew were the last to exit the building. They called and waved. Jolie and Vince waved back. A sleek, black, two-door coupe rumbled up beside them with Boyd hanging out the passenger-side window.

"Hey, you guys want to come over for a while? It's early still."

"Naw, us guys have to work tomorrow," Vince reminded him, "and that includes you."

"Oh, yeah, so it does," Boyd mused, playing dumb.

"Oh, well, my boss is a sweetheart. He won't mind if I'm a little late."

"You just try it, mister, and I'll forget to sign your paycheck."

"In that case, I'll be there bright and early."

"Never doubted it."

Laughing, Boyd rolled up the window, his wife calling out, "See you soon, Jolie!"

"I look forward to it," she shouted at the heavily tinted window.

She and Vince stood where they were until the car pulled away.

"You wouldn't believe it to look at her, but that Sissy's an excellent cook," Vince said conversationally. "On the other hand, you might believe it looking at Boyd."

Jolie chuckled. "They're great."

"Yeah, they are. Did you know that they were high-school sweethearts?"

"So they've been together a long time then."

"Married the day after we graduated."

"But they still don't have kids?"

Vince grimaced. "It's that thyroid thing. They've always said that they would adopt when the time was right. They're looking into it now."

"I see."

"I think they'll take an older child because Boyd remembers too well what it was like to want and need a family and be passed over time and again by couples desperate for babies."

"I understand that," Jolie stated matter-of factly, remembering all too well herself. "Marcus could have been adopted," she went on. "At least he said he could have, but it never happened."

"Wonder why?" Vince mused.

"I always figured that there was something wrong with the family he was with. They'd already adopted two other boys and had two of their own. Marcus never wanted to talk about it."

"Hmm."

They'd reached the truck, and he handed her up into it, then walked around to slide behind the wheel.

"So what are you going to shop for on Monday?" he asked, fitting the key into the ignition.

"That depends on whose name I draw and what that person wants."

He let his hand fall away from the ignition switch and half-turned to face her, one forearm draped across the top of the steering wheel. "I could tell you what I want if you're interested, but you aren't going to find it in a store."

Whatever that meant, she couldn't believe that Vincent Cutler would make an unsuitable suggestion, and she liked the idea that they might trade gifts apart from the family.

"I don't see why we couldn't exchange gifts privately," she said.

For a moment he simply stared through the windshield into the distance. Then he faced her once more.

"Jolie, I've thought about this for a long time. I've prayed about it endlessly."

"That sounds so serious," she said, trying for a light tone even though her heart had begun beating like a jackhammer.

"There's just one thing I want for Christmas," he was saying.

Could he possibly be asking for a serious relationship? she wondered wildly. Were they about to become a formal couple? Surely they were too old to go steady! But not to get engaged. The very thought left her breathless. She was ready for anything—except what he actually said.

"I want you to try to work things out with your brother and sister."

Chapter Fourteen

Jolie rocked back in her seat, feeling as if he'd sucker-punched her. *"What?"*

He repeated himself, word for word, slowly, in case she hadn't heard him the first time. "I want you to try to work things out with your brother and sister."

Anger and disappointment roared through her. How dare he? Who did he think he was to ask such a thing of her? She'd thought he cared about her!

"You don't know what you're asking!" she exclaimed.

"I know it's difficult," he said. "It may be the most difficult thing you ever do, but I believe it's so important for you that I'm willing to take this risk."

"What risk?" she snapped. "It's no risk for *you*."

"Isn't it?" he asked softly, his smoky-blue eyes plumbing hers. Then he sighed and seemed to mentally shake himself. "You can do this, Jolie. I know you can. You're a strong, loving, intelligent woman."

She stared at him with incredulous eyes. "Why are you doing this?"

"Because I truly believe that if you don't make peace with your family, it will color the rest of your life, and I just care too much, Jolie, to let you do that to yourself. Don't you see that you have to at least try to put this pain behind you?"

She pressed her fingertips to her temples. "It seems to me that it's just adding another level of anguish to what I live with every day."

"I don't want you to live this way," he said urgently, "tied up in angry knots for the rest of your life. I certainly can't live like that."

"No one's asking you to!"

"Maybe not, but would you want it for me if it was the other way around?" he asked softly.

He knew. He knew how she felt about him! He wasn't saying it outright—obviously he didn't want to embarrass her—but he knew, And he was trying to show her that he cared for her in his own way, too, in a deeply spiritual way that he had already demonstrated over and over again. Maybe he didn't care for her the way that she wished he did, but the big, sweet lunk really did think that it would be best for her to make peace with her brother and sister.

Maybe it would. She just didn't know anymore. She closed her eyes and such a longing came over her that it was literally physical. It was a longing for the family she had lost, for the nice, normal family that she'd never quite had, and also for the family and life that only Vince himself could offer her.

"Just think about it," he urged softly. "Please, Jolie."

She *was* thinking about it; she couldn't stop thinking about it now. It was as if a hungry little something had lodged itself in the center of her chest, begging and pleading. She put a hand over her mouth. How had she gotten so needy, so weak? This was what wanting Vince in her life had done to her.

She'd been so careful not to want anyone or anything. Her whole life she'd known that to want too much was to face the bitterness of disappointment again and again, and losing Russell had just proven that. Then how could she now want Vincent Cutler? How could she not?

More importantly, what if he was right and by not doing this she would forever curtail her life in some way?

Yet, how could she work out an acceptable understanding with Marcus and Connie? There was Russell, after all. She just didn't know if she could bear to see him with anything approaching regularity and live with the knowledge that he wasn't hers, would never be hers.

Still, if trying was all that Vince asked of her, if he really thought it was best...

Doesn't it make a difference that you wouldn't be coping with it alone this time?

What if this really is best for your nephew? What if knowing his mother loves him is more important than knowing that you love him? And why shouldn't he have both?

"I'll think about it," she finally said, brushing away the tears that she only just realized were on her cheeks. "I can't promise more than that."

"I can't ask more than that," he answered, his voice thick and quivery.

She turned her face away, one hand lifting automatically to ruffle her bangs and smooth them again.

"Let's get you home," he said briskly, starting the engine. "Tomorrow's a work day."

She nodded dumbly, wondering if she was going to get much, if any, sleep that night. Dark fear and bright hope blended together within her, swirling into an ever-changing mosaic of emotions sharp enough to cut her heart to ribbons.

How ironic that in this season of peace she should feel such overwhelming inner turmoil.

Those next days were the longest of Vince's life. He couldn't sleep, couldn't concentrate.

What if he was wrong?

He didn't know Marcus or Connie Wheeler from Adam. They could be the worst sort of hateful, manipulative people. Just because Marcus was a minister didn't mean that he was trustworthy. They could break Jolie's heart all over again, just as she feared they would.

But at least she would have tried, he argued with himself. She would have done all in her power to mend the rift.

Would she, though, come out of it trusting him?

If she allowed him to push her into reconnecting with her brother and sister and then it went badly, she'd have every right to question his judgment. Worse, she might never feel for him what he felt for her.

Pushing her to make peace with her family suddenly seemed a terribly presumptuous, meddlesome, even arrogant, thing to do. He'd told himself that he was acting in her best interest, but had he acted out of selfishness instead? Oh, why hadn't he kept still and bided his time as his father had counseled him?

No longer sure of his own position, all he could do now was pray that God would guide her, give her wisdom and strength in this situation—and the ability to forgive if he was wrong about everything.

She attended church with him and his family on Sunday as planned. Afterward she joined the family for dinner. She smiled and teased and pitched in to help just like everyone else, but it all felt a little forced. She seemed brittle, shadowed, her smile honed to a fine edge. Her gaze felt guarded and diffident, as if she couldn't bear to look at anyone or anything too long, especially him.

When it came time for the family lotto, as it was jokingly called, they all gathered around the table in the kitchen.

Every year his mother baked an elaborate gingerbread display just after Thanksgiving to kick off the season, and the family had long ago incorporated the name-drawing with the gingerbread. This year as a centerpiece for the dining table, Ovida had fashioned a country church, complete with bell tower, steeple and stained-glass windows made of crushed hard candies melted into shapes and designs. For the name-drawing she had made twelve large gingerbread men and seven smaller ones, each with a name written on the back in icing that had hardened before the cookie was turned over to hide them. The children would draw for children's names from the smaller cookies, and the adults from the larger ones.

Before the actual choosing of cookies—and names—began, they all drew slips of paper with numbers printed on them to establish order. Ovida drew the number one, Vince a six, and Jolie a nine. Ovida began the game by choosing the cookie with her son-in-law John's name on it.

"Whoo-hoo! Just pack me a big box of that homemade Christmas fudge of yours," he crowed, patting his middle.

Helen goosed him playfully in the ribs. "And you told me you wanted a new nine iron."

"New iron," Ovida muttered, pretending to write that on an imaginary list. "I didn't even know you were concerned about pressing your clothes, John," she remarked innocently, knowing perfectly well that Helen had referred to a golf club and not a steam iron.

When the laughter died down, the drawing continued. Vince's turn eventually came, and he drew Sharon.

"Okay, I know just what I want," Sharon announced gleefully. She held up one hand as if admiring a ring or bracelet. "I'm thinking three karats at least."

"Three carrots," Vince drawled, borrowing his mother's joke and pretending to take notes in the air. "Would you like peas with that? Green beans maybe? A side of ham?"

"You are the ham," Sharon shot back.

More laughter followed, then Donna drew her own husband's name.

"Rats," he said good-naturedly, "and no, that's not a request, but it might as well be because I'm losing a gift in this deal."

"I'll still get you a sweetheart gift," Donna assured him, leaning into his side as she gently burped the baby on her shoulder.

Marty smiled at their child. "You already have."

"And an expensive gift it is, too," Drew quipped. "You'll be paying on it for a lifetime."

Olivia elbowed him in the ribs.

The laughter and the drawing continued.

When Jolie's turn came, she turned over a cookie bearing Vince's name.

He caught her sudden intake of breath, dimly heard the hum of speculation around them, and wondered again if he had ruined everything for them by urging her so strongly to make peace with her family. He felt the sudden need to blurt that he wanted…something, anything, a new shirt, a garden hose, a picture frame, anything at all except what he'd already said. A glance at his father had him biting back the words, but he made up his mind to take Jolie aside and tell her privately that he was wrong to stick his nose into a situation that clearly was none of his business and that she should follow her own instincts and wishes in the matter.

He never got the chance.

The right moment just never came. They were not even to have a private moment as he drove her home because as they were walking out the door, his mother asked him to drop off a casserole for an elderly friend who had difficulty cooking for herself and Olivia abruptly decided to ride along and say hello.

"You don't mind dropping me at my house after you drop off Jolie, do you, sweetie?" Olivia said, throwing on her coat.

What could he do but smile, shake his head, and tell himself that he would call Jolie later?

Later, however, she seemed to have taken the phone off the hook, because the number rang busy for over an hour before he gave up. It was getting too late to call anyway, and besides, what was the rush?

She'd be over in the morning as usual to do the laundry and work on the house before her shopping trip with his sisters. They would sit down and talk then. He would apologize for butting in, affirm her concerns and they'd be right back where they'd started.

"Oh, Father," he prayed aloud, dropping his head into his hands, "what have I done? What should I do?"

He prayed late into the night, and woke heart-heavy, no closer to certainty than before. Dragging himself out of bed and into his clothes, he went about his morning routine, making coffee and breakfast. He carried a second cup of coffee with him, sipping from it while scraping off his morning beard and combing his hair. He drained the cup before brushing his teeth, and was standing with the brush protruding from a mouth full of foam when the telephone rang.

Quickly, he rinsed and moved into the bedroom to pick up the receiver of the cordless phone beside the bed.

"Hello."

"Vince?"

He knew the instant he heard the quaver in her voice that something had happened.

"Jolie, what's wrong? You okay?"

"I—I'm not sure frankly. Can you come over?"

"Now?"

"Half an hour or so. I-it should be about that."

That didn't make a lot of sense, and when she gulped audibly, it scared the daylights out of him. He started yanking on his boots, the telephone receiver cradled between his head and shoulder.

Everything else was forgotten, especially when she added softly, "Just come over."

"I'm on my way."

He broke the connection and tossed the cordless phone onto the bed, reaching for his jacket.

All the way on the drive over, he prayed that she was all right, that he would have the wisdom and intelligence to deal with whatever had happened. He felt in his bones that it had to do with her brother and sister, and he knew that if he had caused new heartache for her they could both carry the scars of it for the rest of their lives.

Jolie opened the door and almost wilted with relief. "Thank heaven it's you."

Vince strode inside, sweeping the door closed behind

him, and pulled her into his arms, holding her against his chest, her head tucked beneath his chin.

"Are you all right?"

She sighed, relishing the comfort and closeness for several seconds before gulping down the lump in her throat.

"So far. I didn't sleep much, though."

"Me, either," he rumbled. "But tell me what's happened? Why am I here?"

She took a deep breath and looked up at him.

"I spoke to my brother last night."

His reaction was not what she'd expected. Instead of breaking into a smile, Vince stepped back, his hands going to her shoulders, concern clouding his face.

"Jolie, honey, listen. I didn't mean to pressure you. It was wrong of me to meddle in something that clearly wasn't my business."

"You were just concerned for me."

"I know, but—"

Another knock at her door interrupted whatever he'd been about to say. Jolie stiffened, her heart leaping into her throat once more.

This was it then, the moment of truth. They were all about to find out just how strong and daring she was.

For Vince, she told herself, *and for Russell,* but then she was honest enough to add, *and for me.*

Drawing Vince's name had been like a message straight from heaven for her. Once she'd gotten home afterward, she'd plucked up her courage and called her brother. They'd talked for a long while, and she'd come to understand that he'd felt he'd had no choice except to do what he had—and very likely he'd been right. She couldn't blame Connie for wanting her son, and she couldn't blame Marcus for helping her gain custody of him.

In some part of her heart and mind, she'd always known that, but old emotions from the past had been reactivated by the prospect of losing physical custody of the child whom she'd come to love so much, and she'd allowed herself to lash out in pain and anger. Now with Vince on her side, she was ready to put it behind her. The only concern was Russell. She just didn't know how she would react when she saw him again.

Would the past rear its ugly head again? Or was she really ready to go forward? There was only one way to find out.

Squaring her shoulders, she put on a tremulous smile for Vince and whispered, "Merry Christmas," just before she reached for the doorknob.

He gasped and settled his hands upon her shoulders as she opened the door. The weight of them soothed and steeled her, so that she was able to greet her brother and sister with a semblance of control.

"Hello."

"Hello, Jo."

Of average height, Marcus stood just a little over three inches taller than her. He had a lean but solid look about him, and his light golden-brown hair was still damp from its morning combing. In a short while, she knew, it would begin to fall over his forehead from its straight side part as it dried. The poignant smile upon his handsome, beloved face nearly smashed her control, so she quickly glanced away.

Beside him, Connie looked pretty and petite, her golden-blond hair, now cut to chin-length, feathering softly about her face and playing up her big, muted-jade eyes. She wore a vulnerable, uncertain air, as if questioning her welcome, but it was the child in her arms who wrenched the sob up from deep inside Jolie's chest.

She clapped both hands over her mouth in an effort to prevent its escape and felt Vince squeeze her shoulders as she failed. Then Connie abruptly stepped forward and literally shoved her son into Jolie's arms.

"There's your aunt JoJo," Connie said, her voice thick with emotion. "We're so happy to see her!"

Marcus laid one hand on Connie's shoulder and reached for Jolie with the other, clasping her forearm and biting his lips as tears filled his eyes. Russell, God love him, dropped his bright red head onto Jolie's shoulder and wrapped his little arms around her. She sobbed. She couldn't help it. She was so happy to see him, to hold him!

He had grown! He felt heavier, stronger and not at all troubled by the momentous event taking place around him. Aware, yes: troubled, no.

Jolie felt an immense sense of relief. He was well, happy. Whatever they had done to one another, Russell was going to be okay because, she realized suddenly, Russell was loved by those who should love him. What could be better for a little boy than that?

Somehow she felt...*freed* by the realization that she could truly trust this child's welfare to his mother. She hadn't expected that.

Vince lifted a hand to ruffle Russ's short, glowing, coppery locks, and Russell looked up, grinning at this friendly stranger. A watery laugh erupted from Jolie.

"Let's sit down," Vince suggested.

"Yes, let's," Connie replied brightly, blinking back tears.

Nodding, Jolie turned and led them toward the sofa with Russell in her arms.

"What a big boy you're getting to be," she murmured, surprised and delighted when he nodded his agreement. "I'm so happy to see you," she whispered.

He opened his arms wide and hugged her again.

She dropped down into one corner of the couch, Russell in her lap, as Vince introduced himself. She hadn't thought to do it herself.

"Vincent Cutler," he said simply, offering his hand to Marcus, who gave it a hearty shake.

"Jolie's mentioned you," Marcus replied. "And I'm Marcus, of course, and this is our sister Connie."

"Good to meet you," Vince said, nodding at Connie, who folded herself down onto the edge of the chair opposite the sofa.

Jolie was rubbing foreheads with Russell when Vince dropped down onto the arm of the sofa next to her.

"He looks wonderful!" she gushed to no one and everyone.

"He is wonderful," Connie said softly, "thanks to you."

Jolie swiped at her eyes, which kept leaking tears. Words just seemed to be falling out of her mouth. "I've missed him so much!"

"Oh, Jo!" Connie gasped, suddenly launching from her chair to a spot right next to Jolie. "He's missed you, too. We've all missed you. Please come back to us!"

Before Jolie could say anything to that, Connie threw her arms around her, sobbing brokenly, and then Marcus was crouching in front of them, one arm reaching out to each.

"None of us will ever be able to thank you enough for

all you've done, Jo," he began, then he paused to stretch his lips tight over his teeth to control their trembling. "We never wanted to lose you, though. We just want the family back together finally. We've waited so long for that. Decades, Jo. We've waited decades to be together again. Please—" He bowed his head.

"I'm so sorry," Connie wept. "It's all my fault! If I'd been as good as you, as strong as you, none of this would have happened."

Good? Jolie thought. Strong? After wallowing in self-pity and anger all these weeks? Surely if they could over-look and forgive that, she could manage the rest. It might not be easy, but it didn't have to be as difficult as she'd been making it, either. With Russell in her lap, she gathered her brother and sister into her arms as best she could, too overcome at the moment to speak.

"JoJo," she heard Russell say, and then she felt Vince's strong, comforting hand on the crown of her head.

"Yeah, that's our JoJo," he told the boy softly, "and how blessed we all are to have her."

Jolie laughed even as she cried.

"Oh, no you don't!" Marcus exclaimed, launching off the couch to run down Russell, who'd decided that it might be fun to try to climb the curtains.

He brought the boy back dangling between his hands, which were clamped around Russell's little torso beneath his chubby arms. He plopped down on the sofa again, Russell in his lap.

"You are a little chunk."

"I can't believe how much he's grown," Jolie mused wistfully. "He was just an infant last Christmas."

"You don't even have a Christmas tree this year, Jo,"

Connie noted gently, folding the tissue with which she'd been dabbing her eyes.

They all seemed inclined to alternate between bouts of tears and laughter, but in Vince's estimation even the tears were happy now. *Thank You, God,* he said silently, a refrain that he had repeated over and over again as the morning had progressed.

Jolie shrugged and admitted, "I didn't see the point."

"Without Russell here," Connie surmised. "I understand."

"We had a tree last year," Jolie said quickly, and Vince realized that Connie had missed that first Christmas with her son, "but he was too little even to notice."

"He's certainly intrigued this year," Marcus said, doing his best to contain the writhing bundle of toddler energy in his lap. "We bought a four-and-a-half-footer."

"Marcus even built a nice platform for it," Connie added.

Marcus grinned wryly. "Yeah, I had this bright idea that if I made it tall enough and wide enough, he wouldn't be able to reach the tree."

"Which is true," Connie pointed out with a chuckle, "so he just climbs up onto the platform instead."

"And helps himself to the ornaments," Marcus continued.

"The whole bottom half of the tree is bare now," Connie chortled.

"And only God knows how many pine needles he's managed to swallow," Marcus confessed with a wry twist of his mouth.

"Of course, he doesn't have any understanding of Christmas yet," Connie said, mirroring Jolie's smile, "but he loves that tree."

"Tee," Russell echoed happily, kicking out with both legs in an attempt to get to the floor.

Suddenly he stopped and yawned so widely that they all laughed. With a sigh he rolled onto his side and stuck two fingers into his mouth. Connie checked her watch.

"My goodness, it's past his nap time."

Taking him from Marcus, she gathered him against her chest, rocking gently back and forth. He bucked for a few seconds, then dropped his head onto her shoulder, his sleepy eyes smiling at Jolie. Vince curled his hand around hers. It was going to be all right. Everything was going to be all right. *Thank You, God.*

"Speaking of Christmas," Marcus said, leaning forward to capture Jolie's attention. "We were hoping that this year we could all be together."

Jolie sat up a little straighter, flicking a glance sideways at Vince. "Well, I… I've already made plans."

Marcus clamped his jaw and nodded, clearly disappointed.

"That's no problem," Vince piped up, sitting forward slightly. "The three of you will just join us at my parents' house."

Marcus and Connie traded a look. "We couldn't impose," Connie said gently.

"But you wouldn't be imposing," Vince assured her.

"That's kind of you to say," Connie told him, "but your family doesn't even know us."

"That doesn't matter," Vince said. "They'd be delighted to get to know Jolie's brother and sister."

Connie smiled, but she shook her head in refusal. Vince saw Jolie's disappointment; it was mirrored clearly in her brother's eyes.

"Marcus, won't you be spending at least part of the holiday with your foster family?" Jolie asked.

He shook his head, explaining, "Dennis has moved to Colorado with his wife and kids, and Maggie and Dad are going there this year."

"I—I thought Dennis was divorced. He's the oldest one, isn't he?"

Marcus nodded. "Yeah, they got back together. Trying to make a new start in Denver. The folks feel they really have to get behind it."

"Marcus and the other guys insisted," Connie put in.

"Well, that settles it then," Vince declared heartily, "and I won't take no for an answer. I've got to warn you, though. The place is a zoo at holiday time. You've got these two," he said to Marcus, wagging a finger between Jolie and Connie, "but I've got *four*." He held up the appropriate number of fingers in emphasis.

"*Four* sisters!" Marcus yelped.

"Hey." Connie folded her arms in mock outrage. Both men grinned.

"Two older and two younger," Vince confirmed, "which means I get it from both directions."

"Oh, they're wonderful, and you know it," Jolie scolded, slinging an elbow, which Vince easily caught. He grinned at Marcus. The two had just come to a new understanding of one another.

"Did I mention that they're all married?" Vince asked. "That's the good thing about sisters. They give you brother-in-laws."

"Brothers-in-law," Jolie and Connie both corrected.

Marcus and Vince looked at each other and burst out laughing.

"What?" Jolie asked. Connie shook her head, seeming just as mystified as Jolie. Marcus and Vince only laughed harder. "What?" Jolie demanded, finding a soft spot with her elbow this time.

Vince covered his midsection with a forearm, gasping, "It's a brother thing."

"Or rather, a sister thing," Marcus said, still grinning.

"I don't think I like that," Connie muttered, but she was grinning, too.

Marcus lifted a hand placatingly. "Now, now. What would I do without the two of you to correct my grammar?"

"And organize your life," Vince added.

"And redecorate my house," Marcus said.

"Tell me about it!" Vince hooted. "At least your sisters have good taste. Well, Jo does. I assume Connie's is similar."

"Not bad actually."

"Count yourself doubly blessed," Vince told him heartily. "My whole clan is hung up on chintz, which Jolie saved me from, by the way."

"It's not as bad as he's making it out to be," Jolie argued, seeing her brother's raised eyebrows.

"You'll see at Christmas," Vince countered, giving them a little verbal nudge. "Come on. Say you'll be there."

Marcus and Connie consulted each other with another look.

"You're sure your family won't mind?" Connie asked.

"I guarantee it," Vince stated firmly, "and if you refuse, I'll just have to have Mom and the girls badger you into it."

Marcus lifted both hands in a gesture of surrender. Jolie looked at Russell now sleeping heavily on his mother's shoulder.

"Vince has seven nieces and nephews, the youngest born on Thanksgiving Day," she told Connie. "You know Russell would love playing with all those kids."

Connie rubbed his little back. He sighed contentedly, and Connie nodded in acceptance. Vince launched into an explanation of the Cutler family's holiday schedule, and when he got to the Christmas eve church service, Marcus interrupted.

"I conduct a true midnight service, starting around eleven-thirty. Our congregation is small, but nearly everyone attends."

"Where is your church again?" Vince asked.

"Pantego."

"I don't see why we can't make both services. Ours is short. We'll go there first and join you at your church by eleven-fifteen or so."

"You could spend the night with us," Connie said eagerly to Jolie, "and be there for Russ to get his Santa gifts on Christmas morning."

"You can have my room," Marcus added encouragingly. "I'll sleep on the couch."

"Oh, no, I want her to share with me," Connie objected. She looked at Jolie again. "Remember, we always shared when we were little. I had the hardest time learning to sleep without you. It'll be like old times."

"Better," Jolie said, gripping her sister's hand. "Much better."

Vince put his head back, sighing inwardly. It wasn't the first time he'd caught himself teetering on the edge of tears that morning. Sometimes joy came with its own strings attached.

Thank You, God, he prayed again. *Thank You. Thank You.*

If he said it all day, it still wouldn't be enough.

* * *

They stood at the railing on the landing and waved one more time at Marcus, who dropped his own hand and slid behind the wheel of his small sedan, his smile still gleaming white. Jolie felt as if her heart had grown too large for her chest. If she wasn't careful she might float right up into the sky.

Pulling her cardigan tighter against the cold, Jolie turned and ambled back into the apartment. Vince followed, closing the door and propping a shoulder against it, arms loosely folded. He looked very pleased with himself. She'd allow him that.

"Thank you for inviting my family to have Christmas with yours."

"I'm looking forward to it," he said heartily.

"You're sure it'll be all right with your mom?"

"What do you think?"

She thought the Cutlers were just about the warmest, most wonderful people in the world, one in particular.

"And thank you for everything else," she said simply.

Pushing away from the wall, he walked forward and wrapped his arms around her. She laid her cheek against his chest, sighing. She'd never dreamed how lovely just being held could be.

"I am so proud of you," he said. "And you don't know how frightened I was."

"You?" She lifted her head. "Why?"

"If it hadn't worked out…" He licked his lips. "I wouldn't have blamed you for hating me."

Her jaw dropped. "Don't be silly! I could never hate you, not after everything you've done, fixing my car, working out a deal to pay for it, the maintenance agreement—"

"Which you have also paid for," he reminded her, "big-time."

She went on as if he hadn't spoken. "Thanksgiving, the game. And now this." She shook her head. "I wasn't big enough to do this without you. I'd have gone right on being mad at the world and—"

"Hush," he said. Bending his head, he gently pressed his lips to hers as if to stop the flow of her words that way.

Jolie felt her heart take flight. After a moment she drew back, studying his gaze hopefully. Dare she believe that this was more than a friendly gesture?

"Jo," he said. Cupping her face in his hands, he pressed his thumbs beneath her chin and tilted her head back. "No one's ever given me a finer Christmas present." He grinned and added, "I wonder how you'll top it next year?"

Jolie caught her breath. There it was again. *Next year.* He really must mean that they had some sort of a future together. The look in his eyes certainly seemed to say so, but how could she be sure?

"Is that a hint that I should put my thinking cap on?" she asked lightly. "Am I setting a pattern for Christmases to come here?"

He answered her with another question, his voice a deep rumble. "Is that what you want, Jolie, more Christmases to come?"

She didn't know how to answer that, wasn't even quite sure what he was asking, so she backed up a step, flapped a hand through her bangs, chuckled awkwardly.

"Isn't that what everyone wants?"

"I thought you didn't particularly like Christmas."

She shrugged. "Maybe I'm learning to like it."

He laughed. "That's good to know."

She looked down. "That's not all I've learned."

"A wise person never stops learning," he told her. "Life has made you very wise, Jolie."

"I doubt it." She rolled her eyes and caught sight of the clock on the wall beside the door. "Oh, my! Your sisters are expecting to meet me at your house! We're supposed to do lunch before we hit the stores."

"Well, what are you waiting for?" he teased. "Get your coat."

She hurried to do that, thinking that the warmth she felt inside just might be all she'd ever need against a Texas December.

Chapter Fifteen

Dressed in a bright holiday sweater and a long green skirt, Ovida sported a wreath of holly in her fading red hair. She seemed as gay and giddy as the children, who were obviously on a pure sugar high, sweets grasped in their hands. Jolie felt a bit underdressed in her simple brown knit slacks, matching turtleneck and off-white cardigan, but as always Ovida immediately put her at ease, greeting her with a hug. Certainly, she welcomed Jolie and her family with all the warmth that the holiday engendered.

"Thank you so much for coming! What a pleasure to meet you. Good grief, that one could be a Cutler!" she exclaimed, rubbing a hand over Russell's bright hair. "Girls, look at this doll."

Her daughters moved forward, and Connie and Russell quickly disappeared into a gushing gaggle of Cutler sisters. Olivia broke away briefly to look over Marcus and declare him entirely too handsome for a minister.

"And single, too!" she exclaimed after a word from Connie.

That elicited a blush from Marcus and speculative

remarks from the sisters. "Carolina Fowler," someone suggested suddenly.

"Or Audrey Hart."

"Wynona Phillips."

This last suggestion met a chorus of agreement.

Horrified at the obvious matchmaking, Marcus glared at Vince, who covered his laughter with a hand. Jolie shot a conspiratorial glance at Connie and found her fighting her own amusement, a rapt Russell perched upon her hip. Ovida abruptly thrust cups of hot, buttered apple cider into their hands and sent Larry after a plate of elaborately decorated sugar cookies.

This was going to be a Christmas to remember. Tomorrow would bring the delight of watching Russell's face light up when he spied his Santa toys beneath the tree in Marcus's living room, but tonight belonged to the Cutlers.

As usual, it was chaos, exuberant, delightful chaos, and Jolie loved it. She loved everything at the moment. In fact, she'd never been happier.

The last eleven days had been among the brightest and busiest of her life. Between work, finishing Vince's house—she'd wanted it done in time to decorate for the holiday since it was his first in his new home—and getting reacquainted with her family, the days had flown by in a happy blur, much like the children who ran through the room to the flash of John's camera as he wandered around, capturing the celebration on film.

He snapped Larry shaking hands with Marcus, then paused long enough to copy the greeting, while the other brothers-in-law lined up to follow suite.

Smiling, Jolie looked around her.

The Christmas tree, which had gone up in the living

room on the day after Thanksgiving, was surrounded by a miniature mountain range of colorfully wrapped gifts. A cheery blaze flickered in the brick fireplace, and carols wafted softly from speakers placed around the lavishly decorated house. Stuffed angels, handsewn of patterned chintz (of course) and decorated with wisps of organza, velvet, lace and sequins, with yarn for hair, were tucked into every available corner and niche. Vince and Marcus had traded rueful glances over that small fact.

Within minutes of their arrival, the newcomers were all laughing and talking with clusters of the Cutler family as if they'd known one another for ages. Eventually, Bets took center stage, clapping her hands and stomping her feet until she got everyone's attention.

"It's time. It's time," she announced, sounding very adult. "And I want to be Mary!"

"I get to be Elizabeth!" her cousin Brenda announced.

"Tony's Baby Jesus!" one of the boys shouted.

"An honorary role only," his father admonished the infant teasingly.

"Time to read the Christmas story," Vince explained as he escorted Jolie to the hearth, where they perched side by side on plump chintz (what else?) pillows.

The other adults began sorting themselves into seats, couple by couple, more than half on the floor, as Ovida passed out folios bound in red and green construction paper and decorated with bits of rick rack and ribbon. She handed one to Marcus, who took up a spot on the floor next to Jolie, his back to the long, brick hearth.

"You'll read Zacharias for us, won't you, Pastor Wheeler?"

"My pleasure," Marcus said, "but please use my given name."

"Marcus, then." She smiled before turning to her husband. "Daddy, you'll be the narrator. Mark, you're Herod. Matthew, Michael, shepherds."

Connie wound up on a chair next to Donna and Marty, who held baby Tony against his shoulder. Ovida must have handed out a dozen of the bound scripts before passing around simple stapled copies to the others. Jolie and Vince got one to share. Jolie saw immediately that the story was taken from several books of the Bible since the passages were denoted in the margins.

When everyone had settled down, Larry cleared his throat, opened his copy and began to read what was obviously a familiar and beloved story. It began with an encounter between Zacharias and an angel who announced the coming birth of a son for the elderly priest and his previously barren wife, Elizabeth. That child would turn out to be John the Baptist, cousin and forerunner of Christ. Jolie listened and followed along, fascinated. Everyone, she mused, knew the story of the Baby Jesus, but she'd never before heard this part.

The reading, some of which was very dramatic and moving, took all of forty minutes, and when it was done, Jolie marveled at the extent of what she had not known, the fulfillment of prophecy, including the flight into Egypt and Herod's murder of the male children in an attempt to remove any king of the Jews who might one day challenge him for power. No one had ever mentioned to her, for instance, the encounters of Simon and the prophetess Anna with the Holy Infant in the temple.

There was so much more to the story than she had realized! She determined to give the Biblical accounts a careful reading at the first opportunity, including the Old Testament prophecies. It was one of these with which the reading ended, a quotation from the ninth chapter of Isaiah, verse six.

"And His name will be called Wonderful Counselor, Mighty God, Eternal Father, Prince of Peace."

With those final words, a moment of reflective silence descended. Marcus closed his script reverently.

"This is really marvelous," he said. "It's straight from Scripture, but I don't think I've ever seen it arranged so clearly. Could I possibly have a copy to share with my congregation?"

"Take mine," Vince said, handing over his white paper copy.

Bets leaned forward with a mischievous gleam in her eye. "Since we're giving away stuff, can *I* have my presents now?" she asked witheringly.

Laughter and a mild scolding followed, but Larry ultimately made the decision. "Everyone can have their gifts *after* we pray." The whole group quieted, and Larry looked to Marcus. "Would you like to lead us?"

"Oh, no," Marcus answered immediately. "Surely that honor must fall to you."

Larry didn't protest, merely bowed his head and began to speak. He finished by saying, "Most of all, I thank You, Father, for the special ways You've moved in the lives of our family this holiday season. You've always blessed us with amazing and undeserved generosity. You cleanse our souls and mend our hearts, and for that most of all we praise You. Now make us agents of Your love in this season of love and always. These things we pray in the holy name of Your Son. Amen."

"Amen," Jolie whispered, turning her gaze on Vince. He smiled benignly and squeezed her hand before popping up to help the children distribute the gifts.

All of the adults had at least a single gift to open. Due to the so-called "sweetheart" gifts, most had two, as did each of the children, one as a result of the "family lotto" and the other from their grandparents. Ovida and Larry had been good enough even to provide a gift for Russell, as had Jolie. She'd wanted Vince to have something under the tree, too, so she'd bought him a hand-tooled leather cover for his Bible and sent it along with his sisters after their shopping trip. Jolie herself had several gifts waiting for her, one from Sharon, who had drawn her name, and one each from her brother, sister and nephew.

In addition to this bounty, the grown Cutler children had joined together to buy a gift for their parents. This seemed to be a yearly event, and this Christmas the gift was a large-screen television that the sons-in-law carried in from the garage where they'd hidden it earlier. Clearly, Larry was delighted.

"The Super Bowl Party is here this year!" Drew announced, but Vince immediately objected.

"No way. I got my big screen last week, so I've got first dibs. It's already agreed."

"You've agreed," Donna pointed out. "Jolie hasn't."

Jolie glanced around in surprise. "It's not up to *me*."

Obviously that was so, because the matter died instantly. Donna wasn't even looking at Jolie anymore. Instead, she was taking Tony from her husband, and saying something to Connie. Vince had gone back to directing the opening of the gifts.

All the gifts had two tags attached to them, one of which had been removed and deposited into a large glass bowl as the packages were passed out. It was Vince's job to draw the tags, one by one, and announce the name to the assembly. That person could then open the gift of his or her choice, saving the other for next draw. The fun part was the anticipation of hearing one's own name and the absolute delight that everyone seemed to take in watching one another open gifts.

Jolie's name was called early on, and she first chose a package from Marcus. It was a new Bible bound in supple tan leather with pages edged in gold. Inside, he had written an inscription. "To Jolie, one of the two dearest sisters in the world. May God bless you with every good thing, shelter you from harm and fill your life with love. Marcus."

She hugged him and treasured his whispered, "I love you, sis."

"I love you, too."

Next time around, she opened Connie's gift, a touching photo album filled with old pictures of them as children and recent ones of Russell, Connie and Marcus. They spent several minutes with their heads together, looking through the pages, remembering and laughing as they'd done as children.

"I can't believe you managed to save these," Jolie said, brushing her fingertips across a sheet of old photos.

"I can't believe I have my sister back," Connie said softly, blinking away tears.

Jolie trumped her handily. "I have my sister, my brother and my nephew."

"Wanna trade?" Olivia cracked, lightening the mood and making everyone laugh.

"No, thank you," Jolie replied smoothly, widening her eyes as if in horror.

Everyone laughed again. Vince put a stop to it by

plunging his hand back into the bowl. Some time later he finally drew his own name.

Even though he'd said he only wanted to see her re-united with her family, Jolie hoped he'd like her other gift. He broke the ribbon, ripped away the wrapping paper and lifted off the top of the box, batting back the tissue inside. For a moment he simply stared at the leather Bible cover handstitched and dyed with a West-ern motif and embossed with his name. Then he smiled, reached out for her and, to her mingled embarrassment and delight, kissed her soundly on the mouth before showing off his gift to the company at large. Larry es-pecially seemed to like it. He examined the cover in de-tail, murmuring that it was "Neat."

"Thanks, babe," Vince said. "I wasn't expecting that." He slid her an apologetic look and added, "Guess I should've put something under the tree for you, too."

"Oh, that's all right," she said.

She hadn't expected anything from him, certainly not a "sweetheart" gift as it was termed. It would have been nice, true, but she looked at Russell, saw how en-grossed he was with the stacking blocks she'd given him and recognized the understanding smiles on the faces of her brother and sister. It was enough. How could she ask for more?

With his free hand, Vince drew another name and another and another. Eventually Jolie opened her gift from Russell. It was a framed photo of him. He'd been allowed to scribble on the mat with a crayon, which set off the photo charmingly. And finally she unveiled the beautiful silk-blend sweater from Sharon.

"This is beautiful!"

"It's the very color of your eyes," Sharon told her proudly.

Jolie looked at the lovely green sweater and beamed.

When the last gift had been opened, pronounced delightful and appropriately envied, Vince turned over the bowl as a demonstration of its emptiness and placed it on the floor.

"Guess that's it, folks. Pretty good haul, eh?"

General statements of agreement followed. Bets noted that the children still had Santa gifts to look forward to, and her parents teased her about the possibility of her only receiving coal and switches. She didn't seem very worried.

Jolie rose to help Sharon begin gathering up the trash, but Vince stopped her with a hand on her wrist.

"Wait a minute," he said rather loudly, drawing a small gold-foil bag from his jacket pocket. "Looks like we have one more gift, after all."

Jolie laughed, sure that the pretty gold-foil bag was for her, and sank back down onto the hearth next to Connie, who had squeezed in earlier while looking at the photo album. She couldn't help feeling a little thrill because Vince had bought something for her, after all, not a *sweetheart* gift, of course, but it was enough that it was personal.

Marcus left Russell playing happily on the floor and eased up onto the corner of the hearth next to Connie.

Vince placed the small bag in Jolie's hand, and she felt something hard and cubic inside. Pulling the bow from the fringed draw string, she emptied the sack of its contents. A small, white velvet box tumbled onto her lap, just the right size for a ring.

Jolie immediately dismissed the crazy possibility that

popped into her mind. It couldn't be. She'd let her own wishful thinking completely run away with her. And yet… Her heart was beating pronouncedly as she looked to Vince for some clue as to what she would really find inside that tiny box. The glow in his eyes literally took her breath away.

"Oh, no!" she gasped.

Chapter Sixteen

Vince felt his heart plummet to the pit of his stomach. He'd been so sure. Christmas eve, surrounded by her family and his, had seemed the perfect moment. But now…well, there was no backing out now. His whole family knew what he was planning.

He blew out a deep breath, slipped off the hearth, crouching before her, and reached for the jeweler's box in her lap. She hadn't yet touched it. Her hands hovered about her shoulders, as if she feared the thing would bite her.

More likely it would bite him.

Mentally whispering a quick prayer, he closed his hand around it, dropped that hand to his side and murmured softly, "Am I refused before I've even asked, then?"

What was he going to say to his family? They all expected a happy announcement. Jolie clapped both hands over her mouth as if to say that wasn't going to happen.

"Guess I'm not as clever as I thought I was," Vince said with a self-deprecating grimace. He tried for a smile and failed miserably. "That's what I get, going for the grand romantic gesture."

He cleared his throat and would have risen if she hadn't reached out to capture his face in both her hands, forcing his gaze to hers. Tears shimmered in her eyes, eyes that brimmed to overflowing. With love.

And disbelief.

"This can't be happening," she said in a tiny, shaky voice. "Not to *me*."

Vince tilted his head and felt the tremble of her fingers against his skin. Hope blossomed, the hope that he had misunderstood her initial reaction.

"Why not to you?" he asked patiently, aware that everyone else in the room seemed to be holding their collective breath.

Jolie gave her head a truncated shake. "I'm not the sort of person who…we're not like you." She waved a hand broadly, looking up at the arrested assembly. "Cutlers are…you're *normal*."

Relief washed through Vince, relief mingled with a shade of irritation.

"Whatever that is," he snapped. Then he reached for his patience. "Normal is one of those things that can't be easily defined, but all right, so you're not like us. So what? I wouldn't want you if you were."

Only the instant the words left his mouth did he realize how true they were.

Okay, she'd had issues that had needed settling, relationships that had needed mending, but that didn't mean that he wanted her to change who she was. He loved her as she was. She was perfect for him as she was. Why hadn't he told her that earlier?

He sighed, realizing that he'd handled this whole thing

badly. Bowing his head, he quickly prayed for God to give him the right words.

"We're blessed, we Cutlers," he began, trusting God to put the words into his mouth. "We've had nice *normal* lives, wise, caring parents. God must have known that we couldn't handle anything else. Or maybe He was just preparing me for you, the way He was preparing you for me." He fitted his hand around the gentle curve of her jaw, feeling a certain peace, a rightness settle over him. "He gave you a special kind of strength, Jo. You've never had a stable home life, parents who protected and guided you, and yet you're one of the best people I know."

"I'm *not*," she insisted tearfully. "I've been so selfish, so angry."

"So human," he amended. "Honey, the shocker is not that you've had negative emotions as a result of negative experiences, it's that you continue to be so caring, so honorable, so forgiving, so solidly, stubbornly *you*."

"That sounds like the sort of man *you* are," she told him wonderingly, "not the sort of woman *I* am."

"Do you know what sort of woman *you* are, Jolie?" he asked, and then he answered his own question. "You are exactly the sort of woman I need, exactly the sort I could love for the rest of my life if you'll just— Whoa!"

She nearly bowled him over, flying off the hearth and throwing her arms around his neck.

He dropped the box to the floor and caught himself with one hand. Laughter rushed up out of his throat as he steadied them both. He heard gasping and sniffles in the background and the sweetest squeaking in his ear.

"I love you so much!"

Now they were getting somewhere. He hugged her tightly for a moment, torn between elation and relief.

"Let's try this again. Okay?"

"O-o-kay," she managed.

Easing her back onto the hearth, he groped for the box with one hand. At the same time, he was having some trouble getting her to let go of him, but he managed it with little squeezes and pats and tugs. She quaked all over, like the first leaf of spring meeting the last icy blast of winter. He felt a sharp tap on his shoulder. Looking up, he found his precocious niece at his side.

Bets grinned down at him and shoved her hand at his face. On her palm, just beneath his nose, rested the white velvet box that had started all of this. Trust Bets to get herself into the spotlight.

He picked up the tiny box between his thumb and forefinger, saying wryly, "Thanks."

She inclined her head, grinning, spun on her tiptoes and paraded back to her seat, her hands clasped behind her.

"I would make a very good flower girl, by the way," she announced cheekily.

Laughter sputtered, eddied, faded while Vince hung his head in mock chagrin.

Bets had temporarily upstaged him, but he knew who held the major roles. Now it was time for this little drama to reach its climax.

Taking a deep breath, he rocked forward onto one knee, reached out and clapped a hand around the nape of Jolie's neck, steadying both of them and feeling her lovely hair slide beneath his fingers. She had worn it down, a simple rhinestone clip at one temple.

Plain and simple, that was Jolie.

No, not plain.

She had to be one of the most beautiful women in the

world, and—incredibly—she was meant for him. He knew it at the very core of his being, and that certainty gave him strength, peace, joy.

"Jolie Kay Wheeler," he said in a firm, even voice, "will you marry me?"

She made a strangled noise and burst into tears. His heart stopped again, then Marcus grabbed his hand and began pumping it while Connie hugged her sister comfortingly.

"Hang on. Hang on," Vince instructed, wanting this thing settled in no uncertain terms. She hadn't actually said yes yet.

He dropped the box into Jolie's hands. She stared at it for a moment and then began wrenching at it, sobbing or laughing, he couldn't tell which. Impatiently, he snatched the box back, snapped it open and plucked out the ring, holding it up so that the two narrow, red satin ribbons that he'd attached to the band hung down in front of her.

This time, he was sure that it was laughter which shook her. Smiling, he explained himself.

"It comes with strings attached."

"Yes," she said, scrubbing at the tears on her face.

Since he wasn't exactly sure what that meant, he proceeded, lifting one thin ribbon with an index finger.

"This one is love."

She giggled. Jolie, his Jolie, actually *giggled*.

"You have to say it so everyone else can hear it," he instructed around a smile.

"Yeah, otherwise nobody'll believe it," Marty cracked.

Everyone laughed, the sound rich and ebullient.

"I love you!" Jolie declared to mild applause.

Vince was having a really good time now. He hadn't done so badly, after all. He lifted the second ribbon.

"This one is marriage."

Another wave of applause washed through the room as Jolie reached for the ring, but Vince was determined to hear it plainly said, so he jerked the ring back. She caught the tail end of the ribbon, and for a moment they performed a little tug of war. Something told him that it wouldn't be the last.

He couldn't have been happier. God knew he'd be bored inside of a week with a meek, compliant little mouse of a woman. Besides which, the other Cutler women would eat her alive! A prickly, sassy, strong-willed but good-hearted female was exactly what he needed, and even she seemed finally to know it.

"You knucklehead," she said, sniffing, "of course I'll marry you."

The room erupted, as did Vincent's heart. Jolie yanked the ring out of his grasp and threw her arms around him again. He caught her against him, rocking her wildly as blows of congratulations rained down on his shoulders.

Connie sat on the hearth, openly weeping and laughing, her son standing at her knees, while Marcus was on his feet, shaking hands and accepting congratulations as if he was the bridegroom.

Suddenly Vince felt himself close to tears. Jolie seemed to know it instantly.

She pulled back far enough to place her forehead against his and whisper, "I do love you, Vince, with all my heart."

"I know that," he said, hugging her tight once more, "but it's no more than I love you. We're going to be so happy, Jo."

After a moment, they both sank back onto their heels. Vince took the ring, admiring the single, brilliant-cut diamond—not *too* large because Jolie wouldn't like anything ostentatious—and slipped it onto her finger, ribbons and all.

It was a tight fit with the ribbons still attached, but he wasn't ready to remove them just yet. He'd tie them around her wrist if he could. Or his own. He settled for cupping her face in his hands and kissing her firmly.

His sisters were planning the wedding aloud in the background.

"Valentine's Day," he heard Olivia say.

"It's perfect," Donna declared.

Vince climbed to his feet, taking Jolie with him, his anxious gaze on her face, but she put her head back and laughed, saying, "Don't look at me. I'm not about to get in the way of that."

Vince relaxed, Jolie's hand clutched tightly in his, and half teased, "I'm counting on you to keep them from decking me out in ruffles and a red tuxedo."

"On the budget you've given us?" Sharon scoffed. "We'll be lucky if we can get *her* properly outfitted."

"Oh, wait!" Helen exclaimed, rushing over to spin Jolie around and take her measure with a critical eye. Abruptly she nodded. "Mother," she announced, "Jolie can wear your dress."

"That old thing?" Ovida gasped, but even Vince could hear the delight in her voice. "It's from the sixties, Empire waistline, little wedding ring collar, straight skirt."

"And sleeveless," Sharon pointed out. "In February."

"We'll get a little lace jacket," Donna suggested eagerly. "No, velvet, white velvet. Simple, sleek, elegant."

Jolie literally clapped her hands, eyes bright, the lines of her face softened with happiness and laughter.

Suddenly, Vince couldn't contain his joy a moment

longer. He wrapped his hands around her waist, lifted her and literally spun her in a circle.

The Cutlers were big on celebration, big on family, big on faith and big on love. Their collective past was glorious with holiday memories and shared joys, but this was surely a year that would stand out among all the rest. A Thanksgiving baby, a Christmas engagement, hopes and dreams fulfilled. A perfect, God-given love.

* * * * *

UPON A MIDNIGHT CLEAR

Gail Gaymer Martin

Dedicated to my sister, Jan,
who knows the sorrow of losing a child.
And in loving memory of her infant daughters,
Lisa Marie and Beth Ann, who live with Jesus.

Thanks to my husband, Bob, for his devotion,
support and hours of proofreading.
To Flo Stano for her nursing expertise,
and to the Bedford Chamber of Commerce
for their invaluable information.

Then shall ye call upon me, and ye shall go
and pray unto me, and I will hearken unto you.
And ye shall seek me, and find me,
when ye shall search for me with all your heart.
—*Jeremiah* 29:12–13

Chapter One

Callie Randolph scanned the employment ads of the *Indianapolis News*. Her eyes lit upon a Help Wanted entry: *Special child, aged five, needs professional caregiver. Live-in. Good wage. Contact David Hamilton. 555 area code.* Southern Indiana, she assumed. "Live-in" she wanted. But a child?

She raised her head from the ad and caught her mother, eyeing her.

"You've been quiet since you got home," Grace Randolph said, resting back in the kitchen chair. "Tell me about the funeral."

"It was nice, as funerals go. But sad, so close to the holidays." Ethel's death, coming as it did on the footsteps of Christmas, jolted Callie with the memories of a birth six Christmases earlier. Pushing away the invading thoughts, Callie shifted in her chair and focused on her mother. "More people than I would expect at the funeral for someone in her nineties, but I suppose most of the mourners were friends and business acquaintances of Ethel's children. The family has a name in the community."

"Ah yes, when we're old, people forget."

"No, it's not that they forget. When we're *that* old, many of our own friends and acquaintances have already died. Makes coming to a funeral difficult." Callie hoped to lighten Grace's negative mood. "It'll feel strange not taking care of Ethel. She had the faith of a saint and a smile right to the end. Always had a kind word." She raised her eyes, hoping her mother had heard her last statement.

Grace stared across the room as if lost in thought, and Callie's mind drifted to the funeral and the preacher's comforting words. *"Ethel lived a full and glorious life, loving her Lord and her family."* Callie pictured the wrinkled, loving face of her dying patient. Ethel's earthly years had definitely been full and glorious.

In contrast, Callie's nearly twenty-six years had been empty and dull. Her dreams had died that horrible March day that she tried to block from her memory. Her life seemed buried in its own tomb of guilt and sorrow.

"So, about the funeral—"

Callie slammed the door on her thoughts and focused on her mother.

"Tell me about the music. Any hymns?" Grace asked.

Callie eyed her, sensing an ulterior motive in her question. "Real nice, Mom. Organ music and hymns."

"Which hymns?"

Callie pulled her shoulders back, feeling the muscles tightening along the cords of her neck. "'Amazing Grace,' 'Softly and Tenderly.'"

"I can hear you singing that one. So beautiful."

Callie fought the desire to bolt from the room. She sensed an argument heading her way. Instead, she aimed her eyes at the newspaper clutched in her hands.

Grace leaned on an elbow. "So what will you do now?"

"Find a new job, I suppose." She hesitated, wondering what comment she'd receive about her newest resolve. "But I've made a decision." Callie met her mother's eyes. "I'm not going to give elderly care anymore. I'll find something else."

"Praise the Lord, you've come to your senses. Callie, you have a nursing degree, but you continue to waste your time with the deathwatch. You need to live and use the talent God gave you."

Deep creases furrowed Callie's forehead. "Please don't call it the deathwatch. Caring for older people has been a blessing. And I *do* use my talents." She shook her head, amazed at her mother's attitude. "Do you think it's easy to nurse someone who's dying? I use as many skills as I would in a regular hospital."

Grace fell back against the chair. "I'm sorry. I don't mean to belittle your work, but it's not a life for a young woman. Look at you. You're beautiful and intelligent, yet you spend your life sitting in silent rooms, listening to old people muttering away about nothing but useless memories. What about a husband…and children? Don't you want a life for yourself?"

She flinched at her mother's words. "Please, don't get on that topic, Mom. You know how I feel about that."

"I wish I knew when you got these odd ideas. They helped put your father in his grave. He had such hopes for you."

Callie stiffened as icy tendrils slithered through her. How many times was she reminded of how she had helped kill her father? After his death three years earlier, the doctor had said her dad had been a walking time bomb from fatty foods, cigarettes and a type-A personality. Though guilt poked at her, she knew she hadn't caused his death. Yet, she let her mother rile her.

Grace scowled with a piercing squint. "I think it began when you stopped singing," she said, releasing a lengthy, audible sigh. "Such a beautiful voice. Like a meadowlark."

"Stop. Stop, Mother." Callie slammed her hand on the tabletop. "Please, don't call me that."

Grace looked taken aback. "Well, I'm sorry. What's gotten into you?" She gaped at Callie. "You're as white as a sheet. I only called you a—"

"Please, don't say it again, Mother." Callie pressed her forehead into her hand.

"I don't know what's wrong with you." Grace sat for a moment before she began her litany. "I don't know, Callie. I could cry when I think of it. Everyone said you sang like an angel."

Callie stared at the newspaper, the black letters blurring. Her mother wouldn't stop until she'd made her point. Callie ached inside when she thought about the music she'd always loved. She struggled to keep her voice calm and controlled. "I lost my interest in music, that's all." Her fingernails dug into the flesh of her fisted hand.

"Your father had such hopes for you. He dreamed you'd pass your audition with the Jim McKee Singers. But his hopes were buried along with him in his grave."

Callie modulated her pitch, and her words came out in a monotone. "I didn't pass the audition. I told you."

"I can't believe that, Callie. You've said it, but everyone knew you could pass the audition. Either you didn't try or... I don't know. Being part of Paul Ivory's ministry would be any girl's dream. And the Jim McKee Singers traveled with him in the summer all over the country, so it wouldn't have interfered with your college studies. And then you just quit singing. I can't understand you."

"Mother, let's not argue about something that happened years ago."

"But it's not just that, Callie. I hate to bring it up, but since the baby, you've never been the same."

Unexpected tears welled in Callie's eyes, tears she usually fought. But today they sneaked in behind the emotions elicited by Ethel's death, and the memory of the baby's Christmas birth dragged them out of hiding.

Callie had never seen the daughter she had borne six years earlier. The hospital had their unbending policy, and her parents had given her the same ultimatum. A girl placing a child for adoption should not see her baby.

She begged and pleaded with her parents to allow her to keep her daughter. But they would have no part of it. She struggled in her thoughts—longing to finish an argument that held weight. In the end, her parents were correct. A child needed a secure and loving home. Adoption was best for her baby daughter. But not for Callie. Against her wishes, Callie signed the papers releasing her baby for adoption.

Grace breathed a ragged sigh. "Maybe your father and I made a mistake. You were so young, a whole lifetime ahead of you. We thought you could get on with your life. If you'd only told us who the young man was—but you protected him. Any decent young man would have stood up and accepted his responsibilities. For all we knew, you never told him, either."

"We've gone over this before. It's in the past. It's over. It's too late." She clutched the newspaper, crumpling the paper beneath her fingers.

"We meant well. Even your brother and sister begged

you to tell us who the fellow was. You could have been married, at least. Given the baby a name, so we could hold our head up in public. But, no."

Callie folded the paper and clasped it in her trembling hand. She rose without comment. What could she say that she hadn't said a million times already? "I'm going to my room. I have a headache." As she passed through the doorway, she glanced over her shoulder and saw her mother's strained expression.

Before Grace could call after her, Callie rushed up the staircase to her second-floor bedroom and locked the door. She could no longer bear to hear her mother's sad-voiced recollections. No one but Callie knew the true story. She prayed that the vivid picture, too much like a horror movie, would leave her. Yet so many nights the ugly dream tore into her sleep, and again and again she relived the life-changing moments.

She plopped on the corner of the bed, massaging her neck. The newspaper ad appeared in her mind. *David Hamilton.* She grabbed a pen from her desk, reread the words, and jotted his name and telephone number on a scratch pad. She'd check with Christian Care Services tomorrow and see what they had available. At least she'd have the number handy if she wanted to give Mr. Hamilton a call later.

She tossed the pad on her dressing table and stretched out on the bed. A child? The thoughts of caring for a child frightened her. Would a child, especially a sick child, stir her longing?

She'd resolved to make a change in her life. Images of caring for adults marched through her head—the thought no longer appealed to her. Nursing in a doctor's office or hospital held no interest for her: patients coming and going, a nurse with no involvement in their lives. She wanted to be part of a life, to make a difference.

She rolled on her side, dragging her fingers through the old-fashioned chenille spread. The room looked so much the way it had when she was a teenager. How long had her mother owned the antiquated bedspread?

Since college, her parents' home had been only a stop-off place between jobs. Live-in care was her preference—away from her parents' guarded eyes, as they tried to cover their sorrow and shame over all that had happened.

When she'd graduated from college, she had weighed all the issues. Geriatric care seemed to encompass all her aspirations. At that time, she could never have considered child care. Her wounds were too fresh.

Her gaze drifted to the telephone. The name *David Hamilton* entered her mind again. Looking at her wristwatch, she wondered if it was too late to call him. Eight in the evening seemed early enough. Curiosity galloped through her mind. What did the ad mean—a "special" child? Was the little one mentally or physically challenged? A boy or girl? Where did the family live? Questions spun in her head. What would calling hurt? She'd at least have her questions answered.

She swung her legs over the edge of the bed, rose, and grabbed the notepad. What specific information would she like to know? She organized her thoughts, then punched in the long-distance number.

A rich baritone voice filled the line, and when Callie heard his commanding tone, she caught her breath. Job interviews and query telephone calls had never bothered her. Tonight her wavering emotions addled her. She drew in a lengthy, relaxing breath, then introduced herself and stated her business.

Hamilton's self-assured manner caught her off guard. "I'm looking for a professional, Ms. Randolph. What is your background?"

His tone intimidated her, and her responses to his questions sounded reticent in her ears. "It's *Miss* Randolph, and I'm a professional, licensed nurse." She paused to steady her nerves. "But I've preferred to work as a home caregiver rather than in a hospital.

"The past four years, I've had elderly patients, but I'm looking for a change."

"Change?"

His abruptness struck her as arrogant, and Callie could almost sense his arched eyebrow.

"Yes. I've been blessed working with the older patients, but I'd like to work with…a child."

"I see." A thoughtful silence hung in the air. "You're a religious woman, Miss Randolph?"

His question confounded her. Then she remembered she'd used the word *blessed.* Not sure what he expected, she answered honestly. "I'm a Christian, if that's what you're asking."

She waited for a response. Yet only silence filled the line. With no response forthcoming, she asked, "What do you mean by 'special,' Mr. Hamilton? In the ad, you mentioned you needed a caregiver for a 'special child.'"

He hesitated only a moment. "Natalie… Nattie's a bright child. She was always active, delightful—but since her mother's death two years ago, she's become…withdrawn." His voice faded.

"Withdrawn?"

"Difficult to explain in words. I'd rather the prospective caregiver meet her and see for herself what I mean.

Nattie no longer speaks. She barely relates to anyone. She lives in her own world."

Callie's heart lurched at the thought of a child bearing such grief. "I see. I understand why you're worried." Still, panic crept over her like cold fingers inching along her spine. Her heart already ached for the child. Could she control her own feelings? Her mind spun with flashing red warning lights.

"I've scared you off, Miss Randolph." Apprehension resounded in his statement.

She cringed, then lied a little. "No, no. I was thinking."

"Thinking?" His tone softened. "I've been looking for someone for some time now, and I seem to scare people off with the facts...the details of Nattie's problem."

The image of a lonely, motherless child tugged at her compassion. What grief he had to bear. "I'm not frightened of the facts," Callie said, but in her heart, she was frightened of herself. "I have some personal concerns that came to mind." She fumbled for what to say next. "For example, I don't know where you live. Where are you located, sir?"

"We live in Bedford, not too far from Bloomington."

Bedford. The town was only a couple of hours from her mother's house. She paused a moment. "I have some personal matters I need to consider. I'll call you as soon as I know whether I'd like to be interviewed for the position. I hope that's okay with you."

"Certainly. That's fine. I understand." Discouragement sounded in his voice.

She bit the corner of her lip. "Thank you for your time."

After she hung up the telephone, Callie sat for a while

without moving. She should have been honest. She'd already made her decision. A position like that wouldn't be wise at all. She was too vulnerable.

Besides, she wasn't sure she wanted to work for David Hamilton. His tone seemed stiff and arrogant. A child needed a warm, loving father, not one who was bitter and inflexible. She would have no patience with a man like that.

David Hamilton leaned back in his chair, his hand still clasping the telephone. *Useless.* In two months, his ad had resulted in only three telephone calls. One courageous soul came for an interview, but with her first look at Nattie, David saw the answer in the woman's eyes.

He supposed, as well, the "live-in" situation might be an obstacle for some. With no response locally, he'd extended his ad farther away, as far as Indianapolis. But this Miss Randolph had been the only call so far.

He longed for another housekeeper like Miriam. Her overdue retirement left a hole nearly as big, though not as horrendous, as Sara's death. No one could replace Miriam.

A shudder filtered through him. *No one could replace Sara.*

Nothing seemed worse than a wife's death, but when it happened, he had learned the truth. Worse was a child losing her mother. Yet the elderly housekeeper had stepped in with all her love and wisdom and taken charge of the household, wrapping each of them in her motherly arms.

Remembering Miriam's expert care, David preferred to hire a more mature woman as a nanny. The voice he heard on the telephone tonight sounded too young, perhaps nearly a child herself. He mentally calculated her age. She'd mentioned working for four years. If she'd graduated from college when she was twenty-one, she'd be only twenty-five. What would a twenty-five-year-old know about healing his child? Despite his despair, he felt a pitying grin flicker on his lips. He was only thirty-two. What did he know about healing his child? Nothing.

David rose from the floral-print sofa and wandered to the fireplace. He stared into the dying embers. Photographs lined the mantel, memories of happier times— Sara smiling warmly with sprinkles of sunlight and shadow in her golden hair; Nattie with her heavenly blue eyes and bright smile posed in the gnarled peach tree on the hill; and then, the photograph of Sara and him on his parents' yacht.

He turned from the photographs, now like a sad monument conjuring sorrowful memories. David's gaze traversed the room, admiring the furnishings and decor. Sara's hand had left its mark everywhere in the house, but particularly in this room. Wandering to the bay window, he stood over the mahogany grand piano, his fingers caressing the rich, dark wood. How much longer would this magnificent instrument lie silent? Even at the sound of a single note, longing knifed through him.

This room was their family's favorite spot, where they had spent quiet evenings talking about their plans and dreams. He could picture Sara and Nattie stretched out on the floor piecing together one of her thick cardboard puzzles.

An empty sigh rattled through him, and he shivered with loneliness. He pulled himself from his reveries and marched back to the fireplace, grabbing the poker and jamming it into the glowing ashes. Why should he even think, let alone worry, about the young woman's phone call? He'd never hear from her again, no matter what she promised. Her voice gave the telltale evidence. She had no intention of calling again.

Thinking of Nattie drew him to the hallway. He followed the wide, curved staircase to the floor above. In the lengthy hallway, he stepped quietly along the thick Persian carpet. Two doors from the end, he paused and listened. The room was silent, and he pushed the door open gently, stepping inside.

A soft night-light glowed a warm pink. Natalie's slender frame lay curled under a quilt, and the rise and fall of the delicate blanket marked her deep sleep. He moved lightly across the pink carpeting and stood, looking at her buttercup hair and her flushed, rosy cheeks. His heart lurched at the sight of his child—their child, fulfilling their hopes and completing their lives.

Or what had become their incomplete and short life together.

After the telephone call, Callie's mind filled with thoughts of David Hamilton and his young daughter. Her headache pounded worse than before, and she undressed and pulled down the blankets. Though the evening was still young, she tucked her legs beneath the warm covers.

The light shone brightly, and as thoughts drifted through her head, she nodded to herself, resolute she would not consider the job in Bedford. After turning off the light, she closed her eyes, waiting for sleep.

Her subconsciousness opened, drawing her into the darkness. The images rolled into her mind like thick fog along an inky ocean.

* * *

She was in a sparse waiting room. Her pale pink blouse, buttoned to the neck, matched the flush of excitement in her cheeks. The murky shadows swirled past her eyes: images, voices, the reverberating click *of a door. Fear rose within her. She tried to scream, to yell, but nothing came except black silence—*

Callie forced herself awake, her heart thundering. Perspiration ran from her hairline. She threw back the blankets and snapped on the light. Pulling her trembling legs from beneath the covers, she sat on the edge of the bed and gasped until her breathing returned to normal.

She rose on shaking legs and tiptoed into the hall to the bathroom. Though ice traveled through her veins, a clammy heat beaded on her body. Running cold tap water onto a washcloth, she covered her face and breathed in the icy dampness. *Please, Lord, release me from that terrible dream.*

She wet the cloth again and washed her face and neck, then hurried quietly back to her room, praying for a dreamless sleep.

Chapter Two

Christian Care Services filled the two-story office building on Woodward. Callie entered the lobby and took the elevator to the second floor. Usually she walked the stairs, but today she felt drained of energy.

Twenty-five minutes later, she left more discouraged than when she'd arrived. Not one live-in care situation. How could she tell the young woman she couldn't live at home, not because she didn't love her mother, but because she loved herself as much? The explanation seemed too personal and complicated.

Feeling discouraged, she trudged to her car. Live-in positions weren't very common, and she wondered how long she'd have to wait. If need be, she'd look on her own, praying that God would lead her to a position somewhere.

Standing beside her car, she searched through her shoulder bag for her keys and, with them, pulled out the slip of paper with David Hamilton's phone number. She didn't recall putting the number in her bag, and finding it gave her an uneasy feeling. She tossed the number back into her purse.

The winter air penetrated her heavy woolen coat, and

she unlocked the car door and slid in. As thoughts butted through her head, she turned on the ignition and waited for the heat.

Money wasn't an immediate problem; residing with others, she'd been able to save a tidy sum. But she needed a place to live. If she stayed home, would she and her mother survive? God commanded children to honor their parents, but had God meant Callie's mother? A faint smile crossed her lips at the foolish thought. Callie knew her parents had always meant well, but meaning and reality didn't necessarily go hand in hand.

Indianapolis had a variety of hospitals. She could probably have her pick of positions in the metropolitan area, then get her own apartment or condo. But again the feeling of emptiness consumed her. She wasn't cut out for hospital nursing.

Warmth drifted from the car heater, and Callie moved the button to high. She felt chilled deep in her bones. Though the heat rose around her, icy sensations nipped at her heart. Her memory turned back to her telephone call the previous evening and to a little child who needed love and care.

She shook the thought from her head and pulled out of the parking lot. She'd give the agency a couple of weeks. If nothing became available, then she'd know Bedford was God's decision. By that time, the position might already be taken, and her dilemma would be resolved.

Callie glanced at David Hamilton's address again. Bedford was no metropolis, and she'd found the street easily.

Two weeks had passed and no live-in positions had become available, not even for an elderly patient. Her twenty-sixth birthday had plodded by a week earlier, and she felt like an old, jobless woman, staring at the girlish daisy wallpaper in her bedroom. Life had come to a standstill, going nowhere. Tired of sitting by the telephone waiting for a job call, she had called David Hamilton. Despite his lack of warmth, he had a child who needed someone to love her.

Keeping her eyes on the winding road lined with sprawling houses, she glanced at the slip of paper and reread the address. A mailbox caught her eye. The name *Hamilton* jumped from the shiny black receptacle in white letters. She looked between the fence pillars, and her gaze traveled up the winding driveway to the large home of oatmeal-colored limestone.

She aimed her car and followed the curved pathway to the house. Wide steps led to a deep, covered porch, and on one side of the home, a circular tower rose above the house topped by a conical roof.

Callie pulled in front, awed by the elegance and charm of the turn-of-the-century building. Sitting for a moment to collect her thoughts, she pressed her tired back against the seat cushion. Though an easy trip in the summer, the two-hour drive on winter roads was less than pleasant. She thanked God the highway was basically clear.

Closing her eyes, she prayed. Even thinking of Mr. Hamilton sent a shudder down her spine. His voice presented a formidable image in her mind, and now she would see him face-to-face.

She climbed from the car and made her way up the impressive steps to the wide porch. Standing on the expanse of cement, she had a closer view of the large tower rising along the side. *Like a castle,* she thought. She located the bell and pushed. Inside, a chime sounded, and she waited.

When the door swung open, she faced a plump, middle-aged woman who stared at her through the storm door. The housekeeper, Callie assumed. The woman pushed the door open slightly, giving a flicker of a smile. "Miss Randolph?"

"Yes," Callie answered.

The opening widened, and the woman stepped aside. "Mr. Hamilton is waiting for you in the family parlor. May I take your coat?"

Callie regarded her surroundings as she slid the coat from her shoulders. She stood in a wide hallway graced by a broad, curved staircase and a sparkling crystal chandelier. An oriental carpet covered the floor, stretching the length of the entry.

Two sets of double doors stood closed on the right, and on the left, three more sets of French doors hid the rooms' interiors, leaving Callie with a sense of foreboding. Were the doors holding something in? Or keeping something out? Only the door at the end of the hallway stood open, probably leading to the servants' quarters.

The woman disposed of Callie's coat and gestured for her to follow. The housekeeper moved to the left, rapped lightly on the first set of doors, and, when a muffled voice spoke, pushed the door open and stepped aside.

Callie moved forward and paused in the doorway. The room was lovely, filled with floral-print furnishings and a broad mantel displaying family photographs. Winter sunlight beamed through a wide bay window, casting French-pane patterns on the elegant mahogany grand piano. But what caught her off guard the most was the man.

David Hamilton stood before the fireplace, watching her. Their eyes met and locked in unspoken curiosity. A pair of gray woolen slacks and a burgundy sweater covered his tall, athletic frame. His broad shoulders looked like a swimmer's, and tapered to a trim waist.

He stepped toward her, extending his hand without a smile. "Miss Randolph."

She moved forward to meet him halfway. "Mr. Hamilton. You have a lovely home. Very gracious and charming."

"Thank you. Have a seat by the fire. Big, old homes sometimes hold a chill. The fireplace makes it more tolerable."

After glancing around, she made her way toward a chair near the hearth, then straightened her skirt as she eased into it. The man sat across from her, stretching his long legs toward the warmth of the fire. He was far more handsome than she had imagined, and she chided herself for creating an ogre, rather than this attractive tawny-haired man whose hazel eyes glinted sparks of green and brown as he observed her.

"So," he said. His deep, resonant voice filled the silence.

She pulled herself up straighter in the chair and acknowledged him. "I suppose you'd like to see my references?"

He sat unmoving. "Not really."

His abrupt comment threw her off balance a moment. "Oh? Then you'd like to know my qualifications?"

"No, I'd rather get to know *you*." His gaze penetrated hers, and she felt a prickling of nerves tingle up her arms and catch in her chest.

"You mean my life story? Why I became a nurse? Why I'd rather do home care?"

"Tell me about your interests. What amuses you?"

She looked directly into his eyes. "My interests? I love to read. In fact, I brought a small gift for Natalie, some children's books. I thought she might like them. I've always favored children's literature."

He stared at her with an amused grin on his lips.

"I guess I'm rattling. I'm nervous. I've cared for the elderly, but this is my first interview for a child."

David nodded. "You're not much beyond a child yourself."

Callie sat bolt upright. "I'm twenty-six, Mr. Hamilton. I believe I qualify as an adult. And I'm a registered nurse. I'm licensed to care for people of all ages."

He raised his hand, flexing his palm like a policeman halting traffic. "Whoa. I'm sorry, Miss Randolph. I didn't mean to insult you. You have a very youthful appearance. You told me your qualifications on the telephone. I know you're a nurse. If I didn't think you might be suited for this position, I wouldn't have wasted my time. Nor yours."

Callie's cheeks burned. "I'm sorry. I thought, you—"

"Don't apologize. I was abrupt. Please continue. How else do you spend your time?"

She thought for a moment. "As I said before, I love to read. I enjoy the theater. And the outdoors. I'm not interested in sports, but I enjoy a long walk on a spring morning or a hike through the woods in autumn— Do I sound boring?"

"No, not at all."

"And then I love…" She hesitated. *Music.* How could

she tell him her feelings about music and singing? So much time had passed.

His eyes searched hers, and he waited.

The grandfather clock sitting across the room broke the heavy silence. *One. Two. Three.*

He glanced at his wristwatch. "And then you love…"

She glanced across the room at the silent piano. "Music."

Chapter Three

Callie waited for a comment, but David Hamilton only shifted his focus to the piano, then back to her face.

She didn't mention her singing. "I play the piano a little." She gestured toward the impressive instrument. "Do you play?"

David's face tightened, and a frown flickered on his brow. "Not really. Not anymore. Sara, my wife, played. She was the musician in the family."

Callie nodded. "I see." His eyes flooded with sorrow, and she understood. The thought of singing filled her with longing, too. They shared a similar ache, but hers was too personal, too horrible to even talk about. Her thought returned to the child. "And Natalie? Is your daughter musical?"

Grief shadowed his face again, and she was sorry she'd asked.

"I believe she is. She showed promise before her mother died. Nattie was four then and used to sing songs with us. Now she doesn't sing a note."

"I'm sorry. It must be difficult, losing a wife and in a sense your daughter." Callie drew in a deep breath.

"Someday, she'll sing again. I'm sure she will. When you love music, it has to come out. You can't keep it buried inside of…"

The truth of her words hit her. Music pushed against her heart daily. Would she ever be able to think of music without the awful memories surging through her? Her throat ached to sing, but then the black dreams rose like demons, just as Nattie's singing probably aroused sad thoughts of her mother.

David stared at her curiously, his head tilting to one side as he searched her face. She swallowed, feeling the heat of discomfort rise in her again.

"You have strong feelings about music." His words were not a question.

"Yes, I do. She'll sing. After her pain goes away." Callie's thoughts turned to a prayer. *Help me to sing again, Lord, when my hurt is gone.*

"Excuse me." David Hamilton rose. "I want to see if Agnes is bringing our tea." He stepped toward the door, then stopped. "Do you like tea?"

Callie nodded. "Yes, very much."

He turned and strode through the doorway. Callie drew in a calming breath. Why did she feel as if he were sitting in judgment of her, rather than interviewing her? She raised her eyebrows. Maybe he was.

In only a moment, David spoke to her from the parlor doorway. "Agnes is on her way." He left the door open, and before he had crossed the room, the woman she'd seen earlier entered with a tray.

"Right here, Agnes. On the coffee table is fine." He gestured to the low table that stretched between them. "Miss Randolph, this is Agnes, my housekeeper. She's caring for Nattie until I find someone."

"We met at the door. It's nice to know you, Agnes." The woman nodded and set the tray on the highly polished table.

"Agnes has been a godsend for us since we lost Miriam."

"Thank you, Mr. Hamilton," she said, glancing at him. "Would you like me to pour?"

"No, I'll get it. You have plenty to do." With a flicker of emotion, his eyes rose to meet the woman's. "By the way, have you checked on Nattie lately?"

"Yes, sir, she's coloring in her room."

"Coloring? That's good. I'll take Miss Randolph up to meet her a bit later."

Agnes nodded and left the room, closing the door behind her. David poured tea into the two china cups. "I'll let you add your own cream and sugar, if you take it," he said, indicating toward the pitcher and sugar bowl on the tray. "And please have a piece of Agnes's cake. It's lemon. And wonderful."

Callie glanced at him, astounded at the sudden congeniality in his voice. The interview had felt so ponderous, but now he sounded human. "Thanks. I take my tea black. And the cake looks wonderful." She sipped the strong tea, and then placed the cup on the tray and picked up a dessert plate of cake.

David eyed her as she slivered off a bite and forked it into her mouth. The tangy lemon burst with flavor on her tongue. "It's delicious."

He looked pleased. "I will say, Agnes is an excellent cook."

"Has she been with you long?"

He stared into the red glow of the firelight. "No—a half year, perhaps. Miriam, my past housekeeper, took

Nattie—took all of us—under her wing when Sara died. She had been with my parents before their deaths. A longtime employee of the family. She retired. Illness and age finally caught up with her. Her loss has been difficult for us."

He raised his eyes from the mesmerizing flames. "I'm sorry, Miss Randolph. I'm sure you aren't interested in my family tree, nor my family's problems."

"Don't apologize, please. And call me Callie." She felt her face brighten to a shy grin. "Miss Randolph sounds like my maiden aunt."

For the first time, his tense lips relaxed and curved to a pleasant smile. "All right. It's Callie," he said, leaning back in the chair. "Is that short for something?"

"No, just plain Callie."

He nodded. "So, Callie, tell me how a young woman like you decided to care for the elderly. Why not a position in a hospital, regular hours so you could have fun with your friends?"

She raised her eyes to his and fought the frown that pulled at her forehead. Never had an interview caused her such stress. The man seemed to be probing at every nerve ending—searching for what, she didn't know. She grasped for the story she had lived with for so long.

"When I graduated from college, I had romantic dreams. Like Florence Nightingale, I suppose. A hospital didn't interest me. I wanted something more…absorbing. So I thought I'd try my hand at home care. The first job I had was a cancer patient, an elderly woman who needed constant attention. Because of that, I was asked to live in their home, which suited me nicely."

"You have no family, then?"

She swallowed. How could she explain her relationship with her mother. "Yes, my mother is living. My father died about three years ago. But my mother's in good health and active. She doesn't need me around. My siblings are older. My brother lives right outside Indianapolis. My sister and her husband live in California."

"No apartment or home of your own?"

"My mother's house is the most permanent residence I have. No, I have no other financial responsibilities, if that's what you're asking."

David grimaced. "I wasn't trying to pry. I wondered if a live-in situation meets your needs."

"Yes, but most important, I like the involvement, not only with the patient, but with the family. You know— dedication, commitment."

A sound between a snicker and harrumph escaped him. "A job here would certainly take dedication and commitment."

"That's what I want. I believe God has a purpose for everybody. I want to do something that has meaning. I want to know that I'm paying God back for—"

"Paying God back?" His brows lifted. "Like an atonement? What kind of atonement does a young woman like you have to make?"

Irritation flooded through her, and her pitch raised along with her volume. "I didn't say *atonement*, Mr. Hamilton. I said *purpose*. And you've mentioned my *young* age often since I've arrived. I assume my age bothers you."

The sensation that shot through Callie surprised even her. Why was she fighting for a job she wasn't sure she wanted? A job she wasn't sure she could handle? A sigh escaped her. Working with the child wasn't a problem. She had the skills.

But *Callie* was the problem. Already, she found herself emotionally caught in the child's plight, her own
buried feelings struggling to rise from within. Her focus
settled upon David Hamilton's startled face. How could
she have raised her voice to this man? Even if she wanted
the position, any hopes of a job here were now lost forever.

David was startled by the words of the irate young
woman who stood before him. He dropped against the
back of his chair, peering at her and flinching against
her sudden anger. He reviewed what he'd said. Had he
made a point of her age?

A flush rose to her face, and for some reason, she
ruffled his curiosity. He sensed a depth in her, something that aroused him, something that dragged his own
empathy from its hiding place. He'd felt sorry for himself and for Nattie for such a long time. Feeling grief for
someone else seemed alien.

"To be honest, Miss Rand—Callie—I had thought
to hire an older woman. Someone with experience who
could nurture Nattie and bring her back to the sweet,
happy child she was before her mother's death."

Callie's chin jutted upward. Obviously his words had
riled her again.

"Was your wife an old woman, Mr. Hamilton?"

A rush of heat dashed to his cheeks. "What do you
mean?"

"I mean, did your wife understand your child? Did
she love her? Could she relate to her? Play with her? Sing
with her? Give her love and care?"

David stared at her. "Wh-why, yes. Obviously." His
pulse raced and pounded in his temples, not from anger

but from astonishment. She seemed to be interviewing him, and he wasn't sure he liked it, at all.

"Then why does a nanny—a caregiver—have to be an elderly woman? Can't a woman my age—perhaps your wife's age when she died—love and care for your child? I don't understand."

Neither did he understand. He stared at her and closed his gaping mouth. Her words struck him like icy water. What she said was utterly true. Who was he protecting? Nattie? Or himself? He peered into her snapping eyes. *Spunky? Nervy?* No, *spirited* was the word.

He gazed at the glowing, animated face of the woman sitting across from him. Her trim body looked rigid, and she stared at him with eyes the color of the sky or flowers. Yes, delphiniums. Her honey-colored hair framed an oval face graced with sculptured cheekbones and full lips. She had fire, soul and vigor. Isn't that what Nattie needed?

Callie's voice softened. "I'm sorry, Mr. Hamilton. You're angry with me. I did speak to you disrespectfully, and I'm sorry. But I—"

"No. No, I'm not angry. You've made me think. I see no reason why Nattie should have an elderly nanny. A young woman might tempt her out of her shell. She needs to be around activity and laughter. She needs to play." He felt tears push against the back of his eyes, and he struggled. He refused to sit in front of this stranger and sob, bearing his soul like a blithering idiot. "She needs to have fun. Yes?"

"Yes." She shifted in her chair, seemingly embarrassed. "I'm glad you agree." Callie stared into her lap a moment. "How does she spend her day now?"

"Sitting. Staring into space. Sometimes she colors,

like today. But often her pictures are covered in dark brown or purple. Or black."

"No school?"

David shook his head. "No. We registered her for kindergarten, but I couldn't follow through. I took her there and forced her from the car, rigid and silent. I couldn't do that to her. But next September is first grade. She must begin school then. I could get a tutor, but…" The memories of the first school day tore at his heart.

"But that won't solve the problem."

He lifted his eyes to hers. "Yes. A tutor won't solve a single problem."

"Well, you have seven or eight months before school begins. Was she examined by doctors? I assume she has nothing physically wrong with her."

"She's healthy. She eats well. But she's lethargic, prefers to be alone, sits for hours staring outside, sometimes at a book. Occasionally, she says something to me—a word, perhaps. That's all."

Callie was silent, then asked, "Psychological? Have you seen a therapist?"

"Yes, the physician brought in a psychiatrist as a consultant." He recalled that day vividly. "Since the problem was caused by a trauma, and given her age, they both felt her problem is temporary. Time will heal her. She can speak. She talked a blue streak before Sara's death. But now the problem is, she's unwilling to speak. Without talking, therapy probably couldn't help her."

Callie stared into the dying flames. "Something will bring her out. Sometimes people form habits they can't seem to break. They almost forget how it is to live without the behavior. Maybe Nattie's silence has become just that. Something has to happen to stimulate her, to make her want to speak and live like a normal child again."

"I pray you're right."

"Me, too."

He rose and wandered to the fireplace. Peering at the embers, he lifted the poker and thrust at the red glow. Nattie needed to be prodded. She needed stimulus to wake her from her sadness. The flames stirred and sparks sprinkled from the burned wood. Could this spirited woman be the one to do that?

"You mentioned you'd like me to meet your daughter," Callie said.

He swung around to face her, realizing he had been lost in reverie. "Certainly," he said, embarrassed by his distraction.

"I'd like that, when you're ready."

He glanced at the cup in her hand. "Are you finished with the tea?"

She took a final sip. "Yes, thanks. I have a two-hour drive home, and I'd like to get there before dark, if I can."

"I don't blame you. The winter roads can be treacherous."

He stood, and she rose and waited next to the chair, bathed in the warm glow of the fire. David studied her again. Her frame, though thin, rounded in an appealing manner and tugged at his memory. The straight skirt of her deep blue suit hit her modestly just below the knee. Covering a white blouse, the boxy jacket rested at the top of her hips. Her only jewelry was a gold lapel pin and earrings. She stepped to his side, and he calculated her height. Probably five foot five or six, he determined. He stood a head above her.

He stepped toward the doors, and she followed. In the

foyer, he gestured to the staircase, and she moved ahead of him, gliding lightly up the steps, her skirt clinging momentarily to her shape as she took each step.

Awareness filled him. No wonder he'd wanted to hire an elderly woman. Ashamed of his own stirrings, he asked God for forgiveness. Instead of thinking of Nattie's needs, he'd struggled to protect his own vulnerability. He would learn to handle his emotions for his daughter's sake.

At the top of the stairs, he guided her down the hallway and paused outside a door. "Please don't expect much. She's not like the child God gave us."

His fingers grasped the knob, and Callie's soft, warm hand lowered and pressed against his.

"Please, don't worry," she said. "I understand hurt."

She raised her eyes to his, and a sense of fellowship like electricity charged through him, racing down to the extremity of his limbs. She lifted her hand, and he turned the knob.

He pushed the door open, and across the room, Nattie shifted her soft blue eyes toward them, then stared again at her knees.

Callie gaped, wide-eyed, at his child. Pulled into a tight knot, Nattie sat with her back braced against the bay enclosure, her feet resting on the window seat. The sun poured in through the pane and made flickering patterns on her pale skin. The same light filtered through her bright yellow hair.

Standing at Callie's side, David felt a shiver ripple through her body. He glimpsed at his child and then looked into the eyes of the virtual stranger, named Callie Randolph, whose face now flooded with compassion and love.

Chapter Four

Callie stared ahead of her at the frail vision on the window seat. She and David stood in Nattie's bedroom doorway for a moment, neither speaking. Finally he entered the room, approaching her like a father would a normal, happy child. "Nattie, this is Miss Randolph. She wants to meet you."

Callie moved as close to the silent child as she felt comfortable doing. "Hi, Nattie. I've heard nice things about you from your daddy. I brought you a present."

She detected a slight movement in the child's body at the word *present*. Hoping she'd piqued Nattie's interest, she opened her large shoulder bag and pulled out the books wrapped in colorful tissue and tied with a ribbon. "Here." She extended her hand holding the books.

Nattie didn't move, but sat with her arms bound to her knees.

Stepping forward, Callie placed the package by the child's feet and backed away. She glanced at David. His gaze was riveted to his daughter.

He took a step forward and rested his hand on his

daughter's shoulder. "Nattie, how about if you open the present?"

The child glanced at him, but made no move to respond.

David squeezed his large frame into the end of the window seat. He lifted the gift from the bench and raised it toward her.

She eyed the package momentarily, but then lowered her lids again, staring through the window as if they weren't there.

Frustration rose in Callie. The child's behavior startled her. A list of childhood illnesses raced through her mind. Then other thoughts took their place. How did Sara die? Was the child present at her death? Questions swirled in her thoughts. What might have happened in the past to trouble this silent child sitting rigidly on the window seat?

David relaxed and placed the package on his knees. "I'll open the gift for you, then, if you'd like." Tearing the paper from the gift, he lifted the books one by one, turning the colorful covers toward her. *"The Lost Lamb,"* he read, showing her the book.

Callie looked at the forlorn child and the book cover. If ever there were a lost lamb, it was Nattie. The next book he showed her was a child's New Testament in story form, and the last, children's poems. Nattie glanced at the book covers, a short-lived spark of interest on her face.

David placed the books again by her feet and rose, his face tormented. Callie glanced at him and gestured to the window seat. "Do you mind?"

He shook his head, and she wandered slowly to the vacated spot and nestled comfortably in the corner. "I think I'd like to read this one," Callie said, selecting

The Lost Lamb, "if you don't mind." The child made no response. Callie searched David's face, but he seemed lost in thought.

Leaning back, Callie braced herself against the wall next to the window and opened the book. She glanced at Nattie, who eyed her without moving, and began to read. "'Oh my,' said Rebecca to her father, 'where is the new lamb?' Father looked into the pasture. The baby lamb was not in sight."

Callie directed the bright picture toward Nattie, who scanned the page, then returned her attention to her shoes. Callie continued. Nattie glimpsed at each picture without reaction. But the child's minimal interest gave Callie hope. Patience, perseverance, attention, love— Callie would need all of those attributes if she were to work with this lost lamb.

Glancing from the book, she caught David easing quietly through the doorway. The story gained momentum, as Rebecca and her father searched the barnyard and the wooded hills for the stray. When they found the lamb, who had stumbled into a deep hole, Nattie's eyes finally stayed attentive to the page. When the lamb was again in Rebecca's arms, Callie heard a soft breath escape the child at her side. Nattie had, at least, listened to the story. A first success.

"That was a wonderful story, wasn't it? Sometimes when we feel so alone or afraid, we can remember that Jesus is always by our side to protect us, just like Rebecca protected the lamb. I love stories like that one, don't you?" Callie rose. "Well, I have to go now, Nattie. But I hope to be back soon to read more stories with you."

She lay the book next to Nattie and gently caressed

the child's jonquil-colored hair. Nattie's gaze lifted for a heartbeat, but this time when she lowered her eyes, she fastened her attention on the book.

Callie swallowed her building emotions and hurried from the room. She made her way down the stairs, and at the bottom, filled her lungs with refreshing air. When she released the healing breath, her body trembled.

"Thank you."

Callie's hand flew to her chest, she gasped and swung to her left. "Oh, you scared me."

David stood in the doorway across from the parlor where they had met. "You did a beautiful thing."

"She's a beautiful child, Mr. Hamilton. She breaks my heart, so I can only imagine how she breaks yours."

"Call me David, please. If we're going to live in the same house, 'Callie' and 'David' will sound less formal."

She faltered, her hand still knotted at her chest. *If we're going to live in the same house.* The meaning of his words registered, and she closed her eyes. He was asking her to stay. Could she? Would the experience break her heart once more? But suddenly, her own pain didn't matter. Her only thought was for the child sitting alone in an upstairs room.

Callie stepped toward him. "Yes, if we're going to live in the same house, I suppose you're right... David. The 'David' will take some doing," she admitted with a faint grin.

He extended his hand. "I pray you'll make a difference in Nattie's life. In our lives, really. I see already you're a compassionate woman. I can ask for no more."

Callie accepted his hand in a firm clasp. "I hope you'll continue to feel like that." She eyed him, a knowing expression creeping on her face. "You've already seen me with my dander up, as they say." Her hand remained in his.

"Then we have nothing to worry about. I survived."

"Yes, you did. And quite admirably. Thank you for trusting in my...*youthful* abilities."

His hazel eyes captured hers and held her suspended until his words broke the spell. "It's my pleasure."

Callie gazed around her childhood bedroom, facing a new and frightening chapter in her life. Five times she had packed, heading for a patient's home. But tomorrow was different.

Nattie appeared in her mind, the child's face as empty of feeling as Callie's would be when she stepped into David Hamilton's home in Bedford. He was the last person she wanted to have know the fear that writhed inside her. She would step through the doorway with a charade of confidence. She had announced with no uncertainty that she could provide professional, compassionate care for Nattie. And she would.

The sound of Grace's unhappy voice echoed in Callie's head. *"Bedford is too far away. Why must you be a live-in nurse? What if I need you? Dr. Swanson, right here in town, still needs an office nurse."*

She'd heard the same questions and comments since she chose home-care. Tomorrow, another day—a new beginning.

Though she hadn't finished packing, Callie's thoughts dragged through her, sapping her energy. A good night's sleep would refresh her, she thought. With that notion, she crawled into bed.

But Callie couldn't escape her dream. It soon rose in her slumber, shrouded in darkness and mist.

* * *

*In a foggy blur, his stare toyed with her, sweeping her
body from head to toe, and her flush of excitement deepened to embarrassment. His smooth voice like a distant
whisper echoed in her head. "Callie. That's a lovely,
lovely name. Nearly pretty as you are, sweetheart."*

*An uneasy sensation rose in her, unexpected and un-
natural. Why was he teasing her with his eyes? She felt
self-conscious.*

*In the swirling darkness, he flashed his broad, charm-
ing smile, and his hushed voice touched her ear again.
"You're nervous. No need to be nervous." He turned the
bolt on the door.*

The *click* of the lock cut through her sleep. Callie
wrested herself from the blackness of her dream to the
darkness of her room.

"Bedford's only a couple hours away, Mom. I told you
already, I can get back here if you need me." Packing
the last suitcase the next morning, Callie glanced over
her shoulder at Grace. "I don't understand why you're
worried. You've never needed me yet."

Grace leaned against the door frame. "Well, I get
older every year. You never know." Grace's pinched expression gave witness to her unhappiness.

Callie bit back the words that could easily have sailed
from her lips: *Only the good die young.* Her mother was
well-meaning, she knew that, but Callie found a chip
growing on her shoulder when she spent too much time
with Grace. She needed to keep that situation in her
prayers—only God could work a miracle.

Callie chuckled out loud. "We have the same problem, Mom. I seem to get older every year myself. Any idea how we can fix that?"

Grace's compressed features gave way to a grin. "Can't do much, I suppose. I just worry. Your sister lives thousands of miles away. Kenneth is useless. Sons don't care much about their mothers."

"If you need Ken, he can be here in a minute. But you have to call him and let him know. Men just aren't as attentive as women." Guilt swept over her. She hadn't been very attentive, either. And Grace was right—though she wasn't ready for the grave, they had celebrated her sixty-fifth birthday. And no one was getting any younger.

A sudden feeling of tenderness swept over her. She was her parents' "surprise" baby. At the age of forty, Grace had her "babies" raised. Patricia was fourteen, and Ken, eleven. Then came Callie, who was soon deemed the "little princess." All her parents' unfulfilled hopes and dreams were bundled into her. She had let them down with a bang.

A heavy silence hung in the room as Callie placed the last few items in her luggage. When she snapped the locks, she turned and faced her mother. "Well, I guess that's it. I may need a few other things, but I'm not that far away. And at this point, I'm not sure how long I'll be needed."

The words caught in her throat. Already, the face of Nattie loomed in her mind. Her greatest fear was beginning to take shape. This child would continue to linger in her thoughts when her job was completed in Bedford. And could she walk away from another child? She prayed she could handle it.

Grace stood at the doorway, her hands knotted in front

of her. "You'll be coming back occasionally? So I'll see you once in a while, then?"

"Well, sure. I'm not chained to the house. At least, I don't think so." She grinned at Grace, trying to keep her parting light. Most of her previous patients had lived in the area. Living in Bedford would make trips home a bit more complicated.

Grace heaved a sigh and lifted her smaller bag. Callie grabbed the larger piece of luggage and followed her mother down the stairs and out the door.

As Callie loaded her car, she shuddered, thinking of her dream the night before. She drew the chilled, winter air through her lungs, clearing her thoughts. She stood for a moment, staring at the house where her parents had lived for most of her life, remembering...

When she returned inside, Grace had lunch waiting on the table. Seeing the food as another attempt to delay her, Callie wanted to say "no, thank you," but she had to eat somewhere. Noting her mother's forlorn expression, she sat at the table.

"Thanks, this will save time. I should arrive in Bedford in the mid-afternoon, if the weather cooperates. I'll have a chance to get settled before dinner." She bit into her sandwich.

Grace raised the tuna salad to her lips, then lowered it. "Are you sure you're safe with this man, Callie? He saw your references, but did you see his?"

Callie understood her mother's concern. "I think seeing his daughter is reference enough. He's not an outgoing, friendly man. I saw so much sadness in his eyes. Anyway, he has a full-time housekeeper who lives in. She looked comfortable enough. Though once I'm there, I imagine she'll enjoy having the opportunity to go home." Callie sipped her tea.

"You mean you have to keep house, too?"

Callie choked on her sip of tea. She quickly grabbed up her napkin to cover her mouth. "No, Mother. Agnes is from the community. She'll be able to go home and visit her family. Since I'm there, she won't have the responsibility to be the nanny. That's all. He says I'll have my own suite of bedrooms—room, private bath and a little sitting room. And I'll have dinner with the family. Now, don't worry. I'll be fine."

Grace raised an eyebrow. "What kind of business is this man in to afford such a big home and all this help?"

"Limestone quarries and mills. They've been in the family for generations. His grandfather opened a quarry in the middle eighteen-hundreds, I think. Eventually his father took over."

"Family business, hmm? Must be a good one to keep generations at it."

"It is. I was really amazed. I picked up some brochures at the Chamber of Commerce office on my way out of town. So many famous buildings were made with Indiana limestone—the Pentagon, the Empire State Building, lots of buildings in Washington, D.C. So I'd say the family has enough money to get by."

Grace grinned. "To get by? I'd say. One of those aristocratic families…with money to throw away."

"Not really. It's a beautiful house, but David seems down to earth."

"David? What's this 'David' business?"

"Mother." Callie rolled her eyes, yet heat rose up her neck at her mother's scrutiny. "Since we're living in the same house, I suppose he thought 'Miss Randolph' and 'Mr. Hamilton' sounded too formal."

"A little formality never hurt anybody."

"I'm an employee, Mom. And he has no interest in me. The man's not over the death of his wife."

"Accident?"

Callie's brows knitted. "I don't know. He didn't say, and I didn't ask. I'd already asked too many questions for someone who was supposed to be the person interviewed."

"Never hurts to ask questions."

"I'm sure I'll find out one of these days. And I don't expect to be with him much. Mainly dinner. He'll be gone some of the time, traveling for his business. I'm there to be with Natalie. Nattie, they call her. She's a beautiful child."

"Just keep your eyes focused on the child, hear me?"

Callie shook her head. "Yes, Mother. I think I've learned to take care of myself."

She caught a flicker of reminiscence in Grace's expression, and froze, praying she wouldn't stir up the past. Grace bit her tongue, and Callie changed the subject.

"The area is lovely there, all covered with snow. And imagine spring. The trees and wildflowers. And autumn. The colored leaves—elms, maples, birches."

An uneasy feeling rippled down her back. Would she see the autumn colors? Nattie needed to be ready for school. If the child was back to normal by then, her job would be finished.

"It's snowing," Grace said, pulling Callie from her thoughts. "And hard."

"Then, I'd better get moving." Callie gulped down her last bite and drained the teacup.

Without fanfare, she slipped on her coat and said goodbye. She needed to be on her way before she was snowbound. Time was fleeting, and so was her sanity.

Chapter Five

David sat with his face in his hands, his elbows resting on his large cherrywood desk. The day pressed in from all sides. Callie should arrive any time now. He'd expected her earlier, yet the uncooperative weather had apparently slowed her travel.

The day of her interview lingered in his memory. Though Nattie had responded minimally to Callie's ministrations, David was grateful for the most insignificant flicker of interest from his daughter these days. Callie had brought about that infinitesimal moment.

The major concern that lodged in his gut was himself. He feared Callie. She stirred in him remembrances he didn't want to face and emotions he had avoided for two years. His only solution was to avoid her—keep his distance.

Though often quiet, Sara had had her moments of liveliness and laughter. He recalled their spring walks on the hill and a warm, sunny day filled with play when she dubbed him "Sir Knight" with a daisy chain she'd made. Wonderful moments rose in his mind of Sara playing pat-a-cake with Nattie or singing children's songs.

If he let Callie's smiles and exuberance get under his skin, he might find himself emotionally tangled. Until Nattie was well, and he dealt with his personal sorrow, he had no interest in any kind of relationship—and he would live with that decision. But he wished wisdom had been his gatekeeper when he'd extended her the job with such enthusiasm.

On top of it all, today they would celebrate Nattie's sixth birthday. Tension caught between his shoulder blades when he pictured the occasion: a cake with candles she wouldn't blow out, gifts she wouldn't open, and joy she wouldn't feel.

David was reminded of the day Sara had surprised him for his birthday with tickets to see Shakespeare's darkest, direst play, *King Lear.* Yet, he'd accompanied her, looking pleased and interested so as not to hurt the woman he loved so deeply.

But Nattie would not look interested to please him. She wouldn't say "thank you" or force a smile. The lack of response for the gift was not what hurt. She appeared to feel nothing, and that tore at his very fiber.

His wife's death had been no surprise; Nattie's living death was.

Rising from his chair, David wandered to the window and pulled back the draperies. The snow piled against the hedges and mounded against the edge of the driveway. Lovely, pure white at this moment, the snow would soon become drab and monotonous like his life.

A flash of headlights caught the mounds of crystal flakes and glowed with diamond-like sparkles. David's heart surged, and for a heartbeat, he held his breath. Dropping the edge of the drapery, he spun toward the doorway. She would need help bringing in her luggage. He could, at least, do that.

Callie climbed the snow-covered stairs with care and rang the bell. When the door opened, her stomach somersaulted. Her focus fell upon David Hamilton, rather than Agnes. "Oh," she said, knowing her face registered surprise, "I expected Agnes." Her amazement was not so much at seeing him at the door as feeling her stomach's unexpected acrobatics.

"I was keeping an eye out for you, concerned about the weather." His face appeared drawn and serious.

"Thank you. The drive was a bit tense."

He stepped back and held the door open for her.

She glanced at his darkened face. "I hope nothing is wrong. You look..." Immediately she was sorry she had spoken. Perhaps his stressed appearance had to do with *her*—hiring someone "so young," as he had continually reminded her.

"I'm fine," he said, looking past her toward the automobile. "Let me get my jacket, and we can bring in your luggage."

He darted to the entrance closet, and in a brief moment, joined her.

Heading down the slippery porch stairs, Callie's eyes filled with his Titan stature. In her preoccupation, her foot missed the center of the step and skidded out from under her. She crumpled backward, reaching out to break her fall.

David flung his hand behind her and caught her in the crook of his arm, while the other hand swung around to hold her secure. "Careful," he cautioned.

Captured in his arms, his gaze locked with hers, she

wavered at the sensation that charged through her. She marveled at his vibrant hazel eyes in the dusky light.

"Be careful. You could get hurt," he repeated, setting her on her feet.

She found her voice and mumbled a "thank you."

Capturing her elbow, he helped her down the next two steps. When she opened the trunk, he scanned its contents.

"I'll help you in with the luggage," he said, "and I'll come back for the rest."

She nodded. Hearing his commanding voice, she couldn't disagree. He handed her the smallest case, taking the larger himself, and they climbed the steps with care.

Once inside, David set down the larger case and addressed Agnes, who was waiting in the foyer. "Show Callie her rooms, please. I'll carry in the boxes and bring them up."

Agnes nodded and grabbed the larger case. But when David stepped outside, Callie took the case from her. "Please, let me carry this one. It's terribly heavy."

Agnes didn't argue and grasped the smaller case, then headed up the stairs. At the top, the housekeeper walked down the hallway and stopped at a door to the left, across from Nattie's room. She turned the knob and stepped aside.

As Callie entered, her heart skipped a beat. She stood in the tower she had admired from outside. The sitting room was fitted with a floral chintz love seat and matching chair of vibrant pinks and soft greens, with a lamp table separating the grouping. A small oak desk sat along one curved wall, and oak bookshelves rose nearby. A woman's touch was evident in the lovely decor.

Callie dropped her luggage and darted to the center window, pulling back the sheer white curtains framed by moss-colored draperies. She gazed outside at the scene. A light snow floated past the window, and below, David pulled the last carton from the trunk and closed the lid. He hefted the box into the air, then disappeared beneath the porch roof.

Agnes remained by the door, and when Callie turned back and faced the room, the housekeeper gestured through the doorway to the bedroom. Callie lifted her luggage and followed her inside. The modest bedroom, too, illustrated a feminine hand. Delicate pastel flowers sprinkled the wallpaper that ended at the chair-molding. Below, the color of palest blue met a deeper blue carpet.

"Agnes, this is beautiful." She wanted to ply the woman with questions about Sara and how she used the charming rooms.

"Mr. Hamilton hoped you'd like it."

"How could I not? It's lovely. So dainty and feminine."

Agnes nodded and directed her to a door that opened to a walk-in closet; across the room, another door led to a pristine private bathroom, graced by a claw-foot bathtub.

As she spun around to take in the room once again, David came through the doorway with the box.

"Bricks?" he asked.

"Nearly. Books and things."

"Ah, I should have guessed. Then you'd like this in the sitting room."

"Please." Callie followed him through the doorway.

David placed the box between the desk and the bookshelves. "I'll be right back with the other. Much lighter, I'm happy to say."

Callie grinned. "No books."

He left the room, and she returned to Agnes, who hovered in the doorway.

"Miss Randolph, did you want me to help unpack your things?"

"Oh, no, Agnes, I can get it. And please call me Callie. The 'Miss' stuff makes me nervous." She gave the woman a pleasant look, but received only a nod in return.

"Then I'll get back to the kitchen," Agnes said as she edged her way to the door.

"Yes, thank you."

Agnes missed David by a hairbreadth as he came through the doorway with the last box. He held it and glanced at Callie.

"Bedroom," Callie said, before he asked, and she gestured to the adjoining room.

David turned with his burden and vanished through the doorway. Before she could follow, he returned.

"So, I hope you'll be comfortable here. I still want to get a television for you. But you do have a radio."

Callie's focus followed the direction of his hand. A small clock radio sat on the desk. "The rooms are lovely. Just beautiful. Did your wif—Sara decorate them? They have a woman's touch."

"Yes," he said, nodding his head at the sitting room. "She used this as her reading room, and she slept here if she worried about Nattie's health. The bedroom was the baby's nursery then."

"I couldn't ask for a nicer place to stay. Thank you."

He glanced around him, edging backward toward the door, his hands moving nervously at his sides. "Then I'll let you get unpacked and settled. Dinner will be at six. We're celebrating this evening. We have a couple of guests for Nattie's birthday."

"Really? I'm glad I'm here for the celebration. And pleased I brought along a couple of small presents. I'd be embarrassed to attend her birthday party empty-handed." She kept her voice level and free of the irritation that prickled her. Why hadn't he thought to tell her about the birthday?

"I'm sorry. I should have mentioned it." A frown flashed over his face, yet faded as if another thought crossed his mind. He stepped toward the door. "I'll see you at dinner."

He vanished through the doorway before Callie could respond. She stared into the empty space, wondering what had driven him so quickly from the room.

Glancing at her wristwatch, the time read four thirty. She had an hour-and-a-half before dinner. She needed time to dress appropriately if they were celebrating Nattie's birthday.

The word *birthday* took her back. Nattie was six today, so close in age to her own child, who had turned six on Christmas Day. Her chest tightened as the fingers of memory squeezed her heart. Could she protect herself from loving this child too deeply? And why did Natalie have to be six? Eight, four…any other age might not have bothered her as much.

She dropped on the edge of the bed and stared at the carpet. With an inner ache, she asked God to give her compassion and patience. Compassion for Nattie, and patience with herself.

As he waited for Callie's entrance, David prepared his guests for her introduction. Reverend John Spier listened attentively, and his sister Mary Beth bobbed her head, as if eager to meet someone new in the small town of Bedford.

"How nice," Mary Beth said, lowering her eyelids shyly at David. "Since I've come to help John in the parsonage, I've not met too many young unmarried women. Most people my age have already settled down. I look forward to our meeting."

"Yes, I hoped Callie might enjoy meeting you, too."

"Although once John finds a proper bride, I assume I'll go back to Cleveland…unless God has other plans."

David cringed inwardly, noticing the young woman's hopeful look, and wondered if he'd made a mistake inviting the pastor and his younger sister to the birthday dinner. The evening could prove to be difficult enough, depending on Nattie's disposition.

Looking toward the doorway, David saw Callie descending the staircase. "Here's Callie, now. Excuse me." David made for the doorway.

By the time Callie had reached the first floor, he was at the foot of the staircase. Caught off guard by her attractiveness, David gazed at her burgundy wool dress adorned with a simple string of pearls at her neck. The deep red of her gown emphasized the flush in her cheeks and highlighted the golden tinges of her honey-colored hair. As he focused his gaze, their eyes met, and her blush heightened.

"I see the party has already begun," she said. "I heard your voices as I came down the stairs."

"Now that you've joined us, everyone's here but the guest of honor." A sigh escaped him before he could harness it. "I invited our new pastor and his sister. I thought you might like to meet some of the younger people in town." He motioned for her to precede him. "We're in the living room."

She stepped around him, and he followed, watching the fullness of the skirt swish around her legs as she walked. The movement entranced him. Passing through the doorway at her side, he pulled his attention from her shapely legs to his guests.

As she entered the room, John's face brightened, and he rose, meeting her with his outstretched hand. "You're Callie."

"Yes, and you're David's pastor."

"John Spier," he said, then turned with a flourish. "And this is my sister, Mary Beth Spier."

"It's nice to meet you," Callie said, glancing at them both.

The young woman shot Callie an effusive grin. "And I'm certainly pleased to meet you. Being new in town myself, I've been eager to meet some young women who—"

"Have a seat, Callie." David gestured to the love seat. Interrupting Mary Beth was rude, but he couldn't bear to hear her announce again that she was one of the few single women in town. David chided himself. He should have used more sense than to invite a young woman to dinner who apparently saw him as a possible husband.

When he joined Callie on the love seat, she shifted closer to the arm and gracefully crossed her legs. His attention shifted to her slim ankles, then to her fashionable gray-and-burgundy brushed-leather pumps.

John leaned back in his chair and beamed. "I hope we'll see you at church on Sundays. We're a small congregation, but loaded with spirit. Although we could use

a benefactor to help us with some much-needed repairs."
His glance shot toward David.

David struggled with the grimace that crept to his
face, resulting, he was sure, in a pained smile. "Agnes
will announce dinner shortly. Then I'll go up and see if
I can convince Nattie to join us. I never know how she'll
respond." He eyed them, wondering if they understood.
"I've had a difficult time here since Sara… Well, let's
not get into that."

He wished he would learn to tuck his sorrow somewhere other than his shirtsleeve. He turned his attention to Callie. "Would you care for some mulled cider?"

She agreed, and he poured a mug of the warm brew.
He regarded her full, rosy lips as she took a sip. She
pulled away from the rim and nodded her approval.

His mind raced, inventing conversation. Tonight he
felt tired, and wished he could retire to his study and
spend the evening alone.

When Pastor John spoke, David felt himself relax.

"So where do you hail from, Callie?"

Without hesitation, she related a short personal history. Soon, Mary Beth joined in. David listened, pressing
himself against the cushions rather than participating.

To his relief, Agnes announced dinner.

"Well, finally," David said, embarrassed at his obvious relief. David climbed the stairs to find Nattie, as
Callie and the guests proceeded toward the dining room.

Callie held back and followed David's ascent with
her eyes. He was clearly uncomfortable. She wondered
if it was his concern for Nattie or the obvious flirtations
of Mary Beth.

In the dining room, Agnes indicated David's seating
arrangement. Mary Beth's focus darted from Callie to

Agnes; she was apparently wondering if the housekeeper had made an error. She was not seated next to David.

When he arrived back with Nattie clinging to his side, he surveyed the table without comment. Except for a glance at Callie, the child kept her eyes downcast. David pulled out her chair, and Nattie slid onto it, focusing on the folded napkin on her plate, her hands below the table. David sat and asked Pastor John to offer the blessing.

Callie lowered her eyes, but in her peripheral vision she studied Nattie's reaction to the scene around her. Until David said "Amen," Nattie's eyes remained closed, but when she raised her lids, she glimpsed around the table almost without moving her head.

When her focus settled on Callie, their gazes locked.

In that moment, something special happened. Would she call the fleeting glimmer—hope, premonition or fact? Callie wasn't sure. But a sweet tingle rose from the base of her spine to the tips of her fingers. Never before had she felt such a sensation.

Chapter Six

After dinner, Nattie withdrew, staring into space and mentally recoiling from those who addressed her. David blew the lit candles on her cake as they sang "Happy Birthday" and excused her before the gifts were opened, saying she needed to rest. The wrapped packages stood ignored like eager young ladies dressed in their finery for the cotillion, but never asked to dance.

Callie longed to go with the child to the second floor, but refrained from suggesting it. Tonight was her first evening in the house, so she was still a stranger. And Nattie needed her father.

After they left the room, Callie sat uneasily with the Spiers, lost in her own thoughts.

"Such a shame about the little girl," John said, looking toward the doorway. "Has she always been so withdrawn?"

With effort, Callie returned to the conversation.

"Since her mother died a couple of years ago. I'm sure she'll be herself in time."

Mary Beth sighed and murmured. "Such a shame. And poor David having to carry the burden all alone."

John turned sharply to his sister, his words a repri-
mand. "Mary Beth, we're never alone. God is always
with us."

"Oh, John, I know the Lord is with us. I meant, he
has no wife." Her look pleaded for forgiveness, and she
lowered her eyes.

Callie didn't miss Mary Beth's less-than-subtle meaning. "I don't think you need to worry about David. He'll
come through this a stronger person, I'm sure. And don't
forget, Mary Beth…"

The young woman looked curiously at Callie. "Don't
forget…?"

"David's not alone anymore. I'm here to help him."

Mary Beth paled, and a flush rose to Callie's cheeks.
Callie raised her hand nonchalantly to her face, feeling
the heat. Her comment astounded her. She sounded like
a woman fighting for her man.

When David returned to the parlor, the guests rose to
leave, and Callie took advantage of their departure to say
goodnight and head for her room. Confusion drove her
up the stairs. She felt protective and possessive of this
family—not only of Nattie, but of David. In less than a
day, the situation already tangled in her heart.

Callie woke with the morning light dancing on the
flowered wallpaper. She looked around the room, confused for a moment, and wondered where she was. Then
she remembered. She slid her legs over the edge of the
bed and sat, collecting her thoughts. How should she
begin? What could she do to help this child, now bound
in a cocoon, to blossom like a lovely butterfly?

One thing she knew. The process would take time.
She stepped down to the soft, lush carpet and padded

to the bathroom. A shower would awaken her body and her mind, she hoped.

When she finished dressing, she steadied herself, knowing what she had to do wouldn't be easy. She bowed her head, asking for God's wisdom and guidance, then left her room to face her first day.

Across the hall, Nattie's door stood open. Callie glimpsed inside. The child again sat on the window seat, but this time was looking at one of the books Callie had given her. Suddenly, she lifted her head and connected with Callie's gaze.

With her eyes focused on Nattie, Callie breathed deeply and strode purposefully to the doorway. "Well, good morning. Look at the wonderful sunshine."

Nattie followed her movement, but her face registered no response.

"When I woke, I saw the sun dance on my walls. I bet you did, too."

Nattie's attention darted to her wallpaper and back again to Callie. Was it tension or curiosity Callie saw settling there? She longed for a cup of coffee, but she'd made her move, and she'd stick it out. When she ambled toward the window seat, Nattie recoiled slightly. Callie only leaned over and glanced out the window. Nattie calmed.

"Did you look outside? The sun has turned the snow into a world of sparkling diamonds. And I've been told 'diamonds are a girl's best friend.'" She giggled light-heartedly, hoping Nattie would relax. "That's pretty silly, isn't it. I think the *snow* is a girl's best friend. Maybe we could take a walk outside today. We might even make a snowman."

Callie saw Nattie turn toward the window and scan

the fresh, glistening snow. She had piqued the child's interest.

"Nattie, I imagine you had breakfast already." She looked for some kind of response. None. "I'll go down and have a bite to eat. If you'd like to go outside, you can put on some warm stockings before I return. How's that?" Callie swung through the doorway with a wave and headed toward the stairs.

Would the child have the stockings on when she returned? If Nattie didn't want to talk, Callie would find another way to communicate until the child trusted her. Callie's thoughts thundered with questions. But mainly, she wanted to learn about Sara's death.

Silence filled the lower level of the house. She followed the aroma of breakfast and entered the dining room, where a lone table setting waited for her. She filled a plate with scrambled eggs and bacon from a small chafing dish, and poured a cup of coffee. This morning she didn't feel like eating alone. Looking for company, she carried the plate and cup through the door leading to the kitchen.

She found herself inside a butler's pantry, but through an arch, she spotted a stove and counter. Sounds emanated from that direction, and she headed through the doorway.

Agnes spun around, flinging her hand to her heart.

"Sorry, Agnes. I scared you."

The housekeeper's wide eyes returned to normal. "I didn't expect anyone, that's all. Can I get you something? I left your breakfast in the—" Her gaze lowered. "Oh, I see you have your plate."

Callie placed her dish and cup on the broad oak table.

"Do you mind if I eat in here with you, Agnes? I don't feel like eating alone this morning."

Agnes appeared flustered. She rushed forward with a damp cloth to wipe the already spotless table.

"I'm not trying to make work for you. The table's fine. I just thought you and I could get to know each other a little better. We're both employees here, and I'm sure familiarity can make our days more pleasant."

Agnes eyed her for a moment, then her face relaxed. "I sort of keep my place around here. Behind the scenes. You're more involved with Mr. Hamilton and Natalie. Except recently, while Mr. Hamilton looked for someone. But I'm at a loss. I never quite knew what to do for the child." She took a deep breath.

"Do you have a moment to join me in a cup of coffee?" Callie motioned to the empty chair across from her.

Agnes glanced at the chair, then at Callie. "Why, I don't mind if I do." She poured herself a mug of coffee from the warming pot and slipped onto the chair. "Black," she said, raising the mug. "I drink it black."

"Never could drink coffee black, myself. I like a little milk. I say 'cream,' but I prefer milk really." Callie smiled, and for the first time received a sincere smile in return. "So you've been here only a half year, if I remember correctly."

"Yes, about seven months now."

"I suppose following in Miriam's shadow was difficult."

Agnes nodded vigorously. "Oh yes, very hard. Miriam was part of this family forever. She's a wonderful woman. I knew her from church—Mr. Hamilton's church. That's how he knew me. When Miriam had to retire, he asked if I might be interested in the job. I'd been working for a family that had recently moved. Sort of destined, I suppose."

"Do you like working here?" In Callie's view, Agnes seemed to tiptoe around the house. The image didn't imply comfortable working conditions.

"Mr. Hamilton pays me well, and I'm always treated with respect."

Callie eyed her. "But you don't like working here."

Agnes fidgeted for a moment. "It's not that I don't like it here. The place isn't really homey, if you know what I mean. Mr. Hamilton has his moods. He's quiet and so is the child. Like the house is filled with shadows. He travels a lot, and I struggle to relate to the poor little thing upstairs. Yet whether he's here or not, she doesn't seem to notice one way or the other." She paused, drawing in a deep breath. "Now I don't mean Mr. Hamilton doesn't love his child. I'm sure he does."

"Don't apologize, Agnes. I know what you mean. Sometimes he seems as withdrawn as Nattie. Once in a while, I sense a chink in his wall, but he mends it as quickly as it appears."

Agnes's head bobbed again. "You do understand."

Callie nibbled on a piece of bacon. She was filled with curiosity. "Did you know Mrs. Hamilton?"

"So lovely. Yes, she played the church organ."

"The church organ? Well, that explains some things." Callie recalled David's comment about music.

"Such a sad thing, when she died."

Callie's pulse skipped through her veins. "You know how she died, then? I wasn't told."

"She was sick for a time. Cancer. They weren't married very long…maybe six or seven years. Such a shame."

Callie shook her head at the thought of someone dying

so young. "I wonder what caused Nattie to withdraw so badly. All children are close to their mothers, but her behavior seems so unusual. Odd, really."

"Wondered that myself. I didn't know the family real well. Just Sundays, that's all, and being a small town, you hear about troubles. They were a happy family until the missus got sick."

"I'll ask Mr. Hamilton sometime, but I don't want to sound nosy. If I had a clue to Nattie's problem, I'd have someplace to begin with her."

Callie rose and placed her empty plate and cup in the sink. "Mr. Hamilton is at work, I suppose."

"Yes, he left early this morning. Probably relieved you were here."

"I'm hoping to coax Nattie outside. She's in her room too much. She needs fresh air."

"That'd be nice. I hope she goes out with you."

"Me, too," Callie said, wondering what to do if her plan didn't work.

When she returned to the second floor, she found Nattie on the floor with a puzzle. Her feet were tucked beneath her, so Callie couldn't see her stockings. She scanned the room and saw a pair lying discarded on the floor. Her stomach flip-flopped. Had the child put on the thick ones?

"I'm back," Callie called as she made her entrance.

Nattie glanced at her, then turned her attention to the odd-shaped puzzle pieces spread out on the floor. Callie wandered in and sat next to her on the carpet. The child withdrew her hand for a moment, glancing at Callie with a slight frown, then changed mind and continued to locate the pieces.

Callie didn't speak, but searched until she found a

piece, then placed it in the correct spot. They continued until the last piece remained. Callie waited, letting Nattie fit in the last of the puzzle.

"That's wonderful, Nattie, and you got to put in the last piece. I love to find the last piece." She tittered, hoping to gain some reaction from the child.

Instead, Nattie slid the puzzle aside and pulled her feet out in front of her.

Relief spilled over Callie. The child had donned thicker stockings. "Good. I see you want to go outside. Now, it's my turn to get ready. Would you like to come with me to my room?" Callie rose, but Nattie remained where she was. "Okay, then, you wait here, and I'll be back in a minute. You'll need a sweater, too, to wear under your coat."

She slipped quickly from the room to collect her warm coat and gloves, and hoped she could find Nattie's coat, boots and gloves somewhere. She'd ask Agnes.

David pulled down the driveway as dusk settled. Once again, he'd put in a long workday. The sky had faded to a grayish purple, and the ripples of glistening snow he had admired early in the morning now looked dull and shadowed. As he neared the house, he felt a twinge at his nerve endings, and he applied the brake and peered at the snow-covered lawn.

Sets of footprints had trampled through the snow. He shifted into Park and opened his door, intrigued by the sight of the boot marks. The woman's print would have meant little, but beside the larger indentions, he saw the smaller footprint of his daughter.

In a trancelike state, he followed the prints that wove through the evergreens and around the elms. In an open area, he paused. On the ground, he stared at imprints of angels. Heads, wings and bodies pressed into the snow. But, sadly, all adult angels. No seraphim or cherubim. No Nattie. Only the impression of the household's newest employee stamped a design into the fresh snow.

Yet a bright thought pierced his disappointment. Though Nattie had not made an angel, she had been outside and had walked in the snow—more progress in one day than he had seen in months. He should be grateful for each small gift.

He looked again at the fanned angel impressions at his feet. He counted three, four. He pictured the young woman, flinging herself to the ground, flailing her arms and legs to amuse his silent child. Callie's laughter rang in his mind. Angel? Yes, perhaps God had sent a human angel to watch over his daughter.

He dashed to the car and drove the short distance to the house. His eager feet carried him up the steps, and when he opened the front door, the house had come alive. In place of the usual silence, music played softly from a radio or television program in the parlor, and with anticipation he glanced into the room before hanging his coat. Callie sat curled on the sofa with her feet tucked beneath her, a book in her hand.

She heard him, for she raised her eye from the book, and a playful look covered her face. "Hello. You're home late this evening."

From the doorway, he stared at her in the firelight, his coat still clutched in his hand. "Too often, I'm afraid."

"Let me take your coat, Mr. Hamilton."

David jumped slightly and turned apologetically to Agnes. "Oh, thanks." After he released his coat to her care, he strode into the parlor, his eyes riveted to the firelight glinting on Callie's golden-brown hair.

He fell into the chair across from her. "I noticed a slight miracle outside when I came up the driveway."

Her lips parted in an easy smile. "The angels?"

Watching the animation on her face, he nodded.

"Only mine, I'm afraid. I tried." She lifted a bookmark, slid it between the pages and closed the volume.

"Oh, don't feel discouraged. Nattie went outside with you. We haven't been able to move her beyond these doors. In one day, you've worked wonders. I'm amazed."

Her eyes brightened. "I'm pleased then. I thought I was a minimal failure."

"Not at all." A scent of beef and onions drifted through the doorway and his stomach growled. "You've eaten?"

"No." She shook her head, and her hair glistened in the light. "I waited for you."

"That's nice."

"But Nattie ate, I'm afraid."

"Let me run up and see her, and I'll hurry right down." He rose and dashed up the stairway.

Callie watched him hurry away and filled with sadness, thinking of his excitement over something as simple as his child's walk in the snow. Her attention fell to her lap and the book that lay there.

Then his words rang in her head, and she raised her hand to her chest to calm the fluttering from within. "That's nice," he'd said, when she told him she'd waited for supper. Callie closed her eyes. Why did she care what he said? She was an employee doing her job. That was all.

His footsteps left the oriental carpet and hit the shiny

wood floor at the entrance to the parlor, and she looked toward the doorway.

"Agnes says dinner is ready," he said.

She rose, and as they neared the dining room, the aroma stirred her hunger. A low rumble from her stomach echoed in the hallway. She glanced at him apologetically.

"Don't feel bad. My stomach isn't complaining loudly, but I'm starving. You shouldn't have waited, but I'm glad you did."

A flush of excitement rose in her, until she heard his next sentence.

"I'm anxious to hear about your day with Nattie."

I'm being foolish. Lord, keep my mind focused on my purpose in this home. Not on silly thoughts. Her flush deepened in her embarrassment, and she hoped he might not notice in the softened light of the dining room doorway.

As they stepped into the room, Agnes came through the kitchen entrance with a steaming platter. She placed it on the table, then hit the switch as she exited, brightening the lights above the table.

David pulled out a chair for Callie, and she sat, waiting for him to be seated. The platter, sitting before them, aroused her senses. A mound of dark roasted beef was surrounded by sauteed onions, browned potatoes and carrots. She bowed her head to murmur a silent prayer, but before she asked God's blessing, David's warm voice split the silence.

He offered thanks for the food and the day, then he thanked God for Callie's presence in the house. A heated blush rose again to her cheeks. Now in the brightened room, when David looked up from his prayer, she knew her pink cheeks glowed.

"Sorry," Callie said, touching her cheeks, "I'm not used to being blessed along with a roast."

An unexpected burst of laughter rolled from David's chest. Agnes halted in the doorway, balancing a gravy boat and a salad bowl in apparent surprise. She looked from David to Callie, then added a smile to her face as she approached the table.

"This roast looks and smells wonderful, Agnes," David said, the merriment still lingering in his tone.

"Why, thank you, Mr. Hamilton." She placed the items on the table and scurried from the room with a final wide-eyed glance over her shoulder.

"Poor Agnes hasn't heard much laughter in the house since she came. I think I've surprised her." His hazel eyes crinkled at the edges as he looked at Callie.

"Then it's about time," Callie said lightly, trying to ignore the beating pulse in her temples. "'Laughter is good for all that ails you,' my father used to say."

"He was right. Laughter is music everyone can sing."

The word *music* seemed to catch them both off guard, and they each bent over their plates, concentrating on filling their stomachs. They ate quietly, keeping their eyes directed at the meat and potatoes. Callie searched her mind for something to draw him out again and distract her own thoughts.

"I borrowed a book from the library. What a lovely room. And so many wonderful books." She pictured the room next to the library. She'd turned the knob, but the door had been locked. Though curious what the room was, she didn't ask. "I hope you don't mind about the book."

"No, not at all. You're welcome to read every one."

"I'd have to live here forever to do that."

He lifted his eyes to hers. "Yes, I suppose you would."

Silence lingered again, until David asked about Nattie. The rest of the meal was filled with tales of Callie's day with the child. They both were comfortable with the topic, and the conversation flowed easily until the meal ended.

When they reentered the foyer, she said goodnight and climbed the stairs. But the *click* of a door lock startled her, and she spun around. David slipped quietly into the room at the bottom of the stairs. Another faint *click* told her he had locked himself in. The sound bolted her to the floor, as her dreams rose up to haunt her. She stood a moment until she gained composure, then continued up the stairs.

Chapter Seven

After breakfast, Callie knocked on Nattie's door. Since the day in the snow, two weeks had passed with no new breakthrough.

Today, Nattie sat staring out the window with a doll in her lap. Pieces of doll clothing lay at her side, and Callie sensed she had stopped in mid-play. The doll wore a diaper and dress, with the shoes and bonnet waiting in a pile.

Nattie glanced at Callie, but turned her attention to the doll.

Callie ambled to the window seat and sat for a moment before she spoke. "What a pretty baby you have there. But the poor child is only half dressed. What about her shoes and bonnet?"

Nattie ignored Callie, though occasionally she looked curiously at her and then lowered her eyes again.

Callie wondered what would make a difference. How could she get through to the lonely little girl. "Would you like to color? Or maybe we could draw some pictures?" Nothing. Whatever she encouraged Nattie to do, Callie would first do it alone. That much she had learned. She shifted to the floor and pulled out one of Nattie's puzzles. Tumbling the pieces onto the floor, she turned them so all the picture pieces were facing up.

Nattie glanced at her, swiveling so her legs dangled over the window seat. She lay the doll to the side and watched.

Callie began forming the outer rim of the puzzle. When the frame was nearly complete, Nattie slid from the bench and joined her. She peered at the pieces to see if the fit matched, and often they did. Each time the child joined her, Callie felt they had made some progress.

Callie hummed a tune as she worked the puzzle. The sound surprised her. Humming, like singing, had vanished from her life. Today she felt like murmuring the simple melody, and best of all, Nattie eyed her more than usual. The child seemed comforted by the droning sound. Certainly her mother had hummed to her, too. Perhaps the memory soothed her.

Eventually, Callie rose and stared outside. The past days had seemed lonely. David had gone to Atlanta on a business trip, and except for an occasional conversation with Agnes, her world was as silent as Nattie's.

March would be along shortly, and she longed for warmer weather when she and Nattie could go for walks and run in the fresh air. Maybe then the child would warm the same way the summer sun would heat the soil, encouraging new shoots to sprout. Nattie, too, might come alive again.

As David finished his breakfast, Callie entered the dining room. Each time she appeared, a deep longing filled him.

"Good morning," she said brightly, and turned to the buffet.

David returned her greeting and watched as she took a plate and scooped up a serving spoonful of scrambled eggs. With toast and sausage on her plate, she sat on David's left. "How was your trip?"

"Fine. Too long actually, but that's business."

They hadn't talked much recently. All he'd learned was that nothing dramatic had occurred as yet with regard to Nattie. Though his hopes remained high, the process seemed to be taking forever.

"I wouldn't know much about business. I've always been a nurse. Whole different career. Though, we notice how quiet it is when you're away." She lowered her eyes, focusing on her plate and scooping egg onto her fork.

David knew exactly what she meant. Before she had come, the house had seemed a tomb. He sipped his coffee, hating to tell her he would be gone again that evening.

"I have a dinner invitation this evening, so I won't be home. I suppose you can endure one more night without my tantalizing conversation."

As he spoke, her face faded to disappointment. "One more night, huh? When I took the job I didn't have any guarantees of dinner entertainment, so I suppose I can handle it." She put a smile on her face, but David had learned enough about Callie to know the smile was to appease him.

He folded his napkin and laid it next to his plate. "To be honest, I'd rather stay home."

"Business dinner?"

"Probably, but on the pretense of a social evening at the parsonage."

Callie's face gave way to a wry grin. "Ah, an invitation from Mary Beth, no doubt."

A sigh escaped him before he could control it. "No doubt." He eyed his wristwatch and rose, longing to stay and talk. He had forgotten how comfortable it was to sit after a meal and chat. He and Sara had often lingered at the table long after the meal was finished. He could easily do the same with Callie. But his business waited him. "I'd better be on my way."

"I'm sure you'll have fun." Callie tilted her face toward him, and her words sounded to David as if they wavered between sarcasm and wit.

"How about a wager?"

"Sorry, kind sir, I don't make bets. It's sinful, you know."

Her smile sent a tingle through him, and he glanced at his face as he passed a mirror in the entry to see if the unexpected sensation showed.

"I suppose we should have been polite and invited Callie to join us," Mary Beth gushed, after they settled into the cozy living room after dinner. "I don't know where my mind was."

I do, David thought as he gallantly tried to smile at her comment. "I'm sure she understands." Thinking of Callie's wry smile, he realized she understood Mary Beth Spier was looking for a husband—but in the wrong direction.

"Perhaps next time," John said. "We should enjoy each other's company more often. Other than Sundays, I might add."

David enjoyed his private joke. If John were to be perfectly honest, he might also add that he didn't see

David on many Sundays, either. David waited, wondering where John was going from there.

"Speaking of Sundays," John said, "we certainly miss having an organ for worship. Looking back at the records, I see your wife was the organist for a couple of years."

David gathered his wits, keeping his face unemotional. "Yes, she was. I believe a lady named Ruta Dryer filled in for my wife while she was ill...and after Sara died."

"Yes, I noticed that, too. But then the organ needed some work, and I'm afraid financially we haven't been able to make those repairs."

"I see," David said, waiting for the pitch.

"I wonder if you'd considered helping out with that little project. I imagine we could find an organist—but first, we need the instrument."

David bit his lip, struggling to control his emotions. "Sara's death was a tremendous loss for my daughter and me, as you can imagine. I haven't given much thought to the organ since then. I've been concerned about my child, and to be honest, thoughts of the organ music fill me with some raw spots yet. You'll have to let me think about it."

"Oh, certainly, I wasn't suggesting that—"

"I may seem self-indulgent, but the congregation has adjusted to the piano. And I need to deal with my own problems—and my daughter's—before I deal with someone else's."

"Yes. Do take your time. I suppose I should have been more considerate in my request."

"Don't worry about it. How would you know what goes on in my head?"

Mary Beth leaned across the table and latched onto David's arm. "I wish I could help. I'm sure life isn't complete without…well, being alone and with your daughter, too. Hiring a woman to fill in for Nattie's mother is all right, but—"

"Callie is far more than a fill-in. She's a professional nurse, well-trained. I'm very hopeful that her influence with Nattie will bring her out of her cocoon. Callie's full of spirit and a delightful…" He looked at their astounded faces and realized he had gone overboard in Callie's defense.

Mary Beth stared at him wide-eyed. "Oh, I didn't mean she isn't capable. I'm sure she is. I mean your daughter has needs, but so do—"

"David knows what you meant, Mary Beth," John sputtered. "We shouldn't dwell on the subject. Would you care to play a game of Chinese checkers, David?"

Better than the Chinese water torture you're putting me through. David nearly laughed aloud at his thought.

On the first Sunday in March, late in the afternoon, Callie sat curled on the sofa in the library, reading Jane Austen's *Mansfield Park.* She'd read the author's other novels, enjoying the wit and social commentary on the lives of women in the early eighteen-hundreds.

Sometimes, she felt her own life was tangled in social principles.

Today for the first time since her arrival, Callie had gone to church. She had chosen to worship at a new, larger church on Washington Avenue, one with a large vibrant pipe organ. She longed to hear something uplifting, something to take the ache from her heart and give her patience and courage.

Even in church, for the past few years, she had avoided singing. But today she raised her voice, and her spirit lifted with the music. *Sweet hour of prayer, sweet hour of prayer.* Prayer? Had she prayed as she ought to have done? Or had she leaned on her own humble abilities, forgetting God's miracles?

The pastor's voice shot through her mind, like an answer to her question, with the Scripture reading. *"Then you will call upon Me and go and pray to Me, and I will listen to you. And you will seek Me and find Me, when you search for Me, with all your heart."* The morning's message settled into her thoughts. Pray, she must.

Now, as the sun lowered in the sky, Callie snapped on the light. Doing so, a shadow fell across her page. She glanced up to see David standing a distance from her, observing her silently.

He slid into a chair across from her. "Disappointed?"

"Disappointed?"

"With Nattie. I suppose you imagined by now she'd be playing like any six-year-old?" His face told his own story.

"I'm optimistic again. But you're disappointed, I think."

He lowered his head, studying his entwined fingers laying in his lap. "Oh, a little, I suppose. I don't know what to expect, really."

"You can't expect more from her than you do from yourself."

His head shot upward, and Callie swallowed, wondering why she had been so blunt.

"What do you mean?" His brows knit tightly, and his eyes squinted in the artificial light.

Well, here goes. Callie took a deep breath. "You can't

hide behind these walls, totally. Not with your business. But look at you. You aren't living, either. Just marking days off the calendar."

"That's what you think, huh?"

"I suppose I'm too forward."

"I expect nothing less."

His eyes, despite the abrupt comment, crinkled in amusement.

"I should be angry at you, but I imagine you're telling the truth."

"That's what I see. Maybe you have another side, but here, everything is shut off. The doors are closed as if you want nothing to escape. Or is it, nothing to enter? You build walls around yourself…or lock yourself in your secret room."

His face pinched again. "Secret room?"

Callie tilted her head forward. "Yes, the room next door. The locked door."

He released a quiet chuckle. "That's my study. I suppose I've gotten into the habit of keeping it locked. All my business secrets are in that room." He rose. "Come. I'll show you."

Callie felt her cheeks grow hot. "No, I didn't mean—"

"Up, up." He reached down and took her hand, pulling her to her feet. "I don't want you to think I have bodies locked away in there or skeletons hiding in the closets."

"I'm sorry. Really."

But her pleading did no good. David wrapped his arm around her shoulder and marched her to the hallway. He turned the handle, and the door opened without a key. He glanced at her with a playful, smug look and pushed open the door.

Though she felt foolish being led in as if she were a

naughty child, she savored the warmth of his arm embracing her. She longed to be in his sturdy arms, feeling safe and secure. But as she stepped into the room, he raised his hands to her shoulders and pivoted her in one direction, then the other, showing her the room.

"See. Not one body."

His voice rippled through her. She turned toward him, her eyes begging forgiveness. "I wasn't suggesting you had something bad in here. I meant, you lock yourself away. There's a difference."

He looked deeply into her eyes, and her heart stopped momentarily, dragging her breath from her. When the beat returned, its rhythm galloped through her like a horse and rider traversing rocky ground. Faster. Slower. Faltering. She struggled for control.

"You're right, I suppose," he said.

His words unlocked their gaze. But in the lengthy silence, Callie became flustered. "I'm right?"

"Yes, about locking myself away from the world."

He moved into the room. "Since you're here, come in. As you see, your sitting room is directly above this one. It's the tower room."

The tower intrigued her, and she moved voluntarily into the depth of the uniquely shaped room. The heavy wooden paneling darkened his study in comparison to her sunny room. Centered on one wall, his vast desk faced the outer hall. Tall shelves and a row of file cabinets stood nearby. A leather sofa and chair sat in the center of the room on an elegant Persian carpet.

"All man. No woman's touch here," she said.

A fleeting grin dashed across his face. "This room is mine, remember." His right hand gestured toward the tower room, and she wandered through the archway.

Only two windows lit the circular room, smaller than hers above. As she turned, her eyes were drawn to another piano, a console, against an inner wall.

She stepped forward, noticing manuscript paper spread along the stand. She turned to him in surprise. "You write music?"

"Not really."

She felt him withdraw, swiftly rebuilding the wall he had opened when he let her enter his sanctuary. "But this is an unfinished manuscript." Her eyes sought his.

"I used to write music. I haven't touched that in a long time. I haven't played in a long time."

She nodded. Neither had she. She'd let the music in her life die the way part of her had died that terrible day. Yet, today, truth rose from the solemn moment. David would never live again until he lived fully. And neither would she.

A sound caused them to turn toward the foyer. Agnes stood in the doorway of the study.

"Dinner's ready when you are, Mr. Hamilton."

"Fine, we're coming now."

Callie pulled herself from the room. "I'll get Nattie," she said, hurrying into the hallway. She climbed the stairs, trembling over her second revelation of the day. Earlier, she'd considered the importance of prayer. Now, she knew she could ask no one else to join the living unless she lived herself.

After breakfast two weeks later, Callie and Nattie lay together, coloring on the parlor floor. David stepped into the room wearing his overcoat, his briefcase in his hand. He leaned down and kissed Nattie's head. "Goodbye, Nat."

Callie tilted her head and looked at him standing above her.

"We'll see you later."

"Yes, I shouldn't be too late. By the way, this Friday I have a meeting in Indianapolis. I don't know if you need to make a trip home, but you're welcome to ride along. The meeting should run only a couple of hours. Perhaps you'd like to visit with your mother."

Callie rose from the floor, surprised at his offer. "Yes, I'd like that. I know my mother would enjoy the visit, and I have a few things I can pick up while I'm there." Retrieving her lightweight clothing excited her more than did visiting with her mother, but she kept that to herself. Most of all she'd enjoy the private time with David. "I'd love to go, if you don't mind."

"Not at all, I'd enjoy the company. And Agnes said she'd be happy to keep an eye on Nattie."

Their gazes connected, and Callie sought the flashing green specks that glinted in his eyes. A flush rose to her neck, and she looked away from him. "I'll call my mother then, so she'll be expecting me."

He nodded and took a step backward toward the door. "Good." He spun around, and she heard the front door close.

Nattie paused momentarily, almost as if she would speak, but instead, she lowered her head and concentrated on her picture. Recently, her dark-toned coloring had given way to brighter shades, one success Callie had noticed. Nattie used a yellow crayon to color the sun, then traded for a medium green to fill in the grass. Big progress in Callie's view.

She stretched out on the floor again next to the child and turned back to her picture: red tulips, green leaves, yellow daffodils. It reminded her that spring lay on their doorstep. Then, without direction, her thoughts jumped to the changing colors in David's eyes. In the morning light that streamed through the window, the colors had shifted and altered, creating earthy, vibrant hues. Her heart skipped at the vision, and the image hummed within her.

Humming. Callie eased back on her elbows and held her breath. She hadn't been humming, but a sweet lilting melody rose to her ears. Without moving, she listened. Softly, Nattie hummed as she concentrated on the coloring book, her silence finally broken.

Callie's pulse raced, and her joy lifted as high as the prayer of thanks she whispered in her mind for the wondrous gift.

Chapter Eight

With David at the wheel, Callie leaned back and enjoyed the passing scenery. Though spring was yet a few days away, a fresh green hue brightened the landscape, and a new warmth promised things to come.

David, too, seemed to sense Nattie's own promise of things to come. Since hearing of her latest progress, David smiled more often. He referred to Callie as another miracle worker, though she reminded him more than once that God worked miracles, she didn't.

David glanced at the dashboard clock. "I figure we'll arrive about eleven. I'll drop you off and still have time to get to the meeting." He shot her a glance. "I should only be a couple of hours."

"Just come when you're finished. I'll be ready I'm sure." She'd probably be ready sooner. Yet she had to admit, she and her mother had plenty to talk about. She had spoken to Grace only briefly since arriving in Bedford.

"Are you sure? Maybe I should call."

Callie opened her shoulder bag and jotted down the telephone number. "Here you go."

"Slip it in my pocket so I remember to take it with me."

She leaned across the space between them, slipping the note into his nearest suit coat pocket. Her fingers tingled at the touch of the soft cashmere wool, and she warmed at his nearness. *Don't get carried away,* she chided herself.

Romantic fantasies had long disappeared from her dreams. She had never known a man before or after the experience of her child's conception. The thought of intimacy with any man frightened her.

As a teen, she had dreamed of the special day when she would dress in a white gown and float down the aisle as a bride, giving herself to a loving man, exploring and learning about love and passion. The dream had vanished as quickly as her virginity, and in its place, shame and guilt festered like an infected wound.

"You're so quiet," David said.

"Sorry. Just thinking."

"I hope they're nice thoughts."

She closed her eyes and avoided the truth. "Yes, they're very nice." She couldn't tell him the private things that filled her mind. No one would ever hear those thoughts. Another reason she could never fall in love.

After a short distance, the outskirts of Indianapolis spread along the horizon, and David soon left her at Grace's front door. She raised her hand as he pulled away, then she entered the house. She expected her mother to be hanging out the window, waiting for her, but instead the rooms were silent.

"Mom," she called. She wandered to the kitchen, where dishes lay piled on the countertop. Very unlike her mother.

"Mother." She listened and heard a noise above her.

"Callie?"

"You're upstairs, I take it." Callie climbed the steps, and saw her mother standing in the hallway, still in her bathrobe. Concern prickled her. Grace never slept late. "What's up with you?"

"I don't know," Grace answered, seeming confused. "I didn't feel well this morning."

"Or last night," Callie added.

"What do you mean?" Grace shuffled down the hall-way.

Callie stood by the stairs, transfixed. "The dishes. You didn't clean up after dinner last night. That's not like you at all. Something's wrong. You need to see a doctor."

Grace swished the air with her hand as if erasing her words. "I don't need a doctor. Probably just a little spring cold. You know how they can be."

She studied her mother's face. Grace's mouth was pulled to the side in a faint grimace. Dark circles ringed her eyes, raccoonlike against her pale skin. "I don't know, Mom."

"You go down and make us some coffee, and I'll get dressed. I'll look much better when I wash my face and comb my hair."

Callie moved to her mother's side, giving her a brief hug. "Okay, but we'll talk about this when you come down."

When she returned to the kitchen, she put on a pot of coffee and rinsed last night's dishes, then loaded the dish-washer. It hadn't been run for a couple of days. Callie's concern was not the untouched dishes or her mother's appearance. Grace loved to play the martyr. Yet today, she denied valiantly that something was wrong. Callie knew something was *very* wrong.

She started the dishwasher, then looked into the refrigerator. "Old Mother Hubbard's cupboard," she said aloud to herself. Inside, she found three eggs and the end of a bread loaf. When the eggs were scrambled and in the frying pan, Callie popped the bread into the toaster. Her mind worked over the problem. No question. Grace wasn't herself. Living two hours away, she'd have to depend on Ken to keep an eye on their mother. She'd call him after breakfast.

Grace entered the kitchen as the toast popped.

"Perfect timing, Mom. I made us some breakfast." Though Callie had eaten, she joined her mother at the table. She heaped the egg on Grace's plate, giving herself only a tablespoon full.

"Now, I'm not going to leave you without knowing what happened. When did you get sick?"

"Please, Callie, I'm fine. Wait until you're an old woman. Then you'll understand about being tired…and confused once in a while." She nibbled the toast.

"I'm tired and confused now, Mom. Age has nothing to do with it. I think you need to see a doctor. You're not ninety. You're only in your mid-sixties. I'll call Ken before I go."

"I felt fine until yesterday afternoon. I got a terrible headache. Sort of achy in my left arm. I think it scared me. I laid down for a while, and it seemed to pass."

Callie pictured the dishes piled on the counter. The problem hadn't passed as fast as Grace wanted her to believe. Rather than press her mother, she allowed Grace to change the subject, and filled her in on Bedford, her progress with Nattie, and a description of the lovely house.

As the time approached to leave, Callie made a doctor's appointment for Grace and phoned Ken. "I know you're busy, but could you please see Mom gets to the doctor?"

"Are you that worried?" Ken asked, sounding as if he thought she was being foolish.

"Look, Ken, she said her arm ached, and she had a bad headache. We can't play around with symptoms. Let's let a doctor tell her it's nothing."

"I suppose you're right."

"And you really should check with her every day or so, at least until she's feeling better."

"Easy for you. You go off and let me do the work, huh?"

"For a change, it won't hurt you. The thought of leaving her here alone bothers me."

"Where's our dear sister Patricia, when we need her?"

Callie sighed at her brother's complaining. "In California, where she's always been. Quit trying to wheedle out of this. Just check on her once in a while. Can you do that?"

"Okay, I give."

Though his voice was teasing, Ken left Callie less than confident, but there was little else she could do. Before she walked away from the telephone, David called to say he'd be later than expected.

When he finally arrived, Callie hurried out to his car. "Would you mind coming in a minute? Mom insists upon meeting you."

David turned off the ignition and stepped out into the afternoon sunshine, a knowing look etching his face. "We have to make mothers happy."

Callie led him up the porch steps. "I'm worried about

her, actually." She glanced at him over her shoulder and grasped the doorknob.

He paused. "Something wrong?"

"Yes, but I'm not sure what. She seems ill, but she denies it."

David's brows furrowed as Callie led him inside. As they came into the living room, Grace eyed him.

"Mother," Callie said, "this is my employer, David Hamilton. David, my mother, Grace Randolph."

David reached forward as if to shake hands, but Grace's arms remained folded against her chest. Unabashed, he retraced his hand and tucked it into his pocket. "I'm sorry to hear you're not feeling well, Mrs. Randolph."

"I'm fine. My daughter lives so far away she's forgotten what I look like."

"Mother," Callie said, controlling her irritation, "you are not fine. I've called Ken, and I want you to promise to call me after you see the doctor."

"It's nothing. You're making a mountain out of nothing."

Callie rested her hand on her mother's shoulder. "Let the doctor tell me that, okay?"

Grace snorted her protest.

"Promise you'll call," Callie said.

After a lengthy pause, Grace nodded her head.

Callie bent and brushed a kiss on her cheek. "We have to go, Mom. Please do as I say."

Callie gave David a desperate look and stepped backward. David proceeded ahead of her and held the door open while Callie gave her mother a final wave, then stepped outside.

When they had settled in the car, Callie rubbed her

temples. "She won't call. I'll have to call Ken. I pray he knows something. Sometimes brothers are useless when it comes to asking questions."

David glanced at her. "Do you want to drive up and take her yourself?"

Callie sighed. "I don't know. Ken should be able to handle it. I'll call him when we get home. Maybe I'll feel better."

"That's fine, but if you need to come here, Agnes can keep an eye on Nattie for the day."

"Thanks." She caught his image in the rearview mirror. His concern touched her.

Callie leaned her head against the headrest, and they drove in silence until they passed the city limits of Indianapolis. A few miles beyond the Franklin exit, she straightened in her seat. "Sorry. I'm not good company."

"No problem. Did you get a little rest?"

"Yes, I think I drifted off for a minute. I've spent my life in silent battles with my mother, and now that something's wrong, I'm dealing with some guilt. And a lot of worry."

"That's part of life." David drew his shoulders upward in a deep sigh. "I think we all do that, Callie. It's so easy to take things for granted. Complain and grumble. Then when we're gripped by worry, we have all the 'I wishes' and 'I should haves' thrashing around inside us."

"I want to resolve some of those things with my mom before anything happens. I guess this scare reminded me of that."

"Good. Look at the positive side. And speaking of positive thoughts, how's your stomach? Mine's empty. They only gave us coffee and pastries at the meeting. No good wholesome food. Did you eat at your mother's?"

"I made her breakfast, but I only nibbled."

"Then we'll stop for dinner. We should reach Columbus about five o'clock. I think Weinantz opens about then. The food is excellent. I called Agnes and warned her not to cook for us."

A strange shyness filled her. David had planned ahead for their dinner together. She'd chased such thoughts from her foolish dreams, and now he was making her hopes come true. She could deal with fantasy, but reality made her vulnerable. *The boss is taking his employee to dinner. Nothing more.* She repeated the words over and over in her mind until they reached Columbus.

The town proved to be a surprise. In the middle of small, turn-of-the-century communities, Columbus rose like a contemporary misfit. Buildings of modern design filled the city center; buses carried tourists through the streets to view the renowned architecture. The restaurant lived up to David's praise, and after their meal, Callie relaxed over coffee, the worries of the day softening.

David studied her concerned face, as she sipped from the steaming cup. For the first time since they had left her mother's, a slight smile touched her rosy lips. "You look more relaxed."

"I feel better. The meal was wonderful," Callie said.

Her smile warmed him. "I'm glad. I know what worry can do. And I've had the same guilty thoughts myself. I look at Nattie's situation and blame myself. After Sara's death, I wasn't there for her. Such a little girl, and I crept away like a wounded animal. I feel terrible about that."

"I think it's more than that, David. Something happened. Something more than Sara's death. I don't know exactly what I mean, but her silence seems deeper than normal grief. You know, children are usually known for bouncing back."

"They do." Her comment pushed him deeper into thought. "I don't know. I've always blamed myself." Was she right? What could have happened? Sara's death was no surprise. And still, it hit him harder than he would ever have imagined. Then, what about Nattie? Could something else have happened?

He gazed into Callie's perplexed-looking eyes, and felt his chest tighten. Bluer than the sky. Rich, deep and filled with her own secrets. What dark moments hid behind those lovely eyes?

"What you've been able to do for Nattie makes me so grateful," he said. "You've already made a difference in her life." In *my* life, he thought, feeling his pulse waver as he regarded her. "Nattie leaves her room now…and the humming. Something more will happen. I sense it."

Callie's face tensed. She lowered her eyes, then raised them shyly. "Could we talk a little? About things that might bother you?"

A knot of foreboding formed in his stomach. "Like what?"

"Tell me about Sara's death. You've never said anything, and like I said, I suspect something more happened to Nattie than losing a mother. Was Nattie with Sara when it happened? Would she feel to blame for some reason?"

"To blame? No, how could she?" He closed his eyes for a moment, the awful memories rippling through him. "Sara had cancer. Leukemia. Nattie couldn't feel responsible for that. Anyway, she was only four."

"I know, but children overhear things that they don't understand. They fill in the blanks, make up their own stories, and things get out of context. I just wondered if that might be possible."

"No, I'm sure that didn't happen." Though he said no, thoughts galloped through his mind as he wondered if something had been said to make Nattie feel Sara's death was her fault.

"If she misunderstood something, anything, it might explain her silence," Callie repeated. "I suppose I'm grasping for it all to make sense."

"I've done the same. Wondered. Worried."

"When did you learn your wife had cancer?"

An overwhelming sorrow washed over him, and the answer stuck in his throat. Callie's question disturbed thoughts he'd tucked away. Now they came crashing into his memory. Without knowing, she was treading on raw nerve endings and deep painful wounds that had yet to heal.

Her drawn face overflowed with tenderness. "I'm sorry," she said. "I guess I'm dredging up hurtful memories. I just thought, the more I understand, the more I'll know what to look for."

He reached across the table and touched her hand clasped in a tense fist. At first, she flinched at his touch, but in a heartbeat her hand relaxed.

"You're right. On both counts." He drew his hand away, balling it, too, into a fist. "Sara had leukemia before we married…but we were hopeful. Like all young, idealistic couples, we thought love could solve every problem—even cancer."

"Oh, David, I'm so sorry. I had no idea. And then when she got pregnant…" Callie tossed herself back against the cushion with a lengthy sigh. "Never mind, I understand."

He grimaced. "Thanks." But she didn't really understand. Not everything. He was not ready to open all the wounds. He hid behind her misconceptions in safety. What would she think of him if she knew the whole story? He leaned against the seat and folded his arms across his chest. He had told her enough.

Chapter Nine

The following week Callie stayed in the parlor after dinner, trying to concentrate on her book. Concern dogged her as she assessed Ken's surprise telephone call.

"Dr. Sanders thinks Mom may have had a minor stroke."

"Minor stroke? How bad is that? Major. Minor. The thought scares me, Ken."

"He'll know more after he gets the results of the MRI test. It's scheduled for next week. Apparently, it takes some kind of picture of the brain."

"MRI. Yes, it's magnetic resonance imaging."

"Thank you, Florence."

"Florence? Oh, Nightingale." She snickered. "Poor Florence wouldn't know anything about an MRI. Anyway, how's Mom doing? Do you think I should come up there?"

"She's good. I don't notice a difference."

Callie rolled her eyes. "Do you really think you'd notice?"

"Thanks, sister dear."

"You're welcome. You'll call me as soon as you hear something."

"Don't worry. She's okay…really."

When Callie hung up the receiver, she had a tremendous urge to get in her car and go to Indianapolis. At dinner, she told David. Again, he encouraged her to go if she would feel better, but wisdom stepped in. She'd wait to hear the test results.

After the meal, David went to his study to work, and she relaxed on the sofa, her legs stretched on the cushion and her feet over the edge. Staring at the book propped in her hand, she saw only a blur, as her thoughts twisted and turned. Nattie had carried storybooks down with her before dinner, and she lay on the floor nearby, flipping through the pages.

When David stepped into the room, she and Nattie glanced up.

"Hmm? All the ladies have their noses buried in a book, I see." He walked to Nattie and stroked her hair with his fingers.

Callie watched her raise the book toward her father, and her heart stood still when she heard the child's soft, sweet voice.

"Read to me, Daddy."

"Nattie," David gasped. His eyes widened and his face paled momentarily, then brightened with happiness. "I sure will, sweetheart." He scooped her up in his arms and carried her to the chair.

Callie's heart skipped and hammered in wild rhythm. She fixed on Nattie's face, witnessing the special moment of her first full sentence since her mother's death. Where one sentence lived, there were two. Then three. It was only a matter of time.

Glowing with rapture, David read two storybooks without stopping, holding the child in his arms. She hugged him tightly when he finished, and for the first time, Callie witnessed Nattie showing affection. Callie and David shared the special moment with quiet looks of elation, not wanting to break the spell.

After Nattie had gone to bed, David returned, bounding into the room like a man saved from a firing squad. Callie rose at his exuberant entrance, feeling her own joy. In a flash, he closed the distance between them, grasping her in his arms and pulling her to his chest.

"Thank you. Thank you," he whispered into her hair.

His warmth surrounded her, and the heat of surprise rose to her face.

"What you've brought into our lives has been like a miracle. Two years I've waited and longed for a single sentence, and tonight—" he looked into her eyes "—my prayer was answered."

A gasp escaped her, and David stepped back abruptly as if embarrassed.

"I'm sorry," he said. "I didn't mean to frighten you."

"Surprised me was all. Not frightened." Though she said the words, the truth was that she was shaken by his actions. She hadn't been that close to a man since… She remembered her father's arms comforting her, but that had been so long ago.

"No, I scared you. I saw the look in your face. I'm sorry. But I didn't think. Tonight's been so wonderful."

"Oh, David, it is wonderful." Though thrilled with the moment, her reaction concerned her. Had she truly been frightened? In her daydreams, she imagined herself in his arms. She had never expected the fantasy to come true. "I guess I didn't expect—"

"Don't apologize. Any apology should come from me."

But she didn't hear one. And she didn't want one.

Looking into his eyes, she saw a hint of mischief. "Perhaps," Callie teased, "but I don't hear you apologizing."

A wry grin lightened his face. "And you probably won't. It was my way of saying thank you."

She grinned. "And much less expensive than a raise."

While Callie lay in bed that night, thoughts of the evening filtered over her like warm sunshine. Nattie's words, *"Read to me, Daddy,"* sang in Callie's mind like a melody. David's smile and his joy rushed through her, jostling her pulse to a maddening pace. *Stop. I'll never go to sleep.*

Though Callie cautioned herself, she didn't heed her own warning. Again, her thoughts stirred, and she remembered his strong, eager arms embracing her. But with that image, her dreams ended, and her nightmare began.

She stiffened at the thought. What could she do with herself? Frustration dampened her lovely memories, and she threw the pillow over her head, fumbling in her self-inflicted darkness to turn off the lamp.

Her black dreams had lain dormant for weeks. Tonight, like a rolling mist, the nightmare crept silently into her sleep.

As she moved through a fog, a click *resounded in her ears. Then, she saw the lock. He flashed his broad, charming smile. "You're nervous enough, I'm sure. We don't want anyone popping in and making things worse, do we?"*

Her chest tightened, anxiety growing inside her. She nodded, afraid to speak.

His fingers ran over the keys in flourished arpeggios, *and she lifted her voice, following his fingers, up and*

down the scales. Her tone sounded pinched in her ears.
She wished she could relax so he could hear her natural
quality. Suddenly her singing turned to a silent scream.

In the pulsing silence, Callie's eyes opened to blackness. She raised her hand and wiped the perspiration
from her hairline. Again she fumbled in the deep darkness for the light switch. The flash of brightness hurt her
eyes, and she squinted.

"I can't bear this anymore," she said aloud. "Please, go
away and let me live." Her shoulders lifted in a shivered
sigh. She pulled her flannel robe over her trembling body
and slid her feet into her slippers. Milk? Tea? Something
to wash away the dreams.

She dragged herself into the bathroom and rinsed
her face. Her image in the mirror frightened her, her
skin pale as a gray shroud. She turned from the glass
and wandered through her rooms to the hallway. Quietly she edged her way down the stairs. The whole house
slept, and falling down a dark staircase would add not
only grief to her terrible night, but also chaos to everyone else's rest.

At the bottom of the stairs, the moon shining through
the fanlight above the door guided her path around the
newel post toward the kitchen. Deeper in the wide foyer,
darkness closed in, but she kept the carpet beneath her
feet, knowing the door would be straight ahead at the
end.

With her hand in front of her, she touched the knob
and swung open the door. A light coming from the
kitchen surprised her. She hesitated. Having a middle-
of-the-night conversation with Agnes didn't appeal to

her, but despite the thought, the choice seemed better than turning back.

As she stepped into the kitchen, she halted. It wasn't Agnes, but David, who sat at the table, sipping from a thick mug. When their eyes met, he looked as surprised as she must have. "Well," she said. "I thought I'd be the only nightwalker wandering the house. Am I intruding on your solace?"

"No, to be honest, you're a pleasant sight."

She thought of her ashen face and disheveled hair and grinned. "I beg to differ, but beauty is in the 'beholder's eye,' they say."

His gaze swept hers, and warm tenderness brushed her heart.

"Beauty is," he agreed, and took another drink. He held the cup poised in the air. "How about some hot chocolate?"

The aroma reached her senses. "Sounds wonderful."

"I made more than I wanted. Sit, and I'll get it for you."

He rose and pulled a mug from the cabinet. Callie slid into a chair, running her fingers through her hair and thinking how perfectly terrible she must look.

He poured the cocoa and placed the hot beverage in front of her. "There." He sat again, then regarded her. "So what brings you out of a warm bed in the depths of the night?"

"A mind that won't stop, it seems." She avoided the truth.

"I know what that means. Nattie's in my mind… among other things."

"Business?" she asked, looking into the milk-chocolate liquid. Rays from the overhead light glinted in splayed patterns on the surface of her drink. When she experienced his silence, she looked up. His eyes met hers.

"No, not business. I was thinking about you, to be honest."

Protectively, her hand clutched her robe. "Me? Why?"

He shook his head. "You'll never know how much you mean to me, Callie. All you've done for us here. You're like a breath of spring after a long winter." A grin tugged at the corners of his mouth. "Pretty poetic for the middle of the night, huh?"

She couldn't speak. She struggled to keep her eyes from widening any more than they already had. "But that's why you hired me. To help Nattie."

"But you've done more than that." He reached across the table and laid his hand on hers. "You've helped me, too. I feel alive again, like a man released from prison, his life restored."

Callie looked at his hand pressing against the back of hers. Though her initial thought was to recoil, she joyed in feeling the warm pressure against her skin.

His gaze traced the line of her face. "I wish you'd tell me what troubles you. You know so much about me. I know so little about your life."

She drew her hand from under his and tucked it in her lap. "What troubles me? Nothing really. Old problems crop up once in a while. Nothing you can do about them."

"But…sometimes you seem frightened. Is it me? Are you afraid of me? Callie, I'd never hurt you. If you think—"

Lifting her hand, she pressed her finger on his lips to quiet him. "Please, it's me. Not you."

He raised his hand, capturing her finger against his lips. A kiss as gentle as a fluttering breeze brushed across her skin. Her heart stopped, and she drew in a quick breath. He wrapped her fingers in his and lowered his hand. "I pray someday you can tell me. Whatever it is."

She withdrew her hand a second time. He tilted his head, his face filled with emotion. She wanted to touch his unshaven cheeks with her palms and kiss the worry from his eyes. A worry that she knew was for her, not for himself. Everything in her cried out to tell him, but she pushed the urge deep inside her, praying this time the pangs would stay there.

Patches of sunlight glinted through the sprouting foliage. Callie glanced over her shoulder at Nattie running behind her, looking like any happy child. A rosy glow lit her cheeks, and her eyes sparkled in the brightness of the afternoon.

"Can't keep up with me, can you?" Callie called as she neared the crest of the hill.

Nattie stumbled along, her young, inactive legs not used to the rigors of dashing up a hillside. When Callie reached the top, she fell to the grass, laughing and breathless. Nattie reached her, puffing, and plopped down near her.

Though the hillside was sprinkled with trees, the landscape offered a view of a smattering of houses and distant barns. The new grass and tree leaves, sporting their pale green colors, sent a charge of rebirth and excitement through Callie.

Like spring bursting on the scene, so Nattie's blossoming was another new gift. Nattie had opened her silent world a little more, and brief sentences popped from her like the unexpected surprise of a new Jack-in-the-box. Neither David nor Callie knew at what moment the child might add another sentence to those they had already tallied with joy.

With her heart full of the abounding changes around her, she began with a hum, and before she realized she had risen, as if the trees were her audience, and had opened her mouth in song—*"Beautiful Savior, King of Creation."* She began timidly as a lilting murmur. She hadn't sung in such a long time. But by the third verse, her voice soared into the sky.

Nattie blinked, then widened her curious eyes. A glimmer of awareness covered her face. Callie studied her. Had her mother sung to her in this spot? Or was it the song? Something in the child's look gave Callie a sense of connection. Could music be a catalyst to help the child heal from her terrible hurt?

The sunlight shimmered through Nattie's hair, creating a golden halo around her face. Callie's heart tugged at the lovely picture. Lost forever was the sight of her own child. Since arriving in Bedford, she had locked her own sorrow in her heart's prison. How could she help Nattie if she spent all her energies grieving over something that could never be?

But today, the sorrow gushed from her like a geyser pent up in the earth. Did her child have dark hair like her father, or honey-toned tresses like hers? Were her eyes blue or brown? Was she happy? Or was she sad the way Nattie had been? All the questions that she had stuffed away rose, pouring over her.

She let the questions flow, then, with new conviction, forced them away. In her silence, the only sounds were the chirping birds and a distant mooing cow. Then Nattie tilted her head, and a grin pulled at the corners of her bowed mouth. "Sing more."

Hearing the child's voice, Callie's heart skipped a beat. Her voice little more than a whisper, she asked, "Do you have a favorite?"

Nattie shook her head.

"No favorite?" With a chuckle, Callie leaned down and tickled her neck. "I won't know what to sing for you, then." She sank to the ground as near to Nattie as she dared. "Maybe someday you'll want to sing with me."

Callie began humming softly. A favorite hymn tangled in her memory. As the words unscrambled in her mind, her heart lifted like the melody of the song. *"What wondrous love is this, oh my soul."* The years that her voice had been silenced by her battered memories seemed forgotten. *"That caused the Lord of life to bear the heavy cross."* The child only listened, staring at the ground with an occasional glimpse toward Callie's face. She too bore some secret "heavy cross."

A deep sorrow filled the child's eyes, and when the line of the verse had ended, Callie stopped her song. Music had definitely touched the child's heart. But with *sadness*. Callie longed to tell David her discovery.

Chapter Ten

David was out of town again, and Callie felt antsy for
adult conversation. With a short grocery list tucked in
her shoulder bag, she drove into town. Agnes usually
shopped, but today Callie needed fresh air and a distraction, and the housekeeper had graciously agreed to
keep an eye on Nattie.

Outside, spring worked its magic on her spirit. She
wanted to run and play in the bright, new grass, not be
bound to the quiet, closed-in house. She longed to leave
her worries and sadness behind.

Through the trees, she caught a glimpse of the steeple of John Spier's church, and an unexplained urge
tugged at her. She pulled the car into the empty parking
lot, stepped out onto the gravel and looked around. The
young pastor's car was parked in the parsonage driveway. She headed for the door, wondering if Pastor John
might be working inside.

At the entrance, she pushed the handle on one of the
big double doors, and it opened. The bright sunshine
spread inside along the worn carpet in the small foyer.

She stepped inside, pulling the weighty door closed.

Standing still, she waited for her eyes to adjust to the gloom. She listened for a sound, but heard nothing. With hesitant steps, she wandered down the aisle, which was lit by the daylight shining through the deep-toned stained glass. Above the dark walnut altar hung a large wooden cross. But the image that caught in her eye was the piano.

She moved as if drawn to the fruitwood console, which was flanked by chairs for a small choir. A trembling melancholy clung to her as she edged forward. Her gaze caressed the keys, and she slid onto the bench, an old desire surging within her.

A hymnbook lay open on the music stand, and her hands trembled as she placed them on the keyboard. As she followed the music, her fingers felt stiff and uncertain on the keys. Though the grand piano sat in silence at the house, she hadn't been moved to play, perhaps knowing the piano was Sara's.

When the hymn ended, she turned the pages to another, then another. Before she realized it, her voice was lifted in song. *"There's a quiet understanding when we're gathered in the spirit."* She had often sung that song in her church in Indianapolis. Longing tugged at her heart. She had not sung in church for the past seven years, and today, with no congregation, she sang for God alone. When the song ended, she bowed her head.

"That was wonderful."

Callie jumped, her head pivoting at the sound of a familiar voice. "Oh, you scared me."

Pastor John halted. "I'm sorry. I didn't mean to."

"How long were you there?"

Smiling, he shrugged. "About two hymns, I'd say. I didn't want to stop you. You play and sing beautifully."

Her hands slid from the keyboard to her lap. "Thanks. I, um, don't sing much anymore."

"But you should." He leaned toward her, his elbows resting on top of the piano. "You have a real gift. It's a shame not to use it."

Callie's shoulders tensed; she felt cornered. "I… I did years ago."

"We could use a soloist in church some Sundays." He raised his eyebrows in question.

Callie lowered her lids, then raised them. "Yes, well, I've been giving thought to singing again."

"And?"

"And I guess I'm not quite ready."

"Not stage fright? You seem so confident, I can't imagine your being intimidated by an audience."

His tone pushed her for an explanation. "I don't have stage fright. I had a bad experience a few years ago."

"I'm sorry."

She shifted uncomfortably. "Wounds heal eventually."

"Well, I'll keep your…wound in my prayers."

Callie whispered her thanks, relieved to end the conversation.

John lifted a chair from the choir area and swung it next to the piano. He sat, and a need to escape gripped her. Not wanting to be rude, she struggled against the urge.

He leaned toward her. "Have you ever thought about directing a choir?"

She sputtered a laugh. "Direct? No. Never in my life. I take it you need a choir director."

"Pam Ingram, our pianist, is doing her best, but playing and directing is difficult, especially for someone with limited training."

"Yes, it is." Callie's heart thudded, as she wondered how to escape without being utterly rude. "I really should get going. Agnes is waiting for the groceries." A nervous titter broke from her lips. "Today wasn't the best day to stop, but I've never been here, and... I was curious."

"You're a member somewhere else?"

"No, I've been going to, um, New Hope over on Washington."

John nodded. "Ah, the new church. We have a terrible time keeping members here. They have so much. Including an organ."

Callie's attention was drawn to the small balcony and the line of pipes. "The organ needs work, you mentioned."

"Yes, a few thousand dollars. We don't have it. I'd sort of hoped since Sara Hamilton had been the organist—and David directed the choir—he might make a donation."

Callie's stomach somersaulted. "David was the choir director here?"

His eyebrows shot upward. "Yes, I've been reading all kinds of things to learn the church's history. I was surprised. And so are you, I see."

Callie felt defensive. "He's never mentioned it, but why would he? He's still healing."

"That's what he said."

"So you asked him?"

John rose, stepped to the console, then spun around. "Yes, I mentioned it."

Wounds heal. She prayed they would. Music was the way to reach Nattie. Might David refuse to let her try? Time and patience, that's what they both needed. "Give him time. Things will get better, I'm sure."

A grin curled his lips. "And you? Should I give you time, too, to consider my offer?"

"Your offer?"

"To sing for us? Or help with a choir?"

"Yes, time. It's something we all need." She rose abruptly and stepped to the center aisle before turning around. "I'd better be on my way."

She surveyed the surroundings again as she headed for the door, then stopped halfway down the aisle. "Your church has charm, you know," she said, turning toward him. "New Hope doesn't have charm at all. You should stress that. A lot of people still enjoy the 'old-time religion.'" She waved and rushed up the aisle before he asked her any more questions—or favors.

Though David had returned from his trip, he kept himself closed up in his study. Callie was disappointed. She missed him and hoped to talk to him about the questions that filled her mind regarding Nattie. Sitting in the parlor, she looked through the foyer to the closed door across the way.

Since Nattie had already gone to bed for the night, Callie's responsibilities for the day were over. She rose and marched across the hall, but when she reached the door, she halted. Filling her lungs with air, she released a stream of anxiety from her body, then knocked.

Seconds ticked by. A near-eternity passed before she heard David's response.

"Yes?"

She closed her eyes, prayed, and turned the knob.

David sat at his desk across from the door. "Callie, come in," he said.

She stood shyly near the door. "I'm sorry to disturb you."

"Is something wrong?"

"No, I… I wondered if you have a minute to talk."

"Sure, have a seat." After shuffling the papers in front of him, he rose, motioning for her to sit. "I'm sorry to be hidden away again. I've been preoccupied with a ton of paperwork and some big decisions since I came back from the trip."

"I understand, but I've had a lot on my mind, too." She sank into an overstuffed chair. "And…and I wanted to get your opinion."

David joined her, choosing one of the comfortable chairs across from her. He leaned over with his elbows on his knees, his hands folded in front of him, as he listened to her story of Nattie's day on the hillside. His eyes brightened when he heard about the child's interest in Callie's singing. Yet, as always, sadness followed when he learned of her retreat into silence again.

"But I know music is the key," Callie said. "I believe if I encourage that interest, we'll get somewhere. But since it's a sensitive issue, I wanted to check first. I don't want to do anything that might hurt either of you."

David stared at his shoe, moving the toe along the pattern in the oriental carpet. "I appreciate your concern."

She waited.

In time, he lifted his gaze to hers. "I've been selfish in many ways, protecting myself more than thinking of Nattie." Stress tugged at the corners of his mouth. "I'd like to think I've made some progress. So as they say, you're the nurse. I'll trust your judgment to do what's needed. Anything that will make Nattie a happy child again is fine with me."

Callie relaxed. "Thanks for your confidence."

"You're welcome."

His eyes connected with hers again, and a twinge shot through her chest. The connection sparked liked wires charged with unbound electricity. Finally, she found her voice. "What are you thinking?"

He lowered his gaze. "Nothing. I'm sorry."

She longed to know his thoughts. But she had more to ask, and struggled to organize her musings. "Did Nattie have a particular song she liked to sing with you and Sara?"

David leaned his head back for a moment and then tilted it forward. "Oh, some of the children's songs, I suppose. 'Jesus Loves Me,' for one. Something else about 'two little eyes.'"

"Yes, I know them both. I'll see if she'll sing them with me. I'm grasping for anything."

"Yes, even the slightest progress."

Callie knew she should say goodnight, but she longed to be with him, to talk…about anything.

He drifted away in thought. She sensed she should go and leave him with his own reveries, but a playful look glinted in his eyes. "Have you gotten into mischief since I've been gone?"

"Just a little." She grinned. "On the way to town the other day, I stopped by the church. *Your* church, I should say. I talked a bit with Pastor Spier."

"I suppose he's asking you to join the coalition to pry a donation from me."

"No, but he did mention that he'd asked you." She glanced down at her fingers and realized they were tapping the edge of the chair. "He told me you were once the choir director at First Community Church. Is that right?"

David closed his eyes, and lifted his shoulders in a heavy sigh. "Wish I could get my hands on those church records." He peered at her. "Yes, I'm guilty as charged. I did it to help Sara. Playing and directing is difficult. She could do it, but having a director made things easier."

"I just wondered. Was surprised, naturally. But I suppose you have a lot of surprises hidden away that I don't know about."

He flinched. "Only a few. And you seem to pry them out of me daily."

"Good for me." She shifted in her chair. "So, are you thinking about helping with the organ repairs?"

"Should I throw you out on your ear now? Or later?"

A pleasant expression hovered on his face, so she continued. "He paid me good money to pry this information out of you." She rose with a grin. "I'd better leave before you follow through on your threat." She headed for the door. "Good night."

David rose and stepped toward her. "How's your mother?"

She spun around, meeting his questioning eyes. "Mom seems to be fine, but she did have a minor stroke, according to the MRI test. The doctor has her on some new medication. Now all I can do is pray she takes care of herself."

"I'm glad to hear it was minor. God gives us warnings sometimes, a little reminder to take care of ourselves. Problem is, we have to listen."

Callie grinned as she turned the doorknob. "And listening is definitely one of Mom's serious problems." She glided through the door and closed it before he could respond.

Climbing the stairs, she hummed a simple children's hymn. The tune brought back old questions. Did her own child, living somewhere in the world, know the song? Had Christian parents adopted her tiny little girl? A heavy ache weighted her heart. Drawn by her emotions, or perhaps more by her loneliness, Callie opened Nattie's bedroom door and tiptoed inside.

The child lay curled in a tiny ball on the edge of her bed. The rosy night-light sent a wash of pink over her face, her cheeks glowing with the warm hue. Callie had fought her instincts so often to lavish her affection on Nattie, knowing it might not be good for the child when she had to leave, and positive it would not be good for her own throbbing hurt.

But tonight, she leaned over, brushed the child's hair from her cheek with her finger, and lay her lips against Nattie's warm, soft skin. Tears filled her eyes as she backed away and turned to the door. Taking one more glimpse, she stepped into the hallway—and into David's arms.

Chapter Eleven

Callie gasped as David held her in his arms outside Nattie's room. Her body trembled in fear as she pulled away from his grasp and closed the bedroom door.

"I didn't mean to frighten you," he said. Pausing, he searched her face, then raised his fingers to capture her chin. "Why do you have tears in your eyes? Is something wrong?"

"Nothing. Nothing's wrong with Nattie, if that's what you mean." Callie released a trembling sigh and pulled herself together.

"But why are you crying?" he whispered, sounding concerned.

"I'm not crying." She kept her eyes lowered, praying the evidence of her tears would vanish. When she raised her eyes to his, he held her riveted.

David lifted his hand and brushed his fingers across her lashes. "Your eyes are still wet. Please tell me what's wrong."

Callie grasped for something to tell him. "I'm worried about my mother, I suppose. Looking down at Nattie reminds me how my mother hovered over me when

I was a child. I keep praying for my mother, but fears still creep into my thoughts."

He drew a clean handkerchief from his back pocket and daubed her eyes. "You know, Callie, if you need to go home for a few days, I can manage without you. Not that I want to—but Agnes will take care of Nattie. Please, go home. You'll feel better."

Callie's lie had gotten out of control. She remembered her mother's words that a lie spoken becomes a web of deceit that grows bigger and bigger. "No, really. A good night's sleep is all I need. But thanks for the offer. Maybe one of these days I'll visit her for a weekend."

He rested one hand on her shoulder and tilted her face with the other. "If you're sure?"

His eyes again bound her, and her breath quivered through her body. "I'm sure," she whispered.

His fingers touched her cheek in a tender caress before he pulled his hand away and turned toward his own room.

Callie darted into her bedroom across the hall. Overwhelmed, she shut the door and leaned against the jamb. Her cheek tingled where his fingers had touched, and she raised her own hand and pressed her burning skin.

Her mind raced. Was she a fool? Was his touch only kindness, or had his feelings grown? If he cared about her, she should leave now while she still could. She leaned her head back, pressing her eyelids closed. She could offer him nothing. But how could she walk away from Nattie now that the child had begun to leave her shell.

Foolish. Foolish. Her thoughts were nothing but nonsense. She rushed to the bathroom and turned the shower on to a full, heavy stream, stripping her clothes from her shaking body. She stepped into the tub and let the water rush over her, feeling its calming warmth. She scrubbed herself until her thoughts, like the soapy bubbles, washed down the drain.

No man would love her once he knew the truth. She could offer a man like David nothing but her less-than-perfect self. He deserved a lovely, unsullied woman. She dried herself, rubbing the nubby towel over her body until she glowed bright pink. As she brushed her hair with heavy strokes, she stared at herself in the mirror. No one wanted a used, sinful wife.

Callie tossed the hairbrush on her vanity table and crawled into bed, praying sleep would come quickly. In the darkness, her mind drifted, and, as on so many nights, the mist rolled in. His voice came from the shadows.

"Why, Callie, that's a lovely, lovely name. Nearly pretty as you are, sweetheart."

A flush of excitement deepened to embarrassment. He pulled the door closed behind her, and she stepped inside the room, moving toward the black, gleaming grand piano.

He flashed his broad, charming smile. "You're nervous enough, I'm sure. We don't want anyone popping in and making things worse, do we?" The lock clicked.

Her chest tightened, anxiety growing inside her as his fingers touched the keys. She wished she could relax, so he could hear her natural quality.

He winked, then eyed her hand resting on the piano edge. He stopped playing and placed his hot, sweaty fingers on hers. "You just relax there. I can hear you have a pretty voice."

Callie filled her diaphragm with air, and her voice soared from her, natural and strong.

He looked at her with admiration, swaying and moving on the bench as she sang. "Why you're a little meadowlark, aren't you."

Callie's eyes shot open in the darkness, as the name pierced the night like a knife, *Meadowlark, Meadowlark.*

A gentle breeze drifted through the open parlor windows. Callie leaned her head against the sofa back, her attention drawn to Nattie. With an array of crayons and a coloring book, Nattie concentrated on her artwork, her golden curls hiding her face. The afternoon sun glinted through the windows, and rays danced on the child's hair like a sprinkle of fairy dust.

Each time Callie allowed herself to think about the little girl, her heart ached. No matter how hard she tried to avoid the inevitable, her heartstrings tangled more and more around Nattie.

Daily, she prayed for Nattie's healing, yet the reality sent a sad shiver through her. Nattie, healthy and happy, would start school in September, and Callie would have completed her task. She would have to leave Bedford. How could she ever say goodbye?

As if the child knew she filled Callie's thoughts, she sat up, tearing the picture carefully from the book.

She rose, glancing with lowered lids toward Callie, then carried the picture to her side.

"How beautiful," Callie said, holding the paper in front of her. "You color so well, Nattie. Everything's inside the lines. And such pretty colors, too. I love it."

Nattie's timid grin brightened her face. "It's for you."

Her pulse skipped a beat, and she clutched the paper to her chest. "Thank you. This is one of the nicest presents I've ever had."

Nattie slid onto the sofa and nestled by her side. Callie pulled herself together, reviewing the event as if it occurred in slow motion. With caution, she slid her arm around the child's shoulders. Nattie leaned into her arm without hesitation. Longing, delight, amazement swirled through her in one rolling surge.

"Oh, Nattie, you are a gem," Callie said.

Nattie tilted her face upward, her brows knit together.

"You don't know what a gem is?"

Nattie shook her head.

"I didn't say a 'germ,' did I?" The moisture in her eyes belied her mirth. "I said a gem. Like a diamond. You know what a diamond is?"

"Uh-huh," Nattie said, her face glowing.

"You're *my* diamond, Nattie."

Nattie snuggled more closely to her side. Callie savored the moment, wishing and longing for miracles, thoughts she couldn't speak for fear of losing them.

The magic moment evaporated when Agnes called them to lunch, but Callie's mind replayed the scene over and over. Nattie had already made a giant stride forward, though Callie had yet to put her plan into effect to use music to draw her out more completely.

The thought filled her mind, and she decided to begin after lunch. When they had settled back in the parlor, Callie wandered to the piano and lifted the bench lid. Inside, she found music books of all kinds. She ruffled through them, pulling out a bound selection of well-known classics. She lowered the lid and adjusted the bench. Nattie watched her with curiosity.

Sliding onto the bench, Callie propped the music on the stand, and glanced through the pages and found a favorite. Her hands rested on the keys covered with the dust of disuse. She made a mental note to clean the ivory with witch hazel. But for now, she allowed her fingers to arch and press the first notes of the sonata.

The rich, vibrant tone of the piano filled the room. Like a tonal magnet, Nattie rose, drawn to the instrument. She stood at Callie's side, her sight riveted to Callie's experienced fingers moving over the keys. The music held the child transfixed, and Callie continued, her emotions caught in the rhythm and tones of the masterpiece.

When she finished the selection, she sought Nattie's eyes. The child's face seemed awed by the experience.

"Would you like to sit next to me?" Callie held her breath.

Nattie tried to scoot onto the bench, and Callie put her arm around the girl's slender shoulders, giving her a boost.

"There, now you can see much better. How about another song?"

Nattie nodded, and Callie selected a shorter piece, hoping to keep the child's interest. The Bach étude resounded in a bright lilting melody, and when she finished, she turned to Nattie. "Okay, now it's your turn. Would you like to play?"

Nattie's eyes widened, and a small grin curved her lips.

"Good. I'll show you a simple song. And later, I'll pick up a beginner's book for you. We can surprise your daddy."

Again, Nattie's quiet voice broke her silence. "Okay."

Though her word was a near whisper, to Callie the sound was a magnificent symphony.

Callie slid the beginner's book into the piano bench when she brought it home from the music store. In her excitement, she wanted to share the moments with David, but she wondered if the fact would stir up sad memories. And she'd only asked him about singing, not piano lessons. Waiting seemed to be the better option. Yet already, Nattie's natural talent blossomed.

She and Nattie had made a pact to keep her lessons a secret. When Nattie felt ready to play for her father, they would hold a surprise concert. Like true comrades, their secret bonded them.

With the music book stowed in its hiding place, Callie returned to her room. Tonight she wanted to give Nattie and David time alone. Each day the child's progress seemed more evident. With more than three months before the beginning of school, Nattie would be ready for first grade.

Bored with television, she turned the clock-radio dial on her desk. A familiar hymn drifted from the speakers, and the music wrapped around her like a loving arm. She settled into her favorite recliner and leaned back, closing her eyes.

John Spier's request glided into her thoughts. Years had passed since she'd sung in church. But like Nattie, she'd begun to heal. For so long, her throat had knotted when she opened her mouth to sing. Now her voice lifted often in praise to God and in her love of music. Music completed her and made her whole again. At least, almost whole.

Maybe she should consider Pastor John's request. She

could praise God all she wanted on the hillside and in private, but singing in church was a loving testimony. Hymns drifted through her mind, favorites she had not sung forever, it seemed.

Woven into the radio's musical offering, Callie heard a rhythmic sound. She lowered the radio's volume. The tap came again. She grinned to herself. The door—someone had knocked. She strode across the room and pulled it open.

David stood outside, a sheepish expression on his face. "We missed you."

Callie stepped backward. "Missed me?"

He scanned her face, then his eyes focused behind her.

Callie turned around and glanced into her sitting room, trying to figure out what he wanted. "Did you want to come in?"

He shifted from one foot to the other. "If you don't mind—I just tucked Nattie in for the night, and I felt lonely."

Callie teetered backward, opening the door for him to enter. He had never come to visit, and the situation caused her a strange uneasiness. "Have a seat." She motioned to the recliner, but instead, he pulled out a smaller chair from the desk and straddled the seat, resting his hands on the back.

"You're welcome to sit here," she repeated, but he ignored her offer and remained seated. "So." She glanced around her. "I don't have anything to offer you, except tap water." Her nervous titter sounded ridiculous in her ears.

David shook his head. "I didn't come for refreshments. I just wondered why you made yourself so scarce this evening."

"Oh." Callie relaxed. Now she understood. "Well, I

thought since Nattie and I spend a lot of quality time together, you and she deserved a night alone. Sometimes, it's nice for the two of you to be together…without me. I'm a distraction."

Again his gaze traced her face. "But a pleasant one," he finally said.

She felt a rush of heat rise to her face, a blush she couldn't hide. "You embarrass me. I don't know how to handle comments like that."

"I suppose that's one of the reasons I find you so lovely."

Her blush deepened. "See, you're doing it again." She covered her face with her hands, feeling like an utter fool.

"You're beautiful when you blush, Callie. You remind me of a butterfly locked in its chamber, then suddenly released." He rested his chin on his arms. "Sorry, my poetry's running wild again."

Her gaze sought his. "But it sounded lovely. Really."

"I can never pay you for the joy you've brought back to my life. Every day I see Nattie grow more open, like the little child she was before her mother died. If it was Sara's death alone or something else that made her so withdrawn, I don't know. But whatever it was, you're bringing her out of it. And I…love you for it. I'm sorry if I've embarrassed you again, but I have to tell you."

Callie's feelings tumbled into words. "I see the same progress. Each day I watch her open up a little more, and I'm happier than I can tell you. But I have to be honest with you.

"It makes me sad, too."

He studied her. "Sad?"

"When she's herself again, I'm out of a job. Joyful for

her. Sad for me. Do you see the paradox? I long to see her bubbling with happiness like children her age—but then I have to say goodbye. And…she's stolen a piece of my heart." Callie lowered her lids, the tears building along her lashes.

David rose, moving to her side in one giant stride. In a flash, he knelt before her and grasped her hand. "No, not goodbye. Nattie needs you…and *will* need you. You're the one who's making her strong again. You can't just up and leave her. Even when she begins school, she'll need support and someone who loves her…a woman who loves her. Little girls need a mother's nurturing, not a father who bungles his way along. Don't even think of leaving us. Please."

Callie heard his words, but what he said knotted in her thoughts. *A mother's nurturing.* By delaying her departure, she would only hurt herself more. Could she bear it? "I appreciate the nice things you're saying. But, David, I have to look after my own well-being, too. Time will tell what I can handle emotionally. I can't make any promises."

"I'm not asking for promises, just understanding that we need you."

Words left her mouth that she didn't bite back fast enough. "What you need, David, is a wife. That's who should be nurturing Nattie, not me. You need to live again, too. I'm sure somewhere in the community is a fine, single woman just waiting to be someone's wife."

To Callie's astonishment, David laughed.

"Please don't laugh at me, David. I'm speaking from my heart."

Again, he touched her hand. "I'm not laughing at you,

Callie. Please, don't even think such a thing. I forgot to tell you about our invitation."

"Our invitation?" Her forehead wrinkled to a frown.

"Pastor John called earlier this evening. He asked to speak to you about accompanying him to the church picnic. I told him you had already retired for the evening. Then, Mary Beth latched on to the telephone and invited me."

Callie's stomach flip-flopped with his words. "Pastor John asked me to the picnic?" What she really wanted to say was *"Mary Beth asked you to the picnic?"*

David nodded his head. "Yes, I told him to call you tomorrow. But I couldn't come up with an excuse quick enough, so I had to accept Mary Beth's offer. Please accept John's invitation. At least we can be a buffer for each other. You'll save me from a fate worse than…well, from a trying experience."

Though an unexpected jealousy raged inside her, she contemplated his poignant pleading. A protective camaraderie bound them together. "But accepting the invitation isn't kind, David—not if we're making fun of them."

"I don't mean to make fun. I suppose both of them would be a good—how should I put it—catch. But I'm not ready to be caught, and Mary Beth's efforts are so obvious. I'll have to be honest with her. Somehow."

"Honesty is the best thing."

"Then let me be honest. Make my day worthwhile and accept John's invitation. I can bear it if you're there. And Nattie will want to be with you, too. Please."

She lowered her eyes, and when she raised them, her heart fluttered like the wings of the butterfly David had just compared her to. She nodded.

"Thank you from the bottom of my heart." He rose

and stepped back. "I suppose I should let you get back to...whatever you were doing." He turned toward the door.

"David," she said, stopping him in mid-stride. "Could you stay a minute? I'd like to talk."

Chapter Twelve

David faltered when Callie spoke his name. Turning, he faced her, his heart galloping at the sound of her voice. His eyes feasted on her tonight, sitting near him as if she belonged in the house forever. Not an employee, but a woman. A woman who loved his child and who, he prayed, could learn to love him. Startled by his own longings, he shivered.

"I hope I didn't startle you. This has been on my mind for some time now."

He tensed, considering the serious expression on her face. "Is something wrong?"

"No. When I visited the church a while back, Pastor John asked me if I would sing for a Sunday service." She grinned.

"He also asked me to direct the choir, but I'll leave that talent to you."

David halted her with a gesture. "Forget that." He wondered if Pastor John had put her up to the comment.

"Well, anyway, I'm thinking about singing, and I wanted to warn you."

"Warn me? You have a lovely voice, Callie. You should sing."

She halted and searched his face. When she spoke, her voice sounded controlled and thoughtful. "How do you know I have a lovely voice?" Her eyes lit with a questioning brightness, as if she'd learned the answer to a secret.

He'd spoken without thinking. "I've heard you sing with Nattie. The children's songs. I have ears."

"And you? Do you sing, David?"

"I sang long ago. Nothing like you."

She squinted as if weighing his response, then continued. "I just wanted to tell you that I'm accepting your pastor's invitation to sing."

"If you're singing—" He faltered over the words. "I'd like to hear you. I'll attend worship that Sunday."

Her eyes widened. "You don't attend worship?"

"I've felt very lonely at First Community. Too many memories." He thought of his promise to Sara. "Since Nattie's doing better, I'm taking her to Sunday School, but I usually drop her off and wait."

"You wait for her." Her eyes widened even more. "David, you'll never get *less* lonely unless you work at it."

But it was more than being lonely. Much more. "I'm angry, too, I suppose…at God." The words escaped his control.

"Angry? At God?" Her face bent to a scowl. "Because of Sara's death? But you said you knew she had cancer."

"You've asked a whole parcel of questions. Which do you want me to answer?" Despite the tension edging inside him, a quirky grin flickered on his mouth.

Callie eyed him. "It's wrong, you know, to be angry at God."

"I know." He wandered back to the chair he had left a few minutes earlier and again straddled the seat, leaning on the back. "But as I said before, I had tremendous faith that our love would heal Sara's cancer. A young lover's error. But I had faith. When Sara died, I felt betrayed."

The scowl retreated, and her face overflowed with empathy.

Surprised, he felt his eyes mist at his admission. "And when Nattie reacted like she did, I felt devastated. God took my wife, and then my daughter. I couldn't accept that."

"Oh, David, I understand. We shouldn't, I know, but I've been angry at God, myself. When I stopped singing, I wasn't only punishing my parents, but I probably thought I was hurting God, too."

Her own vulnerability wrapped around his thoughts. Questions that he'd tucked back in his mind surged forward. "And why were you punishing your parents, Callie? What secret hides behind your lovely face?"

She paled, squeezing her saddened eyes closed for a heartbeat. When she opened them, fear clouded her face. "Please don't ask. Don't we all have things in our lives we don't want to talk about to anyone?" She lowered her eyes to her hands knotted in her lap, then raised them and focused on him. "At least, not yet."

David nodded, yet his heart tugged inside; he wanted to know what caused her such pain. What stopped her from sharing her grief with him? What scared her when he touched her? Who had hurt her so badly?

"Thanks for understanding," she added. Her eyes softened as she gazed at him. "I'm pleased Nattie's going to Sunday School."

If he were honest, he couldn't even take credit for that. "I promised Sara I'd raise Nattie to know Jesus.

I'm keeping that promise. I take her to Sunday School. But church…my heart hasn't been in it."

"I know you pray, David. Maybe at dinner it's for Nattie, but you do say prayers." Her gaze searched his. "Let's pray for each other, David. Prayers can work miracles. We both need help."

Her eyes glowed with her request as she looked at him. *Prayer.* Such a simple gift he could give her…and himself. "A deal," he said, and rose. "I'll pray for you, and you pray for me. How's that?"

She peered into his eyes. "Not quite what I meant."

Her look penetrated his soul. The guilt he'd hidden under layers of self-pity peeled away, one by one.

"I said, let's pray for each other. 'Where *two* or *three* are gathered,' the Bible says. We need to pray for our *own* needs, too. Still a deal?" Her hand jutted toward him.

He stepped forward and clasped her tiny fingers in his. Their eyes locked as firmly as their handshake, and heat radiated through him like a match flame touched to gasoline, searing his frayed emotions.

He needed her—wanted her in his arms nestled against him. Yet her fear permeated his thoughts. Moving with caution and tenderness, he drew her to his chest. Her body trembled against him. His voice caught in his throat, and his "thank you" was only a murmur. When he'd corralled his emotions, he gently released her and left the room, feeling as if he had left a piece of his heart behind.

David woke in the morning and looked out the window. The weather couldn't have been better for the church picnic. The sky shone a bright blue, with no hint of rain.

If he hadn't accepted Mary Beth's invitation, he might have looked forward to the occasion, but instead, he glowered as he drove to the parsonage with Callie and Nattie belted in the back seat. He wanted, with all his heart, to seat Callie in the front, but protocol determined the spot belonged to Mary Beth.

When their tedious journey to the park ended, John helped tote their gear, and they found a table beneath a large elm tree.

Nattie clung to Callie's side, her timidity obvious in the crowd of gathering church members. Though distressed at Nattie's discomfort, David found pleasure in watching her relationship with Callie. As soon as she opened a folding chair and sat, Nattie slid onto her lap. The love, evident between them, warmed his heart.

Mary Beth unfolded a chair. "Nattie, aren't you too big to be sitting on your nanny's lap?" Mary Beth asked as she eyed the child. "I think it would be nice if you sat on your own chair here by me." She opened another chair. "I'd like to get to know you better."

Nattie shook her head and Mary Beth's mouth dropped in an awkward gape.

"My, my, aren't we a temperamental child." She plopped into a chair and glowered at Callie, whose protective hand cupped Nattie's shoulder.

"Nattie's shy, Mary Beth," David countered. "Give her time to adjust." He wanted to shake the woman for her comment.

Mary Beth beamed at him with a smile as false as her long, well-polished fingernails. "You're right, David. I wasn't thinking. Let's go for a little walk. What do you say?" She rose without waiting for his response.

David glanced at Callie in desperation, hoping she

would intervene. But she only looked at him with an arched eyebrow, and he slumped off, not knowing how to avoid Mary Beth without being rude.

"What did you have in mind?" he asked her, as they moved away from the safe circle of chairs. He realized too late that his question might be misconstrued.

"I'm sorry?" Her pitch elevated.

"I meant, where did you want to walk?"

She let out a minute sigh, her fingers playing with the collar of her blouse. "Nowhere in particular. I thought we might enjoy some privacy."

She had thought wrong, but he allowed her to lead him through the trees and up a grassy knoll. His mind wandered, envisioning Callie and Nattie sitting back under the elm tree.

Mary Beth squeezed his arm. "My, you are quiet today."

Her comment amused him. "Obviously, you don't know me very well. I'm not a live wire, I'm afraid."

His words didn't ruffle her confidence. "You see, then, our little walk is important. We'll get to know each other better."

He shrugged off her statement and uttered a thought of his own. "When are you returning home, Mary Beth?" His blatant question dropped in the air like a cement brick.

His weighted words seemed to squelch her enthusiasm. "I haven't made plans yet. I've considered staying in Bedford for a while. I had hoped to…develop some lasting friendships here."

"I see." *Coward*, David yelled inside his head. How could he tell her with finesse that he didn't want to be one of her lasting friendships. The only friendship he wanted at the moment was Callie. But in her case, he wanted more than friendship.

He tried with discretion to uncurl her fingers from his arm and step away. "I'm sure your brother enjoys your company. And if I recall, the congregation has a number of young women…and men eager for a new friendship. You have a particular young man in mind?"

Her look sought his, sadly pleading, and he wished he could retract his foolish statement, throwing in the white flag. Obviously, she had a man in mind—not a young man, perhaps, but a man. *Him.* "I'm sorry, Mary Beth, my question was much too personal."

She averted her eyes, staring back toward the groups of parishioners gathering under the trees near the pavilion. "I had hoped you already knew the young man I find so attractive."

He pressed his lips together, wondering how to worm his way out of the pitiful situation he'd created. "Sometimes, I'm thick-headed, Mary Beth. My wife's death was two years ago, but I haven't quite thought of myself as single. I've been preoccupied with my daughter's problems. But thanks for your compliment."

Glowing red splotches appeared on her cheeks, and she turned toward their picnic spot beneath the trees off in the distance. "I doubt if anyone will attract your attention until the nanny leaves your employ. You seem to have eyes only for her."

"I beg your pardon?" David might have been less surprised by a kick in the shin. "I don't have a relationship with Callie." *But I want one.* His own realization brought a rush of heat to his neck.

"Your heart does, I think." She turned and headed back toward the picnic tables.

Flustered by her reaction, he followed her. Was his heart that obvious? He could no longer deny his feelings to himself—nor, apparently, to the rest of the world. Perhaps he needed to let Callie in on the news. Or did she know already?

When David walked away with Mary Beth, Callie wished she were the woman on his arm. He had squeezed into her thoughts and into her heart, and she had no way of protecting herself.

A romantic relationship frightened her, even one with David. His innocent touch excited her, yet a prickling of fear crept through her at the thought of intimacy. She had prayed, but had she really given her fear to God?

Callie observed Nattie. The child's gaze, too, followed her father and Mary Beth across the grass. Callie's hand rested lovingly on Nattie's arm, and she brushed the girl's cool, soft skin with her fingers. Her heart swelled, feeling Nattie's body nestled against hers. As David had said, the young girl needed a mother's love, and Callie had so much love to give.

When Callie looked away from Nattie, Pastor John was studying her. Did he see how much she loved the child snuggled in her arm?

"Are you enjoying your life here in Bedford?" he asked. His query sounded innocent, but Callie sensed more behind it.

"Yes, very much."

He nodded with a subtle reflex toward Nattie. "I notice you have other things holding you here, too."

Callie glanced down at the quiet child and back at him. "Pretty obvious, huh?"

"I worry about you. You need to take care of yourself. One day things will change, and you'll be the one left empty-handed. And empty-hearted."

His words washed over her like ice water. "Yes, I know."

"I didn't mean to offend you. I just wish your days could be a little more pleasant for *you*...personally. I'd like to see you if you're willing."

She gave him a blank stare. Obviously, he wasn't referring to church services. Why hadn't she seen this coming? "Well, I've decided to take you up on your Sunday morning offer. I'll be happy to sing occasionally for the worship service."

"Great. I'm pleased to hear that. But...that's not exactly what I had in mind."

"I know, and I'm sorry. For now, let's begin there. I'm not sure how settled I want to get in Bedford. I have family in Indianapolis, and...well, I suppose you understand."

He fixed his eyes to the ground. "For now, then, I'll just enjoy having you sing with us." He lifted his gaze and a half-hearted smile rose to his lips.

"Daddy."

Callie glanced at Nattie, her word a whisper. She looked up to see Mary Beth charging toward them, David following her with a look of helplessness.

Mary Beth shot Callie a glance and plopped into the folding chair. It lurched, giving a precarious bounce to one side. If it hadn't been for John, she might have ended up sitting on the ground.

"Careful," John said, eyeing her and then David. "You could have fallen flat on your face."

She raised her eyes, scanning her audience. "I already have," she sputtered.

Chapter Thirteen

Callie awakened early, knowing this morning she was singing in church. Feeling jittery, she rushed through breakfast and dashed to church before service for a final rehearsal.

Waiting for her solo, she sat in the front row. When the sermon ended, Pastor John gave a faint nod, and she rose and joined the pianist. As the musical introduction to "The Gift of Love" rippled from the keys, Callie faced the congregation.

Already the words of 1 Corinthians 13 filled her thoughts, *"Faith, hope, and love abide, these three; and the greatest of these is love."* Awareness jolted her. Much of her life had been loveless. Not her childhood, perhaps, but her later years—empty, punishing years of feeling unloved by others, by herself and by God.

As she sang, lifting the words in song, her gaze swept over the congregation. Her stomach tightened. David and Nattie sat conspicuously among them. Two pairs of eyes met hers, and like strands of a fragile cord, woven and bound together, she felt strengthened by their presence. The song touched her heart. What was life without love—both human and divine?

When the service ended, Callie rose and turned to where David and Nattie had been seated, but they were gone. Her pleasure turned to disappointment, and she edged her way to the exit.

As Pastor John greeted the worshipers, he caught Callie's hand before she slipped away and asked her to stay until he was free. She hung in the background, waiting. When the last parishioner had left, he joined her.

"Thanks so much for sharing your wonderful voice with us. And I see you persuaded David to worship with us this morning." He eyed her with a wry smile.

"No, I was as surprised as you."

"Then you've been a good influence without trying."

He made her uneasy. "Perhaps," she said, avoiding his eyes.

"I hope you'll sing again soon."

"Sure. I'll be happy to sing once in a while."

He offered a pleasant nod and rocked back on his heels. "And, by the way," he said, his hand sweeping the breadth of the sanctuary, "we had a few more people here today. Your idea seems to have worked."

She sent her mind back, but came up empty. "My idea?"

"The church with charm, remember? You suggested we advertise we're an old-fashioned church. We hung a few posters in the local supermarkets, and I put an ad in *The Bedford Bulletin*. I've already noticed a difference."

"That's great. I'm glad." She sensed he was stalling.

"Well, thanks for the idea." He dug his hands into his navy blue suit pockets. "And have you given any thought to *my* idea?"

She felt her brows knit again. "Your idea?"

"That you have dinner with me."

The floor sank beneath her. She kept her eyes connected to his and swallowed. What could she say? *I'm falling in love with my employer.*

He shuffled his feet and pulled his hands from his pockets. His eyes never wavered.

"You know I can't get away easily. Nattie still needs a lot of—"

"You have a day off? An evening when David's home?"

She bit the corner of her lip and released it immediately. *Trapped.* "Why don't you call, and I'll check my schedule."

He contemplated her words for a moment. "All right, I'll do that." He touched her arm. "Thanks for singing today."

"You're welcome, John… Pastor John."

"Call me John, Callie."

Callie stepped backward toward the door. "John, then." She lifted her hand in a wave and hurried through the door.

When Callie arrived home, David was nowhere in sight. She climbed the stairs to slip out of her Sunday clothes. As she approached her room, she noticed Nattie's door ajar. Listening outside, she heard Nattie singing softly to herself. *"Jesus loves me; this I know."* Her murmured tone was sweet and wispy.

Callie stood still. What might Nattie do if she stepped inside the room? Her heart soared with each note of the song, perfectly in tune. When the melody ceased, she pushed open the door and stood at the threshold.

"Did I hear you singing?" she asked.

Nattie's face sprouted a tiny grin, and she nodded.

"You sing very pretty." Callie took a step forward. "Just like your mom, I would guess."

"Like you," Nattie said.

The child's words danced in her heart. "Thank you." She eyed the scene for a moment. "What are you doing?"

Nattie tilted her head the way David often did. "Playing."

"Playing, huh?" She moved into the room and slid onto the window seat. "I saw you in church. Did you see me?"

Nattie giggled and nodded.

"What's this head nodding? Cat got your tongue?"

Nattie gave another titter, but this time she opened her mouth wide and wiggled her tongue. When she closed her mouth, she added, "You're silly."

"Well, I guess I am."

In one motion, Nattie scurried up from the floor into Callie's arms. Her heart pounding, Callie hugged the child. "Well, what do I owe such a wonderful greeting?"

The child lifted her soft blue eyes to meet hers. "You sang pretty in church."

Air escaped Callie in a fluttered breath. "Thank you, sweetheart. You sounded pretty, too, just now."

The child wrapped her arms around Callie's neck, and Callie drew her to the window seat, keeping her arm around the girl's shoulders. Nattie cuddled to her and laid her head against Callie's side.

"I have an idea. Sometime we can sing together. Maybe on our next walk on the hillside." She glimpsed down at the bright eyes looking up at her. "Okay?"

Nattie nodded, her eyes drooping sleepily.

Callie swung Nattie's legs up on the window seat, and

the child rested her head in Callie's lap. With pure joy, Callie caressed the child's cheek and arm as she hummed a lullaby she remembered from her childhood. As the words rose in her mind, she sang them gently, and Nattie's breathing grew deep and steady as she sank into a restful sleep.

She smiled down at the little girl, and when she raised her eyes, David stood in the doorway watching her. Her pulse galloped like a frisky colt in a spring meadow. She longed to rush to his arms.

But then he vanished, and, not wanting to disturb Nattie, Callie eased herself back, leaning her head against the wall. He would have to wait if he'd wanted to talk to her. She was busy being a...mother. The word moved through her like an angel's song, lifting the hairs on her arms.

Later that evening, Callie found a gift-wrapped package next to her dinner plate. She flushed, wondering if John had sent something over in the hopes she would accept his dinner invitation. As she turned the small box over in her hand, David entered the dining room and eased into his chair.

"I wonder where this came from?" Then she saw the look on his face, and knew.

"Just a small token."

A tenderness that filled his eyes caught on her heartstrings and, like a kite, tugged and pulled until she let the string go, her love lifting to the sky. "For what?"

"Do you have to ask? I picked it up the other day, and was waiting for the right moment. I saw the perfect moment today. You, with Nattie sleeping on your lap."

"Sorry to ruin the lovely picture, but I don't think

Nattie feels well. When I tried to get her ready for dinner, she said she didn't want anything to eat. Her cheeks are a little flushed, too. I'll take her some soup later."

"You can't wiggle out of it, Callie. I saw you holding her in your arms. Please accept my little gift."

She studied the box again, turning it over in her hand.

"Thank you. May I open it?"

"Sure, what do you think I'm waiting for?"

She grinned and pulled the tissue from the box. When she lifted the lid, a delicate rosebud lapel pin lay on a cushion of blue velvet. A rosy shade of gold shaped the bud, and the leaves and stem contrasted in the traditional golden hue. "It's beautiful. I've never seen anything like it."

"The clerk told me the pin was designed in one of the Dakotas. Apparently, they're known for three shades of gold. Sorry, this only has two."

She raised her eyes from the lovely brooch, heat flushing her cheeks. "I do feel deprived. Only two shades of gold, huh?"

"I promise. Your next gift will be three." He locked her in his gaze.

Your next gift. She raised her trembling hand to her heated flesh. "I believe I have two-toned cheeks at the moment."

"I seem to embarrass you, don't I?"

Embarrass? He thrilled her. Her voice bunched in her throat. If she spoke, only a sob would escape. Regaining control of herself, she murmured a simple "thank you."

David rose, and in one stride, stood at her side. He lifted the brooch from the box, unlatched it and pinned it to the wide lapel of Callie's simple summer blouse. "There, now we can eat."

When he sat again, he reached toward her. She glanced at his hand in confusion. But when she saw his bowed head, she lay her icy hand in his, and he asked the blessing. The warmth of his fingers and of his prayer radiated a comforting quiet through her. She whispered her "Amen" with his, then concentrated on dinner, afraid if she thought about anything else, the sentiments of the day might overwhelm her.

As she sat on the wide porch, Callie raised her head from her book at the sound of a car motor. Her stomach tumbled, as Mary Beth stepped from her automobile and crossed to the walk.

"Good morning," she called. "I was passing by and noticed you on the porch. I hope you don't mind that I stopped by."

Callie rose. "No, not at all." If God had wanted to punish her, he could have zapped her with a bolt of lightning for her lie. Of all the people in the world Callie *didn't* want to see, Mary Beth topped the list.

"Beautiful summer day, isn't it?" Mary Beth commented, flouncing up the porch stairs.

Callie cringed. The woman brought out the worst in her. She summoned her Christian manners. "May I get you some lemonade?"

Mary Beth stood uneasily on the top porch stair. "That would be nice."

"Have a seat," Callie said, pointing to a chair near hers, "and I'll be right back."

She dashed into the house, raced up the stairs, pulled a comb through her hair, smeared lipstick across her lips, then flew down the stairs to the kitchen. Holding her chest, she gasped to Agnes, "A glass of lemonade, please."

Agnes stared at her wide-eyed. "Something wrong?"

"No—yes. Mary Beth Spier dropped by for a visit."

Agnes didn't seem to understand, but filled a glass with ice cubes and lemonade. "Here you go," she said, handing it to her.

Callie stood a moment to regain her composure, then turned and did her best to saunter back to the porch. Pushing open the screen door, she glued a smile to her face and handed the drink to Mary Beth. Nattie, playing in the yard, glanced at them, but kept her distance.

"The child seems more adjusted now than when I first came to Bedford," Mary Beth said as she eyed Nattie.

"Yes, she is. We thank God every day."

Mary Beth stared at her lemonade, then turned to Callie. "So then, what will you do with yourself?"

"Pardon me?" Callie got the drift of her remark, but she wasn't going to admit a thing.

"I mean, you're a nurse. If the patient is well, the nurse usually finds a new patient, right?" Her eyes widened, and when Callie didn't respond, she blinked. "Wrong?"

"No, for a physical illness, you're right. Nattie's problem is more psychological. Healing is different."

"So you're planning to stay, then?" Her face puckered.

"For a while." Seeing the woman's face caused her to wonder about her own. She struggled to display what she hoped was a pleasant expression. "I'll leave eventually," she added, not wanting to utter the words. "Why do you ask?" Callie already suspected why, but she wanted to hear the woman's explanation.

"Well, uh, I suppose I should be out-and-out honest with you." Her shoulders raised, and she gave a deep, disgruntled sigh. "David is an attractive man, and available. Nattie needs a mother. Someone to give her love and affection. I realize right now that you're providing for her care, but David needs…well—I don't know why I'm explaining this to you."

Callie stared at her in amazement. "I'm not sure why you are, either."

Mary Beth rose, fists clenched at her side. "As long as you're here, David isn't going to realize he needs a wife and a mother for Nattie. I would make him a good companion. You're hired help, Callie. He certainly can't marry his child's nanny, now can he?"

Her words smacked Callie across the face. Struggling for composure, Callie concentrated on keeping her voice level. "I don't think you or I have any business deciding who David should marry." Mary Beth's hand clutched her chest, but Callie continued. "Am I to understand you want me to leave so David will come to his senses and marry you?"

"I didn't say it quite that way. I said, as long as you're here taking care of—"

"Of Nattie. That's what I do here." Callie raised her hand and fondled the two-tone gold rosebud pinned to her summer sweater.

"Well, I wasn't suggesting… I find it very difficult to talk to you."

"If you're waiting for me to leave, I have a piece of advice for you. Don't hold your breath."

Mary Beth's face reddened, and she bolted from her chair. "That's what I get for being honest. If you cared at all for that little girl and her father, you'd feel differently. I'm sorry you don't understand."

She swung on her heel and rushed down the stairs.

When she reached the sidewalk, she turned and faced Callie again. "And thank you for the lemonade. It was very good." With that, she spun around and dashed to her car.

Chapter Fourteen

Nattie had made wonderful progress on the piano for a six-year-old. She'd begun her second book in only a few weeks, and Callie listened in awe to her obvious talent. The lessons continued to be their secret, so Nattie practiced during the day when David was at work.

While she practiced, Callie sat nearby, her mind filled with Mary Beth's words. Despite her irritation with the woman, Mary Beth had pinpointed the truth. As long as Callie lived in the house, David wouldn't look for a wife and mother for Nattie.

The image of David falling in love with someone else seeped like poison through Callie's thoughts, making her sick at heart. An inexpressible loneliness surged through her. If she had nothing to offer David, she would be kind to leave. Maybe Mary Beth wasn't the woman for him—but somewhere in the world a lovely young woman waited for a man like David and a beautiful child like Nattie.

Callie pulled herself from her doldrums and eased her way across to the piano, as Nattie finished her piece.

"Was that good?" Her shy eyes sought Callie's.

She rested her hand on Nattie's shoulder. "That was wonderful. Your daddy is going to be so proud of you."

Nattie turned on the bench and faced Callie. "I'm tired of practicing."

"You can stop if you want. You practiced a long time."

She placed her hand in Callie's. "Can we go outside now?"

"Sounds good to me. But first, let's go see what Agnes is doing. I think I smelled cookies earlier."

The child's eyes brightened, and she dragged her tongue across her upper lip. "Yummy. Cookies."

Callie pulled her by the hand. "Let's go see if we can have a sample."

Like two conspirators, they marched toward the kitchen. Agnes, apparently hearing their giggles, waited for them as they came through the door. She placed a plate of cookies on the table, then headed for the cabinet and pulled out two glasses. "Milk goes good with cookies, don't you think?"

"I think you're right, Agnes," Callie said, sliding into a chair next to Nattie.

Before Callie could reach for a cookie, Nattie had one half eaten. Agnes put the glasses of milk on the table, and they munched on cookies and sipped milk until the plate was empty.

"Good thing I only put out a few," Agnes said with a grin, shaking her finger at them. "You wouldn't have left any for the man of the house."

"My daddy's the man of the house," Nattie announced.

"None other," Callie agreed, tousling her hair. "Thanks, Agnes. They were delicious."

"Thanks, Agnes," Nattie echoed. They rose and headed for the side entrance.

Callie halted at the screen door. "We're going for a walk up on the hill, Agnes. Tell David we'll be back in a while, if he gets home before we do."

The housekeeper nodded, and the screen slammed as they made their way down the steps.

Nattie skipped on ahead, and as she watched from behind, Callie marveled at the change in her. Only months ago, Nattie had been silent and withdrawn. Today she behaved like any six-year-old. Only on occasion did she slip into a deep, thoughtful reverie that filled her young face with dark shadows of sadness. Callie thanked God those times grew fewer and farther apart.

But today, the child skipped on ahead, and only when she reached the highway did she stop and look over her shoulder, waiting for Callie to catch up with her.

Hand in hand, they crossed the street, then raced up the hill and through the trees to their favorite spot, the spot where Nattie had spoken her first words to Callie. Now the fields were overgrown with wildflowers, and wild raspberry bushes bunched together along an unshaded path. Nattie plucked a black-eyed Susan as she twirled through the field, holding it out in front of her to show Callie.

They plopped down to rest under the shade of an elm, where the leaves and sun left speckled patterns on the green grass.

"Can I pick some more flowers? For Daddy."

"You can, but wait until just before we leave, okay? Wildflowers need water. We don't want them to get limp and die before we get them home."

Nattie agreed, then flopped back onto the grass and raised her hand over her head, staring into the cloudy sky. "I can see pictures in the clouds, Callie."

"You can?"

"Uh-huh." She pointed to a large fluffy cumulus.

Callie stretched out on her back next to Nattie, and together they pointed out dragons and elephants and ladies with long hair. The sun spread a warmth over her body, but not as completely as did the glow of her precious moment with Nattie.

As she lay there, Callie's mind filled with old, old songs she remembered her father singing when she was a child. "Buttermilk Sky." "Blue Skies." Then a hymn came to mind, and she sat up cross-legged, humming the tune.

Nattie rolled over on her side and listened for a while in silence, until she touched Callie's leg and said, "Sing."

Callie closed her eyes, and the song filled the air. *"For the beauty of the earth, for the beauty of the skies, for the love which from our birth…"* As Callie sang, Nattie's face glowed. The soft blue of her eyes sparkled with dots of sunshine. If ever in her life Callie had felt fulfilled, today was the day.

Somewhere in the reaches of her mind, the words to the song tumbled out. On the third verse, she rose, lifting her hands to the sky, and Nattie followed her, twirling among the wildflowers.

"For the joy of ear and eye, for the heart and mind's delight."

Then she heard a voice in the distance singing with her, drawing closer. *"For the mystic harmony, linking sense to sound and sight."*

Nattie said the words first. "It's Daddy." She raced from the spot and darted into the grove of trees. Callie stood transfixed for a moment, then thought better and hurried after Nattie. But she had taken only a few steps, when David came through the elms with Nattie in his arms.

A smile filled his face, and as he neared Callie, his rich, resonant baritone voice finished the verse. *"Christ, our Lord to You we raise this our sacrifice of praise."*

When he finished, Nattie giggled in his arms, hugging his neck. "I knew that was you, Daddy."

Callie stood in a daze. "But I didn't."

He unwound Nattie from his arms and slid her to the ground. Then he sank onto a grassy patch, stretching his legs out in front of him. "This is the life."

Callie, still astounded, sank next to him. "You should sing more, David. You talk about me? You have a tremendous voice."

"Not great. Adequate. I can carry a tune."

Callie looked at him and rolled her eyes. "And I gave Sara all the credit for Nattie's talent."

David checked her statement. "We should give God the credit."

Callie stopped in mid-thought. She turned slowly toward him. "You're right." Since the day David had told her about his anger with God, Callie had worried. But his words today eased her mind. And she leaned back on her elbows and breathed in the fresh, sun-warmed air.

David had surprised himself with his comment. But what he said was true. Neither he nor Sara could take credit for Nattie's talent. He'd given the glory to God. He eyed the child, her face glowing and her golden hair curling around her head like a bright halo.

He had an idea, and with a chuckle, he clapped his hands together. "Nattie, pick some daisies for me. With long stems. I'll make something for you."

She dashed off, bringing back a flower on a long spindly stem. "Is this a daisy?"

"That'll do. It's a black-eyed Susan." He pointed to the patch of white flowers nearby. "Those are daisies over there."

She darted away, then hurried back with a couple of the milky-colored blossoms with yellow centers. He sat and wound the stems together, fashioning a daisy chain. Sara had often created flower garlands, but today, as if God had given him another gift, the thought of her didn't press on his heart. Instead, he longed to make a wreath of flowers for Nattie's hair.

As his fingers worked the stems binding the flowers together, he eyed Callie and saw a look of wonderment on her face.

Amazement trickled through him, too, as he pictured himself immersed in blossoms. "I suppose you never thought you'd see the day that I'd sit and make flower garlands, huh?"

She laughed. "No, you're right. Maybe in a hospital for mental therapy—but not sitting here on the grass. Couldn't have imagined it in a million years."

"See, you just never know."

Nattie darted back and dropped a few more flowers in his lap, and then headed off again.

"Look at that child, Callie. Can you believe it? I hoped for so long, but I had dark moments when I thought she'd never come out of it. Now here she is—like new."

"I know. Watching her lifts my spirits higher than anything."

He raised his eyes to hers. "I'll tell you what lifts my spirits."

She sensed what he would say, and her chest tightened in anticipation.

"You. I believe Nattie came around because you've given her the tender love she needs. Not her mother, maybe. But you're soft and gentle like Sara. You're fair, blond hair, blue eyes."

"Spitting image?"

David shook his head. "Not spitting," he said, giving her an amused grin. "Only a faint resemblance. And you're a whole different person. Sara was quiet, sometimes too thoughtful. Even before her illness, she concentrated too much on things. She had fun, but...you're full of life and laughter."

Her face filled with surprise, and for the first time, he realized Callie had no idea how lovely she was.

"When I first met you, the word *spunky* came to mind."

"Spunky? I always thought I was a bit drab and boring."

"You?" David stared at her, amazed. Never in his life would he think of her as drab and boring. Lively, unpredictable, perhaps a little irritating at times—but never dull and lifeless.

"So what's the grand pause for? You're thinking bad things about me, aren't you?"

Pleasure tumbled through him. "I plead the fifth."

"Swell." She gazed down at the grass and plucked at a blade with her fingers.

"You'll only blush if I tell you what I was thinking. Except for the part about 'irritating.'"

Her head shot upward. "Irritating?" Her brows squeezed together, and she peered at him. "What do you mean 'irritating'?"

"Occasionally."

She arched an eyebrow.

"Once in a while."

She leaned closer, squinting into his teasing eyes.

His heart thundered at their play. "Rarely. Hardly ever. Once in a blue moon." He shrugged. "Okay, never."

She flashed him a bright smile. "See, I knew it."

He felt as if he were sailing into the clouds. He watched Nattie picking daisies, and Callie smiling at him with her glinting, delphinium-blue eyes. He wondered if he'd ever been so content.

When Nattie returned, he rested the daisy chain on her hair and kissed her.

"Am I pretty, Daddy?" She twirled around the way she and Callie had done earlier.

"You're absolutely beautiful."

Her eyes widened. "Like Callie?"

His heart lurched with awareness. "Yes," he murmured, glancing over at the woman who brought unimagined joy to his life. "Just like Callie." He allowed his gaze to sweep over her before he turned back to Nattie. "But we aren't finished here, Nattie. We have another lady who needs a crown."

Nattie regarded Callie with excitement and ran off again, as David's fingers manipulated the stems in his lap.

After a few concentrated minutes, he rested a laurel of flowers on Callie's head, too. Then he rose. "And now, my two princesses, I think we'd better get home. Looking at my sundial, I see Agnes is probably wondering how to keep our dinner warm."

He reached down, extending his hands to Callie. She looked up and took his hands. With one slight pull, she rose as easily as if she were a feather pillow. David smiled at the two most important women in his life, each with sun-speckled hair adorned with a flowered garland.

That night when Callie went to her room, her thoughts drifted back to the three of them in the meadow earlier that day. Each memory brought a warmth to her heart, as she witnessed Nattie stretching herself back into a normal life. But most of all, Callie pictured David, sitting on the grass, weaving flowers into crowns for their hair. She chuckled to herself, remembering the day they had met and his stern, pinched face.

Yet her joy changed to apprehension when she thought about the future. For them, she saw no hope of a life together. Mary Beth had planted a seed in her mind that continued to grow. When September came, whether she wanted to or not, she must leave.

Going home would be the best for David and for Callie. Though she'd warned herself many times, she had done the unthinkable. She had fallen in love with him.

At first, she wondered if her love for Nattie had made her think fondly of David. Yet the more time she spent with him, the more she was sure that wasn't true. She loved him as a man, not as Nattie's father. He excited her. His touch thrilled her.

Yet her old fears crept into her mind when she least wanted them to. Like her haunting dreams, they covered her with empty, hopeless thoughts.

She rose and turned on the lamp in her bedroom. A shower would relax her, and maybe she could sleep. She turned the nozzle on full blast and stepped into the steaming water, letting it wash over her and soothe her tightened muscles. Afterward, when dry, she massaged her skin with the vanilla-and-spice-scented cream that reminded her of Agnes's cookies. Her stomach growled, and she chuckled to herself.

Slipping her feet beneath the blankets, Callie fluffed her pillow and snapped off the light. Behind her eyelids, she saw again the afternoon sky filled with puffy white clouds: animals, people and wonderful imaginary shapes.

Then David appeared, lifting a garland of flowers and resting it on her head. In her imagination, his hands touched her face tenderly and his arms reached out, pulling her to him.

But then as sleep descended, the clouds, too, lowered, turning to a gray, swirling mist, and Callie heard the *click* of a lock. The black dream enveloped her, and David's handsome face changed into the face leering from the shadows.

He winked and placed his hot hand on hers. "You just relax there. I can hear you have a pretty voice. Take a nice deep breath. Throw out your chest and fill those lungs."

She drew a deep breath, her blouse buttons pulling against the cloth as her lungs expanded and her diaphragm stretched.

"That's better." He smiled, gazing at her with admiration.

But when she saw his eyes resting on the gaping buttons, the air shot from her.

His fingers moved across the keys, his body swaying on the bench, as she sang. When he played the final chord, his hands rose immediately into applause. "Why, you're a little meadowlark, aren't you?"

He rose and beckoned her with a finger to a sofa across the room. "Have a seat here so we can talk." She froze in place, his leering eyes riveting her to the floor, and as he reached toward her, a soundless scream rose in her throat.

Callie opened her eyes, her body trembling as she stared into the darkness. *It's only the dream. I'm dreaming.* She wiped the perspiration from her brow and rolled over on her side. Someday the dream would fade. It had to.

Chapter Fifteen

"**W**ell, what do you think?" Callie asked, as Nattie grinned from the piano bench. "Is tonight our surprise concert?"

Her golden curls bounced in the sunlight streaming through the windows. "Uh-huh," she said, giving a nod, "and we'll really surprise him, too."

"We sure will. You play so well already, Nat. I'm proud of you." She rose from the chair and gave the child a squeeze. "Right after dinner, we'll tell him to come into the parlor. Then, I'll be the announcer, and you stand up and take a bow."

Nattie giggled, as Callie described the scene. Filled with their conspiracy, they tiptoed from the parlor and raced up the stairs to wait for David to come home.

They filled their time with puzzles and a storybook, until a car door slam alerted them.

"Daddy's home," Nattie said, peering out the window and turning to Callie with her hand over her mouth to suppress her giggle.

"I heard, but don't forget, we can't let on about the secret."

"Okay," she said, a mischievous twinkle in her eye.

Shortly, his footsteps reverberated on the stairs, and Nattie jumped up and raced to the doorway. "Daddy." She lurched into his arms.

As she did daily, Callie watched their reunion. Since Nattie's return from her quiet world, their day had established a few pleasant routines. At the sound of David's arrival, Nattie dropped whatever she was doing to greet him. Best of all, David's love, once shrouded by his own knotted emotions, had opened as widely as his arms now stretching toward his daughter.

With Nattie captured in his embrace, he looked at Callie over her shoulder. "So what have the two of you been up to, today?"

Nattie let out a giggle and glanced at Callie.

Without giving away their secret, Callie shushed her with a look, then said to David, "Just our usual fun-filled day. Nothing special—puzzles, storybooks, the usual." She figured "the usual" covered the piano practice.

David eased Nattie to the floor. "Well, I think I'll change. Agnes said dinner's in a half-hour."

"We'll see you there," Callie said, grasping Nattie's hand and pulling her back into her room before she burst with the news.

Callie tempered Nattie's excitement at dinner. But as the evening progressed, the child's gaze lingered on her, beseeching her to conclude the meal so the surprise concert could begin.

David, for a change, filled the time with talk about some new business opportunities. Rarely did he bring his work to the table, but tonight Callie listened with appreciation, knowing that the chatter distracted Nattie from blurting their after-dinner plans.

"I have an idea," Callie suggested. "Let's have dessert in the parlor a little later. Agnes made homemade peach pie, and I suspect we all need to rest our stomachs before dessert."

"Sounds good to me," David said, folding his napkin and dropping it alongside his plate. He slid back his chair and rose. "How about you, Nat? Willing to wait for dessert?"

She eyed Callie before she commented. "Yes, because I want to show you something now."

"Show me something? Hmm? What could it be? A picture?"

Nattie jumped from her chair. "Nope. Come on, Daddy, and I'll show you our surprise."

David glanced at Callie. She only shrugged innocently. But when he turned his back, she gave Nattie a wink. The child giggled and skipped off to the parlor.

Callie expected to find Nattie seated at the piano when they caught up with her, but she had remembered their plan and now waited in a chair, her hands folded in her lap. Callie delighted in the heartwarming picture.

"So where's my surprise?" David asked as he entered the room.

"Don't rush us," Callie cautioned. "You sit down right there." She pointed to the chair in good view of the piano. "Are you ready?"

He looked at her, a confused frown knitting his brows. "As ready as I'll ever be."

"Okay, then, let me introduce our entertainment for the evening. Da-da-da-dum!" Callie imitated a drumroll. "Give a warm welcome to Nattie Hamilton, who will perform for us on the grand piano." She began the applause.

David gaped and looked at Nattie, who rose from her chair, bowed and scurried to the piano.

She grinned at her father, then slid a book from under the seat and propped it on the music stand. Easing onto the bench, she adjusted the music book, arched her fingers over the keys and began the song she had prepared: Bach's étude, "Minuet." Her small fingers struck the keys, sending the spirited melody dancing across the room.

With his mouth hanging open like a Venus flytrap, David's attention was riveted on his daughter. When she struck the final note, his quick look at Callie's amused expression prompted him to snap his mouth closed with embarrassment.

Callie burst into applause, praying that David wasn't angry. But in a heartbeat, his surprised expression turned to joy, and he leaped from the chair in a thundering ovation and a cry of "Bravo!"

Nattie slipped from the piano bench, pulled out her pant legs as if she wore a skirt, and took a deep bow.

He bolted to her side and knelt to embrace her. "Oh, Nat, I'm so proud of you. Just like your mom." Turning, his eyes focused on Callie, who was standing in the distance and observing the scene. "And I know I have you to thank for her lessons."

She lowered her lids to hide the tender tears that rose in her eyes. "You're welcome."

"Nat, this is the best concert I've ever heard. You are my personal star."

Nattie grinned and wrapped her arms around his neck. "I'm your star."

"You sure are. Best gift in the whole world." He rose,

taking one of her hands. "So when have you been practicing?"

"Every day," Nattie told him. "After you go to work.
But we couldn't practice on Saturdays or Sundays. Otherwise, you'd hear me. I'm on my third book already."

David turned to Callie. "You've been buying her
music books?"

She nodded.

"You are a gem, Callie. A real gem."

"She's a diamond, just like me." Nattie's voice burst
with excitement. "Callie told me I was her gem. Did you
know that means a 'diamond,' Daddy?"

David raised his hand quickly and wiped what Callie guessed was a tear that had escaped his eye. "I do.
You're both my diamonds."

Nattie ran to Callie's side, hugging her waist. "We're
Daddy's diamonds, Callie."

She looked down at the child's beaming face. "I heard.
That makes us both pretty special."

"Yep," she said, her head resting against Callie's hip.

Callie looked at David. "Before our throats are too
knotted to enjoy dessert, I should probably ask Agnes
to bring in the pie. What do you say?"

He grinned, his eyes glistening with moisture. "I say,
you're not only a diamond, but a very wise woman."

When John Spier called, Callie could think of no excuse. She agreed to attend a jazz concert at the historic
Opera House in Mitchell. When she accepted the invitation, he suggested dinner, as well.

A whole evening with John didn't excite her. But she'd
told him to call, and he'd done what she asked.

Telling David was difficult. She had no idea whether

he cared or not, but *she* cared. And she took forever to harness her courage.

"Tonight?" David asked.

"Yes." She wanted to tell him she'd rather stay home and sit in the parlor with him, but her truthfulness would only embarrass her, and lead nowhere. "But if it's a problem, I'll call him and explain. I didn't give you much notice."

"No, that's fine, Callie. I, ah… I have no plans for the evening."

Disappointment filled her. She wished, at least, that he looked upset or inconvenienced.

He peered at his shoes. "You need a private life. You devote a lot of time to us."

"All right, if you don't mind." She had so much more to say—but if he didn't care, why should she? "I'll go, then. Thank you."

"You're welcome," he said, glancing at her. "Have a nice time."

Suddenly her disappointment turned to irritation. "I'm sure I will," she said, her voice picking up a spark. "I'll go."

"Good."

This time his tone sounded edgy. She turned and left the study. Nattie stood in the hallway, peering at her, as Callie came from the room. She had more than two hours to get ready, but she wasn't going to sit there and feel sorry for herself. She had a date, and she'd enjoy herself if it killed her.

With a final look at David through the doorway, she charged up the stairs and into her room. Plopping on the edge of her bed, she stared into her open closet. What should she wear? Hardly anything she owned seemed appropriate for a date. She needed to go on a shopping spree—but where around here? Shopping meant a trip to Indianapolis. More guilt rose as she thought of her mother.

Though they talked on the telephone, Callie hadn't been home to visit Grace in a while. She should arrange a trip. *Trip?* In September, she would be leaving Bedford altogether. Bleak dread raked through her. But it was a cold, hard fact.

She rose and maneuvered her outfits along the wooden rod, glancing at skirts, blouses, dresses. The Opera House. Was it dressy? She was positive she didn't have anything appropriate. Taking care of Nattie didn't require fancy dress, only casual. She searched through the clothing again, but stopped when she heard a noise at the hall door.

She turned and saw Nattie peering in from the sitting room. "Come in, Nat."

Nattie rarely came to Callie's room, and today she edged through the door.

"Did you need something?"

Nattie shook her head, her eyes focused on the closet. "Are you going away?" she asked.

"Uh-huh," Callie said, peering at a summery dress she held in front of her on the hanger.

"Please, don't go away." Nattie's voice quivered with emotion.

Callie spun around and faced her. Nattie's lower lip trembled, leaving Callie confused. "What's wrong? Don't you feel well?"

She shook her head. "I don't want you to leave. Who will take care of me?"

Callie crossed to her and knelt to hold her. "No, I'm

not leaving for good. Just for tonight, Nat. Your daddy's home, and Agnes. They'll be here. I'll be back later."

Nattie's misty eyes widened. "Oh… I thought you were going away."

"What would make you say that? Heaven forbid. I wouldn't leave you." Nattie lay her head on Callie's shoulder, and the unintended lie she had uttered, like a boomerang, spun back, whacking her conscience. Hadn't she just decided she would leave Bedford in September?

She gazed into the child's sad face and couldn't bring herself to say any more. Instead, she held Nattie tightly to her chest until she felt her relax, then tickled her under the chin. "So, you thought I was leaving you. You silly. Wouldn't I tell you if I were going away for good?"

"But you and Daddy hollered. I thought—"

"No, we were just talking loudly. There's a difference. And don't you worry about that, anyway. I'm not going anywhere, except out to dinner and to a concert with Pastor John."

Nattie tilted her head, staring directly into her eyes. "Why don't you go with Daddy?"

The child's look of sincerity tugged at Callie's heart-strings. Yet, the words made her smile. Sometimes she wondered the same thing. What might it be like to spend an evening with David—on a real date? She took a minute to find her voice. "I suppose because your daddy didn't ask me—"

"Didn't ask you what?"

Her head shot upward, and she felt a flush spill over her face like a can of rose-colored paint. "I didn't hear you."

David stepped into the room. "Yes, I know. So what didn't I ask you?"

"You didn't ask Callie to go to dinner," Nattie offered, still hugging Callie's neck.

"And why would I do that?" He glowered at Callie.

She unleashed Nattie's arms, then rose. "You shouldn't. She's upset because she thought I was leaving—for good. I explained I was going out with John."

"Ah," David said. "She thought that because you were yelling at me."

Callie lifted her chin. "*I* yelled at *you?*"

"Yes. And now she wants to know why I don't take you to dinner and the concert?"

Nattie shook her head, her eyes wide, certainly not understanding all the innuendos.

Callie glared at him. "Yes, that's what she asked." She waited for his arrogant, stinging response.

"I guess," he said, kneeling down to Nattie, "that I didn't think of it first."

Callie's mouth dropped open wider than David's had days earlier at Nattie's concert. Her pulsed raced like an *arpeggio.*

He raised his soft, apologizing eyes to hers, and she faltered backward, grasping the dresser to steady her trembling legs. "You've caught me off guard."

His full, parted lips flickered to a smile. "Yes, I see that. You can close your mouth now." He scooped Nattie into his arms, as she let out a squeal. "We'd better let Miss Randolph get herself decked out for her *date,* Nattie."

"Who's Miss Randolph?" Nattie asked, as he carried her, giggling, toward the door.

He glanced at Callie over his shoulder. "I'm not sure myself, Nattie. I have to figure that one out."

Chapter Sixteen

When Callie arrived home from her evening with John, David's study light glowed through the tower room window. She said goodnight to John and hurried inside. Stopping outside the study door, she paused. She longed to talk to him, but couldn't bolster her courage, so instead she headed upstairs to her room.

The evening had been a strange one. She wondered if, instead of being interested in her, after all, he hoped she could be a liaison between David and the church. Though John said how much he enjoyed her company, the conversation continued to backtrack to the church, the broken organ, and a variety of other congregational concerns.

Callie had decided a pastor's life must be a difficult one, and her heart softened a little as she'd listened to him. She knew the pianist was leaving, and he needed a replacement or, at least, a substitute until a new pianist could be found. Callie sat beside him feeling guilty. He knew she played the piano, and by the end of the evening, she suggested that she might consider helping out "in a pinch."

As well as addressing John's concerns, Callie had her own. She couldn't get Nattie's question out of her mind: *"Are you going away?"* Thinking of the situation, she ached. It was no-win. If she stayed with Nattie, David would eventually fall in love and find a wife. She didn't know if she could bear it.

Still, she knew David's feelings for her had grown. At the thought, her heart soared—until reality smacked her in the face and her feelings nosedived to the ground. How many times did she have to tell herself she had nothing to offer him? She could never allow him to fall in love with her—nor she with him.

With her mind in a turmoil, she climbed into bed. She lay for a long time, her thoughts pacing back and forth like someone waiting for a last meal. She knew she was a loser no matter how she looked at it—and was suffering because her actions would also hurt Nattie.

Finally her eyes grew heavy, and she drifted to a near sleep, awakened again, then succumbed. And as her mind glided into sleep, so the shadows rose from her subconscious.

With his hot hand on hers, she heard him. "You just relax there, little lady. I can hear you have a pretty voice. Take a nice deep breath. Throw out your chest and fill those lungs."

She drew a deep breath, her blouse buttons pulling against the cloth, and she saw his eyes resting on the gaping buttons.

"That's better." He smiled. "Let's try a song."

"We'll do one you know." He handed her some sheet music. "Pick something you know well."

She made her selection and handed him the music. She

heard the introduction clearly and filled her diaphragm with air. She opened her mouth, and her pure, natural voice, filled with strength and joy, soared from her.

He gazed at her with admiration, swaying on the bench, as she sang. When he played the final cord, his hands rose immediately into applause. "Why you're a little meadowlark, aren't you."

He rose, beckoning her to follow him across the room to the sofa. "Have a seat, my little Meadowlark, so we can talk business." Her heart raced at first, then the hammering began. He settled next to her, placing his hand on hers. "Are you more comfortable now?"

"Yes," she said, trying to extract her hand. "A little nervous, I guess."

"How old are you?"

"Just turned nineteen. I'm a sophomore at the University of Indiana."

"You'd really like to sing with our group, wouldn't you? Travel with us in the summer? I'm sure you'd be grateful for a place in our choir."

"Oh, I would. Yes, my father thinks you're wonderful."

"And you? Am I wonderful, Meadowlark?"

His hand slid across her knee, and she grabbed it, holding him back. But his strength overpowered her.

"You want to make your daddy proud, don't you? If you want your daddy to be proud, you have to please me a little. How about a kiss?"

His face loomed above her. Her chest hammered, thundered inside her, and she opened her mouth to scream, but she had no voice. Instead, she couldn't breathe, she was sinking into some deep swirling ocean of icy black water. She heard her blouse tearing and felt her skirt rising on her thighs, and she died beneath the blackness.

* * *

When Callie woke, her hands clasped the blankets and her arms ached from fighting off the monster in her dream. She had kept her secret from everyone. No one knew why she had stopped singing. No one knew what had happened—only she and Jim McKee.

She rolled on her side and snapped on the light, squinting at the brightness. Why had she not pulled herself from the dream sooner? Lately, she'd been able to stop the dream before the end, but tonight the horrible memory wrenched through her. All the filth and pain she had felt these past years lay on her shoulders.

Callie rose from her bed and went into the bathroom, ran cool tap water over her face and arms. She returned to the bedroom and eased herself to the edge of the bed, noticing the clock. Only twenty-five minutes had passed since she'd crawled under the sheets. She needed to talk to David, to do something to make the terrible thoughts go away. But if she talked tonight, she might regret it. The burden she had carried so many years struggled for release.

She leaned back again on the pillow and dimmed the bulb to a soft glow. As she folded her hands behind her head, her mind wandered, and while it strayed, she heard faintly, a soft, lilting melody drift through the room. Her radio? Had she accidentally set the clock-radio alarm?

She rose and strode to the sitting room. The sound was stronger there, louder than in her bedroom. Television? A recording? She listened more closely. A piano coming from below. Was David playing the piano? She had never heard him play. The music rose through the walls, poignant and beautiful.

She slipped into sweatpants and shirt, and opened

her sitting room door. The hallway was empty. No light glowed beneath the second-floor doorways. She followed the stairs down to the dimly lit foyer. A light still shone beneath David's study door, and from outside, she heard the lovely, haunting melody.

Whether wise or not, she turned the knob and eased the door open. Barefoot, she tiptoed into the room, following the music coming from the piano. As she reached the archway, she stood back and watched David's shadow dip and bend as his body moved with the rapture of the music. Her heart soared, yet wept at the haunting sound.

When the last strain died away, he sat with his head bowed, then, as if he sensed her presence, he turned. She stepped through the opening, and his gaze lifted to her face, caressing her, his eyes glistening with emotion.

"Callie, I thought you were sleeping." He rose and moved toward her. "Is something wrong? Did I wake you?"

"No. A dream woke me." She closed the distance between them. "David, the song was beautiful. What is it?" She glanced toward the piano and saw his manuscript spread out on the music stand. "You wrote that, David?" Callie dashed to the paper and lifted the music. "You wrote this." She swung to face him.

He rested his hands on her shoulders. "Yes, I wrote it. It's been playing in my mind for months, but I hadn't written in so long, not since...since Sara died. I didn't think I'd write again. But I couldn't make the music stop roaring in my head until I put it on paper."

Swirling emotion drew her eyes to his, and in them, she searched for an answer. His words promised a release for her. He couldn't make the music stop until he put it on paper. Would her dreams stop if she said them aloud?

She struggled with her thoughts. The truth lay in his heart and in hers. If he knew, could he love her? If she told him, would she be released from her self-made prison? Could she take the chance? She slid the music back on the stand.

"Callie, I could no more fight the music in my head than I can fight the feelings inside me. You should know that I love you. I've been falling in love with you ever since the day we met."

"Oh, please, David, don't say anything that will hurt us."

"Hurt you? Never. My feelings are far too powerful to hide any longer. I've tried to sense how you feel about me. I'd hoped you were learning to love me, too."

"There are too many things you don't know about me, David. Awful things. If you knew them, you wouldn't say you loved me. I've struggled with them in my dreams, but not aloud. They hurt too bad. Please, don't say you love me."

David looked into her eyes, trying to fathom what terrible things she could mean. Her eyes glowed, but with fear. He felt her trepidation in the tension of her shoulders. He drew her to him and wrapped his arms around her.

"Please, Callie, tell me. Do you love me? If you love me, I can handle anything. Whatever you need to tell me. I promise."

She clung rigidly to his arms, and he sensed her panic.

"Don't promise anything until you know the truth," she pleaded. "I couldn't bear to have you reject me."

"Then you do love me? Say it, please."

"I've tried not to love you. For a long time, I told myself I only loved Nattie, but I can't lie. Yes, I do love you, but I can never marry you…or anyone. Never."

He caught her face in his hands and lowered his lips to hers. Her mouth yielded to his, but just as quickly, she pulled away. Instead, he kissed her cheeks and her eyes, tasting the saltiness of the tears that clung to her lashes.

"Callie, if you love me, you'll tell me what's wrong. Let me know what's hurt you so badly. Maybe I can help you."

"Please, let me think about it, David. Play your music for me again. I'd love to hear your song once more. I'll sit right here." She backed up and lowered herself into a chair.

"Promise you'll tell me?"

"I promise I'll think about it."

"Promise you'll tell me, Callie."

"Play for me, David, and I'll try."

David looked with longing into her eyes, and didn't argue, but wandered to the piano and slid onto the bench, shifting the music on the stand. He glanced at her, then lifted his eyes to the music. He played, and the love he'd felt for these past months rose from the keys and drifted through the room.

He sensed her watching him, and he trembled at the thought. As his attention drifted to the last phrase of music, she rose and moved across the floor to stand behind him, her hands resting on his shoulders. He felt the warmth of her hands on his arms, and his fingers tingled with the fire burning in his heart.

On the last chord, he turned to her, and tears ran down her cheeks. Her eyes were focused on the sheet of music resting on the stand. Almost imperceptibly, he heard her whisper, "'Callie's Song.' You named it for me."

He swiveled on the bench. "The music is you, Callie. All the longing and joy, fear, confusion, wonder you brought into our lives here. Nattie, you, me, everything."

She stared at him in disbelief. "Thank you," she whispered.

He stood and placed his hands on her arms. "Thanks to you, Callie." He took her hand and led her toward the door. "Let's sit in the parlor. It's more comfortable there. We need to talk. I'll make us a cup of tea. How does that sound?"

She nodded and followed him, his arm guiding her. When they reached the foyer, he kissed her cheek, aiming her into the parlor as he turned toward the kitchen.

Callie wandered through the doorway, wondering what she would do now. Where could she begin? She had so much she should tell him, yet so little she wanted to admit. He loved her. And she had finally told him the truth: she loved him with all her heart. And Nattie, too. But…

She eased herself onto the sofa, her gaze sweeping the room. The grand piano stood in silence in the bay window, and she thought about the wonderful day, not long ago, when Nattie had played her concert. What happiness she had felt that day. But tonight, though David's song touched her with tenderness, her pulse tripped in fear at the story David wanted her to tell.

Hearing his steps in the foyer, she looked toward the doorway. He came into the room carrying two mugs, and sending a steamy, fragrant mist into the air. Handing one mug to her, he sat by her side, stretching his legs in front of him. "Be careful. This stuff's really hot."

She blew on the beverage before taking a cautious sip, and curled her legs underneath her.

David studied her. "So. Where do we begin?"

She stared at her hands folded in her lap. "I was trying to decide while you were getting the tea. This is very difficult for me. Harder than you can ever imagine. If I get through this, David, you should know you're the only person in the whole world I've told this to."

"I understand. You've suffered far too long for whatever this is about. I'm honored to be the one you trust enough to tell."

A sigh tore through her, and an unbelievable desperation raged inside. A sob escaped from her throat. She swallowed it back, choking on the emotion.

He took her hand in his and brushed her skin with his fingertips without speaking.

Another sigh rattled from her. With a gentle touch, David caressed her hand. Then she began, slowly at first.

"Seven years ago I sang in church, in college—anywhere an audience would listen. I studied music in college. Even thought I might like a career as a musician or singer. But my father longed for me to audition for the Jim McKee Singers. It was made up of college-age students who traveled in the summer. My father was a powerful Christian, and his greatest joy was for me to sing with them during one of their summer tours."

Callie closed her eyes, wondering how far she could get before she lost control. David shifted his fingers to her arm, caressing her the way a father calms his child.

"I arranged for a tryout and waited in an office set up near the college for the local auditions. I felt more and more nervous as each person went in and left. Soon, I was alone. He came to the door and called me in."

"Who, Callie? Who was he?"

She swallowed, struggling to speak his name. "The director... J-Jim McKee." Her lips stammered the name.

"So what happened?"

She felt David tense, almost as if he could guess what she was going to say, but his eyes only emanated tenderness.

She returned to the story beginning with the *click* of the lock. "'You're nervous enough, I'm sure,' he said to me as he bolted the door. 'We don't want anyone popping in and making things worse, do we?'"

As if marching through her dream, she led David through the audition. "Then Jim McKee led me to the couch, and kept calling me his 'little meadowlark.' My poor mother called me that a few months ago, and I panicked. I can't hear that word without remembering."

David leaned over to kiss her cheek. "It's okay, Callie. I love you."

"How can you love me, David? You already know what happened." The sobs broke from her throat, and she buried her face in her hands. "I was a virgin. And he took the most precious gift I longed to share with a husband someday. He raped me, David."

Chapter Seventeen

David drew her into his arms, holding her as she wept and rocked her as he would a child. "It wasn't your fault, Callie. You didn't make it happen. It wasn't your fault."

Seven years of pain and sorrow flooded from her in a torrent of hot tears. His murmured words lulled her. When she gathered her strength, she lifted her head, fearing to look in his eyes, but there, she saw only his gentle understanding.

"I've kept that a secret so long, David."

"Why? That's what I don't understand. Why? How many other young women's lives did that demon destroy?"

"I didn't have the courage to tell my parents. My father idolized the man. He wouldn't have accepted that Jim McKee would do something like that." She searched his face for his understanding. "I thought my dad would blame me, think I had been so awed that I was a willing partner. I don't know. I thought I could wash it away with soap and water and prayers."

"Callie, my love, you suffered too long."

"I read in the paper a few years ago that he died

suddenly from a heart attack. *David, I was happy.* I'm ashamed of myself, but I was happy he died."

David buried his face in her hair. She didn't know what he felt. But his eyes had said he understood, and that's what mattered.

She filled her lungs with healing air and released a ragged sigh. "You know, deep inside I've felt so much guilt. I've wondered if I *did* do something to make him think I wanted him." She sighed. "Do you know what sticks in my mind?"

He shook his head.

"I remember my deep breath and the buttons gaping on my blouse. I kept asking myself, did I tempt him? Did he think I did it on purpose, that it was a come-on?"

David closed his eyes and shuddered. "Callie, how many women in the world take deep breaths and their buttons pull on their blouses? Do you think it's their announcement to the world that they want to be raped? I can't believe you've worried all these years about that."

"I was barely a woman then, naive and so innocent… until that terrible day."

Helplessness washed over her again as she recalled the day she realized she was pregnant. How could she tell her parents then about the horrible event she'd kept from them? That was the moment she decided to let them think the baby growing inside her was fathered by a college student. Why destroy everything they believed? She let them accept her lie.

And now, how could she tell David? He and Sara had chanced everything, even Sara's life, to have a child, and Callie walked away from hers. Maybe the rape wasn't her fault. But losing her child was.

An abortion had been out of the question. God would

never forgive her for taking the life of an innocent child. Despite her supposed wisdom, she'd never forgive herself for agreeing to the adoption. How could she tell David?

The silence lingered, and David held her close in his arms.

"David?" she murmured.

"Yes." He pulled his face from her hair and looked into her eyes, questioning.

"Do you understand why I'm afraid? I don't know if I can ever love a man fully without those memories filling my mind. Even your innocent touch scares me sometimes."

"I sensed your fear, Callie, and I didn't understand. I thought it was *me*."

"Oh, no, it isn't you."

"I know that now. And now that I understand, we can work on it, Callie. We'll take it slow. One step at a time. You can learn that being loved is a gentle, powerful experience. *Love,* Callie—love is a gift from God. A wonderful, pure gift."

Tears rose in David's eyes, and for the first time, Callie saw them spill down his cheeks. Her stomach knotted when she saw his sorrow—sorrow he had hidden for so long.

"You're crying." Callie reached up to wipe away the tears from his cheeks. She kissed his moist eyes and buried her face in his neck.

David's heart reeled at her tenderness. She was not alone in bearing shame for so many years. "I'm crying for both of us. We've both carried secrets longer than we should."

"Secrets? You mean Sara's pregnancy and—"

"Yes, I went against God's wishes and demanded an

abortion. I didn't want her to die, and I knew if she carried the baby, she couldn't have the treatment she needed. But Sara refused, and we waited too long. God punished me for my selfishness."

Callie looked at him, her face filled with confusion. "She was too far in her pregnancy for an abortion?"

He didn't comment, leaving her to accept his silence as his answer. Sara had wanted a baby so badly. He remembered the anger he had felt shortly before she died, how he blamed her pregnancy for her short life. Shaking his fist at God for their losses.

David pulled himself from his sad musings. "Callie, we both have some issues to deal with, but doing it together will give us strength. Love is a mighty healer."

He saw in her face understanding and acceptance. He lowered his lips to hers, and this time, she didn't recoil, but raised her mouth to meet his. Gently their lips joined, and she offered him the love that had lain buried inside her.

When they parted, he held her close, praying that the healing for both of them had already begun.

Callie leaped from bed the next morning. The clock read ten. She'd not slept that late in years. What about Nattie? She threw on her robe and darted across the hall. Nattie was not there. Her bed was unmade, her pajamas in a pile on the floor.

Callie hurried back to her room, completed the most rudimentary cleansing ritual and threw on a pair of slacks and a top. As she dashed down the staircase, she saw David and Nattie at breakfast. Embarrassed at her lateness, she slowed her pace and worked at regaining her composure.

At the bottom of the stairs, a bouquet of fresh flowers sat on the foyer table. At its base lay a card with her name scrawled on the envelope. David caught her eye as she stood in the foyer, and she nodded, touched that he had sent her flowers already, so early in the morning.

But the biggest surprise occurred when she opened the card. The flowers were from John. She flushed, knowing she had to call him immediately after breakfast, to thank him and give him some kind of explanation as to why she couldn't go out with him again.

She hurried into the dining room.

"Callie." Nattie giggled. "You didn't wake me up. Daddy said you overslept."

"Good morning." David eyed her with a searching look. "I believe you overslept."

"I did, didn't I. And why aren't you at work?"

He grinned. "Guilty as charged. And the flowers?"

"You got flowers," Nattie chimed.

Callie nodded. "From John." She wrinkled her nose. "I guess I owe him a telephone call."

"I guess," David said with a hint of jealousy. "What would make him send you a bouquet, I wonder?"

"Guilt? Payola?"

"Blackmail?" His grin grew. "Whatever. Call him, please."

"I will. I promise. By the way, I agreed to fill in as the pianist. Pam Ingram is leaving. She's expecting a baby and doesn't have time to handle the piano and choir right now."

"Pianist and choir director?"

"No. You heard me. *Pianist.* You're the choir director."

"Was."

"We'll see."

"I repeat, *was*."

She gave him a grin, not saying another word. They enjoyed breakfast together, then David hurried off to work. Later in the afternoon, Agnes called Callie to the front door. She descended the stairs with Nattie on her heels and halted in surprise halfway down.

"More flowers?" she asked, gaping at a deliveryman holding a huge package wrapped in floral paper.

"Must be a special occasion," he said. "This is the second bouquet I've delivered here."

She swallowed. "Not really. Just a coincidence." She took the bouquet from him and closed the screen door.

Nattie skipped around her in excitement. "More flowers?"

"Looks like it, doesn't it?"

Callie pulled the protective paper from the magnificent arrangement of mixed flowers: lilies, orchids, roses. John's simple vase looked sad by comparison. She didn't need to open the card to know the source. A grin crept to her lips.

"Who are they from, Callie?"

"Your daddy, I think." Callie pulled the card from the envelope. *I love you. Never forget. David.* She laughed, seeing the sense of competition John's bouquet had aroused. Then her stomach churned as she recalled her promise: she needed to march to the telephone without delay and talk to John.

Callie thanked John by telephone for the flowers and made arrangements to practice on the church piano. Though two pianos were available at the house, her "practice" was an excuse to see him. She reviewed a variety of ways she might tell him about David and her, but nothing felt comfortable.

A cooling air washed over her as she entered the church. The stained-glass windows held the sun's scorching rays at bay. She headed down the aisle, and by the time she reached the piano, John was coming through a side door. But to her dismay, Mary Beth followed behind him.

His sister wore a bright smile painted on her lips, and the look gave Callie an eerie feeling. In a flash, she knew what Mary Beth was thinking. If Callie was dating John, David was "available." She had bad news for both of them.

John stepped to her side. "I appreciate your willingness to fill in here. I'm looking for a regular pianist, I promise, but it may take some time. We don't have too many accomplished musicians hanging around Bedford."

"As long as you know this is temporary," she reminded him.

Mary Beth fanned her face with her hand. "Whew, you saved me, Callie. I play a little, and John was trying to coerce me."

Callie bit her tongue. If she had had any idea Mary Beth played, she wouldn't have volunteered—but it was too late now. "Well, I'm glad to hear you can play, Mary Beth. I do plan to visit my mom in Indianapolis. I haven't seen her in a while, and I'm feeling guilty."

Mary Beth raised her hand to her throat with a titter. "Oh, my, I guess I shouldn't have spoken."

She leaned intimately toward Callie. "And how are things with you? I understand you had a nice evening. And flowers. He sent you flowers." Her voice lilted with feigned enthusiasm.

"Yes, we had a nice time, but I didn't expect flowers."

Mary Beth took a step backward. "I suppose I should leave and let the two of you talk privately."

She needed to act now or never. "No, Mary Beth, don't go. I have something to tell both of you."

John's face brightened, then faded when he looked at her expression. Mary Beth had a similar reaction.

Callie cleared her throat. "I don't want to mislead you. I had a lovely time. The food was excellent, and I enjoyed the concert. But I'm afraid I can't accept any more invitations."

"You can't?" John asked.

Mary Beth's head pivoted from one to the other.

"That evening, David and I came to…an understanding."

Mary Beth gasped. "An understanding?"

"Yes, we realize that we've grown to…care very deeply for each other, and we—we've fallen in love."

"Fallen in love." The words escaped them in unison like the chorus of a Greek tragedy.

Callie looked at them. "I hope you can be happy for us."

"Happy?" John looked bemused, then his brows unfurrowed. "Happy, yes. I'm happy for you."

She watched him struggle to maintain a neutral expression. Mary Beth's face registered pure frustration.

"Well, I hope under the circumstances," Mary Beth said, her face pinched, "that you don't plan to continue living together in the same house."

Callie's heart dropped. The thought hadn't occurred to her. But she had to live here. How would she and David know if they could work through their problems?

Yet how could she explain the situation to others—once Mary Beth spread the news?

Callie leveled her stare at Mary Beth. "We don't live in the house alone, as you know. Agnes and Nattie are both there. I don't believe in premarital relationships, Mary Beth, if that's what you're insinuating." She almost became catty, wanting to add the words, *"Perhaps you do."* But God intervened and removed the words from her lips.

"I'm not insinuating anything. I just wouldn't want others to think differently."

John pressed his sister's arm. "I don't see how others will think anything, Mary Beth. No one knows this, except you and me. And we won't spread idle gossip, will we?"

Mary Beth grasped the neck of her blouse for a second time. "Why…no. I certainly wouldn't spread gossip."

"Then I don't believe we have a problem at all."

Callie wanted to hug him, but instead, she extended her hand. "Thank you, John, for understanding." Mary Beth hovered as if waiting to receive her thank you, but Callie sat at the piano to practice.

Chapter Eighteen

No matter what John had said to make things better, Callie couldn't forget his sister's words. Was it wrong for her to stay at the house now that she and David had admitted their love for each other? Wonderful, fulfilled days passed by, and though they said nothing to Nattie, the child seemed to understand changes had occurred. And her joy had grown as much as theirs.

September was nearly on their doorstep, and Nattie would soon begin school. With her debut into the world of education, Callie faced a decision. What reason did she have to stay in Bedford? The time had come to talk honestly with David.

But Callie's procrastination had blossomed into avoidance. Today she set a deadline. One week. Within the week, she had to broach the subject of leaving. She couldn't stay in the house under the circumstances, no matter what her heart said.

Callie descended the staircase to a flutter of activity. Yesterday David had announced he'd invited their old housekeeper, Miriam, to dinner. With improved health, she had come to Bedford to visit her sister.

At the bottom of the stairs, Nattie clung to the banister, staring at the door and awaiting Miriam's arrival. At the sound of an automobile, Nattie raced to the door and tugged it open.

As soon as Callie saw her, she understood why Miriam held a special place in their hearts. Stepping from the car was a woman who fulfilled everyone's dream of a roundish, warm, lovable fairy godmother. Her face glimmered with animation and love as she threw her ample arms around Nattie and David.

Callie waited inside, allowing their welcome to be unburdened by introductions. David helped Miriam through the door, and Callie met her in the foyer.

The elderly woman moved cautiously forward, a cane in her left hand, and Callie joined her in welcome. "I'm so happy to meet you. I've heard nothing but wonderful things about you."

Miriam's eyes twinkled. "And I've heard nothing but wonderful things about you." She wrapped one arm around Callie's shoulders, giving her a warm hug.

"Come into the parlor, Miriam. We'll sit until dinner's ready." There, David guided her to a comfortable chair. Nattie clung to her side and leaned against the chair arm, as Miriam settled herself.

"I'd hold you on my lap, precious, but I'm not sure my old legs will bear the weight. You've grown so big since I last saw you. It seems years, rather than months."

Nattie stood straight as if pulled by a string. "I forgot. Agnes said I could help set the table." She skipped from the room, as the others chuckled at her enthusiasm.

"David, what a joy to see her so well." Miriam turned toward Callie. "I know we have this young lady to thank."

Callie murmured a thank you, as Miriam continued.

"When I left, my heart was nearly broken, seeing Nattie so distraught. David had already gone through enough without that burden."

"I've enjoyed every moment I've spent with Nattie," Callie said. "I've had the rare pleasure of watching her blossom. It's like a special gift from God."

"I'm sure it is," she said. "And now, David, what's happening with you?"

"Seeing Nattie get better has been amazing. And I might add, meeting Callie has been a blessing for me, too."

A healthy grin curved Miriam's mouth, and her eyes twinkled. "Am I to understand you two have—how should I put it—an understanding?"

Callie glanced at David with a shy grin.

He nodded. "Yes, you could call it that. Callie has brought me back to life as much as she has Nat."

Miriam turned to Callie. "Then, I thank you. You've made an old woman feel very happy."

Callie laughed. "Thanks. We're a pretty happy bunch."

"And we'll be even happier when we eat. Let me check on dinner." David jumped up and left the room.

Miriam checked the doorway, then faced Callie. "While he's gone, I want to thank you privately. I love this family like my own, and my heart was heavy with all the sadness in this house. But today, I feel love—and best of all, promise."

"Thank you. When I first came, I thought David was a grouchy, unloving, hard-nosed man. At times he was, but I soon found the real David underneath all that cover-up."

"David hardened himself. He blamed himself for Sara's death, I know. Letting her get pregnant, and then losing the baby. But when they got Nattie, what joy! She was the answer to their prayers."

"Losing the baby? You mean Sara had a miscarriage. I didn't know that." Callie's stomach knotted. David's words echoed in her mind, *"God punished me for my selfishness."* Is that what he'd meant?

"Oh, yes, such sadness that day."

"I can imagine their joy when Nattie arrived."

"Yes, but short-lived." Miriam's old grief resurfaced in her voice.

"Only four years, I understand."

Miriam lowered her eyes and a look of disapproval swept over her. "Yes, Sara was a lovely woman… David knew she had cancer when they married."

Callie nodded. "Yes, he told me." Obviously, Miriam had stronger feelings than she allowed herself to say.

The older woman regrouped. "But the four years with Nattie were wonderful years for them both. Right up to the end."

David's footsteps signaled his return. He came through the doorway with his hands outstretched. "Dinnertime. Have you ever heard sweeter words?"

Callie helped Miriam from the chair and whispered in her ear, "I always thought the sweetest words were 'I love you'—but you know men."

The two women chuckled, and David raised an eyebrow at them.

They lingered over a dinner of good food, reminiscences and laughter—until the telephone rang.

Agnes summoned Callie.

It was Ken. "It's Mom," he said. "She had another stroke. More serious this time."

"Oh, no, Ken. I've been meaning to visit, but I haven't. I feel so terrible. I'll leave right away."

"You can wait if you'd rather. I'll keep you posted. No sense in rushing here tonight."

Callie clenched the receiver. "No, I want to come now. I'll feel better. I won't sleep a wink if I stay here."

"Okay. Give me a call when you arrive. If I'm not home, I'll be here at the hospital."

"It'll take me two hours or so, Ken. It'll be late. Nine thirty or ten, maybe. So don't worry."

"Callie, drive carefully."

She placed the receiver in the cradle and turned toward the dining room. She hated to put a damper on the visit.

As she entered the room, David rose. "Is something wrong?"

When the words stumbled from her tongue, she fought back her tears. "My mom's had a bad stroke. I have to go home tonight."

"Get ready, Callie, and I'll drive you," David said. "I don't want you to go alone."

"No, I need my car while I'm there. I'm fine, please. You go ahead and enjoy your visit. I'll run up and pack. As soon as I know something, I'll call."

When Callie arrived, she went directly to the hospital. Grace lay sleeping, connected to a machine that hummed and flashed numbers measuring her vital signs. Ken stepped from the bedside and wrapped his arm around Callie.

"She's about the same. She seems to be out of danger, but you can see the stroke has affected her this time."

Callie leaned over the bed and saw her mother's

mouth twisted to one side. "So how much damage? Can they tell yet?"

"No. They'll run some tests in the morning. The doctor said her speech will be affected, at least for a while." He motioned to the chair. "Sit here for a few minutes. I'll take a walk and stretch my legs."

Callie nodded and eased herself into the chair. Pushing her arm through the bed's protective bars, she patted her mother's hand. Tears rose in her eyes, and she felt angry at herself for not having taken the time to come up for a visit.

She rested her head against the high chair back, and her mind filled with prayers. As her thoughts turned to God, she remembered her quandary— whether to stay in Bedford or come home. Maybe this was God's way of intervening. Perhaps her decision would be made for her.

Ken returned, bringing her a cup of coffee. They stayed by their mother's side until their eyelids drooped, then agreed that sitting there all night was foolish. Grace was out of danger, and they needed their rest.

Walking into the night air, Callie looked up into the sky, wondering if indeed God was directing her. If her mother needed her here, she would move back to Indianapolis. She had little choice.

In the morning, Callie called the nurses' station. Grace had rested during the night, and remained the same. Before leaving for the hospital, Callie called David and promised to phone later when she knew more.

By the time she reached the hospital, Ken had not arrived, and Callie stood alone in the doorway of Grace's room. Her mother's eyes were closed, but as Callie neared the bed, Grace opened them with a look of confusion.

"Everything's fine, Mom. You're in the hospital."

Grace opened her mouth, but the muddled words filled her eyes with fear.

"Don't try to talk, Mom. Just rest. The doctor will be in soon, and we'll know more then." Callie adjusted the chair and sat beside her. "If you need me, I'm right here."

She took her mother's hand and gave it a squeeze. And to her relief, Grace exerted a faint answering pressure. Callie clasped her mother's hand, thanking God.

Grace drifted into a fitful sleep, and Callie waited, speaking with nurses as they came in and out to check machines and the IVs, but they said little about her mother's condition.

Ken arrived, and two doctors followed on his heels, then conferred outside the room. Callie rose and met them in the hallway, while Ken stood beside Grace. When they entered, Ken kissed his mother's cheek and joined Callie.

"They suggested we go down for coffee while they examine her. They'll catch us later. Okay?" Callie asked.

Ken agreed, and they hurried to the cafeteria and moved quickly along the food line. Balancing her tray, Callie found a table near an outside window. They ate in silence, until Callie could gather her thoughts.

"I'm trying to decide what to do, Ken. Nattie has improved so much. She'll be starting school in a couple more weeks, and I suppose I should come back home and stay with Mom."

"I thought the last time I talked to you things were going well with you and David. Didn't you say a little romance was cooking?" Ken lifted his coffee cup and drank.

"That's another issue. I'm not sure if I should stay at the house under the circumstances. What will people say?" She leaned back against her chair, her fork poised in her hand. "But if I'm not there, we have little hope for a relationship, either. A two-hour drive each way doesn't encourage a budding romance."

"It's your call, sis."

"I know. But I'm so confused." She placed the fork on her plate and rubbed her temples.

"Well, don't try to make decisions now. Let's see what the doctors say. Mom may be in better shape than we think."

"I don't know if that really solves my dilemma. I still think I should come home." Her hands knotted on the table.

He placed his hand on hers. "Don't ruin your life, Callie. You overthink things sometimes. Try to be patient. Let's take one problem at a time. We're worried about Mom right now."

When they finished eating, they returned to Grace's room and met the doctor outside her door.

"So what do you think, Dr. Sanders?" Callie asked. "Any idea yet what happened?"

"Let me use layman's terms."

"Thanks. But I might mention I'm a nurse."

"Good. That could be helpful. Your mother apparently had an embolism. A blood clot broke loose from somewhere in her body, perhaps the heart. It often travels through the arterial stream into the cerebral cortex. When the clot lodges somewhere along its path, it can stop the flow of blood to the brain. In your mother's case, it did, and the stroke resulted."

Ken's face tensed. "So what happens now? Do you know how bad it is?"

"We'll run more tests, but we know she has some paralysis. She'll need physical therapy, and we'll begin that as soon as she's strong enough. Speech therapy will begin as soon as she's alert. Sometimes we have to wait two or three months before we see if she'll have permanent damage."

Ken's eyes widened. "Two or three months? You mean, we just have to sit and wait?"

"We'll do what we can." He looked at Callie. "And you might be able to speed up the process if you're willing to handle additional physical therapy at home."

Helping with Mom's treatment meant staying in Indianapolis. Nattie's face rose in Callie's mind, and a lonely feeling engulfed her.

"Good. Right now, your mother has IVs, but later she'll be on a variety of medications. An anticoagulant to keep her blood from clotting, and a vasodilator to keep the arteries open. If she has a narrowing or blockage in the carotid artery, she'll need surgery. Right now, your guess is as good as mine. The test will answer a lot of questions."

Ken glanced at Callie.

She shrugged. "We'll wait, then, until you have more information."

The doctor nodded. "You're welcome to visit for a while, but I suggest you let your mother rest as much as possible. Later today, we'll run the tests. Why not stay for a few more minutes, and then go on home? Come back this evening, if you like, and by tomorrow we should have some answers."

Ken nodded. "How about it, Callie?"

She heaved a sigh. "Not much we can do now, I suppose." She looked at the physician. "And we should follow doctor's orders."

With a gentle grin, the doctor rested his hand on her arm. "I only hope your mother's as good at following orders as you are."

According to the test reports, Grace's prognosis gave Callie hope. The week passed during which she was scheduled for daily therapy. Another week or so in the hospital, Dr. Sanders said, and her mother could go home.

The news still lay unsettled in Callie's mind. She sat in her mother's house, staring at the telephone. She had promised to call David, but she had delayed for a full week, wanting to clarify her decision.

David had sent flowers to Grace at the hospital, and another lovely bouquet sat on a nearby table. The brilliant colors should have brightened Callie's evening, but they didn't. Her thoughts were too muddled. She missed David and Nattie. But when Grace was released, she'd need help. Callie knew she had to provide it.

She raised the receiver and punched in the numbers. David's voice echoed across the line.

"How are you two?" she asked.

"We miss you. How are things there?"

"Better. Mom started therapy, and I'm happy to say, she's doing pretty well. Her speech is slurred, but I can understand her. And she forgets words once in a while."

David chuckled. "I do that without a stroke. How about movement?"

"She can't walk by herself yet. But things are promising. It'll take time. She'll have to continue therapy when she gets home."

He sighed. "So that means…?"

"So that means, I'll be coming to Bedford for my things."

Silence.

David finally spoke. "Then you'll go back for a while. I understand. Your mother needs you."

Callie closed her eyes to catch the tears that formed. "Not for a while, David. I'm coming back for good."

Chapter Nineteen

David hovered in her doorway, the blood in his veins as frozen as if he were an ice sculpture. Callie stood at the closet, packing. His wonderful new life was melting away; where his hopes and dreams had been, he saw only empty space.

"Callie, can't you listen to reason?"

"You mean *your reason,* David, not mine."

He strode across the room to her side. "I know your mother needs you now, but not forever. Please, we can't manage here without you, and I don't mean taking care of Nattie. We both love you. You're part of our lives."

She swung to face him. "Please, don't make this harder than it is. I love you, too, David, but we're both dealing with issues from the past. I'm not sure this relationship can go anywhere. Especially now, since someone made me think." Her eyes closed for a heartbeat. "I can't ruin your reputation or mine."

"What are you talking about? 'Ruin your reputation or mine'? That doesn't make sense."

"Yes, it does. Nat's fine now. She doesn't need me. So what purpose do I have living here? I'm a paid…what?

You tell me." She grasped his arms. "I'm a pretty expensive babysitter, wouldn't you say?"

Tears spilled from her eyes and ran down her cheeks.

"Oh, Callie, what do you think you are—a kept woman?" David slid his arms around her back. "God knows that we need you here. I don't care what others might say. And why would they? Who would say anything?"

Callie shook her head without answering.

"Everyone knows about Nattie's problems. For you to walk in and out of our lives when you mean so much to her is unthinkable. She lost her mother, and now you—someone she's grown to love. Who would put such crazy thoughts in your head?"

David's mind swam. *Pastor John? Agnes?* None of it made sense. "You're a Christian. You serve the church. No one would think wrong of you for being here. And what about Nattie?"

"But she's well, David. She doesn't *need* me anymore."

He dropped his arms to his sides and spun away. "No? You think she doesn't need you. Do you know where she is right now?" He whirled around to face her. "She's crying in her room. Nattie loves you. When you came, I didn't think about her loving you. All I thought was that I needed someone to make her better. I never thought I would hurt her."

Callie covered her face with her hands, and remorse spilled over him for the sorrow he had created by his words. "I'm not trying to make you feel guilty. I'm only trying to help you understand how much we love you."

"I'm sorry, David. I've given this a lot of thought. I pray I'm doing the right thing. If I'm wrong, I hope God will help me make it right. That's all I can say. I spent my life bearing a secret anger toward my parents. My mom is the only parent I have left to whom I can make retribution for my feelings. I have to do this."

David closed his eyes and filled his lungs with air. Why did she feel anger toward her parents? He didn't understand her cryptic comment. "I know you want to be with your mother, Callie. And Indianapolis is only two hours away. We'll work things out. Remember our 'deal' a while ago? We agreed to pray for each other. Like Jesus said, 'Where two or three are gathered in my name, I am with them.' We'll leave it in God's hands."

He moved to her side again and held her close. Her heart pounded against his chest, answering his own thudding rhythm. "I love you, Callie." He tilted her face to his. "I have faith in us." His lips touched hers lightly, then he backed away and left, knowing his life would soon be as lonely as the room she was vacating.

Callie struggled to see the road through her tears on her return to Indianapolis. Signing adoption papers had been the hardest thing she'd ever done. Saying goodbye to Nattie was the second. And saying goodbye to David... Callie had no words for the way she felt. She loved them both, but too many things stood in their way. Mary Beth's words hammered in her mind. David still struggled with Sara's death, and Callie had yet to heal from the rape and the adoption. Like someone who carries baskets of bricks up a hill, she carried the weight of Jim McKee's sin on her shoulders.

So often when she looked at Nattie, she imagined her own child. Did her daughter have a halo of blond curls? Was she loved? Was she learning about Jesus? Callie couldn't bear to think the worst. She longed to know—her heart ached. And all the love she had denied herself for years had risen like a wonderful gift and showered down on Nattie. And again Callie was letting a child go. Callie longed for a release. Would telling David about her own child help to heal the wounds? Now she would never know.

Since the telephone call, her thoughts had been filled with worry about her mother. But as she left Bedford, her talk with Miriam drifted into her mind. David hadn't told her Sara had miscarried. Yet he'd told her about wanting the abortion. Callie's head spun with disjointed bits of information, spilled out like pieces of one of Nattie's puzzles. Why didn't David feel God's forgiveness when Nattie was born? Why did he cling to his anger? God had given him a second chance—Nattie.

Finally, she turned her concerns to her present problem—Grace. Would Mom listen to her—as her nurse, and not as her daughter? What might that do to their relationship, which she had hoped to heal? Her head ached with wondering.

The next days flew past with preparations for Grace's return: a hospital bed, therapy training, treatment scheduling, grocery shopping. Yet keeping busy didn't help Callie feel less sad or lonely.

David persisted. He phoned, sent flowers and wrote notes on Missing You cards, but Callie clung to her decision. She believed God's hand had guided her.

Grace's day of homecoming arrived, and Callie stood beside her hospital bed packing her belongings. "Anxious to get home, Mom?"

Grace nodded as she had begun to do, avoiding her distorted voice.

"Talk, Mom. No head-nods. The more you talk, the quicker you'll have your old voice back."

Grace clamped her lips together like a disobedient child.

"Very adult of you, Mom." Callie shook her head in frustration. She had watched hospital films and talked to the psychologist for tips on helping Grace and being supportive. She already felt like a failure.

As she finished packing, Dr. Sanders appeared at the doorway. "So today's the big day? How are you feeling?"

Grace shrugged, then struggled to get out a thick-sounding "Fine."

"Good. I have your prescriptions written out for you. And you're a lucky woman to have a daughter who's a nurse."

"I'm not sure that will go over too well," Callie said. "She's going to resent me."

Dr. Sanders patted Callie's hand. "She'll be fine." He turned to Grace. "Now, you'll listen to your daughter, right? She's trained to help you, and you'll have to mind her. If not, you'll end up back here. I know you don't want that."

Grace's eyes widened, but she kept her lips pressed together.

Dr. Sanders pointed to her mouth. "And you have to speak, Grace. You'll never talk if you don't practice."

He turned to Callie. "We'll send the speech therapist out three times a week, and then count on you to do the rest."

"That's fine. I've had instructions, and I can handle

the therapy—if she'll listen." She directed her last words to Grace.

He spoke for a moment with Grace, and when he left, Callie gathered up the overnight bag and parcels and headed to her car.

Grace was wheeled outside and eased into the car. The trip home was silent, except for Callie's own running monologue. And she breathed a relieved sigh when Ken's car pulled into the driveway behind them.

"Glad you're here," she said, sliding from the car. She closed her door. "I didn't know if I could get Mom in alone. Besides, I need a little moral support."

"You look beat already," Ken said, standing at the trunk, as they unloaded the wheelchair.

She looked at him, shaking her head. "I'm afraid this'll be the undoing of Mother and me. I hoped, coming home, we could smooth out our differences, but she's being terribly belligerent. Like a child."

Ken rolled his eyes. "We'll just have to be patient. She'll come around."

She rested her hand on his shoulder. "And don't forget, I'll need a break once in a while. I can't do this alone or I'll end up in a hospital…and it won't be *medical* hospital."

Ken slammed the trunk. "No one would ever notice."

"Thanks." She poked his arm.

He rolled the wheelchair to the car door, and with his strong arms settled Grace into the seat. Together, they hoisted Grace up the porch stairs into the house and into the hospital bed, as the patient grunted and pointed.

Hands on her hips, Callie stood beside them. "Make her talk, Ken." She scowled at her mother. "We'll have no grunting or pointing in this house."

Grace glowered back as much as her face would allow, and Callie covered a snicker. Her heart broke for her mother, but she knew she'd better learn to laugh if they were to survive.

When Grace was settled, Callie invited Ken into the kitchen for a sandwich. He stretched his legs in front of him, twiddling his thumbs, as Callie buttered the bread. "Do you think you can do this?" he asked.

"Oh, they say God never gives us more than we can handle." She turned to face him. "But I think He's pushing it this time."

Ken threw his head back and laughed. "I was thinking the same thing. Hang in there, and I'll do what I can to help."

"Great, but I won't hold my breath."

David sent two more bouquets the following week—one for her, and the other for Grace. Callie missed him more than she could say. The situation hadn't eased. Grace fought her at every turn, and her nerves pulsed like wired dynamite.

One day, Callie was sitting in the kitchen, nibbling a sandwich that she could barely swallow, when the telephone rang. When she heard David's voice, her hand shook. She longed to tell him how awful things were, but instead she inquired about him, avoiding what was in her heart.

Finally she asked, "How's Nat?"

"Lonesome." A heavy silence hung on the line. "So am I, Callie. Nothing seems worth much anymore."

She refused to respond. She'd say far more than was safe to admit. "How's Nat's school? Is she doing okay?"

She waited. A chill ruffled through her. "Is something wrong, David?"

"I don't want to burden you. You have enough problems."

She stiffened. "Don't leave me hanging, David. What's wrong?" Her voice sounded strained to her ears. "I'm sorry, David, but you've upset me. Is something wrong with Nattie?"

"She's…beginning to withdraw again. Not like before, but she's not herself. I know she misses you. It'll pass with time. Her teacher was concerned, but I explained that…well, I didn't want to get into a lengthy discussion. I said her mother had died recently. I figured that would explain it."

If she'd felt stress before, she felt a thousand times worse hearing his words. "I don't know what to say. Even if I wanted to come back, I can't. Mom needs too much right now, and Ken works full time. He gives me a break once in a while, but I'm it, David. I'm the caregiver here."

He sighed. "I know. I know. I'm trying to think of something."

When she hung up, she covered her face and wept. She felt pity for everyone: Grace, David, Nattie and herself. When her tears ended, she splashed water on her eyes and planted a smile on her lips. Her wristwatch signaled Grace's therapy—and if Callie didn't smile, she'd scream.

"Look at you, Mom," Ken said, as Grace shuffled her feet across the floor while leaning heavily on her walker.

A twisted grin covered Grace's face; she looked as pleased as a toddler learning to take her first steps.

Callie stood nearby, watchful for any problems, but Grace moved steadily along. "Mom's worked hard," she said to Ken. "It makes it worthwhile, doesn't it, Mom? At least, you can get up and move around a little."

Grace grunted a "yes." Her speech had improved, too, turning their hope to reality.

Callie kept her eyes focused on Grace. "See if you can make it to the living room, Mom. You can sit in there for a change."

Grace heaved her shoulders upward as she moved the walker. When she was seated, Callie made a pot of tea and brought out some freshly baked cookies for a celebration. As difficult as it had been, she could see that Grace was mending.

As they talked, the telephone rang, and Callie left the living room to answer it in the kitchen. Something inside her told her the caller was David.

"Don't say a word, Callie, but Nattie and I are coming to Indianapolis to see you."

"Please, David, no. I'm still miserable. I don't think I could bear to see you…and not Nattie. I'll cry for sure."

"Good. Tears soften the heart, Callie, my love. You might as well give up. I'm coming. Nattie will be terribly disappointed if I tell her you don't want us to come."

"Oh, David. Don't say that. Come, then. I'll be here… forever."

"Maybe not. I think I have a solution."

Chapter Twenty

Callie's heart did cartwheels when she saw Nattie through the window. The child darted up the porch before David could catch her. Callie flung open the door and knelt to embrace her; Nattie flew into her arms and buried her face in Callie's neck.

Her small, muffled voice sounded on Callie's cheek. "I miss you."

"I miss you, too, Nat. Terribly." Callie raised her eyes toward David. "I miss all of you."

"Aren't you coming home?" Nattie asked.

The word *home* tore through her. Bedford was more home to her than her mother's house. The answer caught in her throat. She swallowed, and avoided a direct answer. "My mom is sick right now, Nat, and I have to take care of her."

Nattie tilted her head back and searched Callie's face. "Is she going to die?"

"No, she's getting better. But you know what? She won't talk much at all. Do you remember someone who didn't want to talk much a while ago?"

Nattie hung her head shyly and nodded. But her head popped up with her next words. "Is your mommy sad?"

Callie grinned. "No, not sad." She glanced up at David. "More like 'mad.' As mad as a wet hen, in fact."

Nattie giggled at the old saying.

"Well, let's not stand in the doorway. Come in." Callie rose, took Nattie by the hand, and moved so David could enter.

He stepped inside and slipped his arm cautiously around her waist, as Nattie eyed them. "How are you?"

Callie lowered her eyes. "Miserable. And you?"

"Terribly miserable."

Nattie pushed her shoulders forward, squeezing her hands between her knees, and chuckled. "I'm miserable, too."

Her words made them smile. Callie gave her another hug.

"Well, that's good, then. We're all miserable together." She gestured them into the living room. "Have you eaten? Anyone starving?"

"No, we had some breakfast on the way."

"We stopped at Burger Boy," Nattie added.

"Burger Boy, huh?" Callie gave David a disapproving look.

He wiggled his eyebrows. "They have biscuit breakfasts."

"Ah. Well, then, how about something to drink and maybe a cookie or two?"

They agreed, and while they waited in the living room, Callie gathered the drinks and cookies, taking deep breaths to control her wavering emotions. She loved them both, and seeing them today, though wonderful, felt painful, as well.

"Here we go," she said, carrying a tray into the living room and putting the cookies closest to Nattie.

Sinking into a chair, Callie studied David's face. His usual bright, teasing eyes looked shadowed. She gazed at Nattie, longing to speak privately to David. Then an idea struck.

"David, would you and Nat like to say hello to Mom?"

"Sure, if she's up to it."

"Nat, you've never met my mother. I might have a book around here somewhere, and you could show her the pictures and tell her a story. Would you like that? She gets pretty lonely in her room."

Nattie nodded, and Callie hurried to her room. On her bookshelf, she'd kept some favorite children's books. She shuffled through them and located a book of well-known tales and stories illustrated with colorful pictures. Before she returned to the living room, she popped into Grace's room to announce visitors, then left without giving Grace a chance to say no.

In the living room, she handed Nattie the book. "When I was young, this book was one of my favorites."

As soon as Nattie held the book, she flipped through the pages. "I know this story, and this one," she said.

"Good, then let's go in to see my mom."

She took Nattie by the hand, with David following, and headed down the hallway. Grace was staring at the doorway as they entered, looking stressed, probably over Callie's announcement. But when her gaze lit upon Nattie, her face softened. Only the slight tug of paralysis distorted her usual expression.

"Mom, here's David. And Nattie. You've never met her."

David stepped forward, extending his hand. "It's good

to see you, Grace. Callie says you're doing great. A little more time, and you'll be back to normal, huh?"

"Oh, I don't know," Grace said, her speech thick and halting.

Nattie stared at Grace and then glanced at Callie. "I thought your mommy didn't talk."

Callie snickered. "Maybe she just doesn't talk to *me,* Nattie." She peered at Grace. Her mother averted her eyes. Instead, she watched Nattie.

"When I was younger, I didn't want to talk," Nattie said, leaning her folded arms on Grace's bed.

"No?" Grace said, not taking her eyes from the child.

"I was too sad."

"Happy now?" Grace laid her hand on Nattie's arms.

"Uh-huh, except Callie went away to take care of you." Nattie glanced at Callie over her shoulder. "I miss her."

Grace's skewed face formed an angled smile. "You do, huh?"

"Yep." Nattie leaned forward and whispered at Grace. "But we came for a visit to tell her to come home."

Grace raised her eyes toward Callie. "Home?" She reached out and drew her hand over Nattie's blond hair, then nodded. "Yes, I suppose that is her home."

Tears burned behind Callie's eyes, and she quickly changed the topic. "Mom, Nattie wants to show you a picture book. You want to get up in a chair, or would you rather have her up there on the bed with you?"

Grace patted the coverlet beside her, and David boosted the child to the edge of the bed.

"You can get up for lunch, okay? We'll be in the other room for a few minutes. Can you get down by yourself, Nat?"

"I think so." She stared down at the floor.

"If not, give a call, and I'll come running," David said, patting her cheek with his fingers.

Callie and David walked out of the room, leaving Nattie to entertain Grace.

"I think Nat could work wonders with Mother. I haven't seen her so talkative since the stroke. She buttons up when I'm the one she has to talk to."

"But you're the nurse. No one likes nurses. They're too mean, and they make you take medicine and do things you don't want to do."

She returned his tease, rolling her eyes. "Thanks."

"And they always say, 'It's time to take *our* bath.' Have you ever seen a nurse—other than yourself, that is—take a bath?"

She listened to David's chatter, but inside, her stomach dipped on a roller-coaster ride. What would happen now that they were alone? David answered her question. He slid his arm around her waist, drawing her against him. His hand ran up her arm to her face, and he touched her cheek, drawing his fingers along her heating skin to trace her lips.

Her knees wanted to buckle beneath her, and a sensation, beginning as a tingle, grew to an uncontrollable tremor, as his face neared hers. She thought of pulling away, but her desire overpowered her intentions. She met his lips with hers, eagerly savoring the sweetness, and a moan escaped his throat, sending a deepening shudder through her body as her own sigh joined his.

Out of breath, she eased away and gazed into his heavy-lidded eyes. "David, you can't kiss me like this. I can't handle it."

"Good. Let *me* handle things. I refuse to leave this house without knowing you'll come back to us."

"How can I do that? Tell me." She raised her voice overwhelmed by a sense of futility. She longed to be with them in Bedford. No matter what others thought, she loved them and belonged with them.

"Let's sit, and I'll tell you how. I've figured it out. Come." He took her hand and guided her into the living room, and together they sank onto the sofa in each other's arms.

Her first thought was Nattie. What if she saw David's arms around her? "What if Nattie see us?"

"I told her I love you, Callie. And guess what she said."

She could only shake her head.

"She loves you, too. That was her response. And she needs you. She's been so quiet. But as soon as she saw you today, she opened again. Look at her with Grace. She's good for Grace, too."

Callie couldn't deny that. Grace hadn't been so receptive to anyone. Maybe a child's exuberance would bring her out of her self-pitying mode. She thought of her own situation. Nattie had worked a miracle, making her a whole person again.

"So," Callie asked. "What's your plan?"

"Bring your mother to Bedford."

"What?" She scanned his eager face. "I can't do that."

"Why not? Bring her to the house. We have tons of room."

"But it doesn't make sense…does it?"

"It makes all the sense in the world. I've already made arrangements. We'll set the library up as her room. She'll have an easy chair, television, books if she likes to read. There's a telephone there. A bathroom nearby."

"You're overwhelming me." She shook her head in confusion.

"I realized there's no shower on the first floor, except in Agnes's quarters. She said, 'Great, no problem.' So that's solved."

"What about her doctors and medication?"

"Once she's able to get around more, you can bring Grace here for her appointments. And her prescriptions can be filled in Bedford or here. That's not a problem."

Callie stared at him, dazed. "You've thought of everything, I take it."

"Please, don't get upset with me."

"I'm not upset, really. I'm stunned, David. I made a decision that staying in Bedford was the wrong thing to do, and now you're organizing and arranging my life."

"I'm sorry. That was selfish of me to assume that—"

"No, no, I'm not angry. I love you for it, because it means you love me. But I need to think things through."

"I understand, and you'll want to wait until the doctor says it's okay for Grace to travel. But, Callie, we can handle things if we know you're coming home."

"Home?" she said.

"Yes, home." He turned her face to his, and their lips met.

Past fears of intimacy rose inside her, and she tensed for a flickering moment. Then, as quickly, she relaxed her shoulders. With David, she experienced what God meant by loving…giving herself to a special someone and feeling complete.

With his kiss still warm on her lips, Callie rested her head against his shoulder. "David, I can't do anything without Mom's approval. I don't know if she'll be willing to come to Bedford."

"I've prayed." He ran his hand across the back of his neck. "I've prayed, and I believe God heard my prayers. I think Grace will come, Callie. Give her time, but I think she'll come."

She closed her eyes, adding her prayer to David's. Life was nothing without him and Nattie. That's where she belonged. But in all the confusion, she had yet to accomplish what she had set out to do: resolve the hurt that affected her relationship with Grace. She had to forgive and be forgiven.

Forgiving and being forgiven. Such complicated concepts.

She hadn't been totally honest with David, either. Would he forgive her when he learned about her child and the adoption? If only she knew her daughter was happy, maybe she could forgive herself.

But God had given her another child: Nattie. Was this her second chance to make things right?

Chapter Twenty-One

David checked the library for the fifth time. The room looked comfortable. Bed, bedside table, small dresser, all hauled down from an upstairs bedroom. He'd added a television set, and today, a bouquet of fresh flowers had been delivered. He wanted Grace to feel welcome.

The move had been difficult. Callie had been met with resistance from her mother, but finally, Grace had a change of heart. He didn't question the cause, but Callie said it followed on the footsteps of Nattie's second visit to Indianapolis. Nattie had latched on to Grace as she had the first time and had remained at her side. One evening, they sat together in the living room. As David and Callie talked, they grinned, overhearing Grace's and Nattie's conversation from the sofa.

"Tell me about school," Grace said, her speech clearer than it had been on their first visit.

Nattie tilted her head and thought. "Well, the teacher said I'm a good reader for first grade. And I can print my name and some other words…" She paused and raced across the room to Callie. "Do you have paper and a pencil? I want to show your mommy how I can print."

"Sure, I do," Callie said, and pulled a pad of paper and pencil from a lamp table drawer. "Here, you go."

Nattie returned to Grace, nestled at her side and proceeded to demonstrate her printing talents. David listened to Grace's encouraging comments and then returned to his own conversation.

"Any progress with Grace?" David asked in a near whisper, knowing his plans for them to move to Bedford had not set well.

"She's stubborn, David. I suppose I understand. But I haven't given up."

"She seems to be doing well."

"She is. She's using her own bed now, and she walks with the cane, though one leg still isn't cooperating totally."

"I'd hoped once she got around a little on her own, she might think of Bedford as a vacation," he said.

Callie rolled her eyes. "There's where you made your second mistake. Mom isn't crazy about vacations. She's a homebody."

He glanced at Grace and Nattie, the weight of hopelessness on his chest. His life had been empty and futureless without Callie. Though Nattie had withdrawn after she left, their visit two weeks earlier had seemed to work a miracle. All he could think about was his prayer that Callie would come back to Bedford.

Muddled in his thoughts, Nattie's words pulled him back to the present.

"Could you be my grandma?" she asked, looking into Grace's attentive eyes.

David's heart kicked into second gear. He glanced at Callie and saw that she had heard. He waited for Grace's response, his heartbeat suspended.

She lifted her gnarled hand and patted Nattie's leg, which was snuggled close to her own. "I'd like that, Nattie. You can call me Grandma Grace." Her eyes hadn't shifted from the child's face.

"Could I just call you Grandma?"

Grace's face twisted to a gentle smile. "Whatever makes you happy, child."

"Good," Nattie said, and lifted herself to kiss Grace's cheek.

David's heart melted at the sight, and when he turned to Callie, she was wiping tears from her eyes.

"Sentimental, huh?" she asked.

"Just plain beautiful," David responded.

That day had replayed itself over in his mind for the past two weeks. A week after their last visit, Callie had called to say Grace was becoming more receptive to a trip to Bedford. Today, his dream would become a reality.

Now, glancing out the window once again, David grinned, as he saw Nattie gallop through the autumn leaves gathered in mounds under the elms. She was as anxious as he.

Tired of waiting inside, David tossed on his windbreaker and joined Nattie in the yard. Seeing him, she giggled and filled her arms with leaves, tossing them into the air. As the burnished leaves settled to earth, Callie's car came up the winding driveway. Nattie let out a squeal and ran toward him. Together, they followed the car until it stopped in front of the wide porch.

"Grandma. Callie," Nattie called, racing to the car door.

Callie climbed out and gave Nattie a hug. David opened the passenger door and helped Grace from the car.

He longed to take Callie in his arms, but Grace leaned

heavily on him, so he controlled himself. Later, when they were alone, he could welcome her as he longed to do. He eased Grace up the wide steps and across the porch. Agnes greeted them at the door and held it open so Grace had easy access.

"My, now this is what I call a foyer," Grace said, looking wide-eyed around the vast entrance. "Callie didn't quite prepare me for something this elegant."

Nattie jigged around her, encouraging her to follow. "Look, Grandma, here's your bedroom. It's the lib'ary, but now it's your room."

"David didn't want you to climb the stairs," Callie explained. "He has extra bedrooms upstairs. When you're up to it, we can move your things up there, if you'd like."

Grace concentrated on her steps, but shifted her focus for a moment from the floor to Callie's face. "When I can climb those steps, I'll be ready to go back home." She grinned at David. "And you'll probably be ready to kick me out."

Nattie spun around, hearing her words. "We won't kick you out, Grandma. You can stay with me forever."

With a knowing eye, she glanced at Nattie. "Thank you, child. That's the sweetest thing I've ever heard."

Callie leaned close to David's ear. "That's because she doesn't listen to me. Believe it or not, I have said some pretty sweet things."

David winked at her. "I'm sure you have."

Grace raised her head and looked at the two of them. "I may have had a stroke, but I'm not deaf. So quit talking about me."

Nattie grasped her hand. "We have to be nice to Grandma. She's sick."

David and Callie burst into laughter, with Grace's

snicker not far behind. Nattie looked at the three of them, then tucked her hands between her knees and joined them with her own giggle.

Callie hung up the telephone and turned to David. "I gather you told Pastor John I was coming back."

He nodded. "Why? Was it supposed to be a secret?"

"No, but he just called to ask me to sing on Sunday. And he told me about the organ, David. I'm really pleased."

"Give thanks to God, not me. He brought me to my senses."

"What do you mean?"

David took her hands in his and kissed them. "My anger was focused in the wrong direction. I've been angry at God for taking Sara and for Nat's problems, instead of being angry at myself. We knew Sara had cancer, but I expected God to work a miracle."

She nodded. "We can't expect miracles."

"No, we can't expect anything, but we need to have faith. It's the faith that works the miracles. And God hasn't let me down, even when I was being bullheaded. I wanted instant gratification. But sometimes, we have to do a bit of soul-searching before we can appreciate God's will."

"So after some soul-searching, you decided to donate to the organ-repair fund."

"Paid for the repair. I can afford it, and the congregation enjoys the organ music as much as I do."

"It's nice for everyone. I'm glad, David. Oh, and Pastor John mentioned the new organist…with much enthusiasm, I might add." She suspected John valued the organist for more than her musical contributions on Sunday mornings.

"Wait until you see her. She's cute and single. And the right age."

Teasing, Callie arched an eyebrow. "The right age for whom?"

"For Pastor John." He caressed her cheek with the back of his fingers. "*Whom* else?" He gave her a wink.

"Well, I'm glad." She sat next to him on the sofa. "She doesn't happen to have a brother Mary Beth's age, does she?"

"Jealous, are you?" He clasped her hand.

"Should I be?"

"No, but I forgot to tell you what happened while you were gone."

Callie raised both eyebrows this time. "Ah, true confessions?" She curled her legs beneath her and faced him.

"Not quite." His words were accompanied by a chuckle. "But this is about Mary Beth."

Callie's eyes glinted in jest.

"And?"

"A day or two after you left, she called, inviting me to dinner."

"And you accepted, I'm sure."

"Anticipating her motive, yes. I wanted to clear up the issue once and for all…and for no other reason."

"I'm certain." Callie batted her eyelashes at him. David grinned.

"Anyway, to get back to the subject—as I intended—"

"Ah, as you intended."

"Yes, as I intended, she let me know she was interested in making my lonely life less lonely."

"Beautifully said."

"Thank you."

Callie draped an arm around his neck. "And what did you say to that?"

"I thanked her graciously, but declined her offer." He filled his lungs. "Actually, I felt terrible for her. She was embarrassed and flustered. She wasn't quite as blunt as I made her out to be, but she did let me know how she felt."

"I hope you were nice when you rejected her."

"As nice as a rejection can be. I said I was in love with you—but that if I weren't, she'd be a likely second." He tilted his head, giving her a coy look.

"Now that's a rejection."

"I didn't really add the last part." He chucked her beneath the chin. "And I told her I planned to do all I could to bring you back to Bedford."

"You did? Really?"

"I did. She handled it quite well, I'd say."

"No weeping or gnashing of teeth?"

"Only a little."

"Good. She can probably handle it better than I can. With weeping, I'm skilled, but gnashing...?" She gave him a silly grin.

After church on Sunday morning, Callie slipped into her casual clothes and went outside. More leaves had fallen overnight, and winter's chill had put a coating of hoarfrost on everything. She drew in a deep breath of frigid air.

In less than a month Thanksgiving would arrive, then Christmas. On Christmas Day her child would be seven, and little more than a month later, Nat would celebrate her seventh birthday. All the love Callie had kept bundled inside for her own child, she lavished on Nattie. Still, she clung to her secret. And until she had the courage to tell David and Grace, the secret was a barrier between them.

Without question, Nattie had wrought a change in her mother. Grace's critical martyrdom had faded, and in its place, she seemed to have found a joy in living. She would have made Callie's child a wonderful grandmother, after all.

No wedding had been mentioned, but Callie was sure marriage was David's intention. They had settled, without words, into a warm, committed relationship.

But marriage was built on honesty. She wanted to start the new year with the truth. And the longer she waited, the more difficult it would become. The last time she'd set a deadline for herself, she had sensed that God worked to bring it about sooner. Now, she set a second deadline. She would summon her courage, and by the first of January she would tell David about her baby.

Chapter Twenty-Two

Callie and Grace sat in the parlor, a fire glowing in the fireplace. Thanksgiving was still a week away, but the first snow had fallen early and muted the world outside. With David at work and Nattie in school, the house was also quiet.

Callie studied her mother, seated cozily in front of the fire reading a magazine. A year earlier, she would never have believed that her feelings for Grace would change so radically, but they had. And with a renewed fondness welling inside her, she knew the right moment had arrived.

"Mom, could we talk?"

Grace glanced up from the magazine, a look of tenderness etching her face. "I've been wanting to talk to you, too."

"You have?" For the first time in years, she saw her mother with clearer eyes. Grace had always loved her, but her love had seemed doled out in controlled portions, as if she were afraid she might give it all away at one time and have nothing left. Today she seemed different.

Grace tossed the magazine to the floor and leaned

back in the chair. "I didn't want to come here at first. You knew that, of course. And I suppose you saw what changed my mind. That wonderful child. I can understand why you wanted to come back here, Callie, not only because of David, but for Nattie."

"I know. She stole my heart."

"And I think David has, as well. He's a loving man. Kind and generous. You couldn't find a better husband." She peered into Callie's eyes. "I pray that's what the two of you have in mind."

"I pray so, too, Mom. And I'm glad you like him."

"I do. But God gave both of us a gift in Nattie. I look at her, Callie, and all I can think is somewhere in this world there's another little girl just like her. Nattie's so much like you, Callie." Her lips trembled, and she paused, her voice hindered by emotion. "I can imagine what your own little girl is like right now."

Tears stung Callie's eyes. "That's what I want to talk about, Mom. Part is a confession—a terrible secret I kept from you for so many years. Part is to help you understand my hurt and anger toward you and Dad."

"What are you talking about?" Grace's face paled, her eyes narrowed.

"I kept things hidden from you, and I've done the same with David. He doesn't know that I had a child. But I'm going to tell him. He and Sara wanted a child so badly that they took life-threatening chances to have a baby. Sara couldn't continue her radiation or chemotherapy without harming the baby, and without it, she endangered her own life. How could I tell him I had one that I gave away?"

"Oh, Callie, that was a whole different matter. You can't compare the two situations."

"But I can. What would he think of me? I've worried that I'll disillusion him. He expects more of me. I always thought that you and Daddy felt that way, and I couldn't endure that rejection again from someone else I love so much."

Grace threw her hand to her mouth, and her eyes brimmed with tears. "Not rejection, Callie. Your dad and I were so hurt for you. We were irritated that you protected the young man. That's the part that upset us. And naturally, we were disappointed."

"And that's the part that hurt me so much, Mom."

"We had such dreams for you—with all your talents and gifts from God. And your refusal to sing. We felt you were punishing us because we forced the adoption. But we always loved you and thought we were doing the right thing about the baby."

"I know. And my anger at you wasn't fair. Because I never told you the whole story."

Grace's body stiffened. "The whole story?"

"I couldn't tell you the truth, because I knew both of you would be crushed. And to be honest, I wondered if you'd believe me, because I felt guilty thinking I might be partly to blame for what happened." Pressure pushed against her chest and constricted her throat.

"Callie, you're talking in circles. Please, tell me what you mean. You're scaring me."

Strangling on the words, Callie whispered, "The baby's father wasn't a college boy, Mother."

"Not a—" She faltered and clung to the chair. "Then, who?"

"I was raped." The word spilled out of her along with a torrent of blinding tears. Her body shook with the knotted, bitter hurt that had bound her for so many years.

Telling David had been difficult, but telling her mother was devastating.

Grace rose with more speed than Callie could have imagined possible, and made her way to the sofa. She wrapped her arms around Callie and held her with every bit of strength she had. She asked no questions, but she held her daughter with the love only a mother could have for her child.

When Callie had regained control, she told Grace the story, in all its horror. Her mother listened, stroking and calming her until the awful truth was out. A ragged sigh raked through her shaking body.

Tears rolled down Grace's cheeks. No words were needed—Callie understood her mother's grief as well as she knew her own. They talked through the afternoon in a way they had never talked before. Their tears, like a cleansing flood, purified them, purged their past hurt and anger, and united them in love.

Ken joined them for Thanksgiving, and Grace had been content until then. But as Christmas approached, she urged Callie to take her home.

"Look how well I'm doing. My bedroom's upstairs now. I'm getting around. The cane is only a prop—see?" She lifted the cane and took a few steps. "I miss my house. And my things."

"That's why I don't have things, Mom. I've learned to live everywhere without a bunch of trappings."

"That's because all your trappings are with my things—at the house."

She chuckled at the truth. "I'll tell you what, Mom. Christmas is less than three weeks away. Why not stay here through the holidays, and then we'll take you home. You'll have nearly three weeks to get stronger."

"No sense in spending Christmas alone, is there?" David asked.

Grace eyed them both. "You promise? If I shut my mouth, you'll take me home after the holidays?"

"Promise," Callie said. "And think of what a nice Christmas you'll have this year with Nattie around. Christmas is always special with children."

Grace's face softened. "It has been a long time, hasn't it. You were my last baby."

David folded the paper and dropped it beside the chair. "And she's sure not a baby anymore." He winked at Grace.

"Me?" Nattie asked from the doorway, her brow puckered. "I'm not a baby anymore."

David opened his arms to her. "You sure aren't, Nat. But no, we were talking about Callie. She's no baby, either."

Nattie laughed. "I wish we had a baby."

Callie looked from Nattie to David, wondering what his response would be.

"First, we need a husband and wife. Then babies can come."

Nattie glanced at Callie. "You can marry Callie, Daddy. Then you'll be a husband and wife."

David gave her a giant hug. "My girl. She's making all the arrangements." His amused eyes sought Callie's. "We'll have to see about that, won't we?"

"Okay," Nattie said, and dropped the matter without another comment.

But Callie's heart pounded. Marriage seemed the next

step for them, but the words were yet to be spoken. And Callie couldn't answer yes—not yet.

"I have an idea," Callie said.

Three pairs of eyes turned toward her. Surprise lit Grace's face. Callie grinned to herself—did Grace think Callie was about to propose? "Let's go out and buy a Christmas tree."

"Goody," Nattie said, jumping in place at David's side. Her enthusiasm was contagious.

"Before this child knocks me out with her exuberance, I suppose we ought to do just that. A Christmas tree, it is," David said.

For Callie, many years had passed since she'd decorated a house. But this year, she joined in the excitement. The tree stood in the family parlor, covered in lights and bulbs. The house smelled of ginger and vanilla, and every day Callie and Nattie tiptoed into the kitchen to snatch a cookie or two from Agnes's baking.

Four days before Christmas, to Callie's dismay, David had to squeeze in a two-day business trip, returning Christmas Eve.

With David's absence, Callie felt lonely. The house was silent, and she opened her door and glanced across the hallway. Nattie seemed too quiet, and she wondered if the child missed David, too, or if something else bothered her.

She tiptoed across the hall and peeked through the doorway. Nattie was curled on the bed with a book on her lap. She looked up when Callie came into the room.

"So, how are you doing?" Callie asked, sitting on the edge of her bed.

"Okay."

"Just okay? And with Christmas coming so soon? I thought you'd be all excited."

She looked at Nattie's face and saw a question in her eyes.

"Is something wrong, Nat?"

Nattie snuggled down into her bed, turning her head on the pillow. "If you marry my daddy, would you have a baby?"

Callie's pulse skipped a beat. "Only God can answer that, Nattie. Would you like a new baby?"

She nodded yet her eyes blinked as if a fearful thought hung in her mind.

"What are you worried about, sweetie?" Did she wonder if Callie and David had enough love to share?

Nattie lowered her eyelids. "Would you die if you had a baby?"

A ragged sigh shivered through Callie, and she slid her legs onto the bed and curled up next to Nattie. "No, Nattie, I wouldn't die. Are you thinking of your mom?"

Her head moved against the pillow, nodding. "When my mommy was sick, Daddy said he was sorry that I was born, because it made Mommy die."

Callie struggled to contain her gasp. "Oh, Nattie, your daddy wouldn't say that. He loves you so much. Your parents wanted you so badly, and Miriam said that you gave your mom and dad so much happiness. No, no, you couldn't have heard your daddy say that. Maybe you misunderstood."

"Because my mommy was having a baby, she couldn't get her medicine, and she died. So I made her die, didn't I?"

"Is that what's made you sad all this time, Nattie?"

Nattie didn't have to speak. Her face reflected the answer. Callie understood now—Nattie's silence for so long, her burden of guilt that she had caused her mother's death.

She wrapped Nattie in her arms and held her tightly against her chest. Looking at the little girl's blue eyes, nearly the color of her own, she knew this would be what she'd feel for her own child. She couldn't love her own flesh any more than she had grown to love Nattie. And Nattie's hurt was her own.

"Whatever you heard, Nattie, I think, you didn't understand. Your mom had a bad disease for a long time. God was so good to her and gave her four years to spend with you before she went to heaven. Do you remember how much she loved you?"

"Uh-huh," Nattie whispered. "She hugged me like you do." Her small arms wound more tightly around Callie's neck.

"Callie?" Her voice was a whisper.

"What, sweetheart?"

"Could you be my mommy?"

"I think I am already, Nattie. I love you as if you were my own daughter. I couldn't love you more." The words caught in her throat. "And your daddy thinks you're the greatest in the whole wide world.

"So does Grandma Grace."

Nattie nodded. "Grandma loves me. She told me."

"She did, huh? You go to sleep. Your daddy'll be home tomorrow." She nestled Nattie in her arms, singing softly in her ear.

What could Nattie have heard? When David returned, Callie would know.

Chapter Twenty-Three

David stepped into the foyer loaded with packages, and Callie rushed into his arms, suppressing her questions. He lowered the bags, and, despite the snow that clung to his coat, he pulled her to him and pressed his icy lips against her warm, eager mouth. "What a greeting. I should go away more often."

"Don't you dare." She dodged from his damp, chilled arms.

"So where's my favorite daughter?"

He heard a giggle, and Nattie leaped through the parlor doorway into his arms and planted a loud kiss on his cheek.

"You're freezing, Daddy."

"And you're snuggly warm, Nattie."

She wiggled until he released her.

David slid off his coat, and Callie took it from him as he retrieved his packages.

"What have you got there?" she asked, eyeing the parcels.

"Wouldn't *you* like to know?"

"Yes, I would."

"Me, too," Nattie added. "Did you buy me a present?"

"Both of you are nosy. Yes, they're all Christmas surprises, so you'll have to wait. And before I let you two bury your noses in the bags, I'm taking them upstairs right now."

Callie and Nattie pretended to pout, but David ignored them and scooted up the stairs, carrying the bulging shopping bags.

He tossed them into his closet, then changed into his khaki slacks and a rust-and-green pullover. Before closing the door, he glanced with an anxious grin at the packages.

While in Bloomington, he had wandered through a jewelry store, finally selecting a gold locket for Nattie as delicate and lovely as she was.

His heart tripped when he thought of Callie's gift. As well as a gold chain with pearl and garnet beads, David had selected an engagement ring. Christmas Day, he would propose.

After he dressed, David returned to the first floor, admiring the holiday decor. For two years his Christmas spirit had lain dormant. Today, with Callie at his side, he felt complete.

As he neared the bottom of the stairs, Callie beckoned him through the library door, a strange look on her face.

"Something wrong?"

"Push the door closed, would you?" she asked. "I want to make sure we're alone before we talk."

Feeling his pulse quicken, he gave the door a push.

Her face told him she was terribly concerned. "What is it?"

"Something happened while you were gone, and I've

been anxious to talk to you." She glanced over her shoulder at a chair. "Let's sit, okay?"

"Sure," he said, folding his tense body into a nearby recliner. "I see you're upset."

"It's something Nattie said. I think I know what's been bothering her all this time."

His pulse throbbed in his temples. "What is it?"

Callie blurted her story. Confusion and worry tangled in her words, and as he listened, he forced his mind back nearly three years, trying to decipher what Nattie might have heard.

"Callie, I don't know. I can't imagine what she heard. We never talked in front of her. Sara and I were very open about her illness and about her ill-fated pregnancy, but not with Nattie around. I was so angry and guilty when Sara had the miscarriage. But that was a year before Natalie—"

"Could she have overheard you talking when Sara was...really bad. Near the end?"

"If Nattie was listening, I didn't know. Yes, I was terribly upset. I knew Sara's pregnancy was a mistake. Stopping her treatment risked her life, and then we lost the baby, anyway. Oh, Callie, I probably yelled at her, telling her how foolish we were to try and have a child. I was a maniac right before she died."

"If Nattie heard it, she blamed herself."

"But she wasn't to blame. And Nattie should know that. She couldn't have been to blame."

Callie's eyes questioned him, her forehead furrowing in confusion. "Why, David? Sara couldn't have treatment during either pregnancy. Why *wouldn't* Nattie feel to blame?"

David's world crumbled around him. Words he hadn't

said since Sara died rose to his lips. Nattie had been told, but she had been young. Maybe she'd forgotten. They had to raise her to know the truth.

"Answer me, David. Why?"

He struggled to say the words. "When Sara lost the baby, we knew that was our last chance. Nattie isn't my biological child, Callie. She was adopted."

Callie stopped as if struck by a sniper's bullet. Blood drained from her face. Trembling uncontrollably, she raised her hand to her chest. "Adopted?" She rose, her legs quaking. "Adopted?" she whispered. "And you never told me."

"Oh Callie, to me, Nattie was our own. I rarely think about—" He stopped speaking. Callie had dashed from the room and up the stairs.

Weakness overcame her. Callie stood in her room, holding her face in her hands, disbelieving. Why had David lied to her? But…he hadn't lied. He hadn't told her, that was all. A wave of sorrow washed over her. Neither had she told *him* the whole truth.

Adoption. Had David not spoken of it for a reason? Was he ashamed? Her chest tightened, restricting her breathing. She closed her bedroom door and locked it, then threw herself across the bed. Callie's own sorrow tore through her. *Nattie.* This beautiful child, like her own daughter, had been signed away—placed in someone else's home. And somewhere, another mother wondered about *her* lost child. The paradox knifed her. *Why Lord? Why should mothers feel such pain?*

She needed to calm down and reason. Callie closed her eyes, whispering a long-needed prayer to God. Compassion, wisdom, understanding. She needed so much. Yet, so often she wore herself out trying to solve every problem on her own. God had guided her to this house. Was this His purpose?

She loved Nattie as her own, and the child almost could be hers: they had the same coloring and talents. But she knew in her heart, Nattie wasn't. She belonged to someone else.

She curled on her side and prayed aloud. *"Lord, please help me to understand. You tell us to seek You and You'll hear us. With all my heart Lord, I need to find peace and comfort. I want to understand."*

A light rap sounded on the door. *David.* She ignored his knock and his hushed voice, calling her name. For now, she had to think on her own. She could apologize for her behavior and explain her strange reaction later.

Finally, she rose and washed her face, staring at the pale image in the mirror that gaped back at her. Tonight was Christmas Eve, and Ken would arrive soon. This was not the moment for confessions and confusion. Now she needed to look presentable.

She retouched her makeup and tossed a teal-blue dress over her head, cinching the belt around her waist. The rosebud brooch from David lay on her dresser, and she pinned it to her shoulder. *Better? Yes, I look better.* She unlocked the door and descended the stairs.

Ken had already arrived, and called to her from the bottom landing. "Merry Christmas, Callie."

"Merry Christmas, Ken," she echoed.

David watched from behind her brother. Though handsome in his navy suit, tension ridged David's face, and he looked less than merry. She gave her brother a kiss on the cheek, then spoke to David. "I see you're ready for church."

"Yes. You look lovely, Callie." He gave her brother a

friendly pat on the shoulder. "Go ahead, Ken. Let's sit in the parlor with the Christmas tree."

Ken went ahead, joining Nattie and Grace, and David leaned close to her ear as they followed him. "We need to talk."

"Later, David, please. I owe you an explanation."

He nodded, but she felt his arm tense. Tenderly, she pressed his forearm, hoping he understood and forgave her. A faint movement flickered at the corner of his mouth, and she relaxed, believing that he did understand.

With conversations flowing in many directions, the time passed, and Agnes soon announced their early dinner. The children's Christmas program began at seven thirty, and Nattie had to arrive by seven.

At the church, they sat near the front. Beginning with "Oh, Come Little Children," the youngsters proceeded down the aisle, dressed as shepherds, wise men, Mary, Joseph and the angels.

Nattie's halo bounced as she marched past the rows in her white flowing robe and sparkling angel wings. When she saw the family, she raised her hand in a tiny wave.

The children took their places, and families beamed as the little actors spoke with practiced precision. When the angels chorused, "Peace on earth; goodwill to men," Nattie's voice rose above the rest, every word clear and distinct.

At the end of the program, they descended the stairs to the Sunday School rooms, while the children stripped off their costumes.

Nattie dashed to them when they hit the landing. "Was I good? I knew all my lines."

David crouched down and gave her a hug. "We were all very proud of you."

Callie's heart twisted, watching him with Nattie. So much love and devotion for his daughter. Natural or adopted, she was his child.

When David retreated to locate Nattie's coat, a familiar voice sailed toward Callie.

"Well, Merry Christmas."

Turning, Callie cranked her facial muscles into a smile. "Hello, Mary Beth. Merry Christmas."

A man was attached to her arm, and she batted her eyes toward her escort. "Callie, do you know Charles Robinson?"

"Not formally, but I know you from church. It's nice to meet you. And this is my brother, Ken." They shook hands. Saving further conversation, David returned just then with Nattie, now buttoned into her coat. After final amenities, they headed toward the door.

Once home, as they entered the foyer, the parlor clock chimed ten, and eager for Christmas Day, Nattie headed for bed with David's promise to tuck her in. Callie longed to talk with David but she had to join the others for Agnes's homemade cookies and coffee.

The conversation flowed until Callie yawned, followed by David. Finally, they agreed it was time to turn in.

David rose first. "I'd better call it a night. I still have a few 'Santa' things to do for tomorrow morning."

Ken followed and helped Grace up the stairs. As they made their way, Callie turned to David. "Can we talk now?"

He hesitated. "Let me get this stuff set up, so I won't feel hurried. I'll knock on your door when I'm finished."

Disappointment needled her, but he was right. They didn't need to be rushed. Their talk would be important, and she wanted to be emotionally ready. "Okay. I'll be waiting."

Upstairs, Callie paused outside Nattie's room. In the glow of the pink night-light, the child lay in a soft flush of color. Callie stood over her, her hand stroking the golden curls fanned out on the pillow. Nattie slept soundly.

Callie leaned over, brushing Nattie's cheek with her lips, then whispered, "I love you, Nattie." Her heart stirred with loving awareness. It didn't matter whose child she was—Nattie was loved and cherished. God had guided the baby to this house and to a Christian family who loved her.

Brushing the tears from her cheeks, Callie crossed the hall and slipped into a caftan, then waited. Her nerves pitched at each creak of the house, wondering if it was David. Tonight she would tell him about her daughter. How would he feel? And how did she feel? *Peace and understanding, Lord.* Her prayer lifted again. She pushed her door ajar and moved her chair so she could see David approach.

When he appeared, he passed her room and crossed to Nattie's. Surprised, Callie rose, padding softly to the doorway, but he only peeked in and then turned.

"You're waiting. I'm sorry it took so long. You know how it is assembling toys."

A knot tightened in her stomach. No, she didn't know.

"Let's sit," David said, drawing the desk chair beside her recliner. "We have lots to talk about."

Callie sank into the cushion. "I'm sorry, David. I was shocked. I—"

"First, let me explain, please. I wasn't hiding Nattie's adoption. When you first came, the thought entered my mind. But I didn't know you and wanted you to treat her as my own. Then, you grew to love her as I do, and the thought faded. She is my daughter. I love her no differently than I would a natural child."

"Please, David. My shock is more complex than you can imagine. Yes, I was startled when you told me. And then I wondered if you were ashamed of her adoption, and—"

"Ashamed? How could I be? Sara and I chose her. She was ours from her first days on earth. We nurtured her, loved her, cared for her. How could I be ashamed? I thank God for my beautiful daughter, Callie."

Her tears flowed, dripping to her hands knotted in her lap. She raised them to cover her face.

David rose and knelt at her feet. "Don't cry. Please. I don't understand what's happened."

"David, I didn't know how I was going to tell you this. I was so worried you'd hate me or wonder what kind of person I am."

David pulled her hands from her face. "Whatever it is, just tell me." He held her hands captive in his.

She closed her eyes, tears dripping from her chin. "After I was raped, I found out I was pregnant."

"Pregnant—oh, Callie, my love." Tears rimmed his eyes.

"My parents thought the father was a college boy, and I let them believe it. I had a baby girl, David, born on Christmas Day. I placed her up for adoption."

"My love, how could I hate you? You were blameless. And hurt far more than I ever knew."

"But you did so much to have a baby—taking horrible chances. And I didn't fight to keep my child. I haven't forgiven myself. Every day I ask God why it happened— and if she's okay. Is she happy? Do her parents love her?"

David rose, lifted her from the chair, and cradled her in his arms. "Oh, my dear, look around you. Look at the beautiful child that gave Sara and me such joy. Wouldn't God do the same for your child? Trust in the Lord, Callie. You have strong faith in so many things. Believe that God placed your daughter in a home as filled with love as this one."

"I want to believe that." Music stirred in Callie's mind. She paused. The sad song that played within her heart faded, and a new melody filled her—a sense of peace and understanding. And love. "I went to Nattie's room when I came up and looked at her sweet face." The music lifted at the memory. "I couldn't love my own child more, David. I almost feel as if God has given me another chance."

"He has, my love, He has. And He's given us another chance. You've brought such joy to our lives. Nattie and I were shadows when you came, but you breathed new life into us—just as you gave life to your little daughter years ago."

The grandfather clock in the parlor began to chime. *One. Two. Three...* They paused, listening for the last. "It's midnight. Christmas Day." She didn't say what else lay in her heart. His eyes told her he knew.

"Doubt is part of life, Callie. When we first brought Nattie home, I wondered if I could love her. *Really* love her—like a true father. And—"

"You don't have to say it. If anyone was ever a true and loving father, it's you."

"And if anyone was ever a true and loving mother, it's you."

Callie looked into his face, and saw love glowing in his eyes. Her heart felt as if it would burst, and joy danced through her body. "A mother. It's a beautiful thought."

"A mother." Trancelike, David repeated her words and kissed her hair. He tilted her chin upward until their eyes met. "Callie, this is perfect. I planned this for tomorrow, but wait. Wait. Don't move."

He darted from the room, and in a moment returned to drop to his knees in front of her for the second time that night. "I've loved you for so long. You've brought happiness and completeness into our empty world, and, praise God, you've given me a healthy daughter. Nattie loves you so much and so do I. We would like to marry you, Callie. Will you be my wife? And Nattie's mother?"

Tears rolled down his cheeks as he handed her the blue velvet box. Callie knew what was inside, and without hesitating, she whispered her answer. "You know, I love you both with all my heart. Please forgive me for my foolish doubts and fears. I'm so filled with happiness—"

"And?"

She looked into his loving eyes. "And yes, I'll marry you."

His face brightened; the tension melted away. "Open the box, Callie." He turned it in her hand to face her.

She lifted the lid. Inside, a roping of three shades of gold entwined three sparkling diamonds. She raised her eyes. "Three shades of gold. And three diamonds. One for each of us."

"One for each of us. And we can always add a fourth."

His eyes glowed, and with quivering fingers, he took the ring from her and slipped it on her finger. "Perfect." His gaze caressed her face. "Yes, perfect."

She opened her mouth to speak, but he quieted her with his warm, tender lips. Captured in his arms, Callie's fears and shame were gone. Her black dreams could hurt no more. She nestled securely against David's chest, finally whole and at peace.

When their lips parted, they tiptoed, hand in hand, across the hall to gaze at their beautiful child, sleeping peacefully in a rosy glow of light.

Epilogue

On Christmas Day, a month before Nattie's ninth birthday, the family gathered in church. Even Callie's sister, Patricia, and her husband had come from California for the holiday. They arrived, eager to see Randolph David Hamilton, who'd been born in early November.

Grace held the baby in her arms, with Nattie nestled as close as she could without sitting on Grace's lap.

David and Callie stood at the front, their faces glowing with wide, proud grins. David's gaze drifted with admiration to his wife, almost as trim again as she had been before her nine months of "ballooning," as they'd called it. He couldn't take his eyes from her.

"What?" Callie whispered. "Why are you staring at me?"

"Because you're beautiful, and I'm the happiest man alive." He squeezed her arm and tilted his head toward the children, sitting in the third pew.

She teased him with the nudge of her hip. "Well, you'd better focus on the music. We have to sing in a minute."

The organ music voluntary ended, and the ushers brought the offering plates to the front. As they retreated down the aisle, the organist played the introductory notes to the duet.

The opening strains began, and Callie's mind soared back to a Christmas midnight two years earlier—to the moment her past vanished and God's purpose became clear. On that day, a new life began.

Her gaze drifted to Nattie, growing lovelier each day, now looking at her with pure, joyous love. Somewhere on this Christmas night, another young girl celebrated Jesus's birth and her own birthday. Assurance filled Callie, as she trusted that God had guided her own baby daughter to a loving, Christian family.

Callie wiped away an invading tear. Today, with happiness, she looked at her son, the image of his handsome father. Raising her eyes to David's, she felt complete and wonderful. His smile captivated her, and she sighed.

As the last note of the introduction sounded, they each drew in a deep breath, then lifted their voices in the familiar words of an old carol that now rang with new meaning. *"It came upon a midnight clear, that glorious song of old..."*

* * * * *

Get 2 Free Books,
Plus 2 Free Gifts—
just for trying the Reader Service!

Love Inspired®

Save $1.00

on the purchase of any
Love Inspired® book.

Available wherever books are sold, including
most bookstores, supermarkets, drugstores
and discount stores.

Save $1.00

on the purchase of any Love Inspired® book.

Coupon valid until July 31, 2018.
Redeemable at participating retail outlets in the U.S. and Canada only.
Limit one coupon per customer.

52615199

Canadian Retailers: Harlequin Enterprises Limited will pay the face value of this coupon plus 10.25¢ if submitted by customer for this product only. Any other use constitutes fraud. Coupon is nonassignable. Void if taxed, prohibited or restricted by law. Consumer must pay any government taxes. Void if copied. Inmar Promotional Services ("IPS") customers submit coupons and proof of sales to Harlequin Enterprises Limited, PO Box 31000, Scarborough, ON M1R 0E7, Canada. Non-IPS retailer—for reimbursement submit coupons and proof of sales directly to Harlequin Enterprises Limited, Retail Marketing Department, 225 Duncan Mill Rd., Don Mills, ON M3B 3K9, Canada.

U.S. Retailers: Harlequin Enterprises Limited will pay the face value of this coupon plus 8¢ if submitted by customer for this product only. Any other use constitutes fraud. Coupon is nonassignable. Void if taxed, prohibited or restricted by law. Consumer must pay any government taxes. Void if copied. For reimbursement submit coupons and proof of sales directly to Harlequin Enterprises, Ltd 482, NCH Marketing Services, P.O. Box 880001, El Paso, TX 88588-0001, U.S.A. Cash value 1/100 cents.

5 65373 00076 2 (8100)0 12313

® and ™ are trademarks owned and used by the trademark owner and/or its licensee.

© 2018 Harlequin Enterprises Limited

LICOUP0318

HARLEQUIN®

Save $1.00

on the purchase of any

Harlequin® series book.

Available wherever books are sold, including
most bookstores, supermarkets, drugstores
and discount stores.

Save $1.00

on the purchase of any Harlequin® series book.

Coupon valid until July 31, 2018.
Redeemable at participating retail outlets in the U.S. and Canada only.
Limit one coupon per customer.

52615203

Canadian Retailers: Harlequin Enterprises Limited will pay the face value of this coupon plus 10.25¢ if submitted by customer for this product only. Any other use constitutes fraud. Coupon is nonassignable. Void if taxed, prohibited or restricted by law. Consumer must pay any government taxes. Void if copied. Inmar Promotional Services ("IPS") customers submit coupons and proof of sales to Harlequin Enterprises Limited, PO Box 31000, Scarborough, ON M1R 0E7, Canada. Non-IPS retailer—for reimbursement submit coupons and proof of sales directly to Harlequin Enterprises Limited, Retail Marketing Department, 225 Duncan Mill Rd., Don Mills, ON M3B 3K9, Canada.

U.S. Retailers: Harlequin Enterprises Limited will pay the face value of this coupon plus 8¢ if submitted by customer for this product only. Any other use constitutes fraud. Coupon is nonassignable. Void if taxed, prohibited or restricted by law. Consumer must pay any government taxes. Void if copied. For reimbursement submit coupons and proof of sales directly to Harlequin Enterprises, Ltd 482, NCH Marketing Services, P.O. Box 880001, El Paso, TX 88588-0001, U.S.A. Cash value 1/100 cents.

5 65373 00076 2   (8100)0 12314

® and ™ are trademarks owned and used by the trademark owner and/or its licensee.

© 2018 Harlequin Enterprises Limited

HSCOUP0318

Love Inspired®

Inspirational Romance to
Warm Your Heart and Soul

Join our social communities to connect
with other readers who share your love!

Sign up for the Love Inspired newsletter
at **www.LoveInspired.com** to be the
first to find out about upcoming titles,
special promotions and exclusive content.

CONNECT WITH US AT:

Harlequin.com/Community

 Facebook.com/LoveInspiredBooks

 Twitter.com/LoveInspiredBks

LISOCIAL2017